SULZER

The Last Resort

BY THE SAME AUTHOR

The Neon Madonna

THE LAST RESORT

Dan Binchy

St. Martin's Press
New York

Library of Congress Cataloging-in-Publication Data
Binchy, Dan.
    The last resort / Dan Binchy.
            p.   cm.
    "A Thomas Dunne Book."
        ISBN 0-312-08834-5
            I. Title.
    PR6052.I7726L37   1993
    823'.914—dc20   92-41154   CIP

First published in Great Britain by Random Century Group.

First U.S. Edition: March 1993
10 9 8 7 6 5 4 3 2 1

To Joy – whom I love

1

The Eleventh Earl of Gallerick sighed deeply and looked hard at the large man in the blue mohair suit seated opposite him. How in the name of all that's holy could anyone attain such high office and yet be so dense? With another weary sigh, Gallerick started off once more, like a patient but overworked teacher explaining to a backward pupil.

'Look here, Michael old *chap*, it works something like this. You apply to the *blokes* in the European Commission for a Wildlife Grant to support the hunt, and that's all there is to it. As simple as falling off a log! All it needs is a spot of – what do you call it?'

There was a longish pause during which his face contorted with the effort of finding the right word. Then, with a note of triumph in his voice, like someone who has just found a missing sock under the bed, he continued, '*Lobbying*, that's the blasted word I wanted. Then the Brussels chappies say "right ho" or "tout bien" or whatever it is they say when everything is OK and above aboard. After that they start shovelling the money our way, *and Bob's your uncle!*'

Mick Flannery drank deep from the heavy cut-glass tumbler and eyed the speaker with a mixture of pity and affection. Despite the high-pitched accent that at times like these made him sound like an overexcited donkey, Gallerick was a decent enough old skin who could always be counted on for a few quid at election time or when the lads called at his door for the National Collection. No, old Gallerick was all right except for his stubborn refusal to live in the real world. The Earl dwelt in a Celtic Utopia of his very own where foreign Johnnies, at regular intervals, emptied a cornucopia of EC funds into the laps of impoverished gentry like himself. In this instance, the purpose of such generosity was to maintain a pack of hounds whose sole purpose was to dismember foxes – 'in the cause of preserving wildlife'. Mick cleared his throat noisily and started on the difficult path of trying to set Gallerick straight on the matter.

1

'The problem with your scheme, my Lord, is how to convince those shagging bureaucrats in Brussels that tearing a fox into shreds, then plastering its blood all over the youngest rider in the field, quite fits in with Wildlife Preservation. They might just as easily take the opposite view and seek to have fox-hunting outlawed.'

Mick thought he had made his point as diplomatically as possible. When the invitation had come to visit Gallerick Hall, he had anticipated another impossible request whose refusal would throw his Lordship into one of his towering rages. The last time it had been a demand for Government funds to repair the roof of the stately pile. When the money had not been forthcoming, Gallerick had gone into a lengthy, aristocratic sulk.

'Don't talk absolute drivel, Michael, like good chap. Even a blind and deaf mute could grasp the simple fact that fox-hunting is a tool of conservation! When I go out with my hounds, or a gun or a rod for that matter, I am preserving the bloody wildlife round here, not destroying it!'

'Try telling that to Mullarkey!'

'I have done so already as a matter of fact.' Gallerick looked slightly embarrassed at the admission which Mick had wrung from him. Understandably so, for even though the two politicians belonged to the same party, there was intense rivalry between them because they both came from the neighbouring village of Brulagh.

It was now Mick's turn to bridle. 'Oh you have, have you . . . and what did our Deputy Leader and Minister for the Environment say?'

'He said it was the policy of his administration to protect the clean air, magnificent scenery and teeming wildlife of this area. To that end, and I am quoting the little blighter verbatim: "I intend introducing a Wildlife Protection Act at the first possible opportunity".'

'How is that going to help you?'

Gallerick unshipped yet another sigh of exasperation and resumed his kindly schoolmaster role. 'My dear chap, do try not to be a complete chump. I have just explained that very point to you. Do any of you darned politicians ever listen to anybody except yourselves? I'm blue in the face from telling anyone who will listen that the Gallerick pack keeps down the bloody foxes, stops them from overbreeding, interbreeding and God alone knows what else! Survival of the fittest, culling the weak from the fold and all that sort of thing. Surely even you can see that? Mullarkey grasped it right away, I might add.'

'I'm sure he did and all, but did he say that he would actually *do* anything about it?'

'Well no . . . not exactly. As a matter of fact, that's why I asked you to drop in for this little talk. Oh my God, with all this chatter I'm neglecting my duties as host. Here, let me have your glass . . .'

Approximately half a pint of brandy sloshed into the bottom of a glass so large that it might have doubled as an umbrella-stand. The label on the bottle bore the crest of the Gallericks – two unicorns rampant, supporting a ribbon-like banner with the motto *Nil Desperandum*. Their postures suggested that they were about to engage in sexual congress. As for the family motto, the local traders had long ago decided that it meant 'never pay up'. Indeed the brandy, despite its impressive bottle, tasted like paint-stripper and could well have been a modest Spanish Fundador. Even Mick Flannery, whose thirst was a source of awe to all who knew him, was finding difficulty in swallowing it.

Gallerick poured another lethal measure for himself and picked up where he had left off. 'In fact, Mullarkey said you were the very man to loosen the purse-strings of those blighters in Brussels, what with your being a Member of the European Parliament and all that sort of thing.'

'Oh he did, did he?' Mick decided against telling Gallerick that 'those blighters' were far more likely to tighten their purse-strings at the mention of the Flannery name. Only last month he had spent an uncomfortable hour before a disciplinary committee who were investigating the fact that, though paid a generous allowance to cover his overnight expenses in Brussels, Mick had preferred to pass the night on a couch in his office. If they were aware that he had shared it with his secretary, they were far too discreet to mention the fact. He had been let off with a caution and a warning as to his future conduct.

'Yes, he did. He cited the Flannery Leisure Centre as an example. Said if you could raise EC money for that, you could raise it for anything!'

Mick struggled to hide his annoyance. Now, as always, that miserable little bollix Mullarkey never missed a chance to take a cheap shot at him. Long ago, when they were at each other's throats, there might have been some excuse for it, but not now. Mullarkey was not only Leader of the Irish Christian Democrats but the swine was also Deputy Prime Minister and a Cabinet Minister to boot. As for Mick, he occupied a safe seat as an MEP and was therefore no threat to Mullarkey. The bitterness between them was of a purely personal nature. On the surface they were the best of friends, members of the same Government with the shared objective of persuading an increasingly sceptical electorate that yes, another new dawn *was* about to break! Yet the old animus between them remained strong as ever. To make matters worse, Mick's eldest son, Sean, thought the sun moon and stars shone out of Mullarkey's arse. It was whispered that Mullarkey was grooming Sean as his successor.

'Be that as it may, even I can't work miracles . . .'

Mick's reference to miracles was unfortunate, since his wife Maggie had had an experience some time ago in which she fancied she had witnessed a miracle at the nearby shrine.* This resulted in a nervous breakdown from which she had taken a long time to recover. Sometimes Mick wondered if she had ever fully got over it as he pressed on.

'I mean, despite whatever your friend Mullarkey may have told you, the bloody money for this sort of thing doesn't grow on trees, you know. And I can tell you here and now that "bloody money" is just what some of those cute bastards of bureaucrats are going to call it. Brussels is crawling with every kind of shagging lunatic you can think of, and you can bet your sweet life there are plenty of those Animal Rights crazies lurking in the woodwork, just waiting to crawl out at the first sign of money being directed towards blood sports . . .'

He could see that Gallerick was about to protest that his beloved fox-hunting was not a blood sport, despite the impressive array of foxes heads that gazed down on them from the walls of the drawing room in which they were sitting. A watery sun streamed in through the windows and formed a pool of blinding light on the white marble of the huge fireplace. Mick raised his hand to forestall Gallerick's interruption. It was a ploy that had made him a force to be reckoned with in the hurly-burly of politics for longer than he cared to remember.

* See *The Neon Madonna*.

4

'. . . and, my Lord, before you remind me yet again that there is no cruelty whatsoever involved in fox-hunting, save your breath for cooling the soup. I'll take your word for it. The big question is whether the bureaucrats in Brussels will do likewise!'

'Well, of course the silly buggers won't, unless someone like you explains it to them. That's what I'm relying on you to do for me, and the rest of the hunt members.'

The door of the drawing room crashed open, thereby cutting off whatever contribution Gallerick was about to add to the sum of human knowledge. A radiant creature in skin-tight riding breeches and long black leather boots with dark brown tops stormed into the room. Her well-cut riding jacket emphasised rather than concealed her full, rounded breasts. Without so much as glance at Mick, she brushed aside the strands of long dark hair streaming out from under her hunting cap and exploded.

'Daddy, it really is a bit bloody thick! That focking mare ran away with me again. Ran right through McCarthy's cornfield like shit through a goose. Try as I might, there wasn't a focking thing I could do about it. Long Tom McCarthy was out shooting crows. The bastard let me have both barrels just as I jumped out of the field as quickly as I could. Luckily I was about eighty yards away but I swear I have a dozen pellets stuck in my ar . . .'

The precise whereabouts of the pellets were destined to remain a mystery. Mick was sorely disappointed. Being familiar with the tantrums of Gallerick's only child, he was aware that there was always the possibility that she might have been sufficiently in-censed to display her wounds there and then. It was not to be. Gallerick hurriedly interrupted her outburst with a rasping cough, followed by: 'Aphra dear, you remember Mister Flannery, don't you?'

Aphra rubbed her hindquarters gingerly. 'Been trying to put the bite on you for a few quid, has he, Mister Flannery? Hope you can swing it for the poor old darling this time. Daddy, what was that you called Mister Flannery when he phoned to say he couldn't get you the grant to fix the roof? A typical . . .'

'Don't pay the slightest heed to her, Michael. Aphra is a splendid girl in many respects but she does have a rather arch sense of humour. Darling, why don't you run along and phone Dr Buckley? Ask him to come over to have at look at your er . . . wound. After

5

that we can decide whether to complain to the Sergeant about that McCarthy blackguard. Don't you think that would be quite the best thing to do, Michael?'

Mick failed to hear the question the first time it was put to him. He was lost in a happy trance as he stared hungrily at the perfectly shaped, if perforated posterior of Lady Aphra as she disappeared through the doorway. Definitely a front runner in his personal 'Rear of the Year' competition. It wasn't often that Mick Flannery envied Doc Buckley his job, he reflected, as he asked Gallerick to repeat the question.

2

The Porsche was beginning to overheat. Divareli could readily understand why. He and his car were entangled in a procession slower than any funeral. The narrow road with its high ditches on either side of the pot-holed track discouraged any turning round to escape. Because they were all heading in the same direction he shuddered to think what would happen if he tried. Stuck there forever, he expected. They would find his whitened skeleton sitting upright in a rusting Porsche, hands clutching the steering wheel in a vice-like grip, the gearbox forever welded into first gear. To think that he had gulped down lunch lest he should be late for the first race! Niall, the general factotum of the hotel and the possessor of the most spectacular facial acne Divareli had ever seen, had warned him to get to the Point-to-Point well before the two o'clock start.

'You'd be as well to be moving right away, Misther Divareli. Sure the world and his wife will be at the races today. What else have they to do with themselves of a Sunday afternoon, what with the pubs being shut and all?'

Divareli had not attempted to answer what might well have been a rhetorical question. The opening hours of Irish pubs were a mystery wrapped in an enigma, set by laws that were old when Moses received the Commandments. All licensed premises had to close between the hours of two and four on Sunday afternoons. Whether this was to keep holy the Sabbath Day or to allow the innkeeper to grab his lunch and clean his premises before the evening trade remained unclear. It was already ten minutes to two and all he could see ahead was a stream of elderly motor cars snaking away over the distant horizon. His rear mirror painted the same picture in reverse. Since he had turned off what was laughingly called 'the main road' down what appeared to be the dried-up bed of a river, it had been nothing short of a driver's nightmare. Stuttering progress of a few yards was followed by a five-minute standstill, then another lurch forward.

The vehicle ahead had a fine coating of brown mud which cloaked most of its rust and might even have held the contraption together. It contained a large family out for a Sunday afternoon at the races. To while away the time, the younger members were trying to tear each other limb from limb in the back seat. The parents were in front, sitting rigid as statues. Every so often the mother would turn and strike out at the warring offspring behind her with what appeared to be a shoe.

Inching around a sharp bend, he was heartened by signs of activity that might be associated with the staging of a race meeting. A knot of men wearing heavy green anoraks zipped up to their tonsils against the biting wind were gathered at a crossroads. He watched as one of their number detached himself reluctantly from the group to approach a car. Each man carried a leather bag attached to a shoulder strap. Though there was nothing remotely like a racetrack in sight, they were apparently collecting the admission fee. Crumpled banknotes were exchanged for white tickets. Each transaction involved animated discussion. To judge by the collectors' faces, it was not just animated but often downright hostile. Divareli rolled down the window in anticipation. He had no idea how much it might cost to get in. In a perfect world, he reflected, it was they who should be paying him. With the window open, he could eavesdrop on the exchanges between the collector and the driver of the rustbucket in front.

'How much are you looking for, anyway?' The reply from the collector was undecipherable. The driver's voice became shrill with indignation. 'Ah Jaysus, you're joking of course! Sure we're after missin' the first shaggin' race already. What's more, we've got to be out of the place well before the last race. The wife's aunt is coming to tea, if you don't mind. Trust herself to pick the one day the races are on!'

Unmoved by such intimate details of family life, the opening demand must have been repeated by the collector who was showing signs of impatience, a feeling shared by those behind Divareli. Horns tooted gently at first, then rapidly grew to a blaring crescendo. He had to strain to catch the last act of the drama being played out before him.

'A tenner? Christ Almighty, man, are you gone clean out of your mind? Even a blind eejit could see that the kids in the back are barely out of nappies . . .'

A strategic error, it would seem. Before he could press his case any further, the sire was engulfed in a howling chorus of protest from his young, who screamed out their true ages. The end result was drowned in a renewed outburst of hornblowing. Divareli saw what looked like a ten-pound note being stuffed into the pouch without change being offered, and the car with its distressed passengers roared off with a bad-tempered lurch.

Divareli paid five pounds without demur. Conversation was minimal as the collector was keen to confer with four scruffy-looking men in the car behind. They might well have been bearers of 'information'. Niall the boots had impressed on him the absolute necessity of 'information'. To Niall the very thought of betting on a horse because of its form or appearance was laughable.

'Do you know what it is I'm goin' to tell you, Misther Divareli?' The pimply youth had elevated the rhetorical question to the level of an art form.

'Any man . . .', he then repeated this in a higher key, to lend even greater emphasis to his pearl of wisdom. 'Any man who puts a shilling on a horse without knowing at least four tings for sure and certain is a fool, that's what he is. And now sir, if you are going to the races yourself, perhaps you might do me a small bit of a favour. The boss won't give me the day off because he's goin' there himself and he needs me to keep an eye on the place, you know. As I can't ask the auld hoor to put the money on for me as he'd only think he was payin' me too much, I'll have to ask yourself to oblige me by putting on a bet for me.'

He dug deep into a trouser pocket and fished out what appeared to be a crumpled candy wrapper. Placing it on the white linen tablecloth, he ironed it out with the palm of his hand until it was transformed, as if by magic, into a very old five-pound note. It looked as if it had been in the Callahan family for generations.

'Put that on *Flannery's Fancy* in the fourth for me, like the dacent gentleman you are. And if you take my advice, you'll have a cut at it yourself. Only for God's sake get my few quid on first before you drive the odds down with your own bet!'

With a cackle he had vanished before Divareli could discover what the four 'tings' might be. His reverie was disturbed by a scene of utter chaos unfolding before him. Several car-lengths ahead there was a narrow gap cut in the ditch. Inside the gap, there were signs

9

that something was afoot. From what he could see, cars were sprawled rather than parked all over the side of a grassy hill. A few striped marquees formed what had to be the nucleus of the Point-to-Point. The vehicles ahead were spewing out even more exhaust fumes than before, their drivers hunched over the steering wheels as though waiting for the starter's flag to fall. When he again opened the window, his ears were assailed by the revving of engines. It sounded like the starting grid of the Indianapolis 500. Unlike Indy, however, there was another line of cars coming from the opposite direction. The opposing cars jostled for position as they prepared to negotiate the sharp turn through the narrow entrance to the racetrack.

Directing the proceedings like the conductor of an unruly orchestra as he waved each vehicle through the gap, was the uniformed figure of a Garda Siochana. The three stripes on his arm showed him to be a Sergeant of Police. That he was held in some respect by the racegoers was evident from the fact that even the most ardent hornblowers had ceased their tooting. At a signal from the cop the chosen car would leap forward from the pack, engine revving frantically, its driver's face glued to the windscreen in fevered anticipation. Then it would accelerate hard and turn sharply into the gap.

From what Divareli could see, there was a certain amount of mud churned up by the overnight rain. To judge from the screaming engines and the clouds of brownish spray that accompanied each entrance, the gap itself was only part of the ordeal. He wondered how the Porsche would behave in such conditions. He had bought the car in London on the understanding that he would sell it back to the dealer when his stay in Europe was at an end. That was one reason he was keen not to damage it. Then there was the matter of pride. To fail where others had succeeded was not a pleasant prospect.

By the time his turn came, he had laid his plans with military precision. He would approach the entrance in first gear, then accelerate furiously through. This should provide enough momentum to surge through what appeared to be a brown cesspool and then carry on up the hill. In the distance he could see family saloons slewing and slaloming in every direction, in a frantic attempt to reach higher ground.

Suddenly there came an eerie silence. The only sound to be heard was the crackle of static from the Public Address system high on the hill. When not actually informing the racegoers that the horses were now leaving the Parade Ring in a reedy tenor voice that sounded as if it were coming from the bottom of a deep well, it contented itself with hissing sporadically like some enraged electronic serpent. Just then Divareli realised the world had not stopped dead in its tracks. Rather some of its inhabitants were waiting in awe to see how this nattily dressed American in the expensive Porsche was going to negotiate the gap. The sudden realisation that he was not only the centre of attention but was also delaying proceedings caused him to accelerate rather more violently than he had planned.

The car took off like a bat out of hell. He struggled frantically to keep it between the stone walls. Just when it seemed inevitable that the forces of law and order were about to go short one middle-aged Sergeant, Divareli wrenched the wheel to the right. The Porsche slewed around like a well-trained thoroughbred to face the gap. A delicate dab of the throttle should get him safely through. It was not to be. Rather it had the effect of a spur to the flanks of the many horses that lived under the bonnet. They took fright and bolted.

The wheels spun, causing a skid which banged the passenger door off the stone wall of the gap with a metallic clang. Then the engine stalled and showed no inclination to restart. Even if it had done so, it was unlikely that the Porsche would have been able to get out of the mud from a standing start. A discreet tap on the window startled Divareli. It was the Sergeant. Divareli wound down the window. He noticed that the cop was wearing green gumboots.

'That's a fine car you have there, Mr Divareli . . .'

How in the blazes did the cop know his name. *Oh well*, he thought resignedly, *that's his job, I suppose*.

'. . . but I don't see you getting it out of there on your own. There's a man over there on a tractor who'll pull you out. He'll charge you well for it, though. Will I call him?'

Divareli nodded. Getting stuck where rusty old rattletraps, weighed down with snotty-nosed brats and their parents, had sailed through without mishap had left him speechless with embarrassment. A tractor that might have been Harry Ferguson's prototype lurched towards him. Its driver dismounted on the further shore. He was a tall, slightly stooped man who made his way gingerly through the swamp. He was carrying a blue nylon rope with a noose at the end of it. For a moment Divareli feared that the obstruction of punters from backing their choice might be a hanging offence in these parts. To judge by the horns being blown in exasperation, if it were put to a vote, it would have been carried. Then he realised that the rope was merely to drag him out of the mud. The lanky figure, in waders that reached above his waist, was brief but to the point.

'I'm Johnny Slattery. I'll pull you out for a tenner.'

There followed a longish pause, during which it dawned on Divareli that Slattery's outstretched palm indicated a 'cash up-front' situation. He peeled off a purple ten-pound note from a wad of notes and handed it over reluctantly. That it was but a drop in the ocean compared to the cost of a new door for his beloved Porsche afforded him no consolation whatsoever. To make matters worse, it would probably take a lifetime even to get the door shipped from Germany to this goddamn barren lump of rock that called itself Ireland. There and then he resolved to check out of the hotel tomorrow and go back home to the Land of the Free.

3

The twelve horses stalked around the ring as though they owned it. They showed nothing but contempt for those watching their every move in the hope of picking a winner. One animal in particular caught the eye. It had the loping stride of a top model sashaying down the ramp with all her moving parts working in unison like a well-oiled machine. Divareli remembered reading somewhere that Hemingway could smell a winner before it left the ring. As a one-time disciple of the old fraud, he too believed that he had the same gift.

That might have been true where takeovers were concerned. The bank that his father owned had recently gone 'merchant'. All this meant was that they now advanced money as well as advice to companies wishing to buy a stake in other, often larger enterprises. Divareli specialised in selecting wounded companies ripe for a surprise attack. 'Dawn raids', the media had dubbed the ploy. The formula was always the same: grab a foothold stock either by stealth or agreement with the existing management. Then line up the money necessary to buy out the existing shareholders while offering the management a free ride. What with the fees generated by the buyout and the profits from the foothold stock, Divareli invariably made millions both for himself and his bank. Later the subsidiaries would be sold off to the highest bidder, the surplus staff fired and only the valuable core business retained.

Like every other scam ever devised by the greed of mankind, it was good while it lasted. Of late however, the Securities Exchange Commission had taken to scrutinising the deals a little too closely for comfort, while the paper used to finance some of these deals proved virtually worthless in a changed climate of high interest rates. Now, Divareli had decided, would be as good a time as any to take a long break away from Wall Street. He had just disposed of his majority share in Italbank for twenty-seven million dollars while retaining a sufficiently large holding to guarantee his Chief

Executive status would continue. Burnt out from non-stop wheeling and dealing, he had six months leave stacked up which would enable him to see Europe and try to jemmy his way into British Society.

Right now he intended to apply his nose for winners to the Brulagh Inn Maiden Race. According to the race card, entries were confined to horses of six years or more who had hunted regularly with the Gallerick pack of hounds and which had never won a race. Furthermore, all of them were to carry twelve stone and the distance would be about three miles. Presumably should the jockey weigh less, the balance would be made up by putting lead weights beneath the saddle.

In the ring, the mare he had spotted earlier continued to stand out above the rest. She was a big chestnut with a white diamond on her forehead. Her impatience to get on with the proceedings showed in her refusal to walk quietly around like the others. Instead she checked, pranced sideways as she strained at the reins, tossed her head and occasionally lashed out with her hooves at the horse behind her. Her exertions had produced a light sweat that glistened like shot silk in the weak winter sunlight. Divareli was delighted to note that she carried the number seven – his lucky number. Whenever it came up in blackjack or craps, he seemed to win. He saw by the card that the mare's name was *O'Riley* and she was the property of Mrs Margaret Flannery.

He searched through the pockets of the wax jacket he had bought in Harrods, part of his doomed strategy to break into London society. The hunting set, he had perceived, were also the aristocracy. A frosty clique, they set their faces sternly against intruders – even their own kith and kin. He was warned that New Money was anathema to them. What then, he asked plaintively, was the key? Was it endowing hospitals? Underwriting a posh blueblood charity or simply slipping a few hundred grand on the quiet to the Tory party? His mentor in these matters, who ran a merchant bank closely linked to Divareli's, advised him that none of these ploys would work on this side of the Atlantic. Such transparent attempts to buy social status would be scoffed at in Merrie England, but *not so* however, in Southern Ireland – where a more bohemian type of aristocracy still survived. Though their blood was every bit as blue as their British counterparts, they were always short of funds, and this made

14

them more approachable. Money spent with discretion, the banker explained, could secure an *entrée* into the Irish hunting set.

Divareli rummaged through his pockets until he found the torn scrap of notepaper embossed with a fancy crest and old-fashioned lettering that read: *The Gallerick Arms Hotel, Est. 1735.* Scrawled across it was *Flannery's Fancy. Fourth Race. Five pounds Win.* Pinned to the paper was a grimy five-pound note.

If anyone back in New York had heard that Divareli was acting as a bookie's runner for a junior staff member of a clapped-out hotel, they would have laughed themselves into a permanent state of hiccups. He examined the card to find the animal's number. This was not as straightforward as might have been expected. There were forty-three runners down for the fourth race. This was ridiculous! The track could not accommodate half that number – it would be more like a cavalry charge than a race. Then he spotted a notice written with a red marker, hanging from the mast that supported the loudspeakers. This informed the racegoing public that the field had been reduced to the eleven runners listed below.

Divareli wondered what he should do in the event of Niall's selection joining the ranks of the non-runners. He need not have worried. There he was, number thirty. The animal was about half the size of the other horses, more like a king-size pony, in fact, with his ribs showing through half-clipped flanks. He looked as if he had been used as a workhorse all his life, and not a very good one at that. The race card proclaimed him to be *Flannery's Fancy*, the property of Mr Timothy Houlihan, proprietor of the Gallerick Arms Hotel. The breeding was unhelpful. The sire was called *Apparition* and the dam *Brussels Sprout*. The rider was, if anything, even less impressive though his face looked vaguely familiar. The names of the riders had been called out over the defective Public Address system about five minutes earlier as Divareli made his way towards the Parade Ring. He was therefore in blissful ignorance of who it was that was riding his selection or, for that matter, *Flannery's Fancy*. It struck him as odd, however, that one horse should be called 'Flannery' while a different animal was owned by a lady of the same name.

He pushed through the milling crowd towards a line of book-makers. For some reason they advertised their profession as Turf Accountants. They were surrounded by a solid phalanx of bodies, all jostling each other for a better view of the small blackboards with the names of the horses and their odds scribbled alongside. Divareli headed for a bookie who called himself Honest Joe Quinn. The sparse crowd in front of his pitch belied his title. Then again, perhaps the slack trade might have been due to the fact that Honest Joe's minimum bet was five pounds. Divareli shouldered his way through the onlookers until his eyes were level with Honest Joe's toecaps. 'Five Pounds to win on *Flannery's Fancy*, please!'

Honest Joe snatched the money with alacrity while giving him a searching look. It might have come straight out of the pit of the New York Stock Exchange. It asked several questions all at once such as, 'Do you have any inside knowledge?' or, 'Does this bum know something I don't?' For the first time that afternoon, Divareli was beginning to enjoy himself. The bookie turned to his assistant, teetering precariously on top of a plastic crate while clasping a clipboard in one hand and a biro in the other.

Honest Joe sang out in a bored voice, '*Five at twelves for a win on thirty.*'

A ripple of interest ran through the crowd of onlookers. If they did not have the money to bet, then their next best option was to watch someone else doing so. Divareli heard one old man in a tweed cap pulled far down over his nose turn to his companion and shout in his ear: 'Your man there, the Yank, is after havin' a fiver win on the Flannery ting. I wouldn't mind but the world an' his wife know that animal can't run fast enough to warm himself!'

Divareli placed the coloured ticket for Niall's bet in a side pocket. As he did so, Honest Joe produced a green duster with the flourish of a conjuror plucking a rabbit from his hat and wiped the figure twelve from in front of *Flannery's Fancy*. After a moment's thought, he chalked down the figure eight in its place. A bet of five pounds had moved the odds back four points! Divareli took out Niall's ticket again and carefully wrote *12 to 1* on it. Then he turned to Honest Joe and examined his other offerings on what looked like a pretty volatile market. It came as no surprise to see that *O'Riley* was the firm favourite at odds of two to one. Divareli fished out two fifty-pound notes and said, 'One hundred pounds for a win on *O'Riley*, please!'

A hush settled on the kibbitzers behind him. For a second or so, Honest Joe looked as though his assistant had stabbed him in the back. He made a quick recovery but still appeared to be less than delighted about this sudden rush of business coming his way. Again he sang out to his assistant. '*A hundred to win on the favourite, number seven at two's!*'

There was a hostile rasp to his voice. This time there was no hesitation whatsoever before he wiped the figure two from in front of *O'Riley*'s name. To a ragged cheer from the onlookers, he left the space blank and fixed his gaze at something high in the sky. There would be no more bets taken by him on the favourite for the Brulagh Inn Maiden Race.

As he walked away, Divareli noticed several of Honest Joe's colleagues following his example by wiping *O'Riley* off their boards. He placed his own coloured ticket inside a zippered, anti-theft pocket, but not before he had pencilled '*No. 7. O'Riley £100 win at twos.*' He glowed with pride. It was the first time he had forced a bookie to wipe a horse off his board. Not, he reflected, that he visited the racetrack all that often. Still, he had made some pretty heavy bets on the Harvard-Yale game from time to time. These had been sparked by twin objectives. The first was, of course, to make a killing. The other was more subtle. It was designed to suggest, without actually telling the big lie, that he had graduated from Harvard. Whenever he was asked if he had attended that particular seat of learning, he would reply offhandedly, 'Oh sure, I spent time there.' Which was perfectly true. He had gone there for a course in Business Ethics. It had proved useful a few times since then when he was unsure how the Ivy League bankers might react in any given situation.

He leaned over the railing of the Parade Ring to take a last look at his selection. To his consternation, a slim, red-haired girl was climbing aboard *O'Riley*. By the look of her, there would have to be about five stone of lead under the saddle to make up the weight. He asked a fellow onlooker, 'Who's riding number seven?'

The man drew back from him and carefully looked him up and down before answering. 'Mick Flannery's daughter, that's who. And she'd better do what's expected of her though. I'm not telling you one word of a lie but if I were her father I'd never rely on a red-headed woman – even a young wan like herself! Still and all, we can only hope for the best!'

With that, his informant vanished into the crowd. Divareli wished the stranger had been more specific. It would have taken a very

17

sharp man to make much of what he had heard. The loudspeaker above his head exploded to life, giving him quite a start.

'*The horses are now about to leave the Parade Ring. Would patrons please allow room for the horses and their riders to make their way down to the start of the Brulagh Inn Maiden Race. The organisers of today's Point-to-Point would like to take this opportunity of thanking Mister Michael Flannery for the valuable trophy he will present to the winner after this race. With the three hundred pounds prize money on offer by his son, Sean, the ever-popular proprietor of the Brulagh Inn, this race is the major highlight of our racing today.*'

With a click, the PA was switched off, leaving Divareli even more confused than before by the evergrowing Flannery influence. If the trophy and the stake were presented by Flannerys, as well as *O'Riley* being owned and ridden by what surely must be members of the same clan, what did that mean? And why was a horse with apparently no family connection called *Flannery's Fancy*?

He reached for a pack of Camels and applied the flame from his gold Zippo to one of them. He drew the smoke down to his toenails before allowing it to trickle out through his nostrils as he tried, without success, to unravel the mystery. It looked as if he had stumbled across a nice little family set-up. All he had to do was stick around and collect the money. Just like home, he finally decided, as he walked briskly towards the last fence before the winning post.

4

Down at the start, utter chaos reigned. The official Starter, a small fat man in a black bowler hat and a suit several sizes too small for him, stood on the roof of a green van. From there he traded insults with the jockeys and their supporters.

'Will ye start de shagging race before they're scattered to de four corners of de earth?' was the most courteous request launched in his direction. Doubts as to his parentage were raised by those who struggled to keep their mounts in check. Divareli noticed that *O'Riley*, the unwitting partner in his recent betting coup, was cutting a swathe through the other entries in the Brulagh Inn Maiden Hurdle. When she wasn't trying to bite them, her hind legs lashed out at anything that moved. By contrast, her rider the red-haired Flannery female was perched atop her back, her face a picture of utter serenity, oblivious to the confused antics around her. She might as well have been sitting on a wall and watching the world pass by.

Of Niall's selection, there was no sign. *Flannery's Fancy* would have been difficult to spot anyway among horses nearly twice his size. Even with his powerful binoculars, Divareli was unable to pick him out from the seething mass of horseflesh that milled around the Starter. A glance at the race card showed his rider to be wearing *'blue, red stripes on slvs; yellow cap'*. A wider sweep with the glasses located a yellow blob. Yes, there he was, on the outer edge of the crowd and well away from the rest of the horses.

For some reason or other the wearer of the yellow cap had dismounted. Trouble with the saddle, it appeared; a group of men formed a tight scrum around the animal. They were pulling and dragging with some ferocity at the light racing saddle, tightening a girth, perhaps, or adjusting the length of the stirrup irons. A tall lanky individual, who looked very like the one who had relieved him of ten pounds in exchange for pulling him out of the gap,

19

appeared to wrench at something. Shortly afterwards he disappeared into the crowd. The jockey remounted and the Starter, by now purple in the face from shouting at the riders, waved a white handkerchief in the air. The Brulagh Inn Maiden Race had begun.

Much to Divareli's satisfaction, *O'Riley* established an early lead. Horse and rider cleared the fences with feet to spare and barely checked on landing before breaking into a strong gallop towards the next. The jumps were ditches separating the fields with white markers, between which the riders had to steer their mounts. Some were stone walls that had to be cleared in one leap while others were huge earthen banks. The horses had to clamber up one side and then slither down the other. The last hurdle to clear before the winning post had the added problem of a deep water-filled trench on the far side. Each fence had wings to funnel the horses into the narrow jumps, which also prevented stray horses from running loose among the crowd that surged around each obstacle, hurling abuse or encouragement at each rider according to their fancy.

Divareli stationed himself by the last jump. He stood on top of a broken stone wall which gave him a clear view of the proceedings except where the horses disappeared behind a hill just after the start. The race would be three laps of the course. The Public Address system had debugged itself so that the commentary could now be heard quite clearly.

'*Coming to the last, the first time round*, O'Riley *with her lady jockey, has established a clear lead over her rivals.*'

All of these the commentator named individually with a word of encouragement about each. Even those horses already hopelessly tailed off were described as being '*some way behind with ground to make up*'. This might have been due to his charitable nature or to give the backers of no-hopers the illusion that their selections were still in there with a chance. Even the most optimistic of commentators, however, would have been hard put to instil a glimmer of hope in those foolish enough to back *Flannery's Fancy*. The best he could do in concluding his description of the field was to say, '. . . *and bringing up the rear, some distance behind the others, is that gallant small horse*, Flannery's Fancy.'

Indeed, the only point on which a fair-minded observer could take issue with the description was the use of 'gallant'. Twenty lengths behind an exhausted backmarker as he passed Divareli, *Flannery's Fancy* looked to be out for an afternoon's canter. Well, it seemed as though Niall would have to seek elsewhere for his fortune. A fool and his money soon part.

As they thundered past, Divareli trained his glasses on the leaders. It appeared that *O'Riley* was beginning to feel the dead weight of the lead on her back as she approached the halfway stage. She still maintained a strong lead but the backmarkers were beginning to catch up. As they passed him for the second time, there were barely twenty lengths between first and last. Of even greater consequence was that whereas *O'Riley* was now lathered in sweat and breathing heavily as she cleared the fence with only millimetres to spare, *Flannery's Fancy* was galloping along with an easy stride and sailing over the fences like a bird. So much so, in fact, that if Divareli were afforded the opportunity to place another bet on the eventual outcome, he might well have supported Niall's selection despite the animal's shaggy, half-clipped coat. Its rider was equally unkempt, wearing rubber wellington boots heavily encrusted with what looked suspiciously like cow dung.

Four furlongs from home there were only two horses left in the race. Even the commentator confined his remarks to them as the rest of the field had either pulled up or were in danger of being lapped. The girl on *O'Riley* was bent over the animal's arched neck, urgently whispering encouragement into its ear. This was in stark contrast to *Flannery's Fancy* whose jockey was suddenly transformed into a screaming dervish lashing the flanks of his mount without mercy. It had a startling effect, reminiscent of the turbocharger cutting in. *Flannery's Fancy* surged ahead of its rival and, clearing the last fence with feet to spare, raced home an easy winner.

As Divareli followed the two finishers into the unsaddling enclosure he noticed that *O'Riley*'s rider was in tears as she sobbed into the ear of her mare, 'The fucking bastard, the dirty rotten cheating bastard!'

An aristocratic-looking woman in her twenties, dressed in a waxed jacket of indeterminate age and faded jeans tucked inside leather riding boots was trying to console her. Meanwhile the winning jockey dismounted and was engulfed in a crowd of backslapping well-wishers. Among them was the gaunt figure of Johnny Slattery, the tractor driver-cum-salvage expert. As he pushed towards the jockey, he seemed to be clasping something inside his anorak. Moments later he emerged from the throng.

The winning jockey left the winners' enclosure – a corner of the Parade Ring with the numbers one, two and three crudely painted in red on the wooden railing. Clutching his saddle to his chest as though his life depended on it, he was carried along by his jubilant supporters to the Weigh Tent. Out of curiosity, Divareli allowed himself to be caught up in the surge towards the weighing scales. They were of the sort used for weighing bags of coal or potatoes. The jockey, complete with saddle, stood on the platform, and watched the needle on the glass dial sweep around the numbers like a ball dancing on the roulette wheel until it came to rest on twelve. A tall man dressed in heavy tweeds was peering closely at the dial. A badge on his lapel read *Judge and Clerk of the Scales*.

In a plummy accent he announced, 'Well, everything seems in order, eh chaps?'

The chaps seemed to agree as seconds later, '*Winner All Right*' was announced over the loudspeakers. After a pause followed by a burst of earsplitting static, the voice continued: '*Mister Michael Flannery, our Representative in the European Parliament and the husband of the owner of the second-placed horse will now present the trophy so kindly donated by himself to the winning owner, the ever-popular hotelier, Mr Timothy Houlihan . . .*'

The speaker's pause for loud cheering was unnecessary. The whoops of delight at the Flannery name gave way to a light smattering of polite applause when Houlihan's name was mentioned.

'*. . . Mister Flannery will also present a handsome cheque to the winning owner. This was kindly donated by his son, Sean Flannery, the owner of the Brulagh Inn. Sean regrets that he is unable to be here to present it himself so he has asked his dad to do the honours.*'

Another burst of whooping and cheering greeted this news item. Divareli wondered at its cause. He was not to know that Sean Flannery was at daggers drawn with Houlihan because they were both deadly rivals in the same line of business, and that Sean would have preferred to jump over a cliff than present his sworn enemy with anything more than a knee in the groin. If Flannery senior shared his son's views, he concealed the fact well. A large man in an expensive suit and snow-white shirt, he looked as though he was thoroughly enjoying himself as he grasped the microphone and launched into a torrent of what Divareli presumed to be the native dialect.

'*Ahh Card-Juh Gwail, Thaw Awhus moor orrum . . .*' It was a relief when he reverted to a recognisable tongue. 'My friends, I will continue in the language of the Albion for those of you not nurtured in our mother tongue . . .'

This sally drew loud guffaws. Someone behind Divareli shouted, 'Go on outa dat, yew hoor yew. Them's the only few bloody words of Irish yew know!'

If the speaker heard the comment, he chose to ignore it. 'It is my pleasant duty today to present my cup and my son's cheque to the lucky owner of the winner, *Flannery's Fancy*!'

Cries of 'Good man yourself, Mick' and 'For Jaysus sake will you get on with it or we'll be here all day' rent the air. Unperturbed, the speaker continued without pause, 'I have often wondered whether the animal was named after myself or some other member of the family but I suppose that's Tim Houlihan's business and his alone. Anyway, I'm sure you will all agree that it is odd, to say the very least, that my wife's horse should be beaten by another one bearing the family name. Still and all, they tell me all's fair in war and love and those of you that got it at twelves are unlikely to object . . .'

More delighted whoops ensued as Mick Flannery waited for the noise to die down before resuming. 'Anyway, my last duty is to remind you all that the Race Dance is at the Brulagh Inn tonight. Music by the Brulagh Ceili Band, and the good news for all of us is that there's a bar extension till two o'clock in the morning. If ye haven't enough drank by then, 'tis your own fault. Oh . . . and I nearly forgot, there's a disco on at the Leisure Centre for the younger crowd. It is now my pleasant duty to hand the cup and the cheque over to – Timothy Houlihan!'

Divareli looked sadly at his ticket before tearing it into tiny shreds.

'Looks as though you backed the wrong horse, eh?'

Divareli nodded as he sized up the young woman who had posed the question. It was none other than the comforter of the disconsolate jockey a few minutes earlier. She had dark hair tucked inside a silk scarf, framing her high cheekbones. The stained waxedjacket, now carelessly slung over her shoulders, looked as if it had been retrieved from the trash heap, while a baggy sweater hid what appeared to be an excellent figure. The jeans and high boots exuded a couldn't-care-less elegance and a casual sexuality in about equal proportions. He took out his cigarettes and offered her one.

'But it was a good race.'

'Good my arse. The whole focking thing was fixed from start to finish!'

She waved away his Camels with the observation that it was the only brand with a drawing of the factory on the packet before Divareli could regain his composure. As she fished a pack of Dunhill out of her jacket and accepted his offer of a light, he asked, 'I beg your pardon but I don't quite follow you – are you saying the race was crooked?'

'As a ram's horn, that's how crooked it was. The winner never carried an ounce of lead. Even a blind man could see that!'

'Then why didn't someone object?'

'They wouldn't have got much of a hearing, would they?'

'You can't be serious.' It seemed more like the rough stuff he had left behind him.

'Listen, my friend, the crowd running this race meeting could give training courses to that lot. It wouldn't surprise me in the least if that Flannery reptile had his shirt on the winner even though his own daughter was cheated out of the race. So much for the purity of the focking turf! My name's Aphra. You must be the Yank everyone's talking about!'

Divareli dragged deep on the Camel and examined her through half-closed eyes as he exhaled the smoke through his nostrils. She looked like something cut out of the pages of *Country Life*, the magazine he had been boning up on before crossing the Atlantic. Trouble, he decided.

'Hi, Aphra. Good to know you. Luke Divareli.'

'I know. Niall told me.'

'Niall back at the hotel?'

'One and the same! I used to work as a receptionist at the desk for a while until Houlihan started hassling me. Are you coming to the Race Dance?'

'Hadn't really thought about it. Is that an invitation?'

'Could be. If you want to see life in the raw, the Brulagh Inn's the place to be tonight. Sean is a good sort. He and his wife deserve a bit of support. Well?'

This time Divareli could not avoid answering her question. He tried a counter punch. 'I've got a better idea. Why don't you and I have dinner at the hotel, then I'll drive you back to the Brulagh and we can take a peek at this Race Dance?'

5

As they approached the car, Divareli remembered he had forgotten to collect Niall's winnings. 'Hold it – I nearly forgot. I've got to collect my winnings.'

'I thought you said you lost!'

'I did. Niall didn't.'

'Christ, the pimply excrescence must have been in on it, too! I'll find Daddy and tell him that I'm going back with you. You collect Niall's ill-gotten gains and I'll meet you back here in twenty minutes.'

When Divareli proffered the winning ticket, the bookie stared at him long and hard before calling over his shoulder, 'Twelve fives less tax for the gentleman . . .' Then he turned to Divareli and addressed him directly. 'You got a good run for your money. Only for your big bet I would be going home without a penny in my pocket. There was a bundle of money slapped on the winner by the locals just before the "off". Did you have special information about the mare, if you don't mind me asking – or did you just pick her out within a pin?'

Divareli shook his head, not wishing to be drawn into a discussion on what he was now convinced was a fix. It was some consolation that Honest Joe had also taken a hammering on *Flannery's Fancy*, as had his colleagues, to judge by the long queues of smiling punters waiting to collect their winnings. 'I just liked the look of her, that's all!'

'Oh, she's a good-looker to be sure. The mare's not bad, either!'

Honest Joe, it would appear, was a comedian. He handed over the winnings which Divareli placed carefully inside his jacket. It came to just under sixty pounds – considerably more than Niall's wages, Divareli guessed, if Houlihan's appearance was anything to go by. The winning owner and proprietor of the Gallerick Hall Hotel had a lean and hungry look about him. Though he had seen him scurrying around the hotel, Divareli had met him just once in the few days he had been staying there. The john down the corridor from Divareli's room was not working. On receiving this information,

26

Houlihan had become positively oleaginous. Washing his hands nervously with an invisible bar of soap he assured Divareli that he would attend to the matter this very instant. He assured his indignant guest of the hotel's appreciation at his custom and, having declared himself overwhelmed with grief at such an embarrassing incident, promised Divareli his unfailing attention at all times. Blaming the whole thing on the poor quality of the staff available nowadays, Houlihan concluded by swearing on his mother's grave that the fault would be put right within the hour. Two days later the john was still out of commission.

When he got back to the Porsche, Aphra was leaning against it, talking to the gaunt Johnny Slattery. She greeted Divareli with a cheery wave as she introduced him. 'Luke, this is Johnny Slattery. As well as the towing concession, the old darling runs the poteen operation round here, don't you, Johnny?' Slattery extended his hand without comment, but not before wiping his nose with it first. Whether this was a reflex action or a studied insult was impossible to say. Divareli reluctantly gave him a wimpish handshake, nothing like the bonecruncher he'd been taught to deliver. He decided that the opportunity seemed too good to miss.

'Tell me, did you win a lot of money on *Flannery's Fancy*? I saw you helping out with his saddle just before the start.'

Divareli was gratified at the effect of his remarks. Slattery's long jaw dropped as though he had been poleaxed. Hiding his confusion by affecting to look at his watch, he ignored the question completely and turned to Aphra.

'We'd better get goin' if I'm to drag ye out before the next race. There's a horse goin' in it that I kind of half-fancy.'

Divareli opened the damaged door for his passenger and then slid behind the wheel. He sat back, all but helpless as Slattery pulled him through the swamp and out through the gap for the second time that afternoon. In the absence of even the vaguest reference to matters financial, he assumed this to be either part of Slattery's after-sales service or an attempt to buy his silence. Having recovered the tow rope, Slattery drove off noisily in his ancient tractor without so much as a farewell wave.

Divareli drove swiftly between the grey stone walls that fringed the narrow, winding road. This time the traffic was almost non-existent. Even on a dull, overcast day like this the scenery was

27

awesome. The dark brooding purple of the hills rose up to the sky to form the threatening mass of Mount Brulagh. As they drove down towards the village, the grey-blue sea was flecked by frothing white horses that raced across the wavecrests. Whenever the sun made a brief appearance, its brightness was chased across the choppy seas and over the rolling hills by a solid phalanx of black clouds that soon shrouded the landscape. The effect was that of a magic lantern show with the colours changing every time he dared lift his eyes from the potholed track that masqueraded as a road. Aphra's voice cut short his sightseeing.

'You'll have to drop me off in the village. My car is parked outside the Brulagh Inn. Daddy gave me a lift from there.'

'Do you live round here?'

Her confirmation did not encourage further cross-examination. Perhaps her domestic arrangements were a matter of some delicacy. He stole a glance at her left hand. No ring. Not that it meant much these days, he reflected gloomily. Could it be that his passenger had a dislike of such obvious labels? Aphra certainly had a marked curiosity which she made no effort to hide.

'What is an American doing in Brulagh at this time of year? Usually the only Yanks . . .' Aphra clapped her hand over her mouth in mock horror though her voice, as she pressed on, did not sound in the least apologetic '. . . only Americans we get here come in the summer, and even then it's usually because they have lost their way.' Her voice had acquired a faintly mocking lilt. Not enough to be offensive, but sufficient to make him rise to the bait.

'Maybe that's why I like it here. The hotel is goddamn awful but the people, apart from that creep Houlihan, are nice. Also the scenery . . .' He took a hand off the steering wheel to gesture vaguely towards Mount Brulagh, which was yet again undergoing a subtle colour change as the sun broke through momentarily, transforming what a millisecond ago had been a deep purple mass into a green carpet of undulating folds of light and shadow. 'I know it sounds trite but I've never seen anything like it before.'

'Yeeees.' Aphra sounded unimpressed, 'You may have something there. You should meet the Lady Dowager – my Grand-Aunt. She paints most of the time, though nowadays it's flowers and things rather than landscapes. She's mad as a hatter but not a bad painter, come to think of it.'

28

'If she's a Lady Dowager, does that mean I'm in the presence of a titled lady?' Having spent a lot of time and money trying to break into the charmed circle of aristocracy, it would be ironic, Divareli reflected, if he were to crack it now purely by chance.

'Yes, you're in the presence of the Lady Aphra, only child of the Eleventh Earl of Gallerick. Unfortunately I'll never make it to Countess. Only a male, however remote, can inherit – worse luck.'

'Does that mean,' Luke laughed out loud, 'that some guy could come over the hill and say "Here I am, now where's my castle"?'

She looked at him straight with such venom that he almost stopped the car. Long before she opened her mouth to speak, he knew he had said precisely the wrong thing. 'I think of little else night and focking day. It may seem amusing to you, but to me it's a recurring nightmare – and it won't go away.'

Luke shrugged his shoulders and said, 'Sorry,' just once. Then they lapsed into silence for the remaining five minutes of the journey. Just as he was about to set her down in front of the Brulagh Inn, she leaned across and touched his arm with her hand.

'I'm sorry, too. Sorry for snapping your head off. You weren't to know, how could you? I was just taking my absolutely foul temper out on you. It's my father I'm really mad at for getting involved with a pack of scoundrels like that lot in the Weigh Tent. I'm sure he was in on the betting coup along with the rest of them. He's badly strapped for money and probably saw this as a quick fix. Oh the stupid, stupid man!'

Far from being offended by it, he found her flash of temper fascinating. Rather attractive, in fact. He left her to contemplate the stupidity of her father for a moment while he digested what she had just said. 'Are you saying that your father is just a cheap crook – Earl Gallerick or whatever he calls himself?'

The mood had passed like the clouds rolling over Mount Brulagh. She flashed him a smile that warmed his heart. 'Old Gally? Oh no, he's great! You must have seen him in the Weigh Tent. He was the tallish chap in charge of the scales. Greying hair, in his sixties.'

'Jesus, was that him?'

'Yes, that was him. Hasn't two brass farthings to rub together, the old darling. What with a bloody big house falling down around his ears with Yours Truly to support and no male heir, I can tell you

Gally has his work cut out to make ends meet. A nice touch on *Flannery's Fancy* at twelves would be like manna from heaven to him.'

Divareli was outraged. Here he was breaking his ass trying to worm his way into the stately homes of the aristocracy and what happens? The very first genuine blueblood that crosses his path turns out to be a cheap horse-wrangler – and a crooked one at that. When he expressed his surprise that her father could be involved in something like this, Aphra appeared to bristle.

'Well, why ever not? Of course poor Gally was up to his neck in it! Isn't he the Judge as well as being Clerk of the Scales? That means anyone with a gripe, such as the bookies or the poor sods who backed the favourite, have to make their complaints to him. Makes sense, doesn't it?' She paused for a moment before asking, 'Where are you from?'

'New York.'

His name had a familiar ring to it that she couldn't quite pin down. It continued to scratch and scrape around at the edges of her memory in an annoying fashion. He was attractive in a sulky kind of way. He certainly had good taste in cars – the Porsche was divine. She probed further. 'You over here for long?'

'Haven't quite decided yet. I hope to get in some hunting while I'm here.'

'Well, Gally's your man for that! He has his own pack, in fact he's Master of the Gallerick Foxhounds, no less. They've been in the family since Adam was a boy.' She paused for a moment before continuing, 'Why not come to dinner tomorrow night? You could fix up about the hunting at the same time.'

Divareli was delighted by the offer. It was exactly what he wanted. 'Sounds great, but wouldn't it be something of an intrusion? I mean, the man has never seen me before in his life.'

'Oh, not to worry. God only knows who else will be there as well. It happens every so often. Just old Gally strutting his Lord of the Manor stuff. I can bring anyone I want. I don't go for married men, though. You one of those?'

'No . . .'

Before he could say any more she had put one hand on his arm and the other to her mouth as it finally struck her who he was – Luke Divareli the American banker! His face had been all over the

British tabloids as one of New York's most eligible bachelors now that he had made pots of money for selling something or other. She remembered thinking at the time how attractive he looked.

'Oh my God. Divareli – *Luke Divareli*?' He nodded but said nothing. 'Of *course*! Now I recognise you from the papers. "The Wall Street Raider". So *that's* who you are! I had wondered about the car – that explains it. Well, well! It certainly is a small world. Didn't you sell a bank or something for absolutely zillions?'

'Not all of it. The papers played it up to be a real big deal at the time. I came here for a bit of peace and quiet and to get in some hunting. Do you hunt, yourself?'

'Yes, I do. Have to really, though privately I regard it as sheer bloody murder. Grown men and women whooping it up as some poor wild dog gets ripped apart by its distant relatives. The farmers round here don't like it either. They object to a posse of over-dressed and over-privileged nincompoops galloping through their fields, leaving gates open, cutting up the grass and frightening the cattle.'

'That so? How exactly do they object?'

'By putting notices in the *Clarion* – that's the local paper – warning that their lands are preserved. Then of course there's Long Tom McCarthy. He has signs put up on the bounds of his land: *No fucking horses or riders allowed*. Though, to be honest, it's only a few of them. The rest are too fond of old Gally to kick up much of a fuss even if they can't stand the hunting crowd he knocks around with.'

They were approaching the outskirts of a small village. To their left was a shrine of some sort with rusted railings protecting it. Set in a cut-stone wall was a large statue of a woman looking skywards, a flickering neon halo poised six inches above her head. Further on, a large white sign with black lettering proclaimed *Failte go Brulagh*. Underneath it, in smaller letters, *Welcome to Brulagh*. Divareli wanted to hear more about long Tom. 'What about this McCarthy guy?'

'Oh him – nothing much. The crazy bastard just shot me in the arse, that's all.'

'Jesus Christ! Does that happen a lot round here? He might have killed you!'

'No, not really. I was a good bit away when he let me have both barrels, jumping out of his field. He caught me at the crucial

31

moment – just as my backside was in the air with the horse halfway over the fence. McCarthy has had it in for the hunt ever since Gally's father refused to pay him over the odds for a few hens the hounds killed by mistake. One word led to another and there has been bad blood between the families ever since. Here we are. Pull over by the footpath.'

'What about the yellow line? Doesn't that mean No Parking?'

'Not in Brulagh it doesn't. Sergeant Moriarty, the chap directing traffic outside the races, is a decent skin. He won't bother you if you don't bother him. Anyway, he's far too busy trying to catch our friend Slattery moonshining to bother about silly little things like parking on yellow lines. Come on in and I'll introduce you to Sean and his wife. You'll like them.'

They went inside. The bar was patterned on an English pub with lots of mahogany and oak panelling. Divareli liked it immediately, as he did the owner. Sean Flannery looked to be in his late twenties. Before Aphra could make the introductions, Sean stuck his hand out over the counter.

'Welcome to Brulagh, Mister Divareli. I'm Sean Flannery. What'll you have to drink?'

Divareli was taken aback. Aphra rescued him by chirping in a distinct Oxbridge tone, 'No need to show off, Sean. You see Luke, young Niall Callahan was in here last night and he told everyone about this American that had come to stay at the hotel. He didn't tell us that he was going to use you as a bookie's runner though!'

Divareli tried to hide his relief as he answered, 'What I'd really like, Sean, is a whiskey – Irish, of course.'

'One Irish coming up. Did either of you get the result of the four o'clock race? I sponsored it and my mother had a horse called *O'Riley* running in it.'

It suddenly dawned on Aphra that they had left immediately after the *'Winner All Right'*. There wouldn't have been a phone-line to the race course which, for the rest of the year, was just a collection of fields in the middle of nowhere. She continued after a dramatic pause: 'I think I'll let Luke tell you all about it while I go to the loo. I'll give you one bit of advice though, Sean. I'd pour yourself another one of those before you hear the news if I were you!'

With that she disappeared upstairs. Like the smile on the face of the Cheshire Cat, her throaty chuckle lingered in the air for some time after she had gone. Divareli swallowed half his drink at a gulp. He almost gagged as he realised that it did not have any water in it. When he had regained his composure, he adopted his most measured tone as he set about his task.

'Well, it's difficult to know quite where to start . . .'

Shortly afterwards, Sean's shriek of amazement reached the upstairs landing where the ladies' toilet of the Brulagh Inn was located.

6

By the time Aphra came back downstairs, Divareli and Sean were deep in conversation. Seeing their glasses full to the brim with whiskey she decided there and then that she would do the driving to the Gallerick Arms Hotel – and in her own elderly Mini Clubman. As she approached the bar counter, snatches of their conversation drifted towards her.

'I'll tell you one thing for sure, Luke . . .' Sean began to tick off on his fingers the list of EC and Irish grants available to places like Brulagh. Disadvantaged Areas, as Sean called them, apparently attracted endless *largesse* just as long as one third of the funds could be raised locally. Apparently, therein lay the problem. The locals either hadn't the money or were not prepared to risk it. 'My old man assures me that both Brussels and Dublin are busting their guts trying to find projects to spend the bloody money on, could you credit that?'

If Divareli could, he kept the fact to himself. He had heard a lot of 'get rich quick' schemes in his time. Admittedly this was the first time Government Agencies were willing to underwrite two thirds of the cost. He sat back and waited for the catch to surface. Sean broke off to pour Aphra a drink without even asking her first. It was another lethal measure of whiskey. His reward was a polite yet firm refusal.

'I won't drink that, Sean, but thanks for the thought. Why don't you split it between you instead? By the look of the pair of you, I had better do the driving. Perhaps Luke didn't tell you but he has a Porsche outside the door. He's already managed to bash in the passenger door this afternoon. Taking a car like that out on these roads with a bellyful of whiskey is just asking for trouble.'

Sean seemed unimpressed by the information, finding it difficult to hide his eagerness to finish what he was saying. 'I know you two are going out to dinner so I won't delay you. Still and all I want Luke here to know that my old man claims that this sort of grant money won't be on the table much longer, so it won't. That's because us bloody Irish haven't bothered our arses to apply for it, so we haven't . . .'

The three of them fell silent. After a while Divareli stood up and stretched himself. 'Guess we'd better be making tracks if we're to cross that mountain,' he declared.

'And I had better get some work done round here before the band arrives or Jenny will have my life.'

Divareli called from the door, 'We'll be seeing you again later on. Aphra's bringing me to your Race Dance.' As they headed for a wood-panelled Minivan, he asked her: 'You sure you want to take your car?'

'I'm quite sure, thank you very much. Sergeant Moriarty may not mind you parking on those stupid yellow lines but he'll crucify anyone driving with drink taken.'

They drove over the mountain in the gathering dusk, pausing to look back down on the village before they made the descent to the hotel on the far side. Lights twinkled in the village far below them. One, stronger than the rest, was at the end of the fishing pier that jutted out into the tiny harbour. Its reflection bathed the still water in a shimmering pool of light. At the far end of the village, a sharper pinpoint of light, almost dazzling in its intensity, lanced upwards towards them. It was the neon halo of the Madonna at the cross-roads. Between these two focal points, a ragged orange streak on the thin horizon line where sea met sky signalled the last fag-end of sunset. They both gazed at the scene wordlessly, lost in their own very private thoughts.

Divareli congratulated himself on not following through with his earlier intention of getting back to America as quick as his legs – or the Porsche – would carry him. Meeting Aphra had changed all that. As for Aphra, until now she had been bored to distraction. Since packing in her job at the hotel, she had resumed her re-searches into the Gallerick ancestry. It was dirty, boring work for the most part. Dirty because the relevant papers were stored in old plywood tea chests in the basement of Gallerick Hall. There they shared space with last year's surplus apple crop. This meant that not only was everything encrusted with layers of dust but now it also reeked of rotten apples. Her interest was sharpened now that the Gallerick estate was in increasingly straitened circumstances.

35

She wished to find out as much as she could about her inheritance. Johnny Slattery had an aunt living halfway up the mountain who was a fund of local history. Then there were the vague notions Aphra harboured of writing the definitive history of the Gallericks but, despite some very eccentric characters down through the centuries, it was hardly the stuff of best-sellers. Now – all of a sudden – this handsome American enters stage left, promising a welcome diversion both from her dull research work and the gloom surrounding Gallerick Hall and its precarious finances.

They parked the car without difficulty in front of the hotel. The expected influx from the races had yet to materialise. Strolling through the deserted lobby and unmanned reception desk where Aphra had until recently laboured it looked as if either the Black Death had swept through the building or, more probably, the entire staff had gone to the races. The exception was Niall, who was using the bar mirror for a search-and-destroy mission on his blackheads.

'Ah, 'tis yourself, Misther Divareli and Lady Aphra along with you. Sure we haven't seen your lovely face round here for ages, Miss. We thought you had gone from us entirely!'

Aphra did not respond to the flowery compliment. Instead she made for a seat as far as possible from the bar and its talkative minder. Ever the diplomat, Niall knew perfectly well the reason for her abrupt departure but felt that this was not the time to refer to it.

'Tell me this, Misther Divareli and tell me no more: how did my brother make out on *Flannery's Fancy*?'

So that was it!

'He won. How come you never told me your brother was in the saddle? Had I known that, I might have bet on him myself for Chrissakes.'

'Ah, be fair to me now, Misther Divareli. Sure and didn't I advise you to have a cut at it yourself – all I asked you was to get my own few quid on it first.'

Divareli nodded. Niall was right. 'I remember now. Here's your money – almost sixty pounds. Honest Joe Quinn said he stopped the tax on it. I guess I didn't quite understand the system so I had to take his word for it.'

'Oh the melted rogue, that he may not have a day's luck out of it! Still and all, welcome luck. The blessings of God on you for obliging me about the bet, sir. Now you'll have a drink this very minute – out of my winnings, like!'

As Divareli wondered if every move in Ireland were fuelled by alcohol, he could not help noticing that no money went into the till. So they were drinking on Timothy Houlihan after all. Well, that being so Divareli decided, *let's have the other half.* It was a phrase he had picked up from Sean less than an hour ago.

'As we're having it on the house by the look of it, let's have the same again, Niall. Oh and make it large ones this time!'

Niall was taken aback at being found out so easily, especially by a foreigner. However he rallied strongly. 'Begor Misther Divareli, you have the eye of a hawk. We'll do as you say. I'll even join you if you don't mind. Only for the love of God don't tell the boss or I'd be out of here quicker than greased lightning.'

As he was filling the drinks, Aphra asked in a voice as sweet as maple syrup, 'Tell me, Niall – was Tim Houlihan's horse expected to win?'

'Gor I dunno, your Ladyship. Why do you ask?'

'Oh I just wondered, that's all. Curious more than anything, I suppose. I couldn't help noticing that he hadn't been clipped for a year. He looked more like a donkey than a race horse. Then, of course, there's your brother, what's his name?'

'Vincent, your Ladyship. Vincent Aloysius Patrick Callahan.'

Divareli sensed what was coming. Niall might have had an inkling too, if one were to judge by the full and frank answer he gave to the opening question. It would not, in all probability, prevent him from taking the Fifth Amendment if his interrogator pursued this line of questioning much further. Divareli joined Aphra on the distant seat and waited for the fun to begin.

'Well, Vincent Aloysius Patrick was wearing a pair of wellies that looked as if they had just been dug out of a manure pit. What I'm saying, Niall dearest, is that Houlihan's horse was got up to look as if it were entered for the knacker's yard rather than a Point-to-Point. The bookies didn't give it a snowball's chance in hell. You know perfectly well that odds of twelve to one in a race like that are unheard-of, unless the animal's passage is already booked to France inside a can.'

If Niall thought this barb signalled the end of his persecution, he was wrong. Aphra paused but a moment to drain her glass and signal

37

for a refill before expanding on her theme. Niall threw a beseeching glance at Divareli and finding no solace there, fixed Aphra with a glassy stare as she pressed on relentlessly.

'That wretched animal shouldn't have been allowed to enter, much less run in, any decently organised race! I trust you get my meaning?'

If Niall did, he wisely did not admit the fact in open court. With growing amusement, Divareli watched his attempts to wriggle off the hook. He could have told the guy he was wasting his energy, for there was an electrifying pizzaz about Aphra's cross-examination that boded ill for the Accused.

'As God is my judge, Lady Aphra, I don't follow a single word of what you're saying. Sure wasn't I stuck here the whole day while the rest of the staff were off enjoying themselves at the races? How could I know what was goin' on? Surely to God you don't think for one moment that the boss was goin' to let on to the likes of myself whatever trickery he was up to, now do you?' His spirited defence, based on the skilful use of the rhetorical question, might have succeeded but for the reference to trickery.

Aphra pounced on it immediately. It was pure courtroom drama from then on. 'So there *was* trickery going on!'

The triumph in her voice ricocheted around the empty bar. The stragglers from the races had yet to find their way to the Gallerick Arms Hotel. Presumably they would first have to slake their thirst at every hostelry *en route*. The moment of truth had arrived.

'I knew damn well there was something going on from the moment I set eyes on that scumbag Houlihan strutting like a peacock around the ring as though he owned it. He was passing out money over the railings to his cronies like snuff at a wake. Now I suppose you're going to tell me that he didn't fix it so that his nag ran without the lead weights?'

Niall, wisely in Divareli's opinion, did no such thing. Instead he sang dumb and affected an expression of great hurt. A steely glint replaced the smile in Aphra's almond-shaped eyes that she fixed on the unfortunate barman. This did not prevent her from shooting a conspiratorial wink at Luke as she pushed the sword in up to the hilt. Mockery was displacing anger in her cultured tones.

'Well, let me tell you, Niall dearest, that even though half the crooks round here may have been in on the fix, a lot more people

38

like Mister Divareli and myself know exactly what happened. Charley Halpin – the *Clarion* reporter – would give his right arm for a story like this. I'm not worried about the bookies – they are well able to look after themselves. The people I don't like to see getting ripped off are the Flannerys, especially Gillian. She was in floods of tears after the race but she didn't lodge an objection.'

Niall tried one last desperate throw and interrupted with, 'Why didn't she object so if she thought she knew so much?'

Aphra practically screamed at him, 'Because the whole thing was set up by a crowd of bloody men, that's why. From my own father right down to that miserable wretch of a brother of yours, every focking one of them had a piece of the action. A young girl like Gillian could have objected till the cows came home and it wouldn't have made one whit of difference. Both of us saw Slattery slipping the weights out from under the saddle before the start . . .'

This was news to Divareli. Surely she wasn't crazy enough to incriminate her own father? He had better put a stop to this nonsense here and now before the whole thing got out of hand. 'But I thought . . .'

Aphra's hand squeezing his knee quite painfully under the table forestalled whatever nugget of information he was about to contribute to the conversational brawl. It was then that he realised her performance was nothing but a charade designed to frighten the shit out of Houlihan and his ashen-faced barman. Aphra had no more intention of blowing the gaff on the conspirators than she had of flying to the moon, though one might not have thought so by the tone of her voice.

'Oh yes indeed,' she continued, 'it was frightfully clever of him to do it well away from the other horses but there *are* such things as binoculars, you know. *And* telephoto lenses. You can tell that slimy boss of yours that I have some interesting shots of what happened both before and after the race. I have a particularly good one of Slattery sliding back the weights under the saddle your brother is carrying with Houlihan grinning like an ape over his shoulder.'

Divareli chuckled inwardly at the sheer effrontery of it. He knew for a fact that she didn't have a camera of any sort along with her, much less one with a zoom lens. Untroubled by the blatant lie, she pressed on with, 'Now get us a menu, like a good lad, and we'll see what the Gallerick Arms Hotel has to offer in the line of food. As I recall, when I last graced your Reception Desk, the focking chef thought he was cooking for the Borgias.'

Here she nudged Divareli conspiratorially in the ribs before concluding, 'Blackmailers like us get very upset if we are badly fed. Off with you to the kitchen, Niall my boy, and tell Chef to put his best foot forward foodwise. And when Mister bloddy Houlihan returns laden with the spoils of victory, you can tell the miserable bastard that we're celebrating his win by having dinner at his expense. Now let's take a look at the wine list!'

7

Dinner in the Gallerick Arms Hotel was a dull affair of Brown Windsor soup, overcooked lamb and stodgy desserts. It was enlivened considerably by two bottles of champagne which Aphra insisted be on the house in reparation for Houlihan's winning the race in such an underhand fashion – to say nothing of his unwanted attentions. Luke and Aphra had started the meal avidly discussing the events of the day, but by the time they had pushed aside the burnt offerings of the main course, their thoughts were fixed on each other. What began with hand-holding and gazing deeply into each other's eyes escalated rapidly in temperature until all that prevented them from consummating matters there and then on the rather bedraggled dining-room carpet was the fact that the room was quickly filling up with diners. These looked to be the more respectable elements of the race going fraternity – those content with a meal and a quiet drink before going home rather than the motley crowd who were probably whooping it up in the Brulagh Inn.

Meanwhile Timothy Houlihan had returned to his hotel, flushed with victory and the several drinks he had taken in the Weigh Tent afterwards. As he parked his car, he recognised the Mini Clubman as being that of his recently departed receptionist.

It was with some relief that he heard from Niall that Lady Aphra was there because she was dining with a friend and not for any other reason. Nevertheless he elected to give her a wide berth and slipped behind the high, wooden reception desk that looked out on to the hall but was hidden from the dining room. He was in the throes of checking the dinner orders when his attention was distracted by an item for table five. In Niall's recognisable scrawl was written *Two champagne on the house*. As he pondered the possibility that Niall had lost his last few remaining wits and was hell-bent on dispensing the contents of the wine cellar to all and sundry, he was disturbed by a discreet knock on the desk. Raising his head, Houlihan saw that it was the Yank, the one who was bellyaching about the toilet at the end of the corridor.

'At 'tis yourself, Mister Divareli. The plumber would have been here yesterday to fix the . . .'

He was saved the effort of concocting a convincing lie by Divareli asking in a friendly fashion for the key to his bedroom. What Houlihan could not see was Aphra, crawling on all fours past the desk so that she would not be seen on her way to Divareli's room. From the top of the stairs, well out of Houlihan's line of vision, she waved impishly at the impatient Divareli. Practically snatching the key from Houlihan's grasp, he took the stairs two at a time. Outside his bedroom he gave Aphra a long, passionate kiss that was interrupted only by his fitting the key into the door while still locked in her embrace. Once inside, they kissed again with even greater passion as Aphra slipped his coat off and got to work on the belt of his trousers. He nuzzled her ear and whispered, 'I wonder what Houlihan would do if he knew you were here?'

Her loud peal of girlish laughter ensured that they would not have long to wait to find out. When Houlihan heard the unmistakeable laugh of 'her Ladyship' as he sarcastically referred to her while she was in his employ, he darted into the dining room. There was no sign of her. Then he looked out in the car park to check that her car was still there. *So that's what she's at, the snooty bitch! The likes of himself weren't half good enough for her so she had to throw herself at some bloody Yank with dollars coming out his ears.*

Inside the bedroom, Aphra and Divareli were about to remove the last stitch of clothing from each other when a loud banging on the door distracted them momentarily. This was followed by a loud cry of, 'Come outa dere, you hoor you!'

The spell had been well and truly shattered as they looked at one another in amazement. Aphra whispered urgently in his ear, 'Houlihan!'

Divareli swung his legs off the bed and struggled into his trousers, pulling the belt tightly about his waist. The shouting outside on the landing persisted. 'I know you're in there, Divareli. If you don't come out this minute I'll have the law down on you. As for you, Lady Aphra, I'll not be long in telling your father all about this, you brazen hussy!'

Divareli pulled the door open once he was sure Aphra had drawn the bedclothes around her body, naked but for knickers. He wasn't in the mood to provide his tormentor with any cheap thrills. 'What the hell are you roaring about, you stupid bastard?'

Houlihan was almost speechless with fury but managed to stammer, 'There will be none of that carry-on in my hotel, and if the two of ye don't . . .'

His ultimatum never saw the light of day. Divareli caught him by the scruff of the neck and pushed him away from the bedroom door. Houlihan momentarily lost his balance and tumbled head over heels down the stairs. Still fuming, Divareli went back into the bedroom.

'Let's get the hell outa this lunatic asylum. Get into your clothes quick as you can!'

With that he threw a leather suitcase on the bed and emptied the contents of the chest of drawers into it with a furious abandon. Minutes later they stormed out of the hotel, leaving a dishevelled Houlihan staunching the flow of blood from an already swollen nose. Divareli shouted over his shoulder to the injured one, 'Send my bill to the Brulagh Inn!' Seconds later, a battered Mini Clubman with Divareli at the wheel skidded out of the forecourt of the Gallerick Arms Hotel in an angry spray of gravel.

The Black Hole of Calcutta must have been something like this. People were jammed so closely together that they had to drink with their elbows raised to eye-level. Only in that way was it possible to guide glass to mouth. Even then it had to be on a plane parallel to the floor. To get from the door to the long bar counter was a trek not to be undertaken lightly. By dint of repeated Excuse Me's and apologetic smiles Divareli and Aphra had wormed their way through the tightly-packed throng. Everyone was talking furiously but precious few were listening. Above the roar of conversation came the sound of cats being doctored without an anaesthetic in a far-off corner of the bar.

Closer inspection, however, proved the wailing noise to be coming from the Brulagh Ceili Band. Percussion was provided by a king-size tambourine. This was held high in the air with one hand and thumped with the other. Its earsplitting thuds jarred the ears and numbed the senses. It took Divareli a moment or two before he recognised who was pounding its taut skin with such ferocity. Every so often Johnny Slattery, evidently a man of many talents, would wipe his nose with the back of his hand without missing a beat. A cold fear gripped Divareli. What if Johnny doubled as vocalist? 'What do you call that thing our friend is banging?'

They had got almost within striking distance of the counter before Divareli attempted the question. A solid phalanx of backs stood between them and Sean Flannery, perspiring freely as he filled an endless succession of coal-black pints topped off with creamy, frothing heads.

'A bodhran.' She pronounced it Bow-rawn with the emphasis on the first syllable. 'They're made from goat skins. No ceili band worth its salt would dream of performing without one.'

Two large whiskies materialised before them. With a curt, 'On the house. I heard what you did to Houlihan!' Sean was gone to serve another group howling for service. Apparently the jungle drums beat even louder than the bodhran. Taking full advantage of his height Divareli stood on tiptoe to try to get a proper look at the rest of the band. Three figures were huddled round the tall, stooped figure of the bodhran player. One of them, an old man, sawed furiously on a fiddle. He looked quite sad as he gazed fixedly at a spot in the middle distance, oblivious to the seething crowd. The flat cloth cap on his head looked as if it could only be removed under a heavy anaesthetic. A well-dressed man in his sixties with a shock of silver hair stood out like a sore thumb from the others. He was blowing on a tin whistle, swaying to the lilting chords, as he produced musical flourishes that embellished but did not alter the hypnotic rhythm. Seated next to him was a little old lady, her silver hair tied back in a severe bun, with a fresh complexion and a faraway, dreamy smile. She was squeezing what looked like a miniature concertina.

The tune had a rousing swing that set Divareli's feet tapping. He soon realised that his plans to quiz Sean about the EC grants or even to ask him for a room would have to be shelved for the time being. Meaningful communication of any sort from a distance greater than six inches was clearly out of the question. On the drive back to Brulagh after their dramatic exit from the hotel, Aphra had raised the spectre of there being no room for him at the Inn. He wondered that she had not extended an invitation for him to stay at the Hall but decided to let it pass for the moment.

All around them the buzz of conversation and the mind-numbing thud of the bodhran surged ever higher like a tide threatening to engulf them. Occasionally a shout sliced through the wall of sound. 'Give us a pint quick, for Chrissake Sean, before I drop dead of the thirst!' or 'Might as well be in the shagging Sahara as try to get a drink in this place!' Like good barmen the world over, Sean worked steadily and calmly, seemingly unruffled by the abuse being heaped on him. The band were on a raised platform at the far end of the bar. As far as Divareli could see, no one was taking the slightest notice of them or their music.

He and Aphra were standing at the counter, gazing into each other's eyes and rejoicing in even the slightest touch. When he took her hand and clasped it tightly in his, it was almost as though they were making love there and then. Aphra decided that they were just like two teenagers on their first date – tentative but loving – an island of tranquillity in a raging sea of deafening sounds. As for Divareli, he could not remember enjoying himself so much in a very long time. Every now and then a hand would snake between them to claim its drink or to collect change off the marble-topped counter. A tallish man who looked vaguely familiar wedged himself between them and greeted Aphra like a lost sister. She introduced him as Doctor James Buckley.

It was only when Divareli noticed the mouthpiece of the tin whistle protruding from the inside pocket of the Doc's coat that he realised he was in the presence of one of the musicians.

'Hi, Doc. I'm just getting a drink.' He raised an inquiring eyebrow at Aphra to seek her approval before adding, 'Would you care to join us?'

'Love to, but I can only stay for just the one. I'll have to get back up there soon or Johnny will have my life. That's his uncle and aunt playing with him. They only invite me to sit in with them when they're really stuck.'

He turned as a large man, who had been working his way slowly through the crowd, called to him. Mick Flannery's majestic progress towards them had been interrupted every few steps by people grabbing him by the arm or the shoulder and whispering into his ear. When this happened, Mick would adopt a look of intense concentration and nod reassuringly. Divareli recognised a real pro working the room. Vague assurances and unspoken promises

45

bobbed like flotsam in his wake as he moved through the narrow path that had been made for him. Soon he joined them. His voice came deep from inside his barrel chest, hoarse from a thousand speeches.

'Jaysus, that's some crowd Sean has in here tonight . . .'The new arrival mopped his brow with a white handkerchief the size of a sheet.

Emboldened by the whiskey, Divareli thought the opening too good to miss. 'Mister Flannery . . .'

'Mick, call me Mick like a dacent man. They only call me Mister when they want something out of me. I'll call you Luke then we'll be in the same boat.'

'OK, Mick it is. I was just wondering what you thought of that race today.'

Mick shot a quick glance at the Doc before he asked, 'The one Houlihan won, you mean?'

'Yeah, that's the one.'

'Well, now that you ask, I was sorry to see that bastard win it. But then again I had a few quid on his animal so I was glad to see him come in first, I suppose.'

Aphra exploded indignantly, 'You mean to say that you bet against your own daughter?'

If Mick was disturbed by her outburst he didn't show it. If anything, he seemed aggrieved by the suggestion that he might have acted otherwise. 'Of course I did or do you take me for a complete eejit altogether?' It was now Mick's turn to sound indignant. He took a deep breath before resuming, 'Sure the mare was no odds at all – a blind man could see that. The other horse was far better value at twelves even if it did look like it had spent all summer grazing on the mountain. Did you have a bet, Luke?'

'I did. I had a hundred on the mare.'

Mick Flannery was flabbergasted. 'Jaysus, no wonder Quinn wiped her off the board. Any man that loses that kind of money without moaning and groaning about it deserves a drink at the very least.'

'Thank you, Mick.' Fortified by this, Divareli decided to throw caution to the winds and employ the direct approach. 'Sean tells me you're the man to see when it comes to prising money out of the EC.'

The Flannery brow darkened. His voice became wary and full of suspicion. It was not until he realised that this stranger was not trying to put the bite on him that he returned to his old affable self. 'I declare to God but that son of mine's mouth is about three sizes too big for his brain. Still and all I suppose he's right.'

When Mick explained the requirements laid down by the EC, by the simple expedient of putting his mouth to Divareli's ear and speaking into it rapidly for over five minutes without apparently drawing breath, it appeared that Sean had spoken nothing but the gospel truth. The money *was* there, waiting to be taken up – all that prevented this happening was a lack of seed capital and the proper expertise to launch a suitable project. The only fly in the ointment was that the grants might not last forever, but could be withdrawn or severely curtailed in the New Year. Aphra, meanwhile was deep in conversation with Sean's wife, Jenny, during this exchange. From their whisperings and covert glances, it was obvious that Divareli was the topic of their conversation.

When Divareli had digested what Mick was saying, he hinted that he just might be interested in investing in the area, but lest Mick went off at half-cock he warned, 'Don't go away with the idea that this is just the liquor talking. When I say I'll get back to you on it, I mean just that. Now let's have a drink on it. Sean, can I have four whiskeys please, and make 'em big ones!'

Mick leaned over his shoulder and whispered in his ear again just as Aphra rejoined them. 'Two things before we change the subject. Not a word of this to anyone till we firm it up a bit. The other thing is that if you are to even think about coming into this area, you must prepare the ground first.'

Now it was Divareli's turn to become wary. He asked in a voice too low for Aphra to catch, 'Whaddya mean, prepare the ground?'

Mick whispered urgently back at him, 'I mean you've got to make the people round here think you're a good sort, not some cute hoor coming in for a quick kill and then shagging off again before they even get to know you properly.'

Divareli was still uneasy as he inquired, 'So what does that involve? I'm no good at licking ass if that's what you mean.'

For a moment, Mick looked to be mortally offended. Then he explained patiently in a louder voice that Aphra could hear: 'Ah no, for Jaysus sake, that's not what I mean at all. You've just dropped a hundred pounds on a bet this afternoon, am I right?' Aphra's eyes flashed suspiciously at Mick as Divareli nodded without enthusiasm. 'Then it won't break you to spend the same amount on a set of jerseys for the local hurling team. They'll splash it all over the *Clarion*. That'll get you well in with the crowd round here, I can promise you that. Leave a fiver in the collection plate and that ought to take care of the church, though our parish priest, Father Jerry, can be a queer hawk sometimes. He'd make a better friend than an enemy, if you know what I mean.'

Divareli nodded as someone pushed their way through the crowd and whispered urgently in Mick's ear. As he listened, his eyes widened in surprise and he fixed Divareli with a curious stare. When the messenger had vanished into the crowd, Mick suddenly enveloped Divareli in a bear hug as he spoke just loud enough to be heard above the rasp of the music.

'To tell God's honest truth, I had my doubts about you until this very minute. But any man who throws Timothy Houlihan down the stairs of his own hotel is my friend for life. Now I've got to go and sing for my supper . . .'

Meanwhile the Doc had cornered Aphra. 'I would remind you, young lady,' he was saying to her, 'that you are in the presence of no less a personage than the President of Brulagh Golf Club. Kindly remember that when you speak slightingly of the game I love.'

As Mick departed, Divareli could hardly wait to vent his exasperation on the Doc and Aphra. 'Jeez, I don't get it. I really don't. A minute ago Mick was telling me there was no cash round here for any kind of tourist projects. Now you tell me you've a golf-course on your doorstep. Do you know how much it is to join a club in America?'

The Doc shrugged his shoulders. 'No idea. But it's eighty quid here.'

'A day?'

At this the Doc practically choked on his drink. 'Ah Jaysus no, that's for the full year. It's not exactly up to championship standard, you know. In fact we have to share it with the sheep for most of the year.'

It was now Divareli's turn to be surprised though he tried hard to keep it out of his voice. 'Where is it? I mean, is it far from here?'

'About a mile and a half. It runs along the side of the mountain road. I'll show it to you any time you like. The priest, the Sergeant and myself play a fourball whenever Mick is home. You're welcome to join us if you want to.'

Divareli was delighted by the offer and showed it. 'I'd like that. I'm not much good, though.'

The Doc seemed unperturbed by this admission. 'Then you'll be no different from the rest of us. Gus, come over here and meet Luke. Now I had better get back to Johnny before he comes looking for me.'

Moments later the band broke into a lively dance, as the Sergeant greeted him with the question – or was it a statement: 'You got back out through the gate all right then?' Instead of waiting for a reply he went off on a completely different tack, or so it seemed at first. 'I had a call a while ago.'

The statement was left hanging in mid-air as the music reached a climax of such savage intensity that the dancers seemed to melt into a swirling, amorphous mass. Aphra, Divareli noticed somewhat sourly, was enjoying herself, dancing with Mick Flannery as though bound to him by invisible chains.

'Oh yes?'

Divareli couldn't think of anything to add to the pearl of wisdom Gus had dropped into the conversational pool. Another long pause. It was becoming obvious that Gus was not a man to rush headlong into speech. Eventually he again found his tongue.

'From Timothy Houlihan, as a matter of fact. He phoned me up at the barracks to make a complaint . . .' This was followed by an even longer pause. Again Divareli felt that there was nothing he could usefully add to this. He waited for Gus to unburden himself. '. . . against yourself. He claims you were after assaulting him. To be honest, I couldn't understand half of it. Would you say that he had a drop too much taken?'

Divareli did not miss his opportunity. 'If you're asking me was he drunk, Sergeant, I'd have to say that he was out of his mind.'

'I see, begor.' A note of satisfaction crept into the Sergeant's voice as he pursued this line of inquiry. 'But tell me this and then tell me no more: what in the name of God made you throw him down the stairs?'

'Because he was roaring and shouting outside my bedroom. Like I said, the guy was drunk as a skunk!' Gus digested this without comment. Divareli showed that he was rapidly tiring of the charade.

'OK, Sergeant. Now that you've had the word you wanted with me, what are you going to do about it?'

'To be perfectly honest, a lot depends on Timothy Houlihan. If he decides to go ahead and press charges, it could make things difficult for everyone. The matter would be taken out of my hands, if you follow me.'

'Yeah, I see. Well, what would you advise me to do? Go see a lawyer, maybe?'

'Yerrah not at all. Not yet, anyway. With the help of God, the whole thing will go no further. I only mentioned it so you'd be on your guard. They tell me you're not staying at the hotel any more.'

'Correct. I told them to send me the bill on here if that's what you're getting at.'

Gus blushed with embarrassment. 'Yerrah nothing of the sort ever crossed my mind. I'm only thinking that if Sean can't fit you in here, don't be short of a bed. Joe Gallagher has a nice quiet guest-house down by the pier. He only does bed and breakfast but it's good and it's clean. I stay there myself, as a matter of fact.'

'Well, thanks for the offer, Sergeant. I don't believe I've met Joe yet.'

'Ah, you'll like Joe. He's a dacent sort if ever there was one. He worked all his life in America before he retired back here.'

'Now, Sergeant, are you sure you don't want me to hand in my passport or anything like that?'

'Ah, Misther Divareli we're not like that round here at all. I won't need anything of the sort, at least not unless Houlihan is foolish enough to go ahead with this nonsense.'

'What do you think yourself? I mean, do you think he might press charges?'

'Yerrah I'd say probably not. If he was as drunk as you say, he was probably in the wrong by a mile. Apart from his nose, sure the only other part of him that was injured was his pride. Did you have any witnesses, to him being drunk and abusive, I mean?'

'Well, Lady Aphra heard it for sure.'

At this the Sergeant's bushy eyebrows shot halfways up his forehead. 'Oh begor, she was with you, then?' This news took another age to absorb before he continued: 'That's all very well but you can hardly call her into the witness-stand, not if she was in your bedroom. That could be very embarrassing for her, you know.'

'Yes, I see what you're getting at. Hold on a moment . . .' Divareli tried desperately to recall the circumstances of the incident on the landing. 'Maybe Niall heard something. He was downstairs in the lobby at the time, I think.'

'Niall Callahan, you mean?'

'Yeah, the young guy. He must have heard the racket going on upstairs. He certainly would have seen Houlihan coming back drunk after the races.'

'Indeed he might. The only trouble about that is that if his job depends on Houlihan, he's not likely to say anything against him. Anyway we'll see . . .' Whatever he was going to see was interrupted by the return of the two dancers.

Mick's brow was bathed in perspiration. He pulled down his tie and loosened his shirt collar. 'Jaysus I'll tell you something. 'Tis hotter than hell out in the middle of that floor. You'll make a dancer out of me yet, Aphra. That is, if this man here doesn't steal you away from us and take you back with him to America!'

Divareli tried to force a smile as he dropped the bombshell. 'The Sergeant was just telling me that Houlihan filed a complaint against me.'

Mick spluttered with indignation. 'Gus, surely to God you're not going to stand there and tell me you'll take one bit of notice of what that shagger Houlihan says? He couldn't tell the truth even if he tried. This dacent man here . . .' he put an arm round Divareli's shoulders '. . . was perfectly within his rights to throw the shagger down the stairs. The only pity is that he didn't break his bloody neck while he was at it! Aphra was just telling me that Houlihan was pestering her that much that she had to run out of his bloody hotel. Isn't that a fine way for the likes of him to be carrying on?'

Gus was rubbing his jaw pensively as Sean placed a foaming pint before him. Looking at the ceiling and talking aloud to no one in particular, he said, 'Supposing, now just supposing, that Lady Aphra were to complain to me, informally like, that she had suffered harassment at the hands of our friend Houlihan, wouldn't that put a stop to his gallop?'

A long silence followed, broken only by the Brulagh Ceili Band launching into another set. Aphra began to giggle and Mick slapped the Sergeant on the back, nearly causing him to choke on his pint as he growled, 'Gus, I always knew you had a good head on those

51

shoulders. There was a great politician lost in you the day you joined the police force. That's the answer, of course, to stymie the little bollix. Now I really must go and make that shaggin' speech.'

Moments later he held the microphone in his giant fist as though his very life depended on it. His face glistening with sweat, he thanked everyone for supporting the function and expressed the hope that a Flannery horse would win next year. This was greeted with a chorus of catcalls and howls of 'Aha ya boy, ya!' from the floor, from those who must have been privy to the 'arrangement'. Concluding his remarks by welcoming Luke to Brulagh, he thanked him for his promise of a new set of jerseys for the hurling team. As the crowd made for the exits, Mick signalled for Luke and Aphra to follow him into the kitchen. Much later they were still seated round the big wooden table when the back door opened and the gaunt figure of Johnny Slattery, bodhran in hand, stood framed in the doorway.

'I suppose there's no chance of a pint at this hour of the night? I've a thirst on me this minute that'd drown an eel.'

His arrival was greeted with a marked lack of enthusiasm by Sean who exploded, 'Ah, for Jaysus sake Johnny, have a heart. I thought you'd gone home ages ago. Can't you see the bar is closed for the night? Look, I'll get you one drink and only one. Not another drop after that, not even if you got down on your hands and knees and prayed for it. Surely you don't want the Sergeant to catch you drinking after hours, now do you?'

Johnny wiped his nose with the back of his hand and muttered something under his breath about Gus not being able to catch a cold. Divareli had a question he had been waiting to ask all night.

'That's one hell of a drum you got there. What do you play it with?'

'Oh the knuckles, sir, the knuckles. Though there's some that prefer to use a bit of a bone. I prefer the knuckles, though – gives me more of a feel, like.'

To demonstrate, he performed a lightning tattoo on it that made the ware on the dresser tremble. Aphra whispered tipsily into Luke's ear that there were many who would prefer Johnny to play it with a penknife. She might have spoken louder than intended, for Johnny shot her a glare of red-eyed hostility but said nothing as Sean returned with a foaming pint.

'There you are and don't take all night drinking it.'

As if to oblige, Johnny sank half of it at one gulp, leaving a perfect ring inside the glass to mark its passing. Mick asked him, 'How are ye all up the mountain?'

'Oh the finest, Mick. The business is always a bit slack at this time of year, though. They're all saving their few shillings for Christmas. But do you know something? The oul' road is gone to hell entirely. The miserable hoor that fell in for your seat doesn't bother his arse with the likes of us mountainy people. Do you know what it is I'm going to tell you, and it isn't one word of a lie? A flock of sheep could drown themselves in some of them potholes, they're that big. I wish to God they could be fixed again like they were in your time.'

Aphra jumped in with, 'Oh yes, Johnny, just like you fixed that race today, I suppose!'

If he were startled by this, he hid it well. Assuming a look of injured innocence, he swallowed the last of his drink and made for the door. 'God protect us all from sharp-tongued women. I must be on my way. There's still some of us that have work to do in the morning!' The last they heard of him was a hawking spit as he closed the door behind him.

Moments later Sean came in from the bar accompanied by two young women. 'Luke, meet my wife Jenny and my sister Gillian.' Jenny was a petite blonde with an urchin cut. The defeated jockey was taller, a real beauty with flaming red hair. She looked older now than she had done when astride *O'Riley*. Sean explained, 'The girls were looking after the disco bar up at the Sports Centre.'

Gillian interrupted her brother. Nodding to Aphra she said, 'Mr Divareli, is it true that you threw Houlihan down the stairs?'

Divareli looked at Aphra inquiringly before nodding ruefully. The next moment Gillian had rushed at him and, flinging her arms around his neck, planted a kiss on either cheek.

'About time someone did it to the bastard. After what he got away with today, though . . .' she paused to glare fiercely at her father '. . . there's some might not agree with me. Especially when they bet against their own flesh and blood! I'm off home now, Mr Divareli. I'll let you have my bed for tonight as a thank you for what you did to Houlihan.'

Then, grinning impishly at Aphra she added as she disappeared out the door, 'Don't worry, I won't be in it!'

53

Aphra decided that a cruel fate had decreed that their love must never be consummated. First the interruption at the Gallerick Arms, now Sean didn't have a free room in which they might have attended to their unfinished business. It really was, she decided huffily, too silly for words. After Gillian's parting shot there followed a bemused silence that was broken only by a loud knocking on the back door and the familiar voice of Sergeant Gus Moriarty.

'Open up in the name of the law!'

This sparked off frenzied activity wherein all trace of drink was hurriedly concealed and tea splashed into cups with great urgency. The Sergeant, now in uniform, was not there to apprehend them for drinking after hours, however, but rather to impart two items of news. One was that he would not be available to play golf next morning as he had to give evidence at a court hearing. The other was to inform Divareli that he had left the sidelights on in his car.

'Oh shit, the battery will be flat as a pancake by now!'

In bidding them good night the Sergeant pointedly expressed the hope that he had not disturbed them unduly. When he had gone, Mick came to the rescue.

'Don't worry about the car – leave it where it is. 'Twill be safe as a house, especially with a dead battery. In any case there hasn't been a car stolen here since . . .' His voice trailed off as he looked at the others and then changed tack hurriedly. 'I'll be going home in a minute – you can travel with me. We'll just have the binder, then we'll be gone.'

'The binder' was the natural successor to the 'one for the road'. It was so named because of its supposed ability to bind together safely all drinks consumed earlier. On the drive back to Mick's house, the binder failed to live up to its reputation. They had to stop halfway up a hill to relieve themselves against a low stone wall.

Mission accomplished, they turned to get back into their car, only to discover that it had vanished. Mystified, they looked anxiously at each other from either side of the empty road. The vehicle was nowhere to be seen. It was as if an unseen hand had snatched it heavenwards while they were preoccupied with more urgent matters. Just then the moon broke free of a ragged cloud and revealed something large protruding from a ditch at the bottom of the hill.

In his hurry to answer the call of nature, Mick had failed to engage the handbrake. The car had rolled silently down the hill unbeknownst to its erstwhile cargo. They found it unscathed but stuck fast in a bramble bush where it had failed to negotiate the corner. Somewhat unsteadily they finished their journey on foot.

8

Desperate circumstances call for desperate measures. This unoriginal thought crossed Divareli's mind, or that small part of it that was functioning independently of the excruciating pain that had enveloped his entire being. He was watching through half-closed eyes as Mick Flannery prepared breakfast. There was a cupboard directly above the big kitchen range. From it Mick retrieved a package wrapped in stiff brown paper. Placing it on the table, he opened it reverently. As he did so an unmistakeable smell of decay filled the kitchen. It was as though Mick had dug up something that had been in the ground for a long time.

Instead of throwing the contents into a bin, Mick started to sniff the lump of what appeared to be rotting meat then sighed happily, much as a wine-lover might savour a fine claret. From a drawer he took a wicked-looking knife, big as a machete, and began to hack thick slices off what on closer examination proved to be part of a dead pig. The slices fell on the table in orderly fashion like giant, marbled dominoes – allowing Mick to scoop them up on the flat blade of the knife and drop them into a pot of boiling water. For the first time since initiating the breakfast ceremony, Mick broke the silence that hung in the air between them.

'Any time I'm inclined to be a bit sick in myself, I cut a few rashers off a hunk of hardsalt bacon. I can promise you one thing: this pig never saw the inside of a piggery. That's a mountainy pig if ever I saw one.' He was holding up the unsliced portion to the light and examining the cross-section with care. With his finger he traced the pattern of meat surrounded by the creamy grey fat with its thick, yellowing crust. 'Take a look at them for muscles! You have my word for it, he got them from running up and down the mountain like a shagging goat. You won't see flesh like that on some poor hoor that spent all his days cooped up inside a pen!'

Divareli did not question the truth of this assertion. He merely thought that even on this crazy island, anyone caught eating what Mick had just sliced would cop a long stretch in the asylum.

'Once we've the salt boiled out, those will make the finest rashers that ever saw the inside of a frying pan. Throw in a couple of duck eggs and what have you got? A breakfast fit for the High King of Ireland, that's what!'

'Or an instant heart attack.' The thought passed through Divareli's lips as a hoarse, indecipherable croak. The gift of speech had yet to be restored to him. This came as no great surprise for he had woken up in some discomfort, a platoon of construction workers hard at work behind his eyeballs. Armed with noisy and seemingly blunt pneumatic drills, they were digging the foundations for an office block inside his head. For a reason that he had yet to fathom, they were under the supervision of Che Guevara and Madonna. He closed his eyes in the hope that the dream would end and the workers disappear. Then he could sleep again and, on waking, rejoin the human race. But sleep, even of the most fitful nature, would not come. He decided on one last desperate throw of the dice before commending his soul to God. Blinking open both eyes suddenly and without warning, he caught the construction crew unawares and threw them into confusion. In their panic they abandoned their drills and fled, whinnying with fright, over the horizon.

Divareli availed of the lull to take stock of his unfamiliar surroundings. He was in a strange bedroom. The walls were festooned with posters. The nearest one showed Madonna sporting a moustache, felt-tipped in by an unknown hand. A blob of memory bobbed to the surface of his consciousness. Of course, it was coming back to him in awkward sized chunks that he found hard to digest.

Further speculation along these lines was interrupted by the arrival of a stronger signal that took over completely from the previous fuzzy images. A very clear picture of Mick and himself falling about, helpless with laughter, as they tried vainly to drag a car out of a ditch.

A voice plucked him back from the edge of oblivion. He listened with growing concern as his host extolled the virtues of what he was about to serve.

'I'll promise you one thing, Luke. The rashers you get in the shops aren't worth tuppence. Throw them in the frying pan and they shrivel up to nothing. These boyos here . . .', he cocked a thumb at the boiling water that had developed a grey bubbling scum on its surface as the salt and God only knew what else was bleached out of the bacon slices, '. . . are something else entirely. Get outside a few of them with a pair of fried eggs on a cut of fried bread and you won't know yourself.'

He must have seen Divareli blench at the prospect for he changed tack hurriedly. 'Here, swallow this while you're waiting.' Then, noticing his guest's hesitation: ''Tis only tea with a bit of milk and sugar in it.'

This might well have been true but to Divareli's exhausted taste-buds it smacked of high octane, blackstrap molasses. The dark sweet brew coursed through his body in a warming flood. He found he could speak, though his voice sounded hollow and metallic as if a telephone answering machine had taken over his vocal chords. Moving his head, even slightly, still brought short shards of agonising pain that lanced out in every direction from somewhere behind his nose. The robot spoke in a voice he had difficulty recognising as his own.

'Think I'll give the food a miss, if it's all the same to you. I'd like more of the tea, though. It seems to be doing the trick.'

Divareli was in the throes of yet another unfamiliar sensation. The cavity where his cheekbones rose to form the sockets for his eyes seemed suddenly to have filled with cement. This was hardening rapidly and threatened to make eye movement of any sort painful if not impossible. Another mug of tea seemed to arrest the process, if not actually reverse it. His host was speaking again.

'Ah, you can't beat a mug of strong tea. My father-in-law swore by the tea. The poor man, God rest his soul, hardly drew a sober breath for the last twenty years of his life.'

'What did he do? For a living I mean.' Divareli was glad to note that some *timbre* was returning to his voice even if the actual question was rather loose.

'Oh the very same as myself. He represented this area in the Dail. He used to have a grocery and a bar in the village. Back in the War of Independence a troop of Black and Tans threatened to shoot him if he didn't give them information about an ambush nearby. Old Con knew shag all about it and would have told them so if he had even one sober brain left in his skull. Instead, because he was half-drunk as usual, he told them to go and fuck themselves, if you'll pardon the phrase.'

Divareli nodded. In doing so, the head movement provoked another setback of such severity that it caused him to miss Mick's next few words. He had little difficulty, however, in picking up the thread of the narrative.

'. . . Tans were about to put him up against the wall of his shop and shoot him when a senior officer intervened. So they beat him up instead and left him half dead. 'Twas his own fault, of course. If he had kept a civil tongue in his head he would have been all right. Anyway, he became a sort of a hero after that. He told everyone that despite threats of torture and execution, he had refused to turn informer. In the election immediately after the Truce, he won his seat here and held on to it till the day he died.'

'So how did you get the seat from him?'

'Ah, that's a long story. Let's just say that I married his daughter. I used to play a lot of hurling at the time. That helped a bit, too.'

'But aren't you based in Europe now?'

'Yeah, that came about in a funny way. Again it's another long story, too long for now anyway. Jimmy O'Rourke died with four years still to run of his European seat. The Taoiseach, the head of our party in the Dail, offered me the job.'

'Do you enjoy it?'

'Oh sure. The travelling is a bit of a pain in the arse, literally,' Mick Flannery gave a throaty chuckle before continuing, 'but the rest of it is fine. The pay's good too.'

'What do you do for relaxation?' Divareli was sure he knew the answer to that one but thought it polite to ask, nonetheless.

'Drink and golf, mainly. What size shoes do you take? I've a spare pair in the locker room that are just a bit bigger than that. Put on another pair of socks and you'll be fine. What time is it now? Right so, I've a few things to do so would around eleven suit you to play? If we're to get started by then I've a couple of phone-calls to make and you have that battery to look after as well as checking into Sean's place. I can drive you . . . oh Jaysus no, I can't!'

He took a break from shovelling carefully assembled forkfuls of rasher, egg and fried bread into his face to laugh aloud. 'Sure the bloody car is stuck in the ditch. Look's like Johnny's tractor will have to be called into action again. Like I say, I'll pick you up in

Sean's place a bit before eleven and we'll aim to be hitting off the first tee shortly after that. The quicker we finish, the more time we'll have for a few jars before lunch to settle ourselves after last night.'

Divareli had never seen a golf-course like it. Anything further removed from the elegant Country Club with its manicured courses to which he belonged back home would be hard to imagine. As they drove in through the rusting entrance gate, he thought it was to park the car in a derelict field for some purpose known only to Mick Flannery, and it was not until he saw tattered flags flying from poles scattered across the mountainside that it dawned on him that this neglected cow pasture *was* the golf-course!

The first tee was in front of the Clubhouse, a modest building with a corrugated iron roof, green with lichen and age. They did not go inside, opting instead to change their shoes in the weed- infested car park and using the boot of Mick's car as a locker. The others had not yet arrived and there were no other golfers to be seen even though it was a fine, sunlit morning. Divareli would have thought that even in Brulagh, there would have been a queue of players waiting on the tee to hit off. He took advantage of the wait by swishing the Sergeant's golf-clubs, at first tentatively and then with growing confidence. The clubs were old but good. The grips were almost new, which should ensure that the driver would not fly out of his grasp.

The designers of the Brulagh golf-course had achieved the impossible: they had created an arid desert in the middle of a green oasis. The golf-course was a drab strip of land perched uncomfortably among the foothills of the mountain that separated Brulagh from the rest of the world. The road that meandered over it first had to wind its way round a craggy foreland thrusting bravely out into the choppy Atlantic. Even now the light breeze whipped up necklaces of white foam at the base of soot-black cliffs where rolling ocean swells met their first obstruction since leaving America.

Before Divareli could feel homesick, the rasp of a faulty silencer blasting up the winding road heralded the arrival of the opposition. How any self-respecting doctor could drive a rustbucket like that and hope to remain in practice was difficult to understand. In the circles in which Divareli moved, to be seen with the wrong model of the current year's crop of Detroit's finest was to invite social ruin.

After some trouble opening the door, a black-clad figure clambered out of the car. Mick Flannery introduced him as Father Jerry O'Sullivan and continued before anyone could suggest otherwise, 'Luke and myself will play the two of you.'

There ensued a bargaining session of such intensity that Divareli thought they were on the point of coming to blows at least twice. The argument was over how many shots should be conceded, the validity of handicaps and the sum to be played for. Suddenly the storm had passed and terms, meaningless to him, had been hammered out. He took a few more practice swings while the Doc strapped his bag to a trolley. The other two hoisted their bags on to their shoulders and made for the first tee.

Divareli managed a low drive, mercifully straight, that travelled a respectable distance before coming to rest on the fairway. So far so good, he thought. The Atlantic breeze chilled him. He was wearing an open-neck shirt and the cold draught that started around his Adam's apple had worked its way down to his toenails. By using folded newspapers as insoles, he had managed to persuade Mick's golf-shoes to stay on his feet.

This was made more difficult by the unusual nature of the terrain. A seemingly endless series of undulating furrows gave a ripple effect to the fairways. All things considered, he concluded that this might well have been the worst course he had ever played. It was an object lesson in everything that a golf-course should not be. He was not to know that though the other three were well-used to its vagaries, newcomers like himself had been known to stagger off the course scarred for life by the experience. A perfect shot would, for no apparent reason, take a leap at right angles to its trajectory and scuttle like a rabbit into the tall, wiry dune grass that lined the fairways. Divareli's curiosity was aroused. 'What caused the furrows?'

The Doc, as befitted the President of the Club, explained that they had been formed by ridges of potatoes that had never been dug back in the Famine times. 'The spuds rotted in the ground with the blight. Even if they had been all right, the people were too weak from the Hunger to dig them out. Those lucky enough to escape the sickness took the first available ship to America and them that stayed behind mostly died. Where we're walking now was just one of the potato fields abandoned during the Famine.'

61

At that very moment, the Famine was also the subject of Aphra's researches into the family history. Deep in the basement of Gallerick Hall she was immersed in a pile of dusty documents. She tried hard to banish lustful dreams of what it would be like to bed Luke. She wondered if he would be a gentle, caring lover or whether some of the famous Latin passion had survived in his genes, passed on from his presumably Italian ancestors. With a name like Divareli, from where else but Italy could they have come? Surrounded by trunkfuls of dust-laden papers, she decided she didn't really care what sort of lover he turned out to be just so long as he became one at all. At the present rate of progress they would both be in their dotage by the time they finally got into the one bed at the same time without some disaster intervening to spoil the fun.

Determinedly she immersed herself in sorting the wheat from the chaff so that she could begin to write a definitive family history. Thus far, most of the material she had unearthed was nothing more than bills, boring family correspondence and long lists of rents to be paid by the tenants whose tiny holdings dotted the vast estate. For vast it was in the nineteenth century, covering some three thousand acres that stretched from Mount Brulagh to the sea.

As she sorted the various documents to file them she noticed a small square sheet of notepaper. It was a receipt dated 3 May 1866 for the sum of fifty sovereigns, a small fortune in those days. That was enough to dispel the last, lingering dreams of lying in Luke's arms in the warm afterglow of lovemaking. The note, in copperplate handwriting, read '*Received on behalf of the widow Kelly and her daughter Jessica the sum of fifty sovereigns.*' There were no other details except the flowery signature '*David Foley, P. P. The Parochial House, Brulagh.*' The absence of any greeting such as '*Your Lordship*' or a servile ending such as '*Your obedient servant*' or even the minimal '*Yours in Jesus Christ*' indicated that relations between the writer and Aphra's ancestor were somewhat cool. She left it aside from the rest of the material for further investigation. It had caught her eye not only because of the large sum involved but because the Gallericks, then and now, had been members of the Established Church of England since the reign of Henry VIII.

When she phoned Father Jerry, a far from civil Julia May, his formidable housekeeper, informed her frostily that 'His Rivverence' was on the golf-course. From her disapproving tone it was impossible to discover whether Aphra's phone-call or His Rivverence's leisure activities had upset the old cow the most. The only other person who might be of help in unravelling the mystery was living halfway up the mountain. Johnny Slattery's aunt, the little old lady in the Brulagh Ceili Band, was not only a collector of traditional Irish music, she was also a fund of local history. If anyone could adequately explain why an impoverished Gallerick should pay a Roman Catholic priest fifty gold sovereigns that could have been better spent on meeting some of the more pressing demands of his creditors, then it would be the bootlegger's aunt. As Aphra started up the Mini Clubman, she consoled herself with the thought that even if her journey did not bear fruit, the crisp mountain air would clear last night's cobwebs.

The ball dropped down on the sloping green a little too heavily and scampered, like a disobedient puppy, a good six feet past the hole. Father Jerry looked up from the unsatisfactory stroke to see whether the opposition were faring any better. Divareli wore a wall-to-wall grin across his face and Mick Flannery was smacking his lips in anticipation of winning the first nine holes.

'I got this for a birdie – right, partner?' Divareli asked.

Mick Flannery was beaming happily as he chortled his encouragement. 'Right you are. Hole that putt and we win the first tenner, thanks be to God.'

To Divareli's great disappointment, the ball seemed to take on a life of its own after he had struck it. Instead of travelling in a straight line for the hole, it ducked and weaved drunkenly before coming to a halt six inches short of the hole. The one cardinal sin in golf, Divareli reminded himself belatedly, was to leave a winning putt short of the hole. Men had been killed for less. The Doc and Father Jerry exhaled noisily, trying to hide their obvious relief at his miss. They returned to the first tee to begin the second nine. Just as they were hitting off, a woman's voice called to them through the open window of the Clubhouse.

'Mick, Mick, there's a phone-call for you!'

'All right Bernie, I'll be with you in a minute.' He apologised to the others. 'Sorry about this, men. Hold on a moment till I see who it is. It had better be important, I promise you. Monday is the one day in the week that I can call my own.' Because he was halfway to the Clubhouse he could not see the amused disbelief on the faces of his two regular playing partners.

'Oh dear God, I don't know whether to laugh or cry! That bloody fellow . . .', the Doc could hardly get the words out through guffaws of laughter as he pointed to the burly figure disappearing into the Clubhouse, '. . . has the best life of anyone I know,' he managed to complete the sentence.

As they waited on the tee, Divareli reviewed his progress to date. He had started off with a rusty swing that sent the little white ball in any direction but the one he desired. However, over the last few holes it was beginning to come together again. A rhythm, however faint, was creeping into his swing and his approach shots from the corrugated fairways were finishing ever closer to the flagstick. He had saved the last two holes for the partnership when Mick's slashing style of play had left him waist-high in the prickly gorse that, along with the sheep, was not be found on other courses Divareli had visited. Were it not for that last putt that failed to drop for a birdie, they would have been one up at the turn, he reflected as he looked down from the elevated tee upon the village spread out like a scale model below them.

Brulagh looked its best. In the clear winter sunlight, each feature stood out with startling clarity as though in a three-dimensional hologram. The village was clustered round the grey stone of the church, whose spire pointed the way to heaven for the faithful. A large square building nearby housed Father Jerry and his house-keeper, the dreaded Julia May. The priest had alluded to her earlier in the game *à propos* of his having to be finished in good time for lunch.

From this vantage point above the village, Brulagh appeared to be just one street. The Brulagh Inn stood proudly at one end, and further out of town was the crossroads at which stood the grotto to Mary, the Mother of God. When they had passed it on their way to the golf-course, it had shown signs of benevolent neglect in that the paintwork was flaking badly and the protective railings were badly rusted. The shrine was almost directly in front of the entrance to the Flannery farmhouse and did nothing to enhance the landscape, being an unhappy *mélange* of blues and whites. Even from this distance, the grotto clashed violently with countless different hues of green.

Close to the shrine, a mound rose out of the patchwork of fields held together by the low stone walls. Mick had been telling Divareli about it, saying that the mound was the remains of a prehistoric stockade. When attacked by marauders, the local tribe, supposedly possessed of magical powers, locked themselves and their livestock behind high timber palisades set in giant earthworks until the threat had passed. The timbers had long since rotted but the foundations remained. Known as Fairy Forts, legend had it that such places were enchanted. Because of the evil spirits which dwelt within, few were brave enough to enter them or to pluck the plump blackberries that grew on the bramble-covered mound. The more superstitious claimed to have heard strange music issuing from such places on May Eve. Mick had described how the old Canon used to inveigh from the pulpit against such pagan beliefs but that Father Jerry just laughed them away when anyone raised the topic. At the other end of the village, the pier poked a stubby finger into the blue waters of the Atlantic ocean . . .

The Doc interrupted his thoughts. 'Down there across the water from the pier is where we have planning permission for the new golf-course.'

'When do you start work on it?'

'God only knows! It was supposed to be a two-phase plan.' The Doc grimaced his disapproval. 'It included a holiday village of bloody chalets down by the shore. I think there were plans for a hotel and marina as well, as far as I can remember.'

'What happened?'

'In spite of the EC grants and God knows what else, there just wasn't enough money – or interest – to get the thing up and running. I wouldn't mind but Mick had got planning permission and approval for the funding as well.'

9

It had taken Divareli no time at all to realise that the others derived far more enjoyment from arguing about golf than they did from playing. Their current bone of contention revolved around who had actually won and the sum involved. As the argument waxed and waned, Divareli lost interest and gazed out through the Clubhouse window. What greeted his eye was a vista of such piercing beauty that it took his breath away. Starting with the forbidding, slate-grey slopes of the mountain top, the landscape gradually gave way to rocky outcrops and scattered clumps of dark green gorse. This soon changed to brown scrub grass which in turn became tiny squares of green as the terrain joined the blue Atlantic Ocean. Somewhere on that barren mountainside had to be where Johnny Slattery distilled his moonshine. Small wonder that the gut-rot masqueraded under the romantic name of Mountain Dew. Only in such hostile terrain where any movement could be spotted miles away could the likes of Johnny ply his trade despite the attentions of Sergeant Gus Moriarty. As the land continued its headlong plunge towards the sea, the green grass gradually replaced the scrub and bracken of the upper slopes.

More yellowish fields, infertile and weed-choked, with jagged rocks breaking through the thin soil crust contained white blobs that proved to be sheep. Lower down, the landscape became a patchwork quilt of emerald squares inside which black and white cattle were imprisoned by grey stone walls. Divareli had rested on one of these walls while the Doc poked around in the long grass looking for his ball. The large, flattish stone he had chosen to perch on moved to and fro under his weight. Closer inspection proved that each stone was carefully laid on top of another with nothing to bind them except their own weight and shape.

From where he was seated, he saw that his wall – and dozens more like it – sliced up the landscape as though a giant template of squares had been pressed firmly down on the rolling, lumpy terrain.

Many of these walls, which flew straight as an arrow while faithfully following the contours of the mountainside, were topped by an evil-looking fence of barbed wire.

Out of the blue a terrifying thought struck him with the sickening thud of a sledgehammer. If he were to wangle an invitation to hunt with the Gallerick pack, would he be expected to jump these lethal obstacles? Surely not. The rusted wire must slice horse and rider to shreds at the first attempt. From the barstool, he craned his neck in a desperate effort to find even one of the earthen banks which he had been told were the staple fare of Irish foxhunters. They were nowhere to be seen.

And what of the Lady Aphra Gallerick? What, indeed? Was it love or lust that caused him to think of her so often. Long after she had left him, her perfume hung in the air to enchant and distract him. Surely lust must be a transient thing, not a permanent condition like that which now afflicted him so. Of course he wanted to make love to her, and the sooner the better. Never had a promising relationship like theirs been so ill-starred. It was as if the very elements conspired against them. So were his feelings for Aphra just unrequited passion? If and when it was requited, would he still feel the same way about her?

His self-questioning was interrupted by the return of Mick Flannery. Pausing only to call for four more of the same from an invisible Bernie, he fumed, 'Would you credit it? I have to hang round here for another half an hour or so. That was the telephone exchange saying there had been a call for me from Dublin. By the time I got to the phone, they'd got tired of waiting and hung up. Anyway the upshot of it all is that they're to ring me back here shortly.'

Divareli was drawn inexorably back to those menacing stone walls. Well, he decided grimly, he would know his fate by tonight. He wondered what dinner at Gallerick Hall would be like. He wasn't even sure what to wear. What if it were a black tie affair? Anyway Aphra would know. He had asked Sean if she had phoned when he collected the Sergeant's clubs. Apparently not. Yet another gin and tonic in a highball glass appeared before him. It contained a thick wedge of lemon and enough ice to sink the *Titanic*. The real attractions of the Brulagh Golf Club slowly began to dawn on him. He hadn't tasted a drink with enough ice in it since leaving home. Forget about the incredible lousiness of the golf-course, he told himself. His playing partners seemed to have got their priorities right. Undulations and wandering sheep counted for nought. To hell with the corrugated fairways and sheep-piss-stained greens just so long as the creature comforts were up to scratch.

The lady whom Mick referred to as Bernie was in her mid-forties, of cheerful disposition and inclined to fuss more than might have been expected over the Doc. Divareli wondered idly if there were something going on there. As Mick was yet again summoned to the telephone, Father Jerry took a deep draught of his drink that lowered its level by at least three inches and unshipped a sigh of satisfaction that came from somewhere deep down inside his shining black shoes.

'I love this little bar. It's the only place I can take a drink in comfort but I must not be late for lunch. Julia May has me heart-scalded about time. If I'm late for a meal I may well have to fend for myself. Punctuality, she never tires of reminding me, is the courtesy of princes. A doubtful enough proposition, I would have thought myself, but I am not about to argue the toss with her. To be fair to the woman, I might not be alive at all were it not for her feeding me like a gamecock when I first arrived here from Rome.'

'Do you miss it? Rome, I mean.'

'Not any more. I did at the beginning but Brulagh grows on you. Now I wouldn't leave it for all the rice in China. It's got everything I require: peace, solitude and a sensible pace of life. Not that I saw much of Rome itself – the Vatican walls are high. I only visited Rome to play golf with Marcinkus and eat *lepre in agrodolce*.'

The Doc raised his eyebrows inquisitively. 'What in God's name is that – fried leopard?'

'No, not quite. As a matter of fact it's hare in sweet and sour sauce. It also has raisins, pine nuts, chocolate and that sort of thing. Heavenly is the only word for it. My boss in the Vatican was a man who liked his food. Claimed his ancestors invented the dish way back in the middle ages.'

Divareli wanted to get something clear right away. 'You knew Marcinkus? He was a buddy of my father.' Suddenly he wished he hadn't spoken but it was out before he could swallow it back. Damage limitation was now of the essence.

The priest thought for a moment before replying. 'I see, that's interesting. Yes, indeed I knew Archbishop Marcinkus. He was, amongst other things, a very good golfer. Through him we were

68

made honorary members of the Roma Club, which is just a few miles south of the city. At six thousand lire a day it would have been prohibitively expensive otherwise. But then, Marcinkus was always good at that kind of thing. Did your father know him well?'

Divareli replied a little more hurriedly than he had intended. 'No, hardly at all. I believe they did business a long time ago. I just heard him mention the name once or twice, that's all.'

Father Jerry chuckled inwardly. Those ready to claim friendship with the now-disgraced Marcinkus were few and far between. Yet there was a time not so long ago when every bank worthy of the name was inviting the brash American out to lunch. The moment stormclouds gathered and the whiff of scandal attached itself to the burly Archbishop, those same bankers disappeared like snow in springtime. Father Jerry wondered if Divareli's father had been one of those fairweather friends. Anyway, as a result of Marcinkus' misdemeanours their playing facilities at the posh Roma Club were discreetly withdrawn.

Something about the Divareli name intrigued the priest. He tried to mask the curiosity in his voice as he inquired, 'If you don't mind my asking, was your father a banker?'

'Yeah, he owned Italbank in the States. He died a few years back.' Divareli felt no obligation to add that he was no longer a major stockholder. Luckily Italbank did not seem to ring a bell with the priest, nor with the others for that matter. Lack of curiosity was another one of their traits that he liked: the Irish took you as they found you, for good or ill. Now Mick was back among them again, this time cursing fluently.

'You're not going to believe this but those shaggers expect me to be in bloody Strasbourg for a vote at nine o'clock tonight.'

All debate on the outcome of their struggle on the golf-course was abandoned as he vented his fury on the bureaucrats of the EC.

'They want me to vote on some bloody subsidy for the shagging tomato growers of Sicily, would you believe. I wouldn't mind but that lot are the greatest shower of gangsters in the whole community.'

This was greeted by solemn nods all round as Mick paused to drain his glass. 'Anyway, thanks for the game, lads. I don't know how I'm going to get to the blasted airport, though. Maggie needs the car after lunch for something or other.'

Divareli seized on his chance. 'I'll drive you. I've nothing else to do for the afternoon.'

Mick shot him a searching look, then shrugged his shoulders and replied, 'That'll be fine. I'd like a spin in that car of yours. The garage should have the battery charged by now. The flight leaves around six o'clock. Look, I must rush now, if you don't mind. I've a lot to do before we leave. I'll drive you back to Sean's and we can arrange a time for you to pick me up at the house. OK?'

Divareli nodded. He was pleased to get Mick alone in the car where he might further cross-examine him about those grants. He would, however, have been less sanguine had he known that the mention of Italbank had indeed set bells ringing in Father Jerry's mind. Yet if the priest had not been writing that very night to his oldest friend Gianni Manolo Agostini, pastor of the tiny parish of Boggola deep in the vineyards of Tuscany, nothing might have come of it. It was only when Father Jerry ran out of things to write and was left with more than half a page to fill that he cast around and remembered Italbank and Divareli's reference to Marcinkus. He might have done better to have left the page blank save for his usual farewell: *'Yours as ever in Christ, Jerry.'*

10

When they called at the garage, a tin shed guarded by a rusting petrol pump standing like an elderly sentinel outside, it was to be informed that the battery would not be fully charged for at least another hour. As they left, Mick explained quietly so as not to be overheard by the man in greasy overalls: 'I'm not one bit surprised. That hoor doesn't understand the workings of a cigarette lighter, not to mind a complicated bit of machinery like yours. Anyway, what do you want to do now? We can discuss what we were talking about last night again on the way to the airport. I was hoping I could put the application in the moment I got to Brussels. The quicker it's in, the sooner I can get it passed. Then if you still want to go ahead, fine. You would save six weeks or so. If the figures didn't add up, you needn't take the matter any further. Why don't you go for a walk and have a look round? Then you can pick me up at the house around four, if that's okay with you?'

Divareli nodded. He made his way down the steep, cobbled road that led to the side of the pier. The tide was out so he picked his steps carefully down the smooth stone steps cut into the pier. He would have expected them to lead to a moored craft of some sort but instead they petered out on the sandy floor of the harbour. At the water's edge, a fringe of brownish seaweed and stranded jelly-fish formed a crude necklace round the bay. It was quite large, much bigger in fact than he had imagined it to be from the lofty eyrie of the Clubhouse bar. At the end of the crumbling stone pier, in the deeper water of the narrow channel that led to the sea, was moored a smart half-decker. As it bobbed in the gentle swell surging in from the open sea, bright splinters of sunlight glinted off its polished planks. Painted in ornate script on its stern was the name *Sancta Maria*.

Though the sea broke against the far side of the pier, sending plumes of white spray cascading skywards, inside the harbour was smooth as a mill-pond. A pair of swans stared at him haughtily as he strode briskly along the shore to where the still-born marina would have been sited had things turned out differently. Looking around him, Divareli decided that Mick's plan wasn't as outlandish as it had sounded last night at the crowded counter of the Brulagh Inn.

At the top of the gentle rise leading from the basin of the harbour stood the ruins of some kind of tower. From it the eye could see nothing but giant, rolling sand-dunes, fringed with long, wiry grass. Between them and the sandy beach was a thin line of stones washed smooth by the surging tides. It looked to be the finest natural golf-course Divareli had ever seen.

He strolled through the towering dunes, swinging an imaginary club as he visualised the moonscape transformed into a golf-course complete with green ribbons of fairways. Rabbits and a few weird-looking toads were his only companions. It was like a dream sequence in the movies with incidental music scored by the crash of waves breaking on the nearby beach. Overhead the gulls swooped majestically, shrieking mercilessly. He made his way back to the ruined tower and took more careful stock of his surroundings.

Though far from expert at spotting likely resort locations, Divareli was sure that this one had to be a natural. It was perfect for the scheme that had been scratching at the outer edges of his consciousness ever since he first heard about Mick Flannery and his crazy development plan. If the grants were still obtainable, likewise the planning permission, the very spot where he was standing was the ideal site for a luxury hotel. A marina on its very doorstep would be a major amenity, but the jewel in the crown would be the golf-course, an 'autograph' layout designed by a 'name' professional, someone like Jack Nicklaus or Arnold Palmer. It would probably cost at least a million dollars just to get someone of that calibre to lend their name to the course, but it would be worth it many times over in prestige alone.

The course would have to tread the narrow path between championship standard and not being too tigerish to deter the droves of well-heeled hackers who could scarcely hit the little white ball out of their way. Why, even in Europe, the French of all people were opening one golf-course per day. Mick Flannery's good old EC had come up with a set-aside plan whereby the Frog peasantry got paid to grow nothing on their land and thus reduce the mountainous surplus in Europe's bulging grain-stores. Some other branch of the same bureaucracy had dreamt up a 'leisure' scheme whereby agricultural land turned into sports facilities attracted huge grants per hectare. The sport that used up the most acreage with the least capital cost was the game of golf.

Now every dirt farmer from Dunkirk to Perpignan was cutting his grass short, sticking flagsticks into holes and calling his cow pasture a golf-course. Which was fine for beginners until they aspired to something better. Feuds of international proportions erupted when course managers in Britain and Ireland refused to allow sun-tanned Frogs with handicaps of forty permission to desecrate their courses by attempting to play on them. The French, getting it arseways as usual, took this as a studied insult to *la belle France* when the reality was that no golfer with a handicap of forty would be allowed near a half-decent golf-course.

Divareli, a keen skier, had the answer to that one. Instead of nursery slopes and ski instructors, he would run a training facility complete with practice area and professional teachers. He might even persuade the Golfing Unions to allow him to issue handicaps! Think of the attraction to an upwardly mobile Frog, or Jap for that matter, to come back from their vacation in Brulagh with a legitimate golf handicap. So what if they had about the same credibility as some of those degrees from the God factories in the Bible Belt that entitled every headcase who paid one hundred bucks to call himself 'Reverend'. Anyway that was all in the future. Of more immediate concern was to nail down the unquestioning support of Mick Flannery, then get a professional evaluation done of the prospects and the approximate cost. He knew that once these were in place, raising the money would be the least of his problems.

With an international airport just down the road and a stable régime favourable both to America and the cursed Japanese, such a project could scarcely fail. Satisfied that everything seemed OK, Divareli retraced his steps to collect the Porsche, deciding to go back to Sean's and retire to bed for a couple of hours until it was time to drive Mick to the airport. As he walked up the steep cobbled road that led from the pier to the main street of Brulagh, Divareli tried to order his strategy into some sort of meaningful sequence. Of course those silly sods from round here couldn't afford a scheme like that for themselves. In that respect Mick's plan was crazy, regardless of the two thirds grant element. The seed capital just wasn't available in a dump like this.

Divareli had noticed a garish plastic sign that read *Allied Banks of Ireland* outside a building that resembled a rundown pizzeria. The outfit looked as if it couldn't finance a coat of paint for its own premises, much less underwrite a multi-million dollar conference centre. And yet, if he remembered correctly what Mick had said last night, the money would have to be deposited here. He might as well take a look at the bank anyway since he needed Irish currency. The excesses of last night had drained his stock of punts as the Irish Pound was quaintly called. He smiled grimly as he imagined what some of his foul-mouthed Italian-American brokers with their penchant for rhyming slang would christen such a currency, should they ever have to trade it. The bank was closed. He looked at his watch. Two minutes past three.

A small notice was stuck with sellotape, opaque with age, to the frosted glass of the window. It stated baldly that the hours of trading at the Brulagh office of Allied Banks of Ireland were 10.00 am to 12.30 pm and again from 1.30 pm to 3.00 pm. Surprising that the motherfuckers bothered to open the dump at all, was Divareli's reaction as he strode towards the rusty shed that housed the ailing Porsche.

'Your car's ready now, sir.' This was spoken by an elderly man wearing greasy overalls and with a drooping moustache. He had apparently materialised out of the ground, for Divareli would have sworn that he hadn't been there seconds before.

When asked what was owing, the mechanic replied uneasily, 'Do you know what I'm going to tell you, sir, and it isn't one word of a lie – I just don't know. I'll have to be asking the Missus. 'Tis herself handles the money end of things, you see.'

Divareli wondered – not for the first time since his arrival in Brulagh – if he had fallen among a tribe of seriously deranged leprechauns. He inquired politely when the Missus might be back so that the transaction might be brought to a conclusion.

'Only God alone knows that, sir. Look, am I right in thinking that you're going to be around for a while more yet? Well, when I find out how much the job cost, I'll tell young Sean up at the pub and he'll look after the whole thing, if that's all right with yourself?'

'OK by me.'

Divareli sighed resignedly as he climbed into the ca
engine roared to life. He wondered if he was mad to evei
a resort project in a place like this. At least he wouldn't h.... _
here forever himself. The moment everything was up and running
he would be out of here, pronto.

This thought preoccupied him as he spoke to Sean and was shown
upstairs to a bright, airy room with a fine view of the harbour.
Meeting Sean again and the magnificence of the view hardened his
resolve to persevere with the project, but now he worried whether
Aphra had influenced his judgement. As he snuggled under the
duvet and closed his eyes, he asked himself could it be that he was
just looking for an excuse to stay on in this out-of-the-way spot so
that he could have his vile way with her. The last thing he remembered before sleep overtook him was laughing aloud at the very
idea.

By the time he reached Mick's house he was in a rush to avoid
being late, but he need not have worried. His passenger was on the
phone making soothing noises to someone while raising his eyes to
heaven for Divareli's benefit to indicate that this continued to be
one of those days.

'Ah Jaysus, will you cop yourself on. I told you this morning I'd
be there in plenty of time for the shagging vote. And there I'll be,
just as long as the plane does all that's expected of it. Now if you'll
just shag off and let me finish packing, I'll see you later tonight.'
Without further ado, he hung up, grabbed a battered-looking valise
and said, 'Right, I'm ready when you are.'

As he closed the front door behind them, Mick turned the key in
the lock and put it under one of a matching pair of large flowerpots
standing guard outside the front door. They settled into the car and
turned right and away from the village where the entrance to Flannery's joined the road. As Divareli was guiding the Porsche expertly
up the winding mountain road at a rate of knots that made Mick
Flannery shift uneasily in his seat, their progress was halted by a
herd of cows ambling along in the same direction. Passing them on
the narrow road was out of the question.

'They're Johnson's cows. They'll be turning in a gate in a hundred yards or so. You might as well pull into the side till they're
gone out of the way.'

75

Divareli did as he was bid but something bothered him. 'How do you know who owns the cows, for Chrissakes? You're not going to tell me that you can distinguish one of those animals from another?'

'No, of course not. But there are only so many herds of that size round here. The land on either side of the road belongs to Johnsons so they have to be his. For thirty years it was part and parcel of my job to know who lived where, what way they voted last time and what way they'd vote next time out. To do that properly you had to find out what they wanted. Maybe it was a simple thing like getting the road fixed or a job for one of the kids in a Government department. Then again it might be getting a pension or a medical card for someone or hurrying up a grant for a silage pit or an indoor toilet.'

Divareli saw his opportunity to break the flow and asked the question that had been worrying him. 'Speaking of grants, could you just run it past me again – what's available for tourism projects, I mean?'

These were quickly outlined, with the details sketched in where Mick thought it necessary. In all, he spoke for fully ten minutes without interruption. When he had ended, Divareli summed it up thus: 'So what you're telling me is that if I put up the money for something that gets the green light from the authorities, I get two thirds of the capital cost back after it is up and running. Then, in addition there are tax benefits and labour subsidies.'

It was Mick's turn to stare ahead blankly and assume an air of total innocence as though he hadn't been aware right from the start that his driver had swallowed the bait hook, line and sinker. 'That's it in a nutshell. Why, did you have something in mind?'

In every deal, Divareli knew there was the moment of truth. The reason Italbank was still solvent was that he had walked away from more deals than he had eaten hot dinners. Only very few situations met his strict criteria. This looked like one of them. He paused for a while before drawling out his reply, 'Yeah Mick, as a matter of fact I do. That walk along the shore this morning and what you said just now about the grants kinda clinched it.'

Again another pause, even longer than the first. 'What sort of thing had you thought of?'

'A conference centre. Quite like your original plan, in fact. Are the planning permissions for the hotel, marina and golf-course still valid?'

'Oh sure they are. They've at least another two years to run. No problem there.'

'Good, because that's what I had in mind. A big hotel with a marina on the harbour and a championship golf-course in the sand-dunes. There would be holiday villas beside most of the fairways. Timeshare, probably.'

Mick was dumbfounded. The only sound that came from him was a low, appreciative whistle followed by, 'Jaysus Christ Almighty, so it's going to happen after all. I'd given up hope of ever seeing it in my lifetime. Then yourself comes along. 'Twas God sent you and no mistake.'

'Naturally, this is just strictly between ourselves for the moment. I have to okay the idea with my people and get a guy to give the place the once-over. If it all squares up we can start right away.'

'That could be vital – the starting right away, I mean. Some of those grants may not be available after January. No one can tell. It all depends on what's left in the EC kitty at the end of the year . . .'

Easy now, my boy, and don't go trying to land the fish before he's played out. Keep in the back of your mind that if you miss this one, there might not be another along for quite a while.

He tried to make it sound as if the thought had only just occurred to him. 'Like I said, if you want I can file the preliminary application while I'm over there. It will save a month or so by having the paperwork processed immediately rather than being passed from one civil servant to another till they get tired of the game.'

Mick felt that this was neither the time nor place to say that his secretary in Brussels, the compliant Yvette, had a friend in the section that processed such applications. Her task was to weed out the lunatic from the unlikely. It was important to get this scheme underway before the Yank was exposed to the silver-tongued charm of Gallerick and his luscious Aphra. Otherwise Divareli might sink his considerable wealth into a crumbling mansion. Or, worse still, into that pack of mongrels rampaging through the countryside under the supposed control of that assortment of drunks, rams and wastrels collectively known as the Gallerick Hunt. The voice of the 'fish' interrupted further speculation along these lines.

'Good, you do that. I'll see if I can get a guy called Linovitz over here right away. Anything else you want to know at this stage?'

Trying to sound casual, Mick asked the question that had been scratching at his raw nerve-ends. 'Not really. It would be a help, though, if I could put a figure on the whole thing when I'm filing the application, but I suppose it's too soon for that.'

'Not at all. I've been running the numbers through my head but, of course, they're only ballpark figures at this stage. Still, I'd expect the project to come out somewhere close. Want to hear them?'

'I certainly do.'

'Well, for starters there'll be around seven million for the hotel, another three million for the golf-course and maybe about the same for the marina. That's thirteen million US dollars. Better make it fifteen to be on the safe side, just in case we need to build a clubhouse.'

Mick looked out of the window at the blur of the hedgerows as the car powered its way towards the airport. If this guy was genuine, the sooner this thing got off the ground the better it would be for all concerned. Not least for one Mick Flannery whose political future could depend on the success – or otherwise – of the conference centre. In the meantime, this guy was talking about spending *fifteen million dollars*. It looked as though Christmas was coming early to Brulagh this year.

The airport was built beside a river delta. Vast mudflats teeming with long-legged birds stretched as far as the eye could see. Little rivulets of water zigzagged through the brown mud, reflecting the last fag-end of a weak, winter sunset. It reminded Divareli of symphonies in dull grey, captured on canvas by Vermeer, at which one gave an involuntary shudder at the bleakness of the landscape.

A less impressive site for an international airport would have been difficult to find. It did, however, have certain advantages that Divareli was quick to note. No crowds, a good hotel and several restaurants within the complex and, of course, the usual car rental facilities. Mick had introduced him to the Airport Manager before departing for Brussels, and it was from his office that Divareli was now murmuring earnestly on a transatlantic line.

'Look Abe, this is important, no kidding. I need you to get over here right away.'

A protesting squawk came from the other end.

'I don't give a goddamn what you have lined up. Scrub it! There's a situation here that bears looking into, I can say no more than that over the goddamn phone. But right now I want to hear from your own lips that you promise to get over here by Tuesday latest. Here being Shannon, Ireland. You can hire a car and drive down to Brulagh, yeah B for beautiful, R for randy, U for useful, L for loot, A for asshole, G for gin and H for happy. Got all that? No, I don't have a communications network set up at my end yet but I'll have something organised by the time you get here.'

More squawks – this time marginally less frenetic – floated across the broad Atlantic. More explanations were required.

'I was on goddamn vacation, that's why. Then this thing comes up on me outa nowhere. Yeah, you'll be staying at the Brulagh Inn. No, it's not exactly a Holiday Inn but it's okay . . . I'm staying there myself for Chrissakes, Abe, that's how I know! OK, call me when you have a firm arrival date.'

Then he hung up. Abe Linovitz was an investment analyst – at least, that was the flag of convenience under which he sailed. Abe had managed resort hotels in places as far apart as Las Vegas and the Algarve before he realised there was more money to be made by pointing investors in the right direction. When it came to making resorts tick, Abe had forgotten more than the rest of the industry would ever know. The big hotel chains used him all the time as a scout for new locations, or as a doctor for ailing ones.

Major corporations looking for somewhere new and interesting for their next conference would first ask Abe before making a decision. The guy knew better than anyone the ingredients of the elusive formula that would produce a profitable resort operation. If Abe didn't like what he saw, he said so. Not, however, before he had collected a murderous fee. If he liked a project, he demanded a hefty slice of the action and, in return, oversaw the development from start to finish. He could look at a greenfield situation for a minute then reel off what facilities were essential to make it work. In the next breath he would put a number on it that would be within a percentage point or two of the final cost. What made Abe so special was that no one else could pull that trick.

As soon as the place was ticking over nicely and making pots of money for everyone, Abe would sell his stake and move on. The guy had a short attention span. Divareli had used him on several deals and had never regretted it. A lot of bankers avoided Abe like the plague, whispering behind their hands that he was a front man for the Mob while he worked in Las Vegas. The implication was that links like that were not easily severed. Divareli had heard those rumours too but had never believed them. Even if they were true, it had never affected their relationship. Abe, as far as Divareli was concerned, was a streetwise Brooklyn Jew who knew his way round the resort industry like no one else. End of story.

Divareli pushed the buzzer on the desk. A smiling secretary hurried in, notepad in hand and pencil poised expectantly. Divareli gave her the details he wanted sent to Abe and waved her away. His next call was to Italbank. It was brief and to the point. No one talked business over open lines any more in a world where electronic eavesdropping was a growth industry. He used the family code out of habit more than a genuine sense of security – a child could have cracked it within seconds. Yet for Divareli, old habits died hard. As for the message to the Head Cashier, it was brief and to the point: *'Clear soonest ah – one, ah – five US to Allied Banks of Ireland, Brulagh Branch, Ireland. Debit same to new B Project account. Notify ABI two days in advance of arrival. Endit.'*

That was it. A draft for fifteen million dollars would shortly be winging its way towards Brulagh. On his way out to the car, he paused to tip the secretary generously for her help and dash off a polite note of thanks to the man whose office he had been using. Mick Flannery had seen to it that Divareli had been afforded VIP treatment. Apart from the secretarial services, he had arranged for someone from the *bureau de change* to come to the office with Irish money in exchange for a wipe of his Amex card. Divareli decided there and then that if a local were needed to front the Brulagh project, Mick was the right man for the job. He was not to know that the chosen candidate had arrived at that same conclusion some twenty-four hours earlier.

11

The gateway to Gallerick Hall was flanked by two cut-stone pillars. On top of these perched weird, sausage-like objects that might have represented an early Flash Gordon spaceship. The same *motif*, much reduced, was repeated in the terracotta parapet that topped the outer defences of the estate. Just inside the entrance stood a tiny but elegant gate lodge, built of the same stone and festooned with more baby spaceships. Their vast number and unlikely location caused Divareli to speculate idly whether they might not have been intended to depict something of a more personal nature, especially apt should what Aphra had told him of her researches into the murky past of the Gallerick dynasty prove to be correct. In the olden days, it seemed, no female between seventeen and seventy had been safe from the rampant Gallericks. Aphra had promised him the Grand Tour when he arrived for dinner. Even thinking of her aroused him to the extent that he tried harder than ever to concentrate on what lay before him.

The gate lodge was a fine specimen of *bijou* architecture, even if its impact was somewhat lessened by the gaping holes in its roof and the broken panes in the tiny diamond-shaped windows. The avenue meandered ever upwards between post and rail fencing that drooped sadly here and there, pleading for repair. The potholes that pitted the surface were of such magnitude as to oblige Divareli to steer round them. At the end of a long, gentle curve a large lake was suddenly spread out before his eyes, its edges framed by green rushes tipped with rust. The still water mirrored the grey winter sky in the parts where weeds had not taken over and threatened to choke the giant lily pads. A platoon of bullrushes – their beige stalks crowned with brown, velvet mufflers – stood proudly to attention in the shallows. Haughty swans sailed serenely by, disdainful of the throaty burble coming from the twin exhausts of the Porsche. A light finger of mist hung above the tips of the bullrushes – a reminder that autumn had come to Gallerick Hall. It gave everything a spooky, mystical look as though the whole scene might retreat forever from the human gaze – like *Brigadoon* – back into the Celtic twilight.

Out of the mist, a solitary heron flapped lazily across the still water just as a tight wedge of long-necked ducks swooped in to land. Still in close formation, they skidded to a halt on the placid surface. Their bow waves rocked the swans who, studiously ignoring the noisy arrival of the unwelcome intruders, continued to wet their beaks in search of underwater morsels like diners in an expensive restaurant into which a noisy drunk has just lurched.

The avenue skirted the edge of the lake. Divareli braked to a halt to let an otter amble across a low bridge. It disappeared between several largish boulders perched precariously on the low stone parapet. That, too, was in dire need of repair. Some boulders and quite a few of the parapet stones had fallen into the gurgling brook that fed fresh water into the lake. Rounding a corner, Gallerick Hall loomed up before him, catching him unawares.

His first reaction was that it was smaller than might have been expected from the length of its avenue, the second that there was no good reason why one should be in proportion to the other. What stood before him was no ugly barracks of a stately pile but rather a beautifully proportioned gem in a perfect setting of rolling lawns and giant oaks. Next to the last sweeping curve of the avenue before it glided to a halt before Gallerick Hall was another lake, an ornamental one complete with a tiny island, flat-bottomed punt and water lilies. Despite such distractions, it was the house itself that enchanted Divareli.

It was a squat building whose low-pitched slate roof was encased in ornate battlements, again repeating the phallic spaceship motif. Even the elegant chimney-pots echoed this design. The sash windows were huge rectangular affairs, each set in its perfectly sculpted limestone frame. A square porch with six Grecian columns supporting its flat roof, again of carefully chiselled stone, protected the front door. Though obviously modelled on the Acropolis, this miniaturised temple to Apollo did not look out of place. A flight of steps swept up to the raised porch. As the Porsche crunched to a halt on the gravel, Divareli recognised the Doc's battered Ford parked beside a black Mercedes limo whose chauffeur gave Divareli the briefest of nods before returning to polishing its already spotless windscreen. The parking area was cunningly masked from view by the elevated porch. An unseen dog barked a shrill greeting as he climbed the steps. The door opened and a tall figure dressed in brown, crumpled tweed greeted him heartily.

'Good to see you, old man.' Looking back over his shoulder, the Eleventh Earl of Gallerick brayed, 'Aphra darling, this must be the chap you were talking about.'

Suddenly a radiant Aphra was beside him. She was a vision Divareli swore inwardly that he would take to his grave. Long black hair fell about her bare shoulders. Apart from lipstick highlighting the cupid's bow of her full lips, she appeared to wear no make-up. A simple black dress hugged her tall figure, emphasising her sensuous curves. Round earrings big as satellite dishes hung from her ears. A heavy gold chain graced her neck, its Wedgwood medallion lying snug between perfect breasts of luminous alabaster. Divareli decided there and then that he had never seen anyone quite so beautiful – or desirable. She was every bit as much a part of Gallerick Hall as the oaks, the lakes, even the ridiculous phallic spaceships.

While Divareli was devouring her with his eyes, Gally had drawn himself up to his full height, fidgeting with his tie as he sought to attract his guest's attention. Reluctantly shifting his gaze from the vision that was Aphra, Divareli now scrutinised the Eleventh Earl of Gallerick – who was doing precisely the same to him. Aphra had informed him of her new catch, mentioning *en passant* that the Yank with the Dago name was seriously rich. The Machiavelli of the Weigh Tent extended a gaunt hand in greeting. Well into his sixties, the hair was greying at the temples and curled upwards over his collar. A long thin, prominent nose separated tired brown eyes set wide apart under bushy eyebrows. The ears stuck out noticeably above the wide gills of a strong jaw giving a jug-like effect to the otherwise aristocratic features. The mouth was wide and thin-lipped, semaphoring a yellowish, nicotine-stained set of teeth when its owner flashed one of his frequent smiles. The complexion had quite a lot of red in it as if it had been subjected to too much sun – or drink. The fact that the Eleventh Earl was holding a large glass full of amber liquid would seem to favour the latter theory.

'Absolutely splendid of you to come, old chap. Aphra, introduce me to this splendid fella!'

Right on cue Aphra chirped, 'Gally, this is Luke Divareli from New York. Luke, meet Daddy – or the Eleventh Earl of Gallerick, if you prefer.'

Their host protested strongly. 'Oh come on, Aphra darling. Give over the bullshit . . .' Turning to Luke he explained, 'Everyone calls me Gally. Please do likewise, Luke old chap. Step inside and I'll find you something to drink. What will it be?'

'A gin and tonic, please,' Divareli replied, asking himself not for the first time that day whether any form of intercourse, social or otherwise, was possible on this weird island without an accompanying deluge of liquor. Gally sang out over his shoulder as he disappeared into a milling throng of bodies, 'Do come inside this minute and I'll introduce you to the rest of the mob.'

Inside the front door an impressively high-ceilinged hall throbbed with the roar of conversation. To the right, a bar had been set up on a low trestle table that groaned under the weight of an assortment of bottles and glasses of every possible shape and size. Aphra had been swallowed up in the crowd where everyone was shouting, rather than speaking, to each other. This phenomenon fed on itself so that the more noise one group generated, the louder the next one had to roar to be heard above the din. More importantly, very few appeared to be listening. Divareli found himself a reluctant member of this endangered species when a short but very stout lady in her seventies, wearing tweeds from the same medieval loom as Gally, bore down on him.

'Are you Aphra's Yank – the one they're all gossiping about?'

A difficult question to answer – even more so when delivered in a staccato bellow more suited to addressing hounds at the far side of a fifty-acre field. Deciding that the question was unanswerable, Divareli just shrugged his shoulders while eyeing his persecutor warily. She had the complexion of a very old boot and a luxuriant moustache graced her upper lip.

Taking his silence for acquiescence, she introduced herself. 'I'm Gally's Aunt Daphne. You seem pretty quiet for a colonial.'

Curiosity overcame his better judgement – which was urging a continuing silence in the face of this aged harridan. 'I beg your pardon, ma'am, but I don't quite get the colonial bit.'

His host intervened at this stage in the proceedings, bearing aloft what looked like a large glass vase filled to the brim with clear, blueish liquid. On tasting it, Divareli found that the heavy goblet with an impressive coat-of-arms carved in the glass contained almost neat, lukewarm gin. Its provider spoke briskly as though Aunt Daphne had left for another planet. In fact she was standing between them, blinking owlishly when not staring expectantly at Divareli as though waiting for him to pull Old Glory out of his ear.

'What foul luck! I see Daphne the Daft hooked you at the very first cast. Everyone around here avoids her like the plague. Be sure not to take a blind bit of notice of anything she says. She's mad as a hatter and deaf as a post. Did I hear her waffling on about the colonies? Yes, I thought as much. One of the old trout's hobbyhorses, I'm afraid. She regards all Americans as disaffected colonists. Aphra claims old Daff tells every American that crosses her path that it's high time they paid their bally taxes. To the Crown, of course.' His Lordship brayed happily at this.

Divareli thought it only civil to inquire further. 'And what does she say to that? Aphra, I mean.'

'Oh the splendid girl just nods and tells old Daff that she's absolutely right. Did Aphra tell you she's researching the ancestors? All meaty stuff, I promise you. Leg-over merchants to a man – every one of them! Absolutely super girl, don't you agree?'

Before Divareli could concoct an adequate response to this observation, his host was off on a rambling monologue concerning the difficulty in finding a man good enough for his only child. This was cut short by her arrival. Taking Divareli by the hand, she led him away with a parting shot delivered with considerable heat over her bare shoulder.

'Really, Gally, you are the bloody limit. I heard some of that nonsense about the lack of suitable men round here . . .' Turning to Divareli, she shouted in his ear. Even then, it was difficult to catch what she was saying. 'There's a man over there you should meet – Pat Mullarkey. He's the Tanaiste . . .' she pronounced it *thaw-nish-tuh* with an impressive flourish '. . . which is almost the same as your Vice-President, only with much more clout.'

Divareli nodded without voicing his opinion that it would be extremely difficult to have any less. He allowed himself to be led towards a middle-aged couple. The man looked familiar, and much younger than his spouse. Aphra did the introductions.

85

'Mary, this is Luke Divareli, our latest visitor to Brulagh. Luke, this is Mary Mullarkey.'

After some 'pleased to meet you' noises, Aphra pointed him towards Mullarkey. The resemblance was uncanny. The guy looked too much like the late JFK for it to be just coincidental. The same boyish, toothy smile set in the craggy features, why even the hairstyle was identical with the fringe blow-dried across the forehead. Only his taste in wives dented the image. Mary Mullarkey was a pleasant, plump lady in her forty-somethings but by no stretch of the imagination was she a wide-eyed Jackie. 'Pat Mullarkey, meet Luke Divareli.'

Mullarkey had a dry, firm handshake. 'Pleased to meet you, Luke. I hear you have big plans for Brulagh. If I can be of help, please let me know. It's no secret that politicians like to steal the credit for anything private enterprise comes up with – and I'm no exception to that.'

This was delivered with an ironic smile. Divareli began to warm to Mullarkey. 'Yeah, as a matter of fact I do have some ideas at that. Like to hear 'em?' Mullarkey nodded. 'A conference centre with a marina and a golf-course, basically.'

'Keeeerist Almighty! The Flannery Plan resurrected. Well, why not? All it lacked the first time round was money. Do you have money, Mr Divareli?'

'Yeah, some. Enough to do this thing, if that's your question.'

'No, not really. I was just wondering whether you were using your own or someone else's, that's all.'

'My own. Mick Flannery was telling me about the grants available for projects like this. Also the tax holidays and the training schemes. Comes out as a pretty attractive package, to be honest. That is, of course, if all he says is true.'

'Probably is. Mick researched the thing thoroughly a few years back and nothing much has changed in the meantime. The grants may go after Christmas, though. No one knows for sure. Otherwise everything else stays the same. The grants are the main attraction, I suppose?'

It was as much a statement as a question. Divareli saw it for what it actually was – a delicate probe.

'Yeah, you're right. They certainly are a major factor in the equation. Still, if all the other elements didn't gell and I didn't like the idea in the first instance, they would be worthless.'

It was Mullarkey's turn to look puzzled. 'I'm afraid I don't quite follow you.'

'Pat, what I'm saying is that if the location is wrong, or the essential services are missing, or the people unfriendly and the régime either unstable or hostile, then no grants, however generous, are going to attract the serious players. And I, Mr Mullarkey, am a serious player.'

'So I have heard, Luke. I must confess that I checked up on you the moment I heard you were in the neighbourhood. I couldn't help noticing just now that you were too modest to admit that you are one of the most successful bankers on Wall Street.'

'Well, it's good of you to say so but it really isn't true any longer – even if it ever was. I sold most of my shareholding in Italbank a while back. Then there's the security bit. I know damn well that Brulagh isn't Beirut, but you never know nowadays.'

'Yeah, that's true. But not around here, thank God. Still it is a bloody nuisance all the same. The powers that be have just got around to arming my driver – you may have seen him outside. Well, he's a fine driver but I personally wouldn't put him in charge of a water pistol. They gave him an Uzi last week and I haven't let him take it out of the wrapper yet!'

There was a pause before Mullarkey wondered aloud, 'What sort of money is involved in your project – or is that confidential information?'

'Not at all. I don't have the exact figure but somewhere around fifteen million dollars, I expect.'

Mullarkey gave a low whistle and the two women looked suitably impressed. Then the Irishman showed the practical streak to his character. 'If you're talking those sort of numbers, you should make one hell of an impression on our local Bank Manager, that's for sure. Will you be using the local branch?'

'Well, I couldn't help noticing the place was closed today at three o'clock. Seems a little early to put up the shutters, doesn't it?'

'It certainly is, but that's Irish banking for you! Honest to God I sometimes despair of that lot.' Pat Mullarkey's brow darkened as he contemplated the sad condition of institutionalised usury.

Jokingly Divareli suggested, 'Maybe Italbank should open a branch over here.'

'Maybe you should at that. Save yourself a lot of fees on your project, for one thing. Ah, here comes our local banker, Thomas Donnelly, Esquire. I'll be interested to hear what you make of him.'

A tall, balding man with a serious expression on his jowled face was elbowing his way towards them in a determined fashion. Pat Mullarkey introduced them. 'Tom, this is Luke Divareli. Luke, this is Tom Donnelly – Allied Banks of Ireland man in Brulagh.'

Divareli thought he had gripped several small dead fish. Donnelly was not of the Harvard school when it came to handshakes. His accent was rather high-pitched and he looked with glazed eyes at Divareli. Without so much as a nod to indicate that he had heard Pat, Thomas Donnelly got straight down to business.

'I hear you are thinking of going ahead with Mick Flannery's mad scheme down by the harbour.'

'I am.' Divareli had taken an instant dislike to his fellow banker.

'There isn't a bank in Ireland would be prepared to loan a brass farthing to a crazy scheme like that.'

'What's crazy about it?' Divareli's voice was level. This was as good a place as any to test the idea.

'The cost, for one thing. How could anyone expect to get their money back out of something like that? And where would the visitors come from?'

'Oh Japan, America – Europe, I expect.'

Donnelly could not hide the contempt in his voice. 'Just supposing for a minute that they *did* decide to come here, how would they get to Brulagh from the airport? That bloody road is like the bed of a river.'

'They'd fly.'

'Fly? Do you mean . . .' Donnelly could hardly get the words out through the laughter that welled up inside him. The fact that he was rather drunk made what he had to say next even more objectionable. '. . . Someone is going to build an airport here?'

This was accompanied by a loud guffaw. Aphra looked embarrassed by his boorishness and Pat Mullarkey had been about to intervene until he deciphered the message flashed from Divareli's sidelong glance: '*Keep out of this*'.

Divareli seemed oblivious to Donnelly's scorn as he explained in a patient voice: 'That wouldn't be necessary, Mr Donnelly. The visitors would be flown in by chopper if they didn't want to make the road trip. Though personally, I think the drive from the airport to Brulagh is worth the hassle because of the scenery.'

Donnelly persisted in digging himself ever deeper into the hole. 'And who, may I ask, is going to put up the money for all this?' The obvious distaste with which he framed the question made it sound as though he were being asked to bankroll a public toilet. Divareli could not help noticing that the hall had gone silent, ears pricked for what was to come.

'Well, I'm not at all sure that it's any of your goddamn business but, since you ask, I intend to put up the money myself. My bank may be sending you a draft guarantee for fifteen million dollars within the next few days. While we're on the subject, I notice you were closed at three o'clock this afternoon. That is not good enough. I would expect you to provide round-the-clock facilities should I require your services. If you can't see your way to organise that, I'm sure that I can go elsewhere.'

With that he turned on his heel and steered Aphra gently by the elbow towards their host who had been signalling them to come and join his group. Divareli had relished the appalled look on Donnelly's face as the dreadful truth struck home. Just then a loud bang assailed their ears and drowned out the roar of conversation for a split second. It was the dinner gong.

12

The room that Gally ushered them all into was impressive. An elderly figure in formal attire who could have doubled for Boris Karloff swung the doors open from the inside with a dramatic flourish. All that the moment lacked was the crash of thunderous organ music. A carved stone arch surrounding the door-frame led to a large room with, as its centrepiece, a long dining table complete with place settings. In the background, a dull glow came from tiny canopy lights that lit a succession of portraits lining three sides of the room.

The walls were divided at regular intervals by slim marble columns of a dark, greenish hue. Set in the polished wooden floor, they stretched to the ceiling where they were topped by ornate friezes. These in turn supported massive wooden roof-beams. One space in the middle of the long wall was occupied by an enormous marble fireplace whose wide mantelpiece propped up a giant mirror with the Gallerick coat-of-arms carved into the top of its delicate gilt frame. It occurred to Divareli that for someone reputed to be on the verge of bankruptcy, his host did himself proud. At the far end of the dining room was a smaller door, again set in a sculpted stone archway. This presumably led to the kitchens – a possibility now reinforced by the sounds issuing from behind it of pots being vigorously bashed and the general clatter associated with the preparation of a meal.

Divareli tried to focus in on the paintings. They glowered back at him from heavy gilt frames, their stern, bewhiskered faces highlighted by their individual canopy lamps. He observed that not all of the portraits were of men: some were of horses. The artists did not seem to have quite got the hang of painting such animals, however, because even from a distance it was obvious that their necks were far too long. Two things struck him forcibly. All the horses were black and there were no women.

Divareli's seat, it turned out, was near the top of the long table. Between him and Gally – who was ensconced at the head of the table – was Aphra. A more mature blonde lady with an impressive *décolletage* sidled up beside him, and Aphra introduced her as Josephine Donnelly, wife of the bleary-eyed banker.

With a throaty chuckle she inquired sweetly, 'Do tell me, Aphra dearest, just where did you dig up this treasure?'

There was a hint of frost in Aphra's reply which coincided with Gally inviting his guests to be seated. 'Won him at the races, actually. I see you came in first.'

This time Josephine laughed aloud at Divareli's puzzlement. 'Aphra is just being bitchy, as usual. I'm supposed to be the original *Flannery's Fancy*.'

Emboldened by the enormous gin and tonic, Divareli asked innocently: 'And are you?'

Over her bare shoulder she smiled back at him sweetly as he drew her chair out from the table for her. 'That, my friend, is for me to know and for you to find out!'

Divareli hid his embarrassment by manoeuvring Aphra's chair in a like manner. Opposite Gally at the far end of the table, where the hostess might ordinarily have been expected to sit, was Daft Aunt Daphne. In splendid isolation she roared with the best of them, the fact that no one paid the slightest attention not deterring her in the least.

What had once been a fine red carpet, now with moth-eaten tassels at the edges, covered the floor to within a few feet of the walls. Three chandeliers, powered by dim bulbs, were suspended from the massive beams. They were so high up that their effect was ornamental rather than illuminating. A roaring fire blazed in the huge iron grate, where enormous round logs spat out sparks with startling venom on to the marble surround. The flames caused weird shapes to dance around the heavy velvet curtains at Divareli's back. Like the marble pillars, the drapes stretched from heavy wooden pelmets attached to the overhead beams down to the floor. He half-expected them to part at any moment to reveal the set of some long-forgotten Victorian melodrama. Or a Mozart string quartet – though it would have been hard pressed to make itself heard above the racket made by the diners.

The overall effect of the décor was that of decayed opulence. As he settled in his seat, his gaze wandered across the table to the venerable Daphne. She was still bellowing contentedly over Don-

91

nelly's bowed head at no one in particular. In a slightly tipsy flight of fancy, he tried to picture the Gallericks *en famille* communicating with each other across the vast expanse of polished mahogany. Did they use a bullhorn, or merely a telephone? Or perhaps Dracula the butler scuttled to and fro like a frantic Western Union messenger. It was then that it dawned on him that people accustomed to addressing each other from either end of a hunting field would find such a relatively short distance a mere trifle. Perhaps it also explained why his fellow guests brayed at each other so loudly. In any case, Deaf Daphne was now fully occupied in bawling at Tom Donnelly the information that no bank manager worthy of the name could afford not to ride to hounds regularly.

'How else,' she roared, 'can you expect to keep in touch with the victims of your bloody usury?'

If Donnelly had any views on the subject, he was by now incapable of expressing them. Instead he tried vainly to engage Divareli's sympathy by sighing deeply and raising his eyes heavenward in exasperation as the tirade directed against him by Daphne continued unabated.

'Never deal with Irish banks myself. My late husband, God rest his soul, always said they were run by fat little men with red necks and suits two sizes too small for them!'

Divareli turned his attention to his host. Gally was sampling the soup while Aphra and Josephine were deep in conversation behind his back. A large silver tureen had been wheeled to his side. The butler ladled a measure into Gally's soup-plate and the merits of this were now being discussed between servant and master.

'Harmon, there's no bloody salt in this whatsoever. Tastes like cold tea, dammit. Take it back to the kitchens like a good chap and tell Cook to turf in a pound or so of good old sodium chloride. That should make it almost fit for human consumption, eh what?'

'Whatever your Lordship pleases. The Lady Aphra did say to Cook some time ago to go easy on the salt. Something to do with your blood pressure, I believe, Milord!'

Gally looked furtively at his daughter to make sure she could not hear what he was going to say next. 'Absolute bloody nonsense, Harmon. Now push off like a good chap and get that done before our guests faint from the hunger.' Seeing Divareli watching him, Gally evidently felt that an explanation was in order.

'Aphra has a vested interest in keeping me alive. She gets over-protective at times . . .' he interjected a braying laugh at this juncture to forestall any protest from his daughter who had now stopped chatting to Josephine so that she could tune in to what he was saying ' . . . fact is, anyone with even one eye in their head could see that my blood pressure has nothing whatsoever to do with salt but rather too much of this sort of thing.' He broke off to tap his wine glass meaningfully and then eye his daughter warily before risking, 'Isn't that true, Aphra my dear?'

She reacted heatedly. Divareli was unsure whether her peevishness was entirely genuine or more of a token protest. Whatever its cause, he found it strangely attractive. Inwardly he speculated whether that fiery temperament might not make her a tempestuous lover. Further speculation along these lines was cut short by her rebuking her father with, 'Oh Gally, you are such a pain in the arse when you go on with that kind of bloody nonsense.'

'Aphra, do try not to be quite so vulgar in front of Mr . . . oh good, here's the soup at long last. Lash it round the guests, Harmon, otherwise the venison will be burnt to a bloody cinder.'

As might have been expected, when Aphra tasted the soup she exploded with fury. 'Gally, for crying out loud, Cook has poisoned the soup with focking salt . . . You really will have to do something with the silly bitch. I warned her to cut out salt completely and now the focking soup tastes like the Dead Sea. I mean one might as well be talking to the focking wall!'

Instead of making even the slightest effort to explain, Gally pursed his lips and shrugged his shoulders in a gesture of utter hopelessness as he replied. 'I know, my dear, but reliable help is so hard to find nowadays.'

The roar of conversation subsided, only to be replaced by the distinctive slurp of soup being consumed. The major soloist in this movement of the culinary symphony was Daphne. She sounded like a whale trying to escape from a shallow bay. Aphra explained the difficulty as best she could to Divareli now that the servant problem had been shelved for the nonce. Though he did his best to hang on her every word, his concentration was shattered by the awesome sight of her heaving breasts. They rose and fell distractingly as she raised her hands in a gesture of exasperation while explaining, 'Old Daff holds the purse-strings. Gally owns the property but the old bat's the only one of us with any money. When the Hawk laid down the rules of inheritance, he insisted that only a male heir could succeed him. Absolutely focking ridiculous, of course, but true nevertheless. Makes me feel bloody insecure, I can tell you. Who knows what would happen to the place should Gally suddenly cash in his chips. Which is why I nag the old darling about his blood pressure. It also explains why I'm up to my neck in the family archives trying to find out who my surviving relatives might be. Whenever old Daff gets upset, she threatens to leave all her money to the cats' home – or the Association for Distressed Gentlefolk. Bloody ridiculous, isn't it?'

They were still contemplating the injustice of it all when Josephine gave Divareli a sharp dig in the ribs. 'I'm sorry about Tom. He doesn't mean to be rude – it's just that he really is a silly sod when he's drunk.'

Aphra glared at Josephine, not welcoming her intrusion into what was developing into a cosy *tête à tête*. If Josephine were aware of this, she blithely ignored it. By now the soup was being cleared away and Harmon had refilled their glasses, making the change from sherry to a rich Bulgarian claret almost imperceptibly.

Gally was now bellowing across his bows to Josephine. The subject of their conversation, from the snatches that assailed Divareli's ears, appeared to be fox-hunting. Obscure references to 'leaping Doherty's Drain' and 'going to ground in Buckley's Bog' flew between them like errant swallows. Much as he wanted to join in the conversation with a view to his overall objective of getting in some hunting with the Gallerick pack, Aphra's aristocratic sensuality and the seductive huskiness of her voice ensnared him once again.

As for herself, she looked on Divareli as a mixture of many things. A lover, most definitely, if only they could ever order their affairs to make this happen. A possible saviour of the family fortune? Well, that too was a possibility. But care would have to be taken not to make him feel pursued. She was sure that what the tabloids had called 'New York's most eligible bachelor' had sensitive antennae where avaricious *femmes fatales* were concerned. Right now she would be quite content to get into bed with him at the earliest possible opportunity. Fate could look after the rest.

The buzz of conversation faded into the background. It was as though a magnetic field had been set up between them. Other sounds and people intruded into it at their peril, to be hurtled backwards by some invisible force. Divareli sensed that Tom Donnelly was addressing him from across the table, doubtless seeking refuge from the attentions of the deaf Dowager or perhaps in a craven attempt to make amends for his earlier gaffe. Gally was still braying at Josephine and Daphne continued to roar at no one in particular. Harmon had disappeared once more, no doubt preparing the venison for the next course.

Meanwhile, Aphra was telling him of a possible American connection that she had unearthed in her researches, but he was so besotted with her that it was next to impossible to concentrate on what she was murmuring in that deliciously husky voice. Gally's shouting across him did not make it any easier to grasp what she was saying. Suddenly from the kitchens there came a loud bang, not unlike a shot from a gun. Then several things happened at once. First the lights went out, leaving just the candles to faintly illuminate the proceedings. Seconds later Gally exploded, 'Jesus Christ, Harmon the idiot has blown the bloody main fuse!' Last but not least, Divareli felt a slender hand enter his trouser pocket, where it wriggled around for a moment like an inquisitive ferret before homing in on its prey. He was long past caring by the time it dawned on his befuddled brain that the intruder had launched its unexpected assault from the right – where Josephine Donnelly was sitting. Then the lights came on again but the hand remained where it was.

Divareli had heard about 'leaving the men to their port' but hadn't actually witnessed it until now. Without any fuss, the ladies withdrew to the drawing room as Harmon arrived with the port. He closed the doors firmly behind them, checked that the men were amply provided with glasses and cigars and then drifted out silently through the smaller kitchen door.

Gally heaved a sigh of relief and opened the bowling. 'Well chaps, why don't we all move up to this end of the table, now that we don't have to scream at old Daff any more.'

After some shuffling about, the Doc finished up sitting beside Divareli and across the table were Tom Donnelly, Father Jerry and Pat Mullarkey, who was drinking mineral water. The Doc asked Gally when the next hunt meet was scheduled.

'Lawn Meet here, day after tomorrow.' Then he turned to Divareli and asked, 'Do you hunt at all?'

Divareli seized the opportunity with both hands. 'Nothing I'd like more, but I gather that one has to be invited first.'

The question hung in the air for a fateful moment before Gally responded gallantly, 'No problem there, old chap. Be my guest!'

Divareli took a long draught of port. He didn't particularly like the stuff, as it reminded him of old Doc Hooper's cough mixture, but now that he had scored a bull's-eye, the taste didn't seem quite so bad.

'That's great. Thanks, I'd love to. All I need now is a horse.'

'No problem there either, old chap. We will rent you a horse for the day. I'll tell them myself to give you a sound one. Half the hired nags are barely fit for the knacker's yard.'

This was not the time to ask Gally for an armchair animal rather than a lively half-bred hunter. Anything that might jeopardise his chance of hunting with a blueblood with his very own pack of hounds must be avoided. After all, Divareli reminded himself, that was the original purpose of his being here in Brulagh. Swallowing his misgivings, he answered with as much nonchalance as he could muster, 'That's OK, then. I have everything else I need with me.'

'Might even make you Joint Master, if you wish. For a consideration, of course!'

Divareli remained noncommittal in the face of this unexpected offer and the conversation soon became more general. Mullarkey was being cross-examined by Gally about the Wildlife Protection Act he had promised to introduce. His adroitness in avoiding a straight answer was impressive. He explained with great patience that bringing in new legislation to any Parliament was a long and tedious process. In the case of the Dail, this process became even more arduous. Mullarkey explained that the number of societies devoted to the protection of the various species under threat was far greater than one might have thought. By way of explanation, he went on, 'You need look no further than Brulagh. Daphne is a perfect example. She paints flowers and frogs as a hobby. You can bet on it that if she believed for one moment that your foxhounds would harm her orchids or frogs she would hit you with a High Court injunction in the twinkling of an eye.'

The Doc chimed in, 'Same with Joe Gallagher, though I suspect that Joe is more concerned about keeping other fishing boats away from the pier than protecting his precious swans.'

Father Jerry busied himself with packing tobacco into the bowl of his pipe. After a few noisy sucks to make sure it was drawing freely, he applied a lighted match to it with all the reverence of the Pope lighting the Paschal candle in St Peter's Basilica. Gally snipped a neat wedge off the end of his cigar with a silver cutter. He then passed the box to Divareli.

'Bet you can't get those in America.'

This was true. *Romeo y Giuliettas* could be bought only on the black market since the embargo on Cuban goods. Europe did not subscribe to such isolationist doctrines. Divareli was tempted for a moment to light one, then he remembered the agonising cold turkey he had endured while he was trying to break the habit so he passed the box to the Doc who chose one with care. Rolling the leafy cylinder between finger and thumb, he passed it slowly beneath his nose, sniffing appreciatively as he did so. Tom Donnelly had barely uttered one word so far, contenting himself with drinking impressive amounts of wine and requesting second and third helpings of venison. He selected two cigars before shoving the box across the table to Pat Mullarkey. One the creature snipped and lit. The other he placed with some care, oblivious to the stares of his fellow guests, in his top pocket.

This created a conversational vacuum for a minute or so. When it became apparent that the bank manager had nothing to add to the sum of human knowledge, Gally began quizzing Divareli about his hunting prowess. Once he had satisfied himself that the American was unlikely to kill himself or anyone else while riding, he reverted to his own hunting reminiscences.

'Most amazing thing happened a few years back. One of the bitches threw a dead litter. Fine specimens they were too, beautiful markings and sired by the best dog in the whole damn pack. Very sad the whole thing. So what was I to do?'

Though the question was obviously rhetorical, there was an air of expectation as the table awaited the *dénouement*.

'There I was stuck with a bitch bursting with milk and no pups to drink it. The poor old girl would have died on me if it weren't for Johnny Slattery . . .'

'The bootlegger?' Divareli thought it only polite to help his host with what looked to be a fairly complicated monologue. In doing so, however, he felt that this was neither the time nor the place to refer to Johnny's part in fixing the race. Especially when the odds were better than even that the *raconteur* himself had had a hand in the skulduggery.

'. . . One and the same. As luck would have it, Johnny keeps a few pigs. One of his sows had just died giving birth to six of the finest bonives you ever laid eyes on. To make a long story short, Johnny agreed to put the six piglets under the bitch.'

There was a pause here while Harmon refilled their glasses from the huge ship's decanter that had become marooned out of reach in the middle of the table before Gally continued what threatened to be a saga even longer than feared.

'Anyway, where was I, dammit? Oh yes, I remember. It must have been about three months later that the hunt passed close by Johnny's place up in the mountain. The minute the piglets heard the peal of the huntsman's horn, they leapt up from the bitch, jumped the farmyard wall together and were last seen going hell for leather after the hounds. Johnny assures me that he hasn't laid an eye on one of them ever since! In fact the blighter wanted me to compensate him for the loss of the piglets, if you don't mind.'

Amid the general hilarity, Pat Mullarkey rose to his feet. Apologising for having to leave early, he added, 'Before I go, Luke, I want to offer you my office in Brulagh. It used to belong to the Department of Agriculture when I worked for them before I went into politics. I bought the office from them when they closed the place, and only use it now and again as somewhere to meet my constituents. If it's of any use for your project, Mary will give you the key tomorrow. It has a telephone in it, too.'

Divareli was moved by such generosity. 'That's very good of you, Pat. One of the things that worried me was where I would use for a base. If the place checks out, I'd like to lease it from you.'

'Ah, don't worry about that for the moment. If it suits you, that's the main thing. Now I must rush. Does anyone want a lift as far as the village? I have to drop off Mary there and pack a few things before going on to Dublin.'

'Yes, Pat . . .' Father Jerry had got to his feet. He drained his glass with one hand and emptied the ash from his pipe into an ashtray with the other. 'If you will excuse me, I have an early mass to say tomorrow.'

Gally nodded and rose with some difficulty from his chair to shake hands with the two who were leaving. Divareli did likewise but Donnelly and the Doc remained seated. Donnelly threw anxious glances in Divareli's direction every so often but so far had found no pretext on which he might have interrupted Gally's storytelling. As the priest and politician disappeared through the dining-room door, Gally turned his back on the by-now almost incoherent bank manager and gave Divareli his undivided attention.

'Now tell me all about your plans for Brulagh, omitting no detail, however trivial. I only caught bits and pieces of what you were saying to Pat Mullarkey before dinner. A bright boy, that Mullarkey, by the way. Really going places fast. Could well be running this godforsaken country before long – and not before his time, I can tell you! The present leader is living in Cloud Cuckoo Land. Still, that happens to the best of us, myself included I expect.'

'How do you mean?' Divareli was genuinely curious. He had already decided that Gally was for the birds but it came as a surprise to have this view confirmed by the man himself.

Gally leaned over towards him in a confidential manner and explained. 'Well, take the bally house we're in at the moment. Absolutely going to rack and ruin. I had thought of renting it out but never quite got round to it. Not yet, anyway.'

He eyed Divareli hopefully but seeing no sign that he would rise to the bait, continued in a doleful voice, 'All the fault of my ancestors, of course. Especially that cove in the picture up there beside the mirror, the one with the beard and the horse behind him. He lost so much at the tables that he had to sell the lead off the blasted roof to pay his gambling debts. Loved hunting though, so he can't have been all bad. Died of rabies or something like that – silly ass got bitten by his pet fox. Served the old sod right. Insisted that his favourite hunter, the one in the picture, be buried with him. Mad as a hatter, of course!'

'He sounds a fascinating character. Tell me some more about your ancestors.' It was as good a way as any of avoiding disclosing his plans to the Eleventh Earl of Gallerick with regard to the B Project – as he had now labelled it.

'Of course. Come over to the wall and I'll give you the five-cent tour.' They walked over to the first oil-painting in the long procession that stretched around the vast dining room. It depicted a fierce-looking soldier with a pudding-bowl hairdo, wearing a shining breastplate and holding a silver helmet in the crook of his arm. The other hand was outstretched and covered by a heavy falconry glove. Perched on it was a bird of some sort. A wide leather bandolier with a heavy buckle hung over one shoulder while the end of the breast-plate was swathed in what looked like a red silk cummerbund. Blue velvet pantaloons stretched to the knee from where white form-fitting stockings ended in heavy black shoes, again with silver buckles.

'That's the chap who started it all back in the seventeenth century. "The Hawk" Gallerick.'

'Why "The Hawk"?'

'Oh, he came over with Cromwell. One of his foot-soldiers, I expect – though old Daff would have you believe he was a General. Aphra could probably tell you more about him if you're interested. The Hawk ingratiated himself with the boss in some way or other, probably by raping and pillaging better than his brethren. For some reason Cromwell told him that he could have as much of the land round here as his pet hawk could fly over from dawn till dusk. The bird flew so far that the locals claimed he had made a pact with the Devil. The upshot of it all was that he got the land and a castle thrown in for good measure. When that was burned down, another ancestor built The Hall . . .'

Gally skipped a few portraits until he stood before a particularly splendid one and cocked his thumb at the painting of a youngish man, hand resting negligently on a slender rapier with a brass guard protecting its handle. He wore a wide-brimmed black hat from which sprouted a superb ostrich feather. The stylised background included sandy wastes studded with mosques and temples and peopled with what looked to be evil-looking *thugees* wielding curved scimitars in a hostile fashion.

'This bloke, as a matter of fact. They called him "Nabob" Galle-rick because he made pots of money in India. Turned up out of the blue one day and claimed the estate as his. Spent a fortune on the house. Put up the porch, the flight of steps and the fanlight over the door. Shipped over Portland stone from England for the arches and hired Italian sculptors to carve the chimneypieces out of local marble – except for the one in the drawing room which he brought over from Italy. Put in the staircase, too. His wife was a bit eccentric and used to slide down it on a tray to amuse her dinner guests.'

Gally refilled their glasses as he warmed to his tale. 'Nabob eventually took to wandering around the house naked. The vicar persuaded him to wear a cowbell round his neck to warn the maidservants of his approach. Eventually he rode his horse into the lake in the mistaken belief that he had magical powers to keep him afloat.'

'And did he?'

'No, I'm afraid not. Drowned, as you might expect. But the legend persists. He's supposed to reappear every seven years: a ghostly figure wearing a plumed hat gallops his horse across the water, rapier held aloft in triumph until he reaches the middle of the lake. Then the poor bugger sinks gently below the surface for another seven years. Can't say I've seen him myself. Others claim to have done so, Harmon and old Daff among them.'

The rest of the ancestors appeared normal by comparison, being content to add bits and pieces to the Hall until the lead-stripper undid much of their work and necessitated the renewal of the roof. This task was evidently well beyond Gally's slender means and he made no secret of the fact. When they had resumed their seats and topped up their glasses, Gally made his pitch. By now they were both quite drunk and the other three appeared to be in a similar condition.

'Reason I was asking about your plans for Brulagh was that I wondered if the Hall would fit into them anywhere along the line. Not that I would dream of selling it or anything of that nature. I did think that some of your fellow countrymen might like to stay overnight in stately piles like this one, sleep in a fourposter bed and break bread with the local Earl or whatever. I often thought of renting the place out to the kind of people who would appreciate living like a Lord. Aristocratic splendour, complete with butler, acres of woods, rolling pasture and ornamental gardens, that sort of thing. All at a price, of course!'

This last bit was added hastily lest Divareli might get the impression that such services would be rendered free, *gratis* or for nothing – as in the case of Pat Mullarkey's office. Divareli searched around frantically for some way to disabuse his host of the notion that he could be part of Project B. None came to mind so he dissembled as best he could.

'That's very interesting. It may well be of some interest to the promoters but, as you know, the project is still in its infancy. Much

101

more a gleam in the eye than a firm plan at this stage. I had thought
of a golf-course and marina, but a side-trip to a stately home might
well be included. I don't honestly know yet but I'll certainly consider the idea.'

Gally was beside himself with excitement. 'What about hunting,
old boy? Surely the chappies you have in mind would like nothing
better than to do a spot of fox-hunting. Best hunting in the world
round here, y'know. Now please don't get offended when I tell you
that what passes for fox-hunting in America is an absolute joke. As
for Mother England, the lunatics are taking over the asylum. Every-
where there's a meet, a crowd of long-haired, drug-crazed Animal
Rights protesters show up. They lay false trails for the hounds and
throw ball-bearings on the road so the horses will slip on them and
throw their riders. Bloody criminals, that's what they are. And what
do the police do? Sweet damn all. Sweet Fanny Adams. Claim the
crazies have as much right to be there as the hunt. Did you ever
hear such bloody rampant socialism in all your born days?'

Indignation had turned Gally's face a dangerous shade of purple.
In the circumstances, Divareli decided it was just as well that Harmon, who had glided in once more without anyone noticing his
presence, announced in tones more suitable to a funeral: 'Gentlemen,
the ladies await you in the withdrawing room.'

The walls of the drawing room were of carved wainscotting. The
panels near the big white fireplace were perfect but those on the far
side of the room, by the french window, were cracked and stained.
The window stretched from ceiling to floor and was set in the grace-
ful bow that formed the gable wall of Gallerick Hall. Through its
half-closed curtains Divareli could just make out what had once been
an ornate garden, now bathed in soft moonlight. He could see a long
parapet of grey Portland stone, its balustrade supported by the tortu-
ous carved phallic spaceships so beloved of the Gallericks. Little else
was visible except for the giant shapes of giant oaks looming up
menacingly out of the darkness. Soon the draught that whistled
through the warped frame of the window drove him back towards
the blazing fire. Underfoot, some of the parquet tiles that made up
the floor had worked loose and rattled loudly as he stepped on them.

The ladies were seated in a tight group in front of the fire, silhouetted against the dancing flames. It was as though a tableau of
an Edwardian sewing circle had suddenly sprung to life before his

102

eyes. Instead of needlepoint and thread, however, they held heavy cutglass goblets filled with drinks of assorted colours. They nodded perfunctorily to the men as they continued their conversation.

After a while, Aphra waved to him to sit on the couch between her and Josephine. They were directly in front of the white marble chimneypiece. A medallion above the grate had a demonic face leering evilly from behind ornate clusters of grapes. It took Divareli a moment to realise that he was face to face with Bacchus, God of Wine – an especially apt deity to grace Gallerick Hall.

Part of his mind toyed with the possibility that he had fallen in among a lost tribe of suicidal drinkers, or could it just be possible that the rest of the inhabitants of this incredible island also drank to the same extent? As he was about to join the ladies on the couch, Divareli was intercepted by Gally, who led him to a long, elaborately-carved sideboard laden with bottles.

'A spot of brandy, perhaps?'

Divareli nodded and watched as his host half-filled a balloon glass from a bottle whose label showed nothing but two unicorns entwined, the crest of the Gallericks. The brandy was foul – a blessing in disguise. It allowed him to nurse it for the rest of the night and thereby retain his last few remaining wits. No such constraints encumbered his host. Gally drained his glass in one practised movement and refilled it quickly before joining the others. In their absence, some changes had occurred in the seating arrangements. The Doc had insinuated himself between the two women on the couch, and it was apparent that this group were not enlisting new recruits just at the moment. As Gally seemed to have vanished on some errand or other, this left him at the mercy of Deaf Daphne who promptly launched into a well-rehearsed tirade.

She spoke without pause for ten minutes. As far as he could see, she appeared to breathe through her ears. Her chosen topic was the flora and fauna of the locality, especially those she believed to be endangered by the twentieth century. From what Divareli had seen of Brulagh thus far, her fears were premature by at least two centuries. This opinion, however, he declined to share with the Lady Dowager. Instead he commended his soul to God and asked her which species she felt were most endangered by the depradations of modern man. She answered him at even greater length than before. It appeared to involve a Bee Orchid and a toad which now only survived in some sand-dunes. She blamed the threat to their survival on greedy farmers, idle, corrupt politicians and, it seemed, just about everyone else outside this room.

More to dislodge the old broad off her hobbyhorse than from genuine curiosity he inquired, 'What about Mick Flannery?'

She emitted a noise that might well have been 'Pssshaw'. The disgust in her wrinkled face was obvious. She waved a bejewelled claw at Divareli as though to lend even further emphasis to what she was about to say. 'The absolute dregs. Living proof – if that were necessary – that politics is the last resort of a scoundrel. I can't even think of that man without feeling unwell. An unmitigated rascal with a hide thick as a rhinocerous. Still, I'd better keep my voice down, hadn't I?'

'Why?'

Why indeed. Up to now she had been bellowing like a wounded water buffalo. There seemed no good reason why she should suddenly alter the volume at the mention of an absent Mick Flannery. From what Gally had revealed about the Gallerick ancestors, Mick Flannery was an angel complete with wings and halo compared to this lot. Divareli muttered something unintelligible about 'having to rush' and made a bee-line, for the Doc, who flashed him a welcoming smile.

'I see you made a run for it. First his Lordship going on about his ancestors – then trying to put the bite on you for Marshall Aid, followed by half an hour on the endangered *flora* and *fauna* of Brulagh. You certainly have been through the mill.'

At this juncture, Donnelly lurched over to them, mumbling something that might have been intended as an apology. 'Hope you didn't get me wrong back there . . .'

The rest of the sentence tailed off into nothing. Under more normal circumstances, Divareli might have smoothed the banker's path with a noncommittal shrug or even an, 'Aw, don't worry about it,' but on this occasion he preferred to let him suffer a little more. He remembered Mick Flannery telling him that Donnelly's bank had got into trouble by buying up an American Savings and Loan Bank outfit out west. Then fresh from that disaster, it had lost another bundle on a lame duck insurance company. Flannery had claimed that if his government hadn't bailed the idiots out, they would have gone belly-up. Now their Mickey Mouse manager in

Brulagh had the neck to tell a Wall Street veteran that his investment strategy was for the birds. No, Divareli decided, this bag of sleaze should be hung out to dry for a mite longer.

'Yeah, I guess I probably did at that . . .' Divareli adopted a casual drawl as he deftly inserted the knife between Donnelly's ribs. 'Speaking of bum investments, I hear that your people bought a Californian S & L last year.'

Donnelly moved uncomfortably from one foot to the other before admitting that this was so. 'Yes, I believe they did. Didn't work out as well as they had hoped.'

Divareli noted the change from 'we' to 'they'. It was the same all over the goddamn world. Success had many fathers but failure was always a lonely orphan. 'And am I right in thinking that your bank dropped a packet on an insurance company a few years back?'

'Yes, I believe I recall something of that nature.'

'And that you had to get your own goddamn Government to bail you out?' He was shaking his head in mock disbelief, but before Donnelly could reply, he applied the *coup de grâce*. 'By pretending that the whole house of cards would come tumbling down if they didn't underwrite your losses. The miracle is that the politicians swallowed that one. Then, as a final kick in the balls, your board voted its Chairman a hefty salary increase. Am I right?'

This time the wretched man confined himself to nodding.

'Jesus, Tom, if that happened back where I come from, the guy would have finished up at one end or the other of the goddamn street!'

Donnelly finally got the words out. 'I don't understand, Divareli.'

'On Wall Street, Tom, there's a cemetery at one end and a river at the other. Your Chairman would have finished up in one or the other for trying to pull a scam like that on the taxpayer.'

Now that the playing pitch had been levelled – if not actually tilted in his direction, Divareli reluctantly decided to end the game. He would still have to work with this creep in the coming weeks and months. It would be counter-productive to humiliate the guy so much that he would hate Divareli's guts for ever more. 'Don't worry, I was only kidding. I only wish I could pull off something like that and stay outa jail at the same time. Now, that draft I mentioned should be with you in a day or two. I'll be in to see you by then. Now, let me get you a drink. The brandy is particularly fine . . .'

13

'So what do you think?'

Divareli tried not to sound over-anxious. The reply came in a tough New York rasp, far sharper than the squawk of the gulls wheeling overhead.

'Hard to say right off, Luke, but it's sure got some great things going for it. Scenery, layout, unpolluted air, no crowds an' all that. Trouble is that it's halfways up the asshole of nowhere. The airport's fine but the fucking road is a camel track. Looks as if you're right about having to ferry the punters in by chopper. Trouble about choppers is that not only do they fall out of the fucking sky every now and again but in a joint like this, you're goin' to need at least two of 'em 'cos a back-up is vital. That's stickin' two million plus to the capital cost, unless you lease 'em, that is. The good news might be that it's a hook for the punters, the chopper trip, I mean. You might also hire 'em out for sea rescue or scenic trips or God knows what else.'

Divareli was miffed and his voice betrayed this. 'Abe, you just said "*you* might also hire 'em out". Does that mean you're not in on the deal?'

This time the rasp descended into a low growl. 'It means no such thing. I just haven't made my mind up yet. If I do come in on it, I'll want ten points.'

The man had lost his senses. Ten per cent of the action? It was one hell of a consultancy fee. Divareli reacted in knee-jerk fashion by dismissing it out of hand. 'Forget it. If you're being serious, let's just forget the whole thing here and now. Ten points was never heard-of in any deal like this, not even in the middle of the fucking Sahara for Chrissakes! There's five points on the table but not for long.'

Almost before Divareli had finished, Abe cut in swiftly, 'Eight and I'm yours.'

Divareli injected an air of finality into his words. 'Six points – and that's it.'

The small fat man stuck out a chubby hand and grinned from ear to ear.

'Because I like you and the set-up I'll settle for seven.'

Divareli paused only for a second. 'OK, glad to have you aboard. Now, what do you *really* see?'

What Abe saw was money, plenty of it. For twenty million dollars he could build a luxury resort that would attract high rollers. Apart from the marina and golf-course, and luxury hotel, of course, there'd also be swim pools, gymnasia, squash, indoor tennis, a bowling alley . . . cash cows such as waterside bars and restaurants, a ship's-chandler as well as scuba-diving, wind-surfing and jet skiing.

Divareli nodded thoughtfully and then asked, 'What about the hotel?'

'We can go one of two ways. Get a big chain to come in with us as an anchor, or build the fucking thing ourselves. If what you say is correct about the money being out there waiting for us, then the smart move would be to do it ourselves.'

Divareli agreed. 'That's how I see it too. One thing, though. I won't be around tomorrow.'

Abe stroked his chin thoughtfully as he gazed out over the dunes from the vantage point of the ruined tower. 'No problem. I've seen enough here for now. I'd still rather wait for the spring to start the earth-moving, but if those grants might disappear after Christmas then I guess we can put up with a little mud on our boots. You're goin' to have to get building permits and all the rest of the paper-work cleared real quick, my old buddy. The last thing we want is a lotta machinery and men hanging around in a dump like this drain-ing our cash while we're waiting for some goddam piece of paper to come through before we can lift a shovel. I'll fly to Glasgow tonight and meet with McAllister. He's the course architect. We'll draft out something and he'll get over here quick as he can to draw up a proper working blueprint. I'll bring in Jeff Myers from New York to design the hotel and all that goes with it. What are we usin' for money right now?'

'That's set up already. Just let me know how much you want and when you want it.'

Abe seemed pleased at this and said mildly, 'Nuttin' for now. Just get your bank to open an account in my name. I presume we've got a working account here somewhere?'

'Yeah, the local bank.'

'Oh Jeezus!' For the first time that afternoon Abe looked alarmed. 'Do they know anythin' about anythin'?'

On projects like this it was usual to divert some funds to private accounts and that required the cooperation of the banker. Italbank usually set up a temporary branch in the area specifically for that purpose. Where that proved impractical, they used an understanding bank based in Djakarta. After last night, it was hoped that Tom Donnelly would be just as cooperative.

Divareli tried to reassure Abe. 'Not really, but I'm pretty confident that the local guy will do as he's told.'

Abe was still unhappy. 'I sure hope you're right. Anyway, that's your baby. If we leave now, I can get something to eat at the airport before the flight to Glasgow.'

It was Divareli's turn to look surprised. 'Just tell me one thing. How did you know you would be flying to Glasgow?'

'Well, when you mentioned a golf-course over the phone I knew we were gonna need a designer – and McAllister is one of the best this side of the water. He's meeting me off the flight in Glasgow, as a matter of fact.'

Divareli was speechless. Inwardly he cursed himself. He could have had the bastard wrapped up and delivered for five points. Jesus, he must be losing his touch. Well, he would make sure he wrung his money's worth out of Abe. They had said all that needed to be said at this stage. The conversation on the drive to the airport might be strained if he couldn't get the sour taste of having been tricked out of his mouth.

Divareli had that rarest of gifts – the ability to recognise his own frailties. Just in case he let his annoyance at being fooled show through his wafer-thin veneer of politeness and wreck the entire project, he elected to invite Aphra along for the drive. She was fixing up Pat Mullarkey's office for him. He had put her on the payroll just before he left Gallerick Hall in the small hours of the morning. She could write up her ancestral researches just as easily in the office as Gallerick Hall, and she would get paid as well. It violated his code of not messing with the help but he desperately wanted to see more of her. At the time he had befuddled dreams of making love to her spreadeagled across a desk full of papers or while she was answering the phone. These had become less realistic in the cold, sober light of dawn but he still wished to create as many opportunities as he could of consummating what he now believed to be a mutual passion.

The help had indeed been busying herself around the office. Pat's wife had given her the key and told her if she wanted anything to phone her. The view from both windows was surreal. The one beside the door looked across the main street of Brulagh and framed the dark brooding mountain that dominated the tiny village. Somewhere high up on its lofty fastness Aphra hoped that an old crone was racking her brains to recall a name. Just above the mountain a giant, fluffy cloud of greyish-gold exploded skywards to form a spectacular back-drop. Directly opposite, the other window took in the tiny harbour and a vast expanse of blue sea. Seagulls swooped low above the rolling Atlantic swell in search of their next morsel. A gannet dropped like a stone into the sea, emerging seconds later with a small fish wriggling in its beak.

The magic was shattered by a car-hooter blaring outside the door. It was the Porsche. Sitting beside Luke was a small, bald man with twinkling eyes. Luke introduced her quickly and explained that Abe had a flight to catch. He invited her to come with them on the drive to the airport. She would have declined were it not for the pleading look in his eyes.

'Love to, just so long as you can drop me off at Johnny Slattery's place on the way back.'

'That's no problem. At least, not as long as you know the way.'

Her reply took him aback somewhat as he got out to let her clamber into the tiny back seat of the Porsche: 'Of course I do, didn't you know I'm a regular caller at Johnny's place?' Her impish grin deflected any further questions. Anyway Divareli did not especially want Abe to know just how closely he was working with his assistant.

With Abe safely winging his way to Glasgow, the pair meandered slowly back towards Brulagh, so slowly that several drivers gave them a hearty salute as they sped past. It was not every day that a Porsche was seen around here, much less overtaken on the open road. Unconcerned by the antics of other drivers they were content to drink in the scenery and make desultory, disjointed conversation in the manner of lovers the world over. A mile or so before they came to Brulagh, Aphra directed him to take a sharp right turn. For a moment he thought she might be playing a practical joke. What passed for a road was scarcely wider than the car with overgrown brambles lining the ditches on either side. A strip of grass and weeds graced its crown and scraped the underside of the car whenever one of the wheels descended into the cavernous potholes that marked their progress towards the lair of Johnny Slattery.

As if by common consent they did not speak about themselves but rather about the places and people that surrounded them. The events of the previous night were picked over carefully. Aphra laughed gleefully at his description of Donnelly's comeuppance. She mentioned that Josephine Donnelly also called on Johnny's aunt but for a different purpose. The old woman was reputed to have concocted an elixir – a herbal cocktail that delayed the onset of parchment skin and crows' feet around the eyes as well as being an invigorating tonic. So much so that she had confided to Aphra that she was thinking of slipping some into her husband's nightcap. Whether the magic bottle contained any of Johnny's lethal poteen was open to question. If it did, apparently its taste was well masked by the addition of various herbs.

Aphra revealed that the purpose of her visit to Johnny's aunt was to research further the story of a certain Jessie Kelly, a chambermaid who had become pregnant by a Gallerick and was then packed off to America some time in the previous century.

On her last visit, the old woman could not remember the name of the American who had married Jessie all those years ago. It was in the hope that Johnny's aunt might have refreshed her memory in the meantime that Aphra was now directing Divareli through the narrow entrance gate that led into an untidy farmyard.

Rusting machinery, most of it looking as if it had been horsedrawn, lay abandoned in various corners of the yard. A fine selection of nettles and tall weeds with yellow flowers poked their way through the iron spokes of the wheels. Hens ran distractedly to and fro, clucking frantically at the intrusion on their privacy. In stark contrast, a family of ducks waddled importantly towards an evil-smelling pond covered with dark green *algae*, totally oblivious to their arrival. A scrawny-looking sheepdog barked nervously. He gave the impression that he did so more out of a sense of duty than any real aggression.

Nevertheless Divareli opted to remain in the car while Aphra continued her researches inside the whitewashed cottage with the sagging thatched roof. He noticed that as she opened the door, she was met by a blast of smoke coming from within.

110

When Aphra returned after about ten minutes, with streaming eyes and a voice hoarse from the smoke, she was jubilant. The old woman was quite positive that Jessie Kelly had ended her days in America married to someone called Leary, which would have been nothing out of the ordinary, since the surname was quite common, were it not for the fact that she insisted that this Leary had been a foreigner of some sort . . . Divareli might have paid more attention to her story, were he not so preoccupied with wondering how he was going to remain all in one piece while hunting with the Gallerick pack the next day.

The day of the Lawn Meet dawned with a fiery sun escaping from behind the mountains. Yesterday they had been a sombre purple as though in deep mourning but now they were a cheerful pastel of duck-egg blue. A few blobs of grey cloud, tinged with gold, sought vainly to blot out the sunrise. Their failure was marked by angry slashes of orange as the blazing ball of light climbed slowly upwards, changing to a blinding yellow as it did so.

Divareli used a towel to wipe away the condensation from the window caused by the heat of his bedroom clashing with the sub-zero temperatures outside. Tall skeletal trees stood dark against the morning sky. Encrusted with frost, their almost leafless branches supported flocks of menacing black crows, some of whom flapped lazily past the window. He prayed that the frost would not ruin the scent for the hounds. He rang down for breakfast and gazed uncertainly at the unusual clothes he was about to put on. There was only one long mirror in the room. It was on the inside of the door of a huge mahogany wardrobe. The problem was that it would not stay open. As he pulled on his white riding breeches the door swung shut yet again. He looked around for something to prop the damn thing open so that he could monitor the progress of his dressing. Finally he settled on a sturdy chair and placed that carefully against the door. Suddenly he remembered the talcum powder. Gallerick had advised him to use the stuff liberally on his nether regions to avoid chafing during the five hours or so he would spend in the saddle. Even now he could hear the braying voice of the Eleventh Earl as he roared across the port decanter. 'Damned good stuff, that powder. Use tons of it myself. Specially useful when you have got a bad fright and start to pee in your pants . . .'

111

Loud guffaws from round the table had accompanied this. When Divareli had squeezed into his riding breeches for the second time, causing the powder to hang in the sunlight like a minor explosion, he tucked them into long woollen socks, leaving the top of the breeches hanging open. Donning a long-tailed shirt, he pushed the tails down as far as they would go before buttoning up the riding breeches, thus keeping the whole ensemble together. He lifted a snow-white silk hunting stock from its nest of tissue paper and tied it around his throat, securing it with a gold pin. The pin was an elaborate affair that he had paid a lot of money for in Van Cleef's. Carved from solid gold, its bar was diamond-studded and surmounted by the sculpted figure of a horse and rider. He fastened the clasp with great care. He reminded himself that if he were going to hunt with a bunch of blueblooded aristo-crats, then he had better look the part. Just as he was about to pull on the long leather hunting boots there was a gentle knock on the bedroom door. A soft brogue announced the arrival of his break-fast.

Sean opened the door with some difficulty as he balanced the heavy tray with one hand while fumbling for the door-handle with the other. Placing the tray on the bedside table, Sean bade him good morning and was gone.

Divareli placed the first forkful of black pudding into his mouth, taking care not to let the grease from it spill on to the spotless hunting stock around his neck. The breakfast laid out on the tray consisted of three chunky rashers encircling a delicately fried egg, two long thin port sausages, a length of both black and white pud-dings sleek and shiny from frying in their own juice, two wedges of fried bread and four halved and fried tomatoes. A piece of liver and some tiny kidneys completed the still life on the plate. A rack holding eight slices of toast, several thick cuts of homemade brown bread, a dish of butter and a choice of marmalade or honey com-pleted the array. From experience he avoided the orange juice and the coffee. Neither tasted remotely like the real thing. The rest, however, was irresistible.

As he ate, he reflected that the Irish, despite eating and drinking to excess, did not appear any fatter than their counterparts back home. Gallerick, for instance, could have acted as a pullthrough for a rifle, though Mick Flannery certainly showed the effects of the good life. Like most athletes, he had probably let himself go to seed once his playing days were over.

Wiping his mouth with the big linen napkin, Divareli set about the tricky task of pulling up his boots. They had looped thongs attached to the polished brown leather tops. Into these were placed what looked like an elongated corkscrew. Instead of the steel spiral there was an L-shaped device that fitted into the thong. To put on the tight-fitting boot, this had to be pulled upwards. At the first attempt, the ends of his riding breeches rode up over the woollen socks causing a painful bulge inside the boot. Taking the boot off would have been impossible without another gadget – a small wooden plank with the vee cut in it. The vee held the boot firmly as the foot was withdrawn. After considerable grunting, the boot shot across the floor like a cork out of a bottle. He smoothed out the offending wrinkle and pulled the long sock over the end of the riding breeches with greater care than before. This time the boot slipped on like a well-fitting glove.

He then shrugged on the black hunting jacket with the double vent at the back to allow for easy movement in the saddle, and checking his appearance in the mirror, decided that he cut a dashing figure. All that remained, he told himself ruefully, was to stay in the saddle without either trampling Gallerick's beloved hounds or killing himself. He had been told that the etiquette of the hunting field was more complicated than that of being presented to Royalty. Pausing only to put his wallet in the jacket hanging in the wardrobe, he made his way downstairs.

The lawn at Gallerick Hall swept down to a post and rail fence some distance from the house. The wide gravel crescent in front of the steps leading to the portico was gridlocked with horse-boxes and an assortment of towing vehicles ranging from sleek Daimlers to Johnny Slattery's familiar tractor. Many of the cars looked incapable of pulling the skin off a rice pudding, much less a horse-box containing a half ton of horse-flesh. It was five minutes to eleven on a sunny morning. The purple mountains might have beencardboard cutouts carefully glued to the pale blue backdrop of a cloudless sky. The bevy of locals present found at least one topic on which they were in complete agreement: if you could see the mountains that clearly, it meant rain – and plentyof it – before evening.

The converse of this theorem was almost too obvious to state. If you couldn't see them, it was already raining.

Even the most cynical of those leaning against the wooden railing, hoping that the trays of mulled wine would come their way, had to admit that the Lawn Meet made a colourful spectacle. Divareli watched in awe as the Whip in his pink coat herded the foxhounds into the same corner as he had parked the Porsche two nights ago. An occasional flick of the snake-like lash kept them there, panting and agitated like a college football team about to take the field. Occasionally a brown and white hound would sidle away from the pack to beg a cocktail sausage from one of the hangers-on. The Pink Coat would storm after the animal and crack the whip loudly in a manner that sent the guilty hound slinking back to its mates and caused the provider of the sausage to redden with embarrassment. Short of actually riding over them, even Divareli was aware that the worst thing one could do to foxhounds was to feed them spicy sausages just before a hunt. It ruined their scent.

The riders affected black riding jackets, white or beige jodhpurs and a snow-white stock pinned to their throat by a pin. This invariably featured either a gold horse or fox. The whole *ensemble* was crowned by a black hunting cap that incorporated a crash helmet. Until recently, the more aristocratic of the riders wore silk top hats that required almost as much grooming as their glistening mounts. Then one of their number fell heavily on a road and cracked his skull. The coroner, Dr James Buckley – better known as the Doc – recommended so strongly that arrogance should give way to prudence in the matter of headgear that the Hunt Committee hastily drafted a rule stating that '*Hunt Members are obliged to wear headgear similar to that worn by jockeys and showjumpers. Farmers and other hunt followers may wear headgear of their choice.*' This edict was carried in full by the local paper, the *Clarion*, whose Editor had a field day at the expense of the Gallerick Hunt.

Only Daft Daphne rode side-saddle. The leather-skinned veteran had never bothered to switch to the more orthodox riding style when it became socially acceptable to do so. She wore a three-quarter length riding coat, threadbare with age, over a voluminous black skirt, topped off by a tall silk hat, sleek of coat as a well-fed kitten. As might have been expected she was engrossed in conversation with herself. With everyone seemingly determined on giving her a wide berth, she formed an invisible barrier between the well-dressed and those who were less so. The latter, Divareli guessed, were the local farmers who formed the link between the Hunt and those whose land was hunted over. They, too, wore riding caps but the fabric had often worn through to reveal an obscene plastic helmet underneath. Among this group, quilted sleeveless anoraks, faded jeans and rubber gumboots were the order of the day. To Divareli's astonishment, they gulped down the lukewarm stirrup cups with apparent relish. It was not until he noticed a bottle of clear liquid being passed around surreptitiously to replenish the wide variety of gas station glasses that the mystery was solved.

A long trestle table at the bottom of the steps groaned under the weight of bowls filled to the brim with the boiling, Bulgarian brew. This was ladled out in assorted glasses to the riders and to some hangers-on, dispensed by Harmon who was now attired in the garb of a grave-digger. The two ferocious terriers at his heels and the shiny spade boded ill for any fox desperate enough to go to ground. When those milling around the gravel had been served, a tray of wine glasses and cocktail sausages was despatched 'with his Lordship's compliments' to the *hoi polloi* looking on from a respectful distance.

It had not escaped the notice of these hawk-eyed watchers that a favoured few were ushered up the wide stone steps and into the Hall itself where hospitality of a more substantial nature was on offer. Their suspicions were proved correct when the familiar figure of Mick Flannery, attired in an electric blue mohair suit of brightest hue was seen to emerge with a tumblerful of amber liquid clutched to his bosom. With a quick glance around to make sure he was well seen, he gave a friendly, all-encompassing wave to no one in particular before disappearing back inside the Hall.

Divareli was not relaxed. The mare provided for him by the hunt turned out to have come from Houlihan and seemed to possess all of the vices but none of the virtues of a beautiful but highly-strung woman. She had a nasty habit of craning her neck around in a u-turn. To what purpose, Divareli had yet to ascertain but suspected that it might have been so that she could sink her teeth into his thigh. If she could be this troublesome while parked, as it were, he did not care to dwell on what she might get up to in the heat of the chase. Rather like driving the Porsche flat out on black ice, he suspected.

He wished she would stand still long enough for him to swallow his wine and solicit another sausage or two from Harmon.

He watched a grizzled old man in a torn raincoat holding a riderless horse with one hand while consuming two plump sausages on a cocktail stick with the other. To his amazement, having wolfed down the sausages, the old guy then ate the stick with equal relish. Divareli's mount was in a state of perpetual motion whereas the rest of the horses looked as if they had been carved from marble. The mare was forever changing feet, whinnying aggressively at the other horses and tossing her head in a most annoying fashion that obliged him to pull hard on the reins. In so doing, he spilled some of the claret on his white riding breeches. The stain made it look as though he had just been stabbed in the groin.

Everyone seemed on first-name terms. Knots of people were engaged in animated conversation. The men shared a deep braying laugh whereas the women affected a yelping cry – not unlike that of the hounds – that incorporated the word 'bloody' at least twice in every sentence. They seemed totally unconcerned by the fact that their mounts were moving beneath them. They controlled them – almost subconsciously – by deft movements of the knees and heels. Divareli envied them their practised ease almost as much as he did their *camaraderie*.

He was entirely alone. Apart from that brief glimpse of Mick Flannery in the porch, he neither knew nor even vaguely recognised anyone. He wondered how Mick had fared in Brussels. The very least the guy could have done was to phone, he thought sourly, until he remembered he had not been in the office that morning, leaving it in Aphra's hands while he organised himself for a day's hunting. Gally was nowhere to be seen, though a sleek black stallion was being held at the steps of the Hall by a groom with too much hair-oil. It was not unreasonable to assume that this was the Master's steed. Its owner was presumably within, entertaining those whom he considered worthy of his hospitality to proper food and drink rather than the rubbish on offer out here. To be fair, Divareli consoled himself, it was quite likely that Gally was unaware that he was languishing outside.

On the other hand, it was just possible that the point was being subtly made that if Divareli were to invest money in the hunt and become a Joint Master, he would be invited into the inner sanctum as a matter of course. The question he had to ask himself as an investment banker of some repute was, whether it was worth paying good money for the dubious privilege of being invited inside the ancient pile of stones that called itself Gallerick Hall. Gally had failed to disclose how many other Joint Masters he intended to appoint in his latest scheme to raise money.

With a surge of relief, Divareli recognised Niall Callahan among the rogues' gallery of unshaven and unwashed faces that stared back at him.

'Hello Niall, how are you today?'

The object of his attention adopted an awkward pose as he readied himself for the role of the obsequious but cunning stage Irishman so beloved of moviegoers since Barry Fitzgerald first opened his mouth in *Boy's Town*. 'Sure if I was any better, Misther Divareli, I'd have to go and see Doctor Buckley himself, so I would.'

This sally elicited loud guffaws from his fellow yokels. Buoyed up by his success, he inquired in noticeably less deferential tones, 'Will ye be crossing McCarthy's land?'

The very last thing Divareli wanted was to expose his ignorance before this gang of panhandlers and layabouts. The name McCarthy had a familiar ring but ... 'Hard to say, really. What do you think yourself?' He employed much the same technique back home when quizzed about a little-known stock.

'Well now, sir, between you, me and the wall, I wouldn't be in any hurry to jump into Long Tom McCarthy's few acres if I were you. He takes the gun to the hunt, you know!'

'Does he now?' From Callahan's tone of voice, Long Tom might as well have brought along sandwiches and a flask of coffee to sustain him through the long day.

'Oh indeed he does, so he does. His Lordship was the lucky man he didn't get the head blown off himself, so he was. Sure Tom was only just out of the hospital after such a bout of drinking that he didn't know for sure whether he was comin' or goin'. Fair play to his Lordship, though. When Long Tom pointed the gun at him to keep him out of the field, didn't his Lordship give a roar at him as would waken the dead. "Out of my way, McCarthy you blackguard, I'm jumping into that field even if there were fifty more like you waiting for me behind the ditch. If you shoot you'll have to shoot me in the back!" Then off with his Lordship like a scalded cat.

McCarthy raised the gun but someone knocked it out of his hand, thanks be to the Holy God and His Blessed Mother!'

Further discussion of the heroic deeds of the Eleventh Earl of Gallerick were interrupted by the appearance of the hero himself. The entertainment within must have been something out of the ordinary because the colour of his Lordship's face almost matched the fiery red of his coat. With some assistance from the hair-oiled groom, he was hoisted unsteadily aboard the sleek black stallion.

In a moment, the hounds were bounding down the long avenue, baying loudly in their excitement. Almost on their tails cantered Gally, closely followed by the Whip. At a discreet distance behind, the main body of the hunt followed, chatting animatedly among themselves. For some reason best known to herself, Divareli's mare refused to budge. Having spent the previous half hour in perpetual motion, she now adopted the pose of an equestrian statue cast in bronze. With the Hunt already halfway down the long avenue, Divareli was beginning to fear that he had been left at the post. Then Fate, in the form of Niall Callahan, took a hand. Or rather a blackthorn stick. This he applied to the mare's flanks with such ferocity that she sprang forward like a shot from Long Tom McCarthy's gun. Divareli hung on for dear life as horse and rider closed rapidly on the main group who were proceeding at a leisurely trot down the avenue to draw the fox covert at the entrance to Gallerick Hall.

As the distance between them lessened alarmingly, it became clear that the mare had neither the ability nor the desire to stop. Already they were passing out the backmarkers. The post and rail fencing lining both sides of the avenue became a blur. Just when it seemed that the mare was about to crash headlong into the main body of riders and almost certainly reduce the prized pack of foxhounds to raw hamburger beneath her flying hooves, she suddenly took fright and shied violently.

Still hanging on for grim life, Divareli could hardly believe his eyes as the mare performed a perfect right-angle turn at high speed and cleared the post and rail fence with feet to spare. She was now in a large field with some Hereford cattle viewing their progress with an interest that almost matched that of the rest of the hunt. A quick look round her and the mare was off again, this time streaking straight as an arrow for the high stone wall that bounded the estate. She seemed to know the lie of the land better than her rider. A storm had caused an elderly oak to crash through the estate wall on to the road. Though the tree had long since been removed, the gap in the wall remained. It was still a formidable leap but again the mare cleared it as though Divareli's hefty frame were a mere horsefly on her back. Landing on the tarmac road with a thud that jarred every bone in his body, they narrowly avoided an oncoming truck and were last seen by an amazed driver heading at high speed down the road.

Gally turned to his Whip. 'Amazing fellow that Yankee chap. Pal of Aphra's, actually. Can't quite remember his name but she says he's absolutely dripping with dollars. Now he seems set on killing himself. That mare of Timothy Houlihan's is mad as a hatter. Safest place for her is the inside of a tin. I don't know why on earth Houlihan was so insistent that the Yank had her. Anyway, let's hope he doesn't kill himself. Not until he's pushed a few dollars in this direction, eh what? Can you see where she's carrying him at all?'

The Whip squinted through his field-glasses and then looked again to be quite sure. As he lowered the binoculars, his face wore a look of surprised amusement. 'I can as a matter of fact, your Lordship. They have just jumped into Long Tom McCarthy's front field.'

14

The mare finally ran out of steam in the middle of a muddy field. At the far end stood a house with a sagging thatched roof. A crude passage led from it to a gate quite close to where the horse and rider had come to a panting halt. Divareli had never been so frightened in all his life. The gigantic leaps, the near-miss with the truck, the terrified expression on the face of its driver as for one split second he thought he was going to be joined in the cab by Divareli and his steed and not least of all, the appalling exhibition he had made of himself all conspired to leave him in no shape whatsoever to cope with the next thunderbolt about to be hurtled at him by an unkind Fate.

A shrill cry like that of a wounded crow preceded a loud bang. A small dishevelled man wearing a torn overcoat tied at the waist with a length of thin rope was busily reloading a shotgun. Its rusted barrel, from which a thin wisp of smoke spiralled upwards, was bound to its wooden stock by strands of wire. From under a flat cap a face contorted with rage glared up at him with coal-red eyes. Where this apparition had emerged from was something Divareli had neither the time nor the inclination to work out for himself. While relieved that the opening salvo had been fired into the air, it was as yet unclear what the target might be for the fresh shell currently being inserted in the breach. Thus far the gun-toting lunatic had uttered nothing more meaningful than a series of menacing grunts. These were further embellished by an irregular line of spittle that meandered from the side of his mouth to the tip of his unshaven chin before dropping earthwards at irregular intervals. Even more ominous, Divareli concluded, were the patches of whitish foam forming at the corners of his mouth.

By now there was not the slightest doubt in Divareli's mind that he was dealing with Long Tom McCarthy. The words of Niall Callahan echoed in his ears: '*His Lordship was the lucky man not to get the head blown off himself, so he was. Sure Tom was only just*

120

out of the hospital after such a bout of drinking that he didn't know for sure whether he was comin' or goin'!' If appearances were anything to go by, Tom still had some way to go before his rehabilitation was completed. This view was reinforced by his taking a quick swallow from a small bottle he produced from the folds of his ragged coat before unsteadily pointing the gun at Divareli's midriff. If Long Tom McCarthy could point his gun at a Peer of the Realm and a next-door neighbour to boot, he was not likely to harbour any reservations about discharging it at a total stranger.

Divareli desperately scrabbled around the hidden corners of his imagination to come up with something that might deter this maniac from pulling the trigger. Nothing other than straightforward bribery came to mind and he was stretching a gloved hand backwards to the hip pocket of his riding breeches when he suddenly remembered that he had left his wallet in the bedroom. How dearly he longed to be there now, snug beneath the duvet rather than preparing to meet his Maker in the middle of a wet field. There was so much in his life that remained undone – not least of which was the small matter of consummating his devouring passion for the Lady Aphra. What had he ever done, he asked himself plaintively, to deserve a painful death in the middle of a muddy field in the middle of nowhere? Especially without fulfilling what had now become his mission in life – that of making slow, passionate and uninterrupted love to the Lady Aphra Gallerick.

For Luke Divareli to die for want of a twenty-dollar bill would be the supreme irony in a tragedy of Greek proportions now fast approaching its final curtain. Was McCarthy sufficiently demented to squeeze the trigger? If the small bottle from which he was yet again wordlessly refreshing himself contained Johnny Slattery's poteen then anything was possible. As Divareli debated with himself whether a reasoned plea, indeed any form of speech on his part, might not further exacerbate an already delicate situation, he fell to reflecting how much of the blame for his predicament could be laid at the door of Timothy Houlihan. He should have been suspicious from the first of the too-hearty greeting of the oily hotelier.

'Do you know what I told his Lordship the moment he phoned me about getting a mount for yourself? Says I to his Lordship – and may I rot in hell for the rest of my born days if I speak one word of a lie – you can tell Misther Divareli from me that I'll give him the best animal I have in the livery yard, so I will. "Fit for a king, she is, your Honour" were the exact words I said to the dacent man. The mare, I says to myself, is the only animal fit for a fine gentleman like Misther Divareli and he after comin' all the way from America to honour us with his presence.'

Before Divareli could reflect any further on Houlihan and his weird speech patterns, the mare decided to take a hand in the proceedings. Whether it was from boredom or the fact that, like her rider, she had already had more than enough of Long Tom McCarthy and his smoking gun, she surged forward. This caught Divareli unawares but he managed to hold on and remain in the saddle. Long Tom was not so fortunate. The mare's flank struck him amidships, knocking him to the ground. The gun implanted its barrel in the soft, wet earth rendering it harmless. Had Divareli risked taking one hand off the reins, he would have patted the mare gratefully. The Seventh Cavalry had never made a more timely entrance than the mare's sudden decision to resume her rightful place at the head of the hunt.

As she sought to catch up on the hounds, a large ditch loomed up before them. It was covered with scrawny trees and bedraggled bushes. A 'double' ditch, as Sean explained to him later, was one that people used as a path on their way to mass in the village. This explained why it was almost twenty feet wide, with a deep drain on either side. It might well have been the Black Trench about which Gally had waxed so lyrical at his dinner party, when he'd unleashed something that sounded like a 'Harrumphh' and pointed to a bewhiskered ancestor staring stonily back at them.

'That silly bugger came a cropper in the Black Trench. Bloody horse refused to jump the damn thing without warning so the poor sod sailed across the Trench on his own and landed on a stone on the far side. Broke his neck, in fact.'

'You must have been very upset by that.'

'Who me? Not on your life. Had it coming to him. Wasted his fortune on wine, women and song which was fine but when he started losing estates on the throw of a dice the rest of the family decided he was taking things a bit far. They were on the point of packing him off to the Colonies when he saved them the bother by breaking his neck. Quite the best thing he could have done in the circumstances. Oh, as for me being upset, well that didn't really arise. You see all this happened over two hundred years ago.'

'Oh, I see. I didn't realise . . .'

'Gally often refers to the past as though it were in the here and now. I find that quite fascinating, don't you?'

Aphra had looked at them both with innocent, wide-open almond eyes. At the time Divareli had thought her the most beautiful and desirable object he had ever laid eyes on, but he could not make up his mind whether she was being serious, naive or simply teasing him unmercifully. Suddenly, more pressing matters intervened to distract him from his memories of the dinner party.

The large trench had to be negotiated before a foothold could be established on the earthen bank. In their headlong flight to make up lost ground the mare had already sailed over a brush fence and two stone walls, one of which was topped with a strand of evil-looking barbed wire. All these obstacles she had cleared with the utmost ease but now the immensity of the task ahead caused her to slacken her gallop somewhat. The slower pace gave Divareli a chance to compose himself and give some appearance of being in charge of his steed. The respite did not last for long. The sound of the huntsman's horn in the next field sent the mare into a further frenzy.

Time stood still as she gathered herself for a mighty leap that left her perched, flanks quivering and bathed in sweat, on the top of the broad ditch. Divareli, whose heart had scarcely left his mouth since first entering Long Tom's field, was deeply grateful for the generous dousing of talcum powder he had given himself before leaving the Brulagh Inn. Through the dense brambles, the main body of the hunt were now visible in the next field. To join them, would involve jumping an even wider trench, filled with mud. Had Divareli been able to spy a gap in the bushes wide enough to lead the mare down by the reins, he would have dismounted and done so. It was infinitely preferable to get soaked to the skin rather than drown under the mare.

Yet again the decision was taken out of his hands. Unseen by him, another rider had followed him up on to the bank. This unexpected arrival caused the mare to start violently. With an angry whinny, she launched herself out into space. With her neck at full stretch she forced aside the branches and the thorny brambles with her head. These snapped back into place again just in time to snatch greedily at Divareli as she forced a passage through the dense undergrowth.

A downward glance at the trench did nothing to reassure him. Already there were at least three loose horses thrashing around in the quagmire. Their riders were nowhere to be seen. Now horse and rider faced a fresh difficulty. The jump had been massive but despite her best efforts, the mare landed just short of the far bank. With flying hooves and Divareli clinging on to her neck for dear life, she slid down backwards into the foul-smelling slime.

What seemed like an age but was probably not more than five seconds later, the second horse and rider landed with a resounding splash beside them. The latest arrival, however, managed to remain upright. Divareli became submerged and clawed his way frantically back to the surface, completely blinded by the mud. As he took a firm grip on something yielding he discovered that what he had attached himself to was not solid ground, as he had hoped, but a loose garment of some sort. Like a shipwrecked sailor clinging frantically to the wreckage, he refused to release his grip despite protesting shouts and what felt like kicks being rained down upon his hunting cap.

The last thing he glimpsed through the film of slime before losing consciousness was the purple face of Deaf Daphne, still mounted side-saddle on her horse. She was trying to steer the animal towards the far shore that led out of the morass. All that restrained her progress was Divareli clutching the hem of her garment. This quickly resolved itself. As Divareli lost consciousness, he still retained a vice-like grip on the rough cloth, enough for a topsail on a four-rigger. Daphne, her wrinkled countenance ablaze with rage and embarrassment, dismounted when she had reached dry ground, her lower regions unadorned save for a voluminous pair of cami-knickers not seen in public since Victory Day in Trafalgar Square in 1945.

15

If this were the Hereafter, Divareli decided, then it was not anything like it had been cracked up to be. For one thing the noise was deafening. An engine of some sort was roaring. In the brief instant that he regained consciousness, he sensed that he was lying on the floor of some sort of pick-up truck that was bumping its way along a rough track. Voices made themselves heard above the din. One of them was much louder than the other – possibly God's. If so, then it confirmed what he had for long suspected. God was a woman.

As his brain cleared momentarily, he recognised the voice as that of Deaf Daphne. She was addressing the driver but it was almost impossible to catch what she was shouting above the engine noise and the waves of nausea that were threatening to engulf him.

Just before he slipped back into oblivion he heard: '. . . Some dreadful jumped-up Dago that Gally simply had to bring out hunting so that he gets pots of money out of him. To make matters worse, Aphra's dead keen on him. The blighter's a bally sex maniac, if you ask me. Had the skirt off me before I knew where I was. God alone knows what would have happened if he hadn't passed out in the trench. Drink, I expect. None of those Dagos could hold their liquor, Harmon, not like my late husband, God rest his soul. Will you ever forget the night he . . .' But the drinking feats of Daphne's departed spouse remained a secret as Divareli lost consciousness again.

Suddenly, without explanation, he was back home, sitting in the garden with his mother. In a quiet, soft drawl she was telling him her favourite story – the one in which Eileen, her mother-in-law, met Luca Divareli. Eileen was married to Kevin Farrell, a young Irish firebrand who was trying to horn in on the profitable Divareli liquor-smuggling operation across the Canadian border. Of course the Italians didn't like it. Didn't they have the bootlegging business all sewn-up for themselves? But with the Irish growing in power and numbers every day, why should Luca have it all to himself? As usual the answer was obvious to everyone in the street, except

Kevin. It was quite simply that the Italians ran the neighbourhood. They owned the politicians, the police, the speakeasies, the cathouses and most of the Church. Who passed round the collection box for The Propagation of The Faith in the big draughty St Joseph's pro-Cathedral every Sunday? Not Kevin Farrell or one of his Mick cronies but Luca Divareli, that's who!

Luca was always hovering around, smiling and talking quietly to other men in tight suits. She rarely addressed him and never returned his smouldering glances. Certainly not since she married Kevin. Yet the change in her marital status did not deter Luca from semaphoring unspoken messages in her direction at every opportunity. Even from the aisle of the church as he leaned forward to position the collection box in front of young Charley. Then one day Luca turned up on her doorstep with O'Mara, the cop. From the look on their faces she knew something was amiss.

Luca spoke first. 'Eileen, Andy here has somethin' to tell you.'

Though Luca's voice was steady, the cop's was less so. 'Mrs Farrell, I'm real sorry but your husband had an accident . . .'

She put down young Charley lest she might drop him with the shock. He meandered back into the house, singing happily to himself. 'Oh Holy Mother of God, what sort of an accident?'

'A bad one, I'm afraid, Mrs Farrell.' O'Mara reached into the top pocket of his tunic and fished out a tired-looking notebook with pages that curled up at the edges. 'I gotta tell you that your husband was shot while resisting arrest at our side of the border.'

There was the sound of a loud, rushing wind and she felt a lightness in her head. When she came to, she was lying on the sofa of the front parlour. Luca and the cop were bending over her as Charley screamed tearfully, 'Momma, Momma, wake up, wake up!' followed by some chatter that he alone could understand.

Luca was holding a cup of water and encouraging her to drink from it as though it were one of the fine brandies he brought in from Nova Scotia. 'There, there, Eileen. Take it easy. You've just given us a helluva fright going off and fainting like you did just now. Drink some of this and we'll take you down to the Polyclinic.'

'I'm OK, I don't need to go to no hospital . . .'

Luca's voice dropped so that young Charley wouldn't hear what he said. 'I know that, Eileen, but it's Kevin we're talkin' about. You

126

gotta identify the body. You see, that's where they brought him after he got shot.'

This precipitated a fit of hysterics which frightened Charley even more than her fainting had done. She knocked the cup of water from Luca's hand and started to pound O'Mara's burly chest.

'You shot Kevin, you and your lousy friends. He was only trying to make an honest buck and you bastards shot him. I hate you, I hate the both of you!'

Then she fainted again.

Now there was a bright light dazzling Luke Divareli. He opened his eyes only to squeeze them shut against the glare. A familiar voice was saying, 'The pupils seem OK, equal and reacting. The worst he'll have is a bit of a headache. If he had drink taken before the accident, the injection I gave him could make him hallucinate a bit. Other than that, he'll be right as rain. Give me a call if he shows signs of memory loss or complains of a persistent headache. Ah, thanks be to God, he's coming round now.'

Divareli was tucked up in bed. The Doc was shining a pencil-torch into his eyes. Aphra was in the background, watching and listening as she tried to hide her concern. The Doc's voice was hearty.

'Welcome back to the land of the living. As soon as you feel up to it, you should try to make it to the bath. You seem to have a good deal of Mother Earth still attached to you. You've just got a bit of concussion, that's all. Get some rest and you'll be right as rain again in no time. How do you feel now?'

'A bit dizzy, otherwise all right. How did I get here? What happened?'

'You fell off a horse. I'll leave Aphra to fill in the details. I must be off.' He snapped his bag shut and was gone.

Divareli laid his head back on the pillow, stared at the ceiling and allowed his mind to drift back again to his mother's story. Her soothing tones wrapped him a warm cocoon, safe from runaway horses and loud-mouthed aristocrats who called him rude names when they thought he wasn't listening.

After Kevin's funeral, she said, life returned to what passed for normal. Normal, that is, if one ignored the war being waged on Eileen's doorstep. Luca Divareli was making his move. The smaller gangs were no match for him and in a matter of weeks their tattered

127

remnants had either sued for terms or fled. Lines were redrawn and a little room was grudgingly made for the new arrival by the older *capos*. When they saw that he was a man of honour despite his lowly birth – he was not Sicilian – they reluctantly accepted him.

The Farrells, too, were regarded with suspicion by their fellow countrymen in the ghetto. It was rumoured that Kevin's mother had come over from Ireland, heavy with child. Someone she had met on the boat pretended to be her husband. That was good enough for the Immigration Officers at Castle Garden. An unaccompanied pregnant woman would have been sent back to Ireland on the next coffin ship. The priests in St Paul's Presbytery had taken pity on her and placed her under their care. When her time was near they sent her to the Polyclinic, the same one that now held her dead Kevin. Ironically the poor girl died giving birth to the same Kevin. It was no wonder that nowadays Eileen crossed to the other side of the street rather than pass the grim building on her way to and from the sweatshop. It had been a mausoleum for the Farrells since they set foot in the New World.

There were many who linked Luca to the killing. The cops had been expecting Kevin and blew him away when he failed to stop at their roadblock. Speculation raged through the Irish bars and speakeasies as to who might have tipped them off. What made Luca clear favourite was his presence on Eileen's doorstep immediately after the shooting with O'Mara, the crookedest cop in the precinct. Ah to be sure, it was whispered knowingly, poor Kevin had plenty of enemies. But Luca not only saw the Irishman as a rival but also lusted after his wife. For Eileen was indeed a beauty. Of late her undeniable prettiness had given way to something more enduring. She possessed a serenity that was the envy of every woman on the block. When she walked along the sidewalk, head erect with a scarf knotted at her throat, she might have been a queen striding purposefully among her loyal subjects.

Maybe it was his fear of rejection that made Luca proceed with such caution. To have been sent packing by the impoverished widow of a dumb Irish rum-runner would have been more than flesh and blood could take. Luca, like a good general, realised that young Charley was the weak link in Eileen's defences. When he dropped the kid off after a trip to Coney Island or skating in Central Park he would gaze wistfully at Eileen and say, 'You know somethin'? Nuthin's too good for that kid of yours. He's got more brains than the rest of the kids on the block put together. Do you know, he read out most of the goddamn newspaper on the trip back here? I can tell you that's really somethin'! I got guys workin' for me right now that can't read as good as young Charley here!'

He never came right out and said he could offer the boy a better life. His invitations never went beyond asking her out to dinner – not unreasonable requests but yet she declined each and every one of them. Eileen had no kinfolk to turn to after the funeral. Her own family had long deserted Hell's Kitchen, leaving the ramshackle house to her. They had moved to Boston to be with other relatives who enjoyed a marginally higher standard of poverty. As far as she was concerned, they might as well have gone to the moon. Or back to home to Ireland, for that matter. She had never seen the place nor had she any desire to – despite the mawkish ballads that entreated her to do so.

'Come back to Erin, mavourneen, mavourneen,
Come back Aroon to the land of thy birth.'

These were the stock-in-trade of nasal tenors at every wake or wedding yet Eileen was unmoved by these musical tugs on her heartstrings. America was the land of her birth and she regarded herself as a full-blooded, one hundred per cent proof American citizen. That was another difference between Luca and herself. Luca was an Italian first and foremost, with all the hang-ups both religious and cultural that Latins collected.

He came to in the bath, its warm water cocooning him like a giant womb. The previous owner of the Brulagh Inn had been an Irish-American. Though his obsession with shamrocks had by now been almost obliterated from the *décor*, he had left behind a more enduring legacy – American plumbing. Aphra had already changed the water in the giant bath three times, but there were still traces of mud in the bathwater.

'You were ranting and raving again. Damn nearly called the Doc back, you gave me such a start. What were you mumbling about?'

'Nothing much, just thought I was back home for a moment there. Any phone calls?' Even had he wanted to enlighten her as to his past, his mind was far too confused to make any sense of what was a rather jumbled tale.

'Yes. Italbank want you to call them back as soon as possible. Abe asked me to book someone called McAllister and himself into an hotel. As Sean is full up, I couldn't think of anywhere except the Gallerick Arms, much as I loathe putting business Houlihan's way. The only other place is Joe Gallagher's but they might find that a bit basic. They can always move there if they can't stand Houlihan. By the way, what possessed you to ride his mare? Everyone knows that the focking animal is even crazier than he is!'

Before he could think of an answer to this, she was off again. 'Oh I nearly forgot. Mick Flannery phoned just before I left the office: the applications have been okayed by Brussels. Now I suggest that you get out of the bath and back into bed. The Doc warned me that you needed to sleep off the effects of the injection. Now I really must get back to work. See you tomorrow!'

When she had gone, he dragged himself painfully out of the bath. He was surprised at how weak he felt. Exhausted, he tottered to the bed and slipped once more beneath the covers. Almost immediately he fell into a deep but far from dreamless sleep.

The Divareli home was situated in a leafy suburb. Though less than a half-mile from where she lived, Eileen had never seen it before now. An elegant brownstone, it was set among other impressive houses on Chestnut Boulevarde. A manicured lawn sloped to the whitewashed kerb that separated the property from the leaf-strewn sidewalk. Large black cars choked the gravel sweep in front of the house. Beefy men lounged inside them, smoking and chatting to each other in a relaxed yet watchful manner. Luca had persuaded her to be his guest at his sister's wedding reception which was being held in the back garden where guests were already milling around, protected from prying eyes by a high wall topped with broken glass.

He and Eileen approached a large man in a suit two sizes too small for him who stood in the doorway like a bouncer at a ghetto wake. He looked curiously at her and then said to Luca in a deferential manner, 'We were wondering where you'd got to. They're just about ready to cut the cake.'

Luca nodded without saying anything and led Eileen by the hand into the enormous back garden. It was like walking into another world. He introduced her to his parents. The father, a squat elderly man, impeccably dressed in a double-breasted suit with wide lapels, just nodded silently. He smiled at her with his mouth but not with his eyes. His wife was small and wrinkled but with a sharp eye that took in everything at a single glance. Eileen wondered if the old lady could see the careful stitching on her borrowed frock. It wasn't until much later that she realised Luca's mother was vetting her as a prospective daughter-in-law.

She steered Eileen towards the shade of a large tree with a wooden seat built around its base to provide an ideal place for a private conversation. To Eileen she voiced a mother's concern that her 'boy' had not yet found himself a 'proper' girl. Like the Irish, she also used 'boy' to describe a son who would never again see the right side of thirty. Eileen warmed to this small wrinkled creature. Soon she was telling her of Kevin, his untimely death and the problems of bringing up Charley in Hell's Kitchen. She said all this in an unemotional voice without a hint of complaint though from time to time the older woman clucked in sympathy but said nothing that might break the flow of words. When Eileen had finished, they both rose wordlessly and rejoined the guests.

By now, the wedding had taken on a familiar pattern. As the evening wore on it seemed to divide into two separate groups; those who drank until they keeled over and those determined to prevent their doing so. As rows erupted between tipsy husbands and their wives, Luca and Eileen slipped away quietly. When they got back to Eileen's house, a small crowd had gathered around her door. Before either of them could discover the reason, two or three men broke away from the huddle and ran towards the red Cadillac. They pulled hand-guns from under their jackets and fired at Luca in through the open windows. They screamed in accents that were unmistakeably Irish, '*Kill the fucking Dago. Give him one in the balls for Kevin Farrell. Kill that whore of a widow too while you're about it. The bitch is sleeping with an Italian stallion!*' before running off down the warren of backstreets.

Eileen escaped with a grazed shoulder but Luca collected multiple wounds. She nursed him back to health and they married shortly afterwards. She had little choice in the matter since her own people had now totally rejected her because of the shooting and the suggestion that she was Luca's mistress.

They moved to an Italian neighbourhood. Luca was crippled and impotent, leaving young Charley sole heir to the family fortune.

They changed his name to Cesare. Being a cripple meant Luca could focus to the exclusion of all else on expanding his empire. In time he came to believe that wealth and power were meaningless without respectability. He got out of the prostitution and protection rackets to concentrate on the numbers and loansharking. He needed a friendly bank to launder the flood of money from these operations. When he couldn't find one he bought a banking licence. By the time Cesare came of age, banking had become the core business of the family and old Luca put him in charge of it. Banking brought respectability. Cesare became a man about town – the darling of the gossip columnists. Old Luca never did approve of this gadding about but nonetheless it made for excellent contacts when it came to attracting wealthy clients for Italbank.

Divareli became a respected name, so much so that when old Luca died, the Mayor of New York and the Vice-President of the United States showed up for the funeral. His mother's voice took on a note of pride as she ended her tale. 'When you were born, what else could we call you but Luca? Later I persuaded Cesare to change it to Luke, for Luca sounded too much like a *Dago* . . .'

He came to muttering the word *Dago* over and over to himself. Blinking awake he tried to snatch at the wisps of the fast-disappearing memory. He hadn't thought of his mother in ages, but now it was as though the years had been rolled away. Something was gnawing at the edges of his subconscious. *Dago*, that was it! He hadn't heard the word since he left school. Then its sharp, rasping vowels cracked about his head like a whip. He had fought a thousand unequal battles because of that hated word.

Now Gallerick, the idle bastard, had called him a Dago! Well, not quite to his face but that crazy old broad had scarcely concocted her story out of thin air. First that clown Houlihan had tried to kill him by mounting him on a crazy mare, now a bankrupt blueblood thought he could get away with insulting him and trying to rob him into the bargain! Well, Divareli decided, the time had come to show these guys a thing or two. Now fully awake and seething with indignation, he leapt out of bed and started to dress. It wasn't until he reached the office that he wondered if Aphra was part of her father's ridiculous scam.

16

The Eleventh Earl of Gallerick was in his study. The roll-top writing desk at which he sat was overflowing with paperwork, mostly bills and letters demanding immediate payment of same. He felt like throwing the lot of them up in the air, then picking one lucky winner for settlement. The rest would have to go whistle for their money. If they objected too strenuously, they would not be included in next month's draw. No matter how hard he tried to make ends meet, they had the uncanny knack of snapping back even further apart than ever, just when he thought he had got them together.

Nothing, absolutely bally nothing, seemed to work. Try as he might, every scheme he dreamed up to raise money seemed doomed from the start. Take the venison project, he reflected gloomily. That had looked promising for the first year or so. Then poor handiwork, by Harmon, of course, though the damn fellow would never admit it, in repairing a gap in the orchard wall allowed twenty-three deer to sample the heady brew of freedom. Save for one that injured itself in the break-out, they now roamed the estate at will. Now and then he would glimpse a bobtail scurrying into the undergrowth or a set of proud antlers peering at him anxiously before streaking off over the horizon. Tom Donnelly, husband of the delectable Josephine, had provided the seed capital for the deer project and was now pressing for recompense. It was only fitting therefore, Gally had decided, that he be amongst those present to sample the only result to date of his bank's investment. Harmon had found the unlucky doe with a broken leg and taken her out of her misery with a well-aimed bullet. She had featured as the main course of the dinner party of a few nights ago.

Then there were the two hundred pheasants he had reared, again inside the high-walled orchard. In the Nabob's time it had been the jewel in his crown. Giant blocks of limestone handcut by a dozen craftsmen and slotted carefully into place were topped off by a parapet into which iron spikes were sunk to protect the Cox's Pippins from the village brats. One strong door was the sole access to fruit trees that stood erect and in perfect line like a well-drilled regiment. Against the south-facing wall, made of firebrick to retain the sun's warmth, intricately arranged *espaliers* of pear, plum and damson stretched their arms out like giant fans.

Today the orchard was a sorry sight, with many of the trees either cut down or growing wild. The carefully tended *espaliers* had long since grown into gnarled, deformed stumps of trees in their own right. Scattered here and there were the remains of the cages built by Harmon to hold the pheasants – some of which had been intended to star as the main attraction on the menus of hotels and restaurants throughout the land. The remainder should have been targets for a shoot at one hundred guineas per gun. Sadly, the cages had yet to be paid for even though the birds had long since flown. Some idiot, probably Harmon, had left the door to the orchard open and the foxhounds had gone on a rampage, turning over the cages in their pursuit of the birds. Those lucky enough to escape the hounds flew away forever.

Timothy Houlihan removed pheasant from his dinner menu and demanded the thousand pounds he had advanced towards the scheme. Thus far Gally had managed to keep him at bay by asserting that the money was the hotelier's investment in a joint venture – and therefore forfeit – rather than a straightforward loan. But the creature persisted in penning wheedling letters in which phrases like '*as your Lordship knows only too well, I am not a wealthy man*' and ending with: '*A cheque at your earliest possible convenience would be more than welcome . . .*' Because Houlihan rented out his spavined nags to the Hunt via Gally, to be ridden by unsuspecting visitors like the Yank, this ensured that he would not pursue the matter through the courts, but it was nonetheless an irritant that Gally could have well done without.

Something was niggling him like an itch that would not go away. Yes – the Yank, that was it! He had been watching him carefully during the dinner party and it was as plain as the nose on his face that the blighter was dead keen on Aphra. Which was all to the good, especially if the rumours of his vast wealth proved to be correct. Not that the fellow showed any urge to shove any of his *largesse* in Gally's direction. The offer of a Joint Mastership had been greeted with a marked lack of enthusiasm. Gally had expected him to jump at the chance. He had always thought Americans drooled at recognition, however faint, from genuine aristocrats like himself. Not Nuvolari, or whatever his name was. Well, dammit, there must be some way of putting the bite on him. The thought of all that money made Gally's mouth water. He hoped the matter of Houlihan's mare and his attempt to indecently assault old Daff would not cause a rift in their relations. Only time would tell. Gally was trying to think of some tactful way of suggesting to Aphra that she encourage the Yank's advances without making it sound as though he was advising her to sell herself to the highest bidder, when a determined knock on the study door interrupted his thoughts. Harmon drifted in like a wraith. The ability to materialise out of thin air was a disconcerting trick of his.

'Well, Harmon, what is it now? I have here yet another missive from Timothy Houlihan, Esquire. He's still looking for his money back for those pheasants – the ones you let the hounds get at, if you recall.'

Harmon chose to ignore the accusation. He had other fish to fry. 'I have been meaning to speak to you for some time, Milord, on the subject of my wages. The simple fact of the matter is that I can no longer continue to live on . . .'

'Oh for heaven's sake Harmon, not that same old bloody nonsense again. I'm blue in the face from telling you that you're drawing more out of this blasted place than I am!' He broke off to wave 'a piece of paper at the butler. 'Donnelly tells me that I lost fifteen thousand last year. Two thousand of that went to paying you, don't forget. So there you are, old chap. Minus fifteen for Yours Truly and plus two for yourself. Plain as a pikestaff! You can't argue with figures, I always say. Anyway, even if you were entitled to a modest increase I fear it is completely out of the question for the foreseeable future.

'This load of . . .', here he paused to wave towards the pile of papers, '. . . bumf here consists solely of bills and rude letters from creditors who have expressed in no uncertain terms a strong desire to be paid forthwith. Some of them have even gone to such lengths as to threaten the full rigours of the law, whatever they mean by that. If they think that someone who has fearlessly faced down Long Tom McCarthy wielding a shotgun is going to be scared by a mere writ, then they have another think coming. How is he, by the way?'

135

Harmon was confused by the direction the conversation was taking. At all costs he must think of a means whereby it might be steered back to the matter of his inadequate remuneration. Now his Lordship had scurried down yet another burrow. Gone to ground like a fox. He would have to be dug out before he could be chased and caught.

'How is *who*, Milord?'

'Why the Yank, of course. Old Daff told me that you and she fished him out of the trench – after he had debagged her, of course. Can't have been a pretty sight that, eh Harmon?'

'No, Milord, it was not. We brought him back to the Brulagh Inn and young Sean took over from there. I believe Doctor Buckley and the Lady Aphra are attending him.'

'Hope the bloody fellow is all right. I have high hopes for him – absolutely stinking with money, by all accounts. The Lady Aphra seems to have taken quite a shine to him too, I'm glad to say.'

'So it would seem, Milord. She was most distressed when I told her of his mishap. She blamed Timothy Houlihan for the whole thing.'

'Yes, well she may be right there though I can't for the life of me see why Houlihan should want to kill him off. Come to think of it, he *was* rather insistent that he take the mare. Very odd. Did I hear something about him stalking out of the hotel?'

'Indeed he did. But not before he had first thrown Houlihan downstairs, Milord.'

'Great God, why would he do a thing like that?'

'It's a long story, Milord, that reflects no credit on either party if my information is correct. Now, about what we were discussing earlier. My present remuneration goes nowhere near meeting my . . .'

The door of the study opened suddenly – a heaven-sent intrusion from Gally's point of view, though Harmon seemed less than pleased at the unexpected arrival of the Lady Aphra.

'Oops, sorry. Didn't realise there was anyone with you. I can come back later.'

Gally was out of his seat in a flash. 'Not at all, my dear. Come right in. Harmon was just leaving, weren't you, Harmon?'

Nodding to Aphra, an unhappy Harmon took the hint. When the door closed behind him, Gally mopped his brow. 'Phew, that was a near thing. Looking for an increase in wages, if you don't mind. You arrived just in the nick of time.'

'Well, the poor old darling probably deserves it. When did he last get a raise?'

'Can't remember. Anyway it's not on now, that's for sure. Every tradesman for miles around is screaming for his pound of flesh. Not to mention Donnelly and the various tax blokes. We really are in the soup this time.'

He heaved a deep sigh and watched Aphra out of the corner of his eye as he said in sepulchral tones, 'Looks like we'll have to sell the place if something doesn't come up soon. Any luck in your researches?'

'Yes – that's what I came to see you about. That and poor Luke. What in God's name possessed you to let him up on that mad animal?'

'I dunno really. Didn't think anything of it at the time. It becomes more sinister now that Harmon has just told me that what's-his-name threw Houlihan down the stairs of the hotel. What would he want to do a thing like that for?'

It was Aphra's turn to be unforthcoming. She changed the subject. 'I went to see Johnny's aunt – about the American connection I was telling you about, remember?'

He didn't but nodded just the same. Anything for a quiet life. When Aphra got going on the family tree, there was no stopping her. The best course was to let her have her head until she ran out of steam.

'Well, the upshot was that the aunt remembered that Jessie Kelly, the servant girl that became pregnant by young Rodney while working here, ended up married in America to someone called Leary. Davey Leary, she thought, but she couldn't be sure. Now, if we could trace that bloodline over there, we might just unearth a male heir absolutely dripping with dollars, isn't that exciting?'

Privately Gally didn't think so. With the luck he was having, the trail would end at some filthy wino propped against a fire-hydrant and clutching a bottle wrapped in brown paper. Still, one didn't want to discourage the young, especially when she had just become employed again – by that fellow with the funny name. As Aphra waltzed out of his study, full of the joys of life, Gally racked his brain to remember the Yank's name. Davey Leary? No, for God's sake, that was the spouse of the pregnant Jessie a hundred years ago. Try again. De Valera? No, he was a former President who lived almost as long as Methuselah. Divareli, that was it! Quite similar to the other two, in fact. A gleam came into his eye. Both Aphra and Harmon would have recognised the look immediately. The Eleventh Earl of Gallerick had just had another of his brainwaves.

17

Divareli had scarcely any time to brood for long on the insult to his name by Gally. Abe Linovitz had moved into the Gallerick Arms, along with McAllister, where he waged a non-stop guerrilla campaign against Timothy Houlihan. The first night he dined there set the tone for the rest of his stay. According to Niall Callahan who was on duty in the dining room, Abe sent back the soup twice, the steak four times and finally poured his coffee on the carpet with the comment, 'Fucking sump-oil!'

When Houlihan tried to remonstrate with the New Yorker, he was grabbed by the tie and subjected to a torrent of abuse, rich in expletives, delivered in the staccato accents of the Bronx.

'If ya tink you're gonna fob off Abe Linovitz with this kinda shit, then you've got it wrong, ole buddy.'

To lend emphasis to what he was saying, Abe tightened Houlihan's neckware another notch, which caused McAllister and the other diners to fear that they were about to witness a garrotting. The tourniquet round Houlihan's throat made for a rather one-sided exchange of views. Even without such an impediment, it was doubtful whether he would have been able to get a word in edgeways. Abe Linovitz in full spate did not brook interruption.

'I've eaten in some asshole joints in my time, but never before have I been given lukewarm horsepiss for soup, overdone carpet tiles for fillet steak and sump-oil for coffee. Now if you and I are to live on the same goddam planet you had better get somethin' straight right here and now. You may get away with slappin' up trash like this to the rest of these nice folks here . . .', he paused to give an expansive wave of his free hand that encompassed both diners and staff before warming to his theme, '. . . but it ain't goin' to work on ole Abe here.'

Lest anyone should be under the impression that he was referring to another of the same name, Abe helpfully stabbed his own chest with a stubby forefinger before bringing his remarks to a conclusion.

'And that goes for Mr McAllister too. In future when I order a goddam fillet steak, I expect it to be part of some critter that walks around on four legs and says "moo". Then I want you to wound it slightly and walk it through your goddam kitchen. That's what I call a rare fuckin' steak, geddit? Not somethin' that's been left overnight in a fuckin' crematorium.'

He took a deep breath – something Houlihan would have loved to do were he able – before adopting a more conciliatory note. 'Now you just pull yo'self together and kick ass in that kitchen of yours until they fix me somethin' that's fit for human consumption. I don't much care what it is but just make sure I can eat it this time round!'

With that he released the stranglehold and Houlihan staggered off towards the kitchen, dragging air back into his starved lungs in mighty gulps while inwardly cursing every visitor from the New World, regardless of age, sex, colour or creed.

Later Abe would employ much the same tactics when work started on the dunes, the moment McAllister had completed his blueprint for the golf-course. Jeff Myers, the hotel architect, would take longer but then he had to draw up three plans, one of them so outlandish that the authorities would have no option but to turn it down forthwith. This was done on Mick Flannery's advice. If he were to be believed, the Planning Board had to be fed a sacrificial lamb so they could be seen to flex their muscles as protectors of the environment and guardians of all that was best and most beautiful in Brulagh. Though Mick's original scheme had secured outline planning permission, that was for something on a far more modest scale than was envisaged for the B Project.

The preliminary applications had been processed with commendable speed, thanks to the efforts of Mick and Pat Mullarkey. To qualify for EC grants, however, these would have to be converted to 'full' planning permission. Despite Mick's repeated assurances that such was a mere formality, Divareli would not sleep easy until this had been granted. It could only be delayed – or refused – should someone file a formal objection within a month of the application being advertised in the newspapers.

The work on the golf-course could start as soon as Divareli gave the word. Many tons of topsoil and gravel would have to be deposited at strategic points in the dunes, preparatory to transforming them into short strips of undulating highway that, when covered with a layer of rich topsoil, would result in lush fairways streaming out like emerald ribbons between the mighty sandhills. The greens and tees would be similarly constructed though with even more elaborate drainage and gravel layers than the fairways. The foundations of the hotel would be pegged out close by the ruined tower. An annexe of the hotel, overlooking the first tee and last green, would serve as a clubhouse.

Aphra had discovered that the ruin had once been the stronghold of the McCarthys – a family of wealthy smugglers who defended their franchise from its fortified walls and stimulated trade by luring ships on to the nearby cliffs. They accomplished this by waving storm lanterns at those fighting their way through the Atlantic gales. The Crown authorities took exception to such trading practices and to demonstrate their displeasure, burned the McCarthy stronghold to the ground. Divareli did not have the heart to inquire if Long Tom McCarthy was a descendant of this bloodthirsty tribe.

The financial end of things was also proving more difficult than expected. The ongoing SEC investigation into the affairs of Italbank made it necessary to channel the development money through banks in Zurich and Djakarta before it could trickle, as required, into Tom Donnelly's more modest establishment in Brulagh. By now the headquarters of the B Project, Pat Mullarkey's one-time office had become bedlam incarnate. Three telephones jangled incessantly. The walls were covered with drawings, blueprints and work schedules. Yellow hard hats and protective clothing of every sort were heaped in a far corner. Aphra presided over the whole circus with a serenity that surprised and delighted the now fully-recovered Divareli.

'Don't forget that today you are to present the jerseys to the Brulagh hurling team after the game. Mick Flannery phoned to say he would meet you in Sean's after lunch.'

'Oh Christ, I'd completely forgotten about that. Did the stuff arrive, the jerseys, I mean?'

'All twenty-one of them. They're stacked in the corner over there. Will I put them in your car in case you forget them?'

'Thanks, if you don't mind. Do I have to make a speech?'

'I dunno. Mick Flannery will fill you in on the correct procedure. He's the expert where that sort of thing is concerned. Convenient that Pat Mullarkey is away in Dublin, isn't it?'

They both laughed. The rivalry between the two politicians was a source of endless amusement. Pat did everything by the book, slowly and surely. This ensured that whatever he achieved – be it planning permission or work permits for Abe and the two architects – was in perfect order. Mick, on the other hand, worked by arm-twisting and cajoling to find shortcuts through the tangled undergrowth of bureaucracy. While this proved quicker, it was often less reliable.

True to his word, Mick strolled into the Brulagh Inn on the stroke of two-thirty. 'Are ye both ready for the sporting occasion of the century?'

Divareli nodded but Aphra made her excuses. 'Sorry, but I can't make it. Too much to do back in the office. Someone has to mind the store.'

Mick appeared not to be unduly put out by her defection. 'I believe you, girl, when thousands wouldn't. Yerrah you're as well off . . .' he dropped his voice to a low, conspiratorial note '. . . because our shagging minor team wouldn't win an argument, not to mind a match. Mullarkey's supposed to be training them for God's sake. That man couldn't train ivy up a wall!'

On that confident note, they left in Divareli's car for the hurling pitch. St Fintan's GAA Park stood a short distance outside the town. Divareli already knew that GAA stood for Gaelic Athletic Association, the group that ran hurling and gaelic football in Ireland. He also knew that Mick Flannery was a legend in his own lifetime for winning four All-Ireland medals in succession. This was a feat comparable to Bobby Jones' impregnable quadrilateral of four golf Opens in the same year, and about as likely to be repeated. It had also laid the foundations for Mick's three decades in politics. To be fair, Mick never referred to it and looked genuinely embarrassed when someone brought the subject up in conversation. As they walked through the gates and approached the stand, Divareli noticed that it was called the Flannery Leisure Centre.

'What's with the Leisure Centre, Mick?' For a brief moment Divareli wondered if this were an embryo scheme to rival the B Project. Then he dismissed the notion as being too ridiculous by far.

'Ah, they had to call the new stand something so they called it after me. The Leisure bit is underneath. They have a hall which they use for social occasions like bingo and card games, as well as changing rooms and showers. And a bar, of course.'

142

'Of course,' Divareli chorused dutifully. It would have been too much to expect that sport could function without the lubricant of alcohol.

'Speaking of which, would you like a drink? We've a few minutes to spare before they start – just what we need to keep out the cold.' Mick gave a nod to a local worthy lounging beside a nondescript door that led in beneath the stand. The man produced a key from his pocket. A quick look round as he unlocked the door with a furtive air and they were inside. A short walk to another door which yielded its secrets to the same key and they were in a small, spartan bar.

Their guide slipped behind the counter and inquired, 'Well now, lads, what'll it be?'

Mick looked at Divareli and asked, 'Would a hot whiskey be all right?'

Divareli nodded and watched as the man did something with a small microwave oven and produced two steaming glasses in less time than it took him to ask of Mick, 'What do you think of our chances today?'

'Dunno. What're Ballybay like?'

'Nothing wrong with that lot, I can tell you. Mountainy lads the lot of them. I'd swear they live on a diet of broken glass and barbed wire. You played a fair few games agin 'em yourself in your day, Mick, so you did.'

Mick sighed as he inspected the hot whiskey approvingly before putting it to his lips. 'True enough, but my day wasn't today or yesterday, not by a long shot. Ballybay were always a team that would rather see you bleed than sweat. I warned my young lad to keep the ball on the ground. Those shaggers would murder their mothers for a high dropping ball. I hope to God Mullarkey told 'em the same before he left for Dublin.'

'Begor I don't think he did an' all. All I heard him telling them was for them to play their hearts out for the honour and glory of Brulagh. He told them if they had to lose, then let it be by fair means rather than foul.'

'Ah sweet Jaysus, you're codding me. Martin, my youngest, told me the same thing this very morning but I thought he was only trying to get a rise out of me. If they play the way Mullarkey told them, they'll be beaten out the bloody gate. Here, give us two more of those hot ones. No bird ever flew on one wing!'

As they were draining their glasses, the sound of a band warming up filtered in from outside. 'Time to go. We'll have to take our seats before the band parades in front of the stand. Remember to stand to attention and look serious when they play the National Anthem. You might even pretend you know the words if you want to make a good impression. Don't worry if you don't understand them. They're in Irish and most of the crowd haven't a clue what they mean either. You present the jerseys after the game. I'll do the talking unless you really want to say something?'

Divareli *had* wanted to say a few words, but the coolness of Mick's invitation made him change his mind. Divareli had thought this would be a good time to mention the Brulagh Project to the general public, but evidently Mick did not share his view. So be it, he thought as they made their way up the concrete steps that led to the seats in the stand. A section over the tunnel from whence the players emerged had been cordoned off for the Press. There appeared to be only one representative of the Fourth Estate, a small tubby man writing furiously in a spiral notebook. He greeted Mick in a curious sing-song accent.

'How's it goin', Mick? D'you tink we'll win today? I see by the team list that your young lad's the captain. Is he as good as his auld fella, would you say?'

Mick paused for a brief moment to answer the question before taking his place two rows back from the reporter and next to the Doc and Father Jerry. The Press Box also served as a VIP area. Right above the halfway line, it gave a perfect view of the whole pitch. Two tall uprights with a crossbar, just like that for American football, stood guard at either end of the playing surface.

'Who can tell, Charley, who can tell? Whatever lies you write about the match, though, be sure to give plenty of coverage to Mr Divareli here presenting the team with a new set of jerseys.'

Charley jumped out of his seat with alacrity. His voice took on an even higher pitch when he was excited. He made straight for Divareli with an outstretched hand. 'Nice to meet you, Mr Divareli. I've been trying to get an appointment to interview you but some lassie in your office keeps putting me off. Now that I have you in my hand, so to speak, will you give an exclusive interview to the *Clarion*?'

'Of course, Charley. Will we say eleven o'clock tomorrow morning, at my office?'

'Fine by me, Mr Divareli, sir. I wanted to ask you about an article old Daphne has sent to my editor. In it she says that your new golf-course will destroy some class of an orchid that she wants protected. In another bit, she quotes Joe Gallagher as saying that your marina will frighten away his swans . . .'

Before he could divulge any more, the band struck up *Amhrán na Gaeil*, the National Anthem. Divareli was so thunderstruck by what Charley had just said that it was well into the second verse before he started mouthing the words as instructed.

18

A whistle shrilled. The referee threw in the ball and battle commenced with the forwards of both teams attacking the ball, and each other, with slashing hurling sticks. The spectators lined the pitch, leaving the Flannery Stand barely half-full. As it faced into the wind, Divareli guessed it was warmer at ground-level. The biting wind sought out the smallest chink in his furry armour. He was glad of the hot whiskies, though their warming effects were being quickly dissipated by the strong Atlantic gale.

After the most cursory of greetings to priest and doctor, Divareli settled down to watch his first hurling match. After five minutes, two things were already abundantly clear. One was that hurling was a violent game in which assaults perpetrated anywhere else but on the field of play would have earned the aggressor a five to ten stretch in the Pen. It was a miracle that heads were not split open or fingers sliced off as the players fought for possession of the ball. The other thing was that Brulagh, as predicted by Mick, were being 'beaten out the gate'.

Roars of encouragement drifted up from those surrounding the pitch.

'Go on outa dat, Brulagh, and hurl the bloody ball!'

'For Jaysus sake will ye watch the ball and not the man!'

'Go on, young Flannery, show 'em a bit of class!'

'Will someone give the shaggin' referee a jersey and be done with it!'

Divareli had some difficulty in deciphering other instructions, always delivered at the top of the voice and with a sense of great urgency. 'Pull on it!' or 'Hook him quick before he gets away from you!'

Mick sat hunched in his seat, the picture of misery, saying absolutely nothing. He would groan every so often at a particularly poor effort by the Brulagh team. This usually preceded the opposition scoring again so that Mick's utterances took on a Cassandra-like quality for the home team.

One player on the Brulagh side stood out head and shoulders above the rest, in every sense. From the roars of, 'Come on, Flannery, get stuck into him for Jaysus sake!' Divareli gathered that he was Mick's offspring. Try as he might, young Flannery was unable to stem the tide. The Brulagh team seemed strangely listless and had no appetite for the contest. The Ballybay side, in stark contrast, were playing as if their lives depended on it. Small, wiry youngsters possessed of boundless energy, they swarmed all over the Brulagh defence.

Those around him seemed lost in their own thoughts. Father Jerry, wearing a heavy black overcoat, a thick woollen scarf and a fur hat of the type favoured by well-heeled Muscovites, looked to be far away in a world of his own. Had Divareli but known, the priest was furtively eyeing him from time to time as he reflected on the unexpected phone call he had received that very morning from Gianni Manolo Agostini – erstwhile Vatican troubleshooter and current shepherd of the tiny Boggola flock in deepest Tuscany.

There was a time when both Father Jerry and Agostini had been forces to reckon with, working as they did at the very heart of Vatican intrigue. When Divareli had let slip in the golf-club that his father was a friend of Marcinkus – and the one-time owner of Italbank – alarm bells reverberated inside the priest's head. It annoyed him that he could not pinpoint the precise reason for his disquiet. At the very end of his monthly letter to Agostini, Father Jerry mentioned Divareli's reference to Archbishop Marcinkus and Italbank. Now Agostini had replied with details on a Cesare Divareli who appeared to be Luke's father. However, it was what he had to say about his son that was of more immediate concern to Father Jerry. Put in its simplest terms it boiled down to this: Italbank was a sink of iniquity whose continued existence was only tolerated by the regulatory agencies in the US because its money-laundering activities provided useful leads for the Narcotics Bureau, among others, back to the dope smugglers and Mafia types who used its services to transform their ill-gotten gains into respectable bonds. Sophisticated and new-fangled bonds, it would appear, were the house speciality of Italbank.

The alchemist who had performed this modern equivalent of turning dross into gold was none other than the tall, good-looking American sharing some of Mick Flannery's agony at the inept display of the Brulagh Minor Hurling Team. By turning hot money into respectable property bonds of a much lower temperature, Divareli had created a financial instrument that enriched not only Italbank but lined his own pockets to the tune of many millions. The inevitable fly in the ointment was that the Securities and Exchange Commission harboured an intense dislike for this type of conjuring trick and were doing their damnedest to have it declared null and void. Should they succeed, Italbank would come tumbling down like a house of cards. And along with it would collapse the first real chance Brulagh had been offered of joining the twentieth century.

This, in turn, spawned yet another dilemma for the troubled cleric. Did Brulagh really want to join the twentieth century at all? Wrong question – 'kindly rephrase', as his old boss Cardinal Castelli would have put it. He wished he had Castelli's ear this minute. The crafty Milanese would have mapped out a Byzantine solution whereby the wrongdoers ended up penniless and in jail while Our Holy Mother the Church – and Brulagh – found themselves suddenly awash with newly-laundered and sweet-smelling dollars.

As Castelli could not be consulted, Father Jerry was going to have to wrestle with the problem all on his own. If he wanted to blow the entire B Project skyhigh and expose Divareli for what Agostini claimed he was – a cheap crook who made fortunes from recycling drug money – then Father Jerry had to look no farther than two rows down the stand. There in the person of Charley Halpin, sat the conduit whereby the news could be splashed across the local and national papers, and the whole scam exposed.

In a world full of moral dilemmas, Father Jerry consoled himself that one thing was sure and certain: Brulagh were having the daylights thrashed out of them. He shifted his gaze from Divareli to Mick Flannery to see how he was savouring the bitter cup of defeat. Not well, if one were to judge by the agonised expression on his face as he writhed uncomfortably on the hard bench.

Mick Flannery viewed the drama that was unfolding before him with growing unease. Brulagh weren't a bad team, it was just that they were employing the wrong tactics against a smaller, more physical side. Still and all, trailing by two goals and several points, the Brulagh side were like a lighthouse in a bog – brilliant but shagging useless! What they needed was a rip-roaring talk at half-time. But Mullarkey wasn't there and even if he were, he'd probably tell them poor little bastards that it was more important to compete fairly than to win!

Something had been irritating his mind ever since the match began and now he put his finger on it at last. The Brulagh side reminded him forcibly of the very last team he had captained before hanging up his boots: all class but no balls! The years rolled back as if by magic and he was once more treading on the hallowed turf of Croke Park, the Mecca of the GAA. The frantic voice of the commentator breathlessly informed a vast radio audience that with the All Ireland Hurling Final already into injury time, Mick Flannery's team were trailing by two points.

To make matters even worse, Mick had not played well in what surely must be his swansong. Perhaps he had been trying too hard and had lost that smooth, stylish rhythm that had once been such a feature of his play. Or maybe the sportswriters were right after all. *'Hurling's Dinosaur'* was one of the kinder comments that splashed across the Sports pages. He was too old for the game, or so they wrote, all of them except the *Clarion* and its fledgling reporter, Charley Halpin. Being the local paper it could do little else but support the local hero.

Whatever Charley's motives, Mick was grateful to him when the other scribes, once so fulsome in their praise, had thrown him to the wolves. In its last edition before the Final the *Clarion* proudly reminded its readers that Michael J. Flannery was the only native son of Brulagh to play for his country, much less bring home three All-Ireland medals in a row. That record alone should be sufficient to put him into the Hall of Fame.

Still and all, a fourth medal would have capped it all. It had never been done before . . . In a moment of vivid recall, he lived again the closing moments of that last agonising game when, purple-faced and lumbering like an elderly steam train, he had snatched victory from the jaws of defeat.

Now he was less than ten yards from goal. If only the bloody keeper would move off his line, Mick might, with luck, steer the ball past him and into the back of the net. But the cunning bastard had been around too long to fall for something like that. He waited on his line, crouched like a Sumo wrestler and watching every movement that Mick made.

149

Now Mick had to shoot. Any further delay and he would be caught up among the defenders in the goalmouth who would make short work of him. No referee in his right mind would ever award a penalty in the dying seconds of an All-Ireland Final. Especially if it were to alter the result. He might as well have signed his own death certificate! No, if a goal was to be scored, Mick would have to do it all on his own. Aiming for the left corner of the goal, too late Mick saw the goalkeeper coming off his line to block the shot. Mick's hurley met the ball with a familiar thud but the shot felt wrong, like a bad golf-shot. An electric shock surged up the shaft of the hurley, making his wrists tingle. Oh Mother of the Divine Jaysus, I've mishit the bloody thing!

Which he had. Instead of going to the left – where it almost certainly would have been saved by the goalkeeper, who had read his intentions as though they had been blazoned in giant, neon letters across Mick's forehead, the ball skidded gracelessly to the right. It had just enough impetus to find the net six inches inside the right goalpost. The Dinosaur of Brulagh had scored the winning goal in his last match.

Above the roar of the crowd Mick heard two welcome sounds that would live with him for the rest of his born days. One was the shrill peal of the full-time whistle. The other was the crack of the goalkeeper's stick being smashed in frustration against the offending goalpost.

Charley Halpin was sucking hard on a cheap plastic biro, trying to decide between 'stalwart' or 'tenacious' as the most suitable adjective to describe the futile efforts of the Brulagh defence, even though the match was but twenty minutes old. 'Hopeless' would have been the *mot juste* but the constraints of having to work among the citizens of Brulagh prevented him from telling the whole truth. Anyway, Charley consoled himself, it was early days yet, though it would require a miracle to save the home side.

When the whistle blew for the half-time interval the score had not changed. Young Flannery was still bearing the brunt of the attack, clearing his lines with difficulty and occasionally embarking on solo runs when none of his team-mates showed any interest in the ball. These forays invariably ended in a hurley cracking against his head or body, causing the ball to run free. Then it was scooped up by the other side and so the arduous process of fighting for it started all over again. The game was cursed with the inevitability of a Greek tragedy.

The oaths directed at the referee from the sideline seemed not to bother him in the least. He was one of the old school, who believed in letting the game run its course with the minimum of whistle-blowing. That his performance was being watched by one of hurling's living legends did not seem to worry him either. Mick was nudged out of his daydreaming by Father Jerry.

'I'm going to have a word with the team. Do you want to come with me?' He didn't. As far as Mick Flannery was concerned the game was a lost cause and the sooner it was over and done with, the better for all concerned. He would have to come up with a better excuse than that, however, to satisfy the troubled priest.

'I dunno. I don't think that Mullarkey would take kindly to my interfering in the running of his team.'

'Well, unless someone says something to the poor lads now during the interval, they're going to go into the record books as the Brulagh team with the biggest score run up against them for the past hundred years. And by Ballybay, their sworn enemies, to make matters even worse. You're the President of the club and I'm supposed to be the Chairman so we really must do something to help. Don't tell me you're going to stay sitting here on your backside while I have to think of something to say to them. They know I can't tell one end of a hurley from the other.'

Mick was looking at the seagulls wheeling against the evening sky. The horizon was tinged with red and it would be dark with the hour. The priest wasn't sure if he had Mick's attention as he pressed on.

'Look here, I'll tell you what we should do. I'll attend to the spiritual side of things by having a quick word with The Almighty if you promise to go down there and give them a bit of sensible advice. No one expects them to win but they might at least try to put a respectable look on the scoreboard before full-time. Come on, Mick, we'd be failing in our duty as officers of Fintan's GAA Club if we didn't do that much, at the very least.'

Mick grunted. 'I suppose you're right. But neither Mullarkey nor yourself are likely to approve of what I'm going to tell them.'

The priest grinned ruefully. 'Nothing to do with me, thanks be to God. I'll be well out of the way up here, trying to get the ear of the

Almighty so that He may look down with pity on the suffering children of Brulagh in their hour of trial!'

Mick made his excuses to the Doc and Divareli and scrambled down the concrete steps and out through the narrow iron gate that led on to the pitch. The Brulagh team were huddled in an unhappy group, chewing orange slices and arguing among themselves as to where the blame lay for their poor showing. When Martin saw his father striding through the gate, he strolled over to him with an anguished look.

'We seem to be having a bit of a problem in the midfield, Pa.'

'You can put that to music! You have problems in every part of your team, but it's a bit late in the day to start worrying about that now.'

'What'll we do so? Mullarkey told us to play our hearts out and go down fighting.'

'Yeah, well, maybe he's right about the fighting bit. But there's not much sign of heart in the team at the minute. Right now ye couldn't fight your way out of a paper bag. The Ballybay forward line is murdering ye. The Legion of Mary would do a better job against them than you lot. Their full forward has got so many presents of the shagging ball he must think Christmas has come early. He's been scoring all round him without as much as a finger being laid on him.'

'I know that, Pa, but how do we stop him?'

'Oh sweet Jaysus, give me patience! I never thought I'd see the day when a son of mine would ask a stupid question like that. You give him a good dig in the ribs with the butt of your hurley the next time he goes up for the ball, that's what you do. Even the dogs in the street know that much, for God's sake!'

'But Pa, if the referee sees me do that, he'll send me off for sure. Then Mullarkey will give out yards to me. More than likely he'll suspend me for the next three games as well. It'll be all over the *Clarion* and then what will Ma say?'

'Will you cop yourself on and act like a man? Can't you see that this is no time to be worrying your head about Mullarkey, your Ma or the bloody *Clarion*? As for the referee, don't go bothering yourself about him either. He's been in charge of more matches than you've had hot dinners. He's not about to start sending young lads off the field for a little thing like a belt from a hurley. You go off

152

about your business now and tell the rest of those idle shaggers on your team to start playing like men rather than little girls or it's a set of nappies, not jerseys they'll be getting from Divareli after the game!'

As he left the pitch, the referee was gnawing pensively at an orange section. Mick sidled up beside him and muttered in a low tone, almost without moving his lips, 'I think our side might be playing a bit different in the second half. You won't mind, will you?'

'No, Mick, I won't mind in the least.' The referee was gazing at something of interest above the roof of the stand as he finished, 'It's about time someone had a word with them. I was afraid I'd lose track of the score if Ballybay ever got properly into their stride!' With that he made for the centre spot on the halfway line and blew the whistle to start the second half.

Within a minute, the lanky Ballybay full forward realised that he was in a different game. Fielding a high ball at full stretch he was struck simultaneously by two Brulagh defenders. One drove the butt of his hurley into the space between his third and fourth ribs. The other, a puny youth whose only public display of aggression thus far had been to pick his nose defiantly as the game swirled round him, swung his hurley like an axe at the ankles of the still airborne player with such venom that the stick broke in half. Brulagh conceded a further point from the resulting free to put them two goals and five points behind.

On the plus side, however, it was noticeable that the centre forward seemed to have lost all appetite for the game and was content to rest on the laurels he had earned in the first half. This process was repeated five or six times in rapid succession to other prominent players in the opposing forward line. Since the first free there had been no change in the score but the balance of play had shifted slowly but surely to the home side. Martin rallied his forwards with commendable zeal and a long period of unremitting pressure by Brulagh on a now thoroughly intimidated opposition left them trailing by just two points when the final whistle sounded. Honour – if not the day – had been saved. Whether Pat Mullarkey would have agreed had he actually witnessed the encounter rather than read about it in Charley Halpin's purple prose some days later was open to question. As for Father Jerry, he was heard to describe the resurgence of the Brulagh Minors as the greatest comeback since Lazarus.

The presentation of the jerseys took place in front of the stand immediately after the cessation of hostilities. A section of the Ballybay supporters in the crowd chose to voice their dissatisfaction at the way in which Brulagh played the second half by heckling Mick's opening remarks, but this did not appear to trouble the orator in the least as he put his arm round Divareli and introduced him to the throng packed like sardines round the entrance to the dressing rooms.

'*Ah Chord-dew Gale*, my good friends, today it is both my privilege and pleasure to introduce you to the man who is going to put Brulagh on the map – Luke Divareli. Like many before him, Divareli has come from a distant land but in a short time has become more Irish than the Irish themselves . . .' Here Mick paused for breath while Divareli drew hard on his cigarette and leered at the masses with an inane grin intended to convey the soulful, slightly wistful mien of the true philanthropist.

A heckler saw his chance and roared at Mick: 'What about the fish processing factory by the pier or Japanese microchip . . .'

He was drowned out by angry shouts of, 'Tell him be quiet!' and 'Throw the shagger out!' Whether these were intended for Mick or his persecutor remained unclear.

Mick looked in the general direction of the interruption and said in a matter-of-fact tone, 'Yerrah can't you let the poor eejit alone. Don't we all know that they only let him out for a half an hour every day while they're cleaning his cage . . .'

This had the dual effect of silencing the heckler and causing a ripple of good-natured laughter to replace the friction between winners and losers.

'Now, some of you may have already heard of the great plans Divareli has for Brulagh. As they are still in the early stages I can only say at this point in time that they will mean wealth and prosperity for every man, woman and child in this area. That, I need hardly tell you, includes our good friends and neighbours from Ballybay . . .'

This raised a ragged cheer and some half-hearted clapping. The heckler had either retired to lick his wounds or been advised to remain silent.

154

'At this stage I must congratulate them on their fine win today
. . .', renewed clapping and cheering, this time of a more enthusiastic
nature, '. . . though to be fair to our own lads, in the heel of the hunt
Ballybay only barely scraped home against a good Brulagh team!'

This time the air was filled whoops and roars, each set of supporters finding something to applaud in the skilful phrasing. When
some semblance of calm had been restored Mick pressed home his
advantage.

''Twas many a match I played against the men of Ballybay myself
and, fair dues to them, win lose or draw I always found them to be
gentlemen both on and off the field.'

By now the reaction bordered on pandemonium. It dawned on
Divareli that Mick was not just an excellent mob orator but that he
was also carefully massaging the electorate.

'However I know my friends and neighbours from the next parish
will understand if I direct my closing words at the men of Brulagh.
Oh yes, when I say men I mean it – because today they truly came
of age and played like real *men* . . .' This time the wall of noise
threatened to engulf them, and Mick fought to make himself heard
above the racket. 'At least, that's true of the second half anyway!'

This caused loud guffaws, and some unprintable comments. Mick
put on a spurt. 'So in conclusion I just want to say a heartfelt thank
you to Mr Divareli for the grand set of jerseys he has donated to
the Brulagh players. I now call on my son Martin as captain of the
losing team to give three cheers for the gallant winners and also for
the generosity of my friend here . . .' Again he wrapped an arm
around Divareli in a friendly bearhug before ending with, 'Mister
Luke Divareli!'

The cheers were still ringing in their ears as they made their way
down from the stand and slipped once more into the now crowded
bar almost directly beneath where they had been sitting.

19

Right on the stroke of eleven o'clock, Charley Halpin was tapping on the frosted glass of Divareli's office door, bearing an article submitted by Deaf Aunt Daphne, written in the form of a letter – and a long one at that. Divareli read it through.

Dear Editor
It may have escaped your notice that work is about to commence on transforming the dune land by Brulagh Harbour into a luxury resort, complete with golf-course, enormous hotel and marina. This will wipe out the Bee Orchids, Natterjack Toads and Whooper Swans. Why must progress always be at the expense of endangered species such as these? As I am aware that space in your excellent newspaper is at a premium, I will be as brief as possible and confine my remarks to one of the rarest plants in existence; Ophrys Fuciflora *– the Bumble Bee Orchid. This rare species grows on the Brulagh sand-dunes and nowhere else that I know of on this island. It survives by making itself look like a bee. The real bee buzzes around the plant and settles on what it imagines to be the female but is, in fact, the orchid. Being an excitable male, he copulates enthusiastically with the flower and carries pollen from one flower to another, thereby cross-fertilising them. However, the idiot soon discovers his error and transfers his affections to the real thing. This makes the fertilisation of the Bee Orchid an uncertain exercise at the best of times. If that weren't enough, its life cycle cannot begin until the dune turf builds up enough humus to support the growth of fungi. While most other plants store enough food to germinate within a matter of days, these orchids take several years before the germinated seed sprouts its first leaves. Even then a large percentage of those that do flower will have died off long before they get a chance to reproduce. The rare ones that do reproduce are therefore to be treasured. It is scarcely surprising, therefore, that this beautiful wild flower is included in the EC Wildlife Protected Species List!*

I pen this letter in the hope that it will alert your many readers to this serious threat to the environment on their own doorsteps. The fact that the Minister for the Environment, Patrick Mullarkey, is a native son must surely have some bearing on the granting of planning permission. I would point out that while Tourism is an important element in our country's economy, it should not be so sacrosanct that entrepreneurs can stampede roughshod over the delicate eco-systems of our foreshore. Generations to come will not thank us for destroying our natural heritage in exchange for a golf-course – especially as we already have a perfectly good one. Unlike the proposed new course, the existing one not only provides pleasure for golfers but also a safe haven for mountain sheep in time of inclement weather!

Yours indignantly
Daphne Fitzgerald-Gallerick

Having read it through, Divareli looked closely at Charley. 'Is your editor going to print that?'

'As far as I know, that's his intention. It is, after all, a matter of public interest.'

'It certainly is. I had no idea that the place was a kind of wildlife sanctuary. Why the hell didn't someone tell me before now?'

When Charley made no effort to answer the question, Divareli continued, 'I can appreciate the lady's concern and I can guarantee that those species she mentioned will be protected to the very best of our ability. The problem right now is that we already have outline permission to go ahead with the project. We have been virtually guaranteed full planning permission but that won't come through for another month or so. If we wait that long we miss all our deadlines and finish up shit creek. As well as that, the delay could have us miss out on those EC grants which would make the whole project a dead duck – or should I say swan?' Neither of them laughed at the feeble attempt at levity.

'What do you want me to do?' Charley's voice was already ascending the scales to ever higher notes of concern.

'Well, you're going to have to print that damn letter, I suppose. Freedom of the press and all that sort of thing. But you're gonna have to give me the right of reply and print it right next to Daft Daphne or whatever the hell you call her.'

'That's fine, no problem there. Just what I want, in fact. Why don't we do it in the form of an interview?'

'That sounds fine by me. Now?'

'This minute, if I'm to get it in this week's edition.'

In pursuance of the time-honoured policy of the Clarion *in affording 'the right of reply', the following is the text of an interview conducted between Mr Luke Divareli and our reporter, Charley Halpin.*

'Now that you have read the letter, what are your reactions?'

'Well, Charley, I have quite a few as it happens. Let me say at the outset that this is the first I have heard of the three species the lady mentions as being endangered.'

'So what have you to say to her – and our readers – that might set their minds at rest?'

'It seems to me that what we need here is a second opinion. If the lady wishes, she is free to select her own environmentalist to make a full, scientific report on the project and its likely impact on the sand-dunes. As for my side of things, I will ask the Department of the Environment to run their ruler over what we are doing here. If it is found that our proposal will in any way harm the environment, then we will take whatever steps are necessary to ensure that the orchids, toads and swans are properly protected, possibly setting aside a designated area where they can continue to survive in the wild state, undisturbed.'

'Who will pay for all this?'

'I will.'

'And in the meantime, what happens?'

'Oh, the work goes ahead, of course. I intend to set up a company that will manage the entire project. It will be headed up by some local personalities though Abe Linovitz and I will have a small stake in that company. This means that control of the project will rest with the board – most of whom will be local people!'

'What about the EC grants?'

'They only come into play on completion. There is a possibility that they may not be available for much longer, which is why we put in our application at the earliest possible moment, and why we want to get started now rather than wait for better weather in the spring of next year.'

Father Jerry looked out on row after row of empty chairs. He had offered to open the Community Centre in good time for the meeting. As he waited for the first arrivals he tried hard to collect his thoughts.

After several sleepless nights, the priest was still undecided as to his best course of action. To confront Brulagh's benefactor with his murky past could cause Divareli to shake the dust of the village from his feet and seek elsewhere to invest his money, while Pat Mullarkey would require stronger evidence than a mere phone-call from an elderly cleric. As for warning Tom Donnelly, that would just be a waste of time. The man was sporting a grin on his face that stretched from ear to ear. Mick Flannery couldn't care less where the money came from, Charley Halpin would plead a timid editor as his excuse for spiking the story, and Gus Moriarty could do nothing until a crime had been committed within his jurisdiction.

Or could it be that Pat Mullarkey had had second thoughts? It was he who had suggested a public meeting to discuss Divareli's plan – thus providing an opportunity for people to hear exactly what was going on from the lips of the man responsible for the project. Then those who might have objections to the plan could air their views. Indeed, he was rumoured to be under pressure from his own Department. Here in Brulagh, Mullarkey must appear supportive of anything that would boost the local economy, but he would also have to pay heed to his environmental role.

Unless the meeting rejected the idea by a clear majority, it would be assumed that there were no serious objections and full planning permission would be granted as a matter of course. Thus, Mullarkey would be fireproofed. If the people were for it, so was he. If not, well, democracy had won the day and Brulagh would have to wait for another fairy godmother. The Press, in the person of Charley Halpin, would be present to record the proceedings for posterity.

Then there was Joe Gallagher. His fishing and guesthouse business would be affected by the marina – and what about his swans? He would not be drawn on the matter, however, and nor would a lot of other people. Sean Flannery, for instance. Would he view the project as a threat or a godsend to his business? Timothy Houlihan was another who was sure to have strong views on the subject but nobody knew what they were. Mick Flannery, of course, was the exception. Everyone knew where he stood on the matter. After all, this was the realisation of all those promises he had been making to the voters of Brulagh down through the years. To any suggestion that Divareli's dollars might be tainted, Mick would reply that one man's money was as good as another's. Already it was being whispered that he was on a hefty retainer from the Yank.

The hall was beginning to fill up though the stage where Father Jerry was sitting in solitary splendour behind a long table and facing out into the hall was still empty. Meetings of the Development Committee were usually held in the front room of the Doc's house, as were those of the myriad other organisations which, as Parish Priest, he was *ex officio* Chairman. When he had first arrived from Rome, he could not see what all this had to do with saving souls, especially his own. It had taken some time to realise that his main task was that of social worker and unpaid convenor of meetings. Jobs that no-one else would touch with a forty-foot bargepole were his by right. It amused him when he read that priests in Ireland had their finger in every pie. Announcements off the altar invariably concerned bingo sessions and meetings of various associations to be held during the coming week. Those even remotely connected with religion could be counted on the fingers of one hand. It was something one just had to get used to, like Julia May's cooking.

His superiors in Rome had sent him back to Ireland to die. *Ulcerative colitis* was incurable but, given a stress-free life and plenty of food and exercise, it could be held at bay for many years. At first Julia May stood beside him, arms folded and watching him swallow every morsel. Now he was four stone heavier and she no longer supervised his every bite. He needed a three mile walk every day just to keep his weight down to that level. The walk also allowed him to read his daily office, a chore to be sure but nothing as tiresome as the one he was about to perform. At his back stood a large flip chart, balanced precariously on an easel which was bathed in a spotlight provided by the Amateur Dramatic Society. They too had found a new benefactor. Divareli had presented them with a new lighting system. Father Jerry was among the first to hear of it because he was Chairman of that society too, though his input had rarely gone beyond recommending that for their next production it might be wiser to stage something less ambitious than a four hour production of *Antigone*.

From his lonely perch, Father Jerry spied the Doc seated near the back of the hall, strategically placed for a quick exit. The chairs were of tubular steel with wooden strips for the seat and back support attached to the frame with rivets. Some of these had either worked loose or fallen out, making their movement a noisy business. Still no sign of Divareli or Linovitz, not to mention the other two supposed to share the platform, Pat Mullarkey and Mick Flannery. Of late they seemed to have patched up their differences. Mick's apparent reluctance to offer advice to the junior hurling team was but one example of his newfound sensitivity to the feelings of his onetime foe.

Father Jerry wished he could make up his mind about Divareli and his plans. There was a time when he would have prayed to his Maker for guidance, but not now. Age had diminished rather than increased his faith in a merciful God who would intervene in the affairs of mankind. If He could manage to stand aside from famine, pestilence, torture and war, it was unlikely that He would intervene to guide His servant, Jeremiah O'Sullivan, through this particular minefield.

From the back of the hall the Doc watched the foursome approach the stage – the two politicians followed by the familiar figures of Divareli and Abe Linovitz. His thoughts echoed those of Father Jerry. For him, however, there would be no agonising – Brulagh was just fine the way it was. His practice was anything but frenetic, allowing him to indulge in golf, fishing, fowling and fox-hunting as the fancy took him. Most of his patients were elderly and required regular attention. Their treatment involved listening sympathetically rather than plying them with the latest miracle of modern medicine. They rarely paid in cash, opting instead for a system of medieval barter. He had a freezer bulging with pheasant, salmon, trout, bass, geese and turkeys – all for services rendered. In the basement, cunningly hidden under an old blanket, were four cases of poteen – payment for visits to the Slattery household on the slopes of Mount Brulagh. As a doctor he could scarcely recommend it as a cure for all ills, nevertheless by putting sloes into the bottles to steep for a year or so it developed into a passable liqueur. For the elderly he used it as an embrocation and found it just as effective as the proprietary rubs. After a good hunt, such as the one where the Yank had finished up in the Black Trench with Deaf Daphne, he would use it to rub down his horse.

Johnny Slattery had approached him, worried that hordes of tourists would mean an increase in police activity. Even now, Johnny insisted, he was under so much pressure from Gus that it was affecting his nerves. Sergeant Moriarty was the bane of the bootlegger's life. Though he had yet to find the still, hardly a month passed without Johnny's farm and the surrounding area being raided. The most intensive searching had failed to turn up anything more incriminating than a few bags of potatoes, some barley and several stalks of rhubarb. Though all these were ingredients for the manufacture of poteen, of themselves they did not provide sufficient evidence for a conviction. Johnny, therefore, would oppose Divareli even though he could not reveal the true reason behind his objection.

Daphne would feel no such restraint. The fact that she was deaf as a post would ensure that the scurrilous comments being passed behind her back as she launched into the life and times of the flora and fauna of the sand-dunes would go unheeded.

As President of the Brulagh Golf Club and its sixty-three members, the Doc wondered if he should view the arrival of a de luxe version on their doorstep as a threat. In fact he didn't. The old Clubhouse badly needed a new roof and the fairway mower was falling to bits. Any influx of golfers from Divareli's resort would help pay to replace these items. The only snag was that some of them might take six hours or more to complete a round of golf. Well, so what? he asked himself. Hardly anyone played on the damn course anyway except at weekends. For the rest of the time, Divareli's golfers could take as long as they damn well liked to hack their way round the old course. Just so long as they paid for the privilege and kept away from the place on Saturdays and Sundays. Yes, that was it! Let the visitors use the old course much as skiers used 'nursery slopes' to find their feet before venturing on to the more difficult runs . . .

As Father Jerry was about to start the proceedings, Divareli felt surprisingly nervous. He had a feeling of being watched by a sceptical yet courteous jury, who would hear him out and then retire to consider their verdict. It was as if their final decision would depend on his performance tonight. An air of indecision hovered about them, as tangible as the dense pall of tobacco smoke.

Father Jerry broke off from adding to the pollution by removing the huge, curved meerschaum pipe from his mouth and tapping it

162

carefully against the ashtray to get the attention of the gathering. Stiffly rising to his feet, the priest cleared his throat and called the meeting to order.

'Good evening, everyone. I'm glad to see we have a good crowd here tonight because this could be the most important meeting ever held in this hall. As you all must know by now, Mr Divareli . . .' he waved vaguely in the direction of the two Americans '. . . and his colleague Mr Linovitz have big plans for our village. Their technical drawings for a holiday complex on our foreshore are on permanent display at the back of the hall. Everyone should examine them closely as this might be the last chance you'll get to air your views. The plans have been filed with the EC in Brussels where approval for them is expected any day now. My duties as Chairman are to remain impartial and run an orderly meeting. In a moment we will have a quick word from Mick Flannery and Pat Mullarkey, but first I must remind you that the purpose of this meeting is to hear from as many of you as possible and then try to form a consensus. Only in that way will we find out what the majority want. Every man, woman and child here has a right to say what they think. There is not one among us whose life will not be touched – for better or worse – by this proposal.' He paused to let his words sink in and then continued, 'I now call on Mick Flannery to say a few words. Then Pat Mullarkey will address you briefly before Mr Divareli takes over.'

There was a smattering of applause. Divareli was not sure whether this was for the priest or in anticipation of what the two politicians were about to say. In fact they said very little. Mick, as was to be expected, gave the project his wholehearted support and encouraged everyone else to do likewise. Pat Mullarkey was more guarded, pointing out that the environment would have to be protected, but ending by giving the project his qualified blessing.

Now it was Divareli's turn. He opened with a detailed outline of the whole project. Drawings of the hotel-cum-indoor leisure centre, the marina and the golf-course were thrown up on a screen at his back. Abe operated the slide projector and fielded technical questions about bore-holes for the foundations, the amount of topsoil required for the fairways and the number of piles that would have to be sunk in the harbour to erect the walkways for the marina. His answers impressed everyone, including Divareli. Abe had proved

163

that he could put on an expletive-free act when the occasion demanded.

When Divareli ended his presentation, he invited questions. After a brief lull in which feet shuffled and papers rustled like leaves, Daphne struggled to her feet. The space between the seats was cramped, and meant that anyone wishing to stand had to push their chair backwards, scraping it noisily along the floor and rapping those behind painfully on the knees. Daphne wore a crumpled hat of soft tweed jammed firmly down on her head. A heavy scarf was tucked inside a very old jacket secured at her navel by an overworked button. Perhaps because of her previous encounter with Divareli she wore baggy trousers rather than a skirt. The overall effect was that she had swopped garments with a scarecrow *en route* to the meeting. She chose to address the audience rather than the platform.

'As you all know, I'm deaf as a post so I didn't hear one blasted word he said. That does not prevent me from having my say as I saw the plans up on that picture thing and I have read this piece of paper . . .', here she waved the publicity handout aloft, '. . . in which I had hoped to find some reference to conservation, but sadly there was none. It is now crystal clear that the Bee Orchid, the Natterjack Toad and a myriad other species – not to mention Joe Gallagher's poor swans – are doomed if Mr What's-his-name gets his way.'

She then launched into a replay of her dinner-party spiel which was similar to the letter she had written to the *Clarion*. It took a good twenty minutes before she brought her remarks to a close with: 'I appeal to my good friends in Brulagh to reject this reckless scheme until its promoters can give us firm guarantees as to the safety of these endangered species. As things stand, they are certain to perish under the onslaught of those horrid bulldozers and the hordes of tourists we are led to believe will follow.'

It was over. There was no applause. All round the hall, people jerked awake from their private dreams. They had heard her party piece so often that they could recite it word for word. Father Jerry thanked her loudly for getting the ball rolling, then asked were there any other questions.

The Eleventh Earl of Gallerick uncoiled himself from his seat, coughed to clear his throat and brayed from the back of the hall, 'I would like to ask Mr Divareli two questions. How exactly is this thing being funded, and will there be any spin-off effects for local sporting facilities?'

Divareli, alerted by Aphra, was expecting that one but elected to answer Daphne first. 'Before I talk money, I would like to reply to the previous speaker,' he bellowed. 'I can guarantee everyone here tonight, including the Minister for the Environment, that all possible precautions will be taken to protect the species mentioned. Indeed, it is our intention to seek the advice of the Minister and his officials as to the best means of not only preserving the flora and fauna, but of nurturing it to the extent that the whole foreshore will become one vast wildlife preserve. Funds have already been allocated for this and we would welcome any assistance the lady speaker could give us in this matter. As promoters of the project, Abe and I fully realise that a wildlife preserve would enhance, rather than hinder, our plans for the area. As a lasting reminder to us all of the importance of this, I propose to call our development "the Orchid Project" . . .'

A smattering of applause, initiated by Mick Flannery, gave Divareli the chance to catch his breath before pressing on. 'Now, as for his Lordship's questions, the answer to the first one is that I am putting up the money out of my own resources. If anyone has any doubts as to my creditworthiness, I think Mr Donnelly of your local bank will be able to reassure them on that score. As to the question of spin-offs for local sporting facilities, I assume his Lordship is thinking of fox-hunting. I'm sure that many of our guests would welcome the opportunity, as I have done, to hunt with one of the finest packs in the country, and that this could be included in our programme of activities. Any more questions?'

Another long pause followed, complete with more shuffling of feet and rustling of papers. Then Sean Flannery rose.

'I would like to know something of the prospects for local employment. As things stand, our young people are leaving in droves to seek work abroad. How many jobs does the speaker envisage during the construction phase, and how many permanent ones will be available to local people when the project is up and running?'

Divareli turned to Abe and said, 'Abe, that's one for you. I can answer the second part and say that somewhere between thirty and forty permanent, all-year-round jobs will be available on the day we open for business. Between now and then the National Training Authority will be running courses in this hall, so that we will have fully qualified, local staff available to us from day one. Again I have to congratulate both our politicians here tonight for setting this up so quickly. As for jobs on the construction sites, I'll let Abe Linovitz answer that.'

Abe got to his feet. His right leg had gone to sleep and he wished he could have joined it. So far this meeting had a maximum yawn factor. He tucked his shirt inside his belt, hiked up his slacks and replied in the broadest Bronx accent, 'Hiring, as you probably know, has already started. When work begins on the hotel site, we plan to use sub-contractors who will be told to hire locally. Any of you with friends or relations in the building trade should let them know that there is steady work available here at full union rates. Total workforce on the hotel construction will vary but it should never be less than thirty at any time. We are particularly interested in bricklayers, carpenters, plumbers and plasterers. So to answer your question, in the initial phase the overall jobs figure for a minimum of one year will swing between fifty-five and a hundred. OK?'

Sean nodded and sat down again, as did Abe Linovitz. Timothy Houlihan was on his feet, waving his hand to get the attention of the Chairman. He dived straight in without any preliminaries.

'How do we know for sure if this will be of any lasting benefit to the ordinary people of Brulagh?'

It was news to his listeners that he included himself in this category. He had always considered himself a cut above the rest. A stint at boarding school followed by a year at university had given him a superiority complex, which was reflected by his stance next to the radiator rather than taking a seat with the rest of the audience.

'I myself have stayed in several resorts of the type I imagine is planned by these two, and in every instance, I might as well have been on a cruise liner for all I saw of the ordinary people. Sure we went sightseeing, but from an air-conditioned bus. We stopped only at places selected by the resort operator. Souvenirs, trinkets, a bit of traditional dancing to take care of the cultural aspect and that was it. An over-priced drink or two, five minutes for a photo-opportunity and then back to the resort. We might as well have come from outer space for all the locals saw of us or vice versa. As for boosting the local economy – forget it. Sure, there might have been low-grade staff recruited thereabouts, but the good jobs were imported from outside. We spent damn-all locally because the complex provided everything we needed. And I'll tell you something else – you can bet your life that the profits we generated were transferred to some nice little offshore account . . .'

At this point Father Jerry raised his eyes to Divareli, signalling the unspoken query: 'Do you want me to stop him?' It wasn't that the priest disagreed with what was being said, but rather the manner of its saying. To be honest, much of what Houlihan said had been at the back of his own mind. It was just that he could not think of any tactful way of posing the question without insulting the promoters or infringing the impartiality expected from a Chairman. To his relief, Divareli shook his head ever so slightly. So be it. A shrewd move, in the priest's view. Give someone like Houlihan enough rope and he was certain to hang himself. This he now proceeded to do.

'. . . which brings me to the questions I would like to ask of the promoters of this ill-conceived scheme. Question number one is, where does the money come from to pay for all this? I heard, along with the rest of you, that Divareli is putting up his own money and that our own Tom Donnelly is reputed to be quite happy with the arrangements. I notice, incidentally, that the banker in question is not with us tonight. Be that as it may, it still doesn't answer the basic question of where the money is coming *from*. I, for one, would like to know how and where he made it before he tells us how he now proposes to spend it. Question number two relates to the profits. Will they be transferred back to America or stashed away in some cosy little offshore bank on a Caribbean island that no one has ever even heard of?'

As Houlihan was speaking, mutterings of 'Shut him up, for God's sake' and 'Who the hell does he think he is, talking like that?' could be heard from different parts of the hall. Father Jerry nodded to Divareli who, sensing the mood of the meeting, ignored Houlihan's rudeness and concentrated on answering his questions.

'I'm glad you asked me about the effect our development will have on the village. One of the main features we will emphasise in the marketing of the Orchid Project is the friendliness of the local

167

people. Having experienced it myself, I don't intend keeping it a secret from our guests. To answer your original question, Mr Houlihan, I know that our guests will want to mix with everyone in the village, sightsee, drink in the pubs, watch your sports, go to the races, fox-hunt and participate in anything else that may take their fancy. They will be in the higher income bracket and, for the most part, aged over forty. For those of you who may be interested, there will be many opportunities to service their needs. I am thinking of things like limousine hire, pony-trekking, deepsea angling, escorted shooting and fishing trips, that kind of thing. As for how I made my money, well, that's an easy one. Hard work – plain, old-fashioned hard work. You should try it yourself some time. Does that answer your questions?'

Houlihan was back on his feet. From his expression it was unclear whether he had finished his diatribe or was merely gathering strength for a further onslaught. An air of expectancy hovered over the audience like a giant bird. By now there were few who doubted that his hostility was caused by the threat apparently posed to the Gallerick Arms Hotel. It was also becoming clear that a growing section of the crowd, except for the riffraff at the very back of the hall, did not approve of his aggressive approach. There were suggestions – some of them loud enough to reach the platform – that he should be ejected from the meeting forthwith. Much as Father Jerry might dislike Houlihan's rudeness, however, as Chairman he could only request the hotelier to moderate the tone of his comments. So with Agostini's warnings ringing in his ears, he was content to watch as Houlihan continued with his ill-tempered remarks.

'Well, it answers one of my questions though, frankly, we all know that talk is cheap. I'll believe what you have said about the tourists mixing with us locals when I see it – and not before then. I have a man here with me tonight . . .' as yet no one could establish the identity of the mystery witness since he declined to stand, preferring to remain seated and therefore hidden from all but those next to him '. . . who claims that he owns the land on which you are going to build. Long before Columbus discovered your country, there was a McCarthy Castle overlooking Brulagh Harbour. That noble clan ruled the land for miles around until the Saxon invader drove them out to roam the four corners of the earth and . . .'

Whatever flight of fancy Houlihan was about to take off on was interrupted by a roar from behind him. The gaunt figure of Long Tom McCarthy was gesticulating violently, and banging a heavy blackthorn stick against the steel frame of his chair.

''Tis not a word of a lie that the McCarthys were driven out by the foreigner and that sham squires now live like kings on the same land my ancestors fought for at the point of a sword . . .'

Father Jerry had heard this saga several times before. It proved beyond doubt that Long Tom was dangerously drunk and once more about to declare war on foreigners of every stripe but especially the Gallerick family. That it had been at least five centuries since the last of the McCarthy tribe had lived in what was now nothing more than a heap of rubble did not concern the speaker. Neither did he accept that his admission of the castle being won and lost at the point of the sword in any way weakened his claim to it a half a millennium later.

'So bejaysus if anyone thinks that Long Tom is goin' to stand aside and let another crowd of foreigners drive him off what was once rightfully his, then they had better think again. I took the gun to shaggers like that before and I'll do so again.'

During his outburst, some elements from the back of the hall had been egging him on with shouts of 'Go on Tom, you tell 'em' and 'Aha ya boy ya, McCarthy, I wouldn't doubt ya!' Divareli was pondering on how best to counter this while praying that Long Tom had not brought along the gun which had played such a major role in their dealings to date. Perhaps the Chairman had been thinking along the same lines for he shot an inquiring glance at Divareli as though to ask 'Would you like me to call a halt to the proceedings?' Before they could decide the matter was taken out of their hands in dramatic fashion. Long Tom had drifted, unnoticed, towards the back of the hall where his most vocal supporters lurked. Prepared for just such an eventuality, one of them had smuggled his gun into the hall. Suddenly Long Tom, still roaring like a bull, was waving it around in a threatening manner. Someone next to him tried to wrest it away and this caused the barrel to jerk upwards. As it did so, the gun went off with an impressive bang. A shower of plaster fell from a gaping hole in the ceiling, covering those below with a fine white coating of dust, but missing Long Tom, who had made his escape during the shocked silence that followed.

169

This was shortlived. With a noise that jerked everyone in the hall back to their senses, Father Jerry banged his pipe hard against the big glass ashtray beside the microphone and in as steady a voice as he could manage, declared the meeting adjourned *sine die*.

20

When the crowd had dispersed hurriedly, the stage was left to Father Jerry and the two promoters. Divareli gathered up his notes while Abe folded away the projector and put the flip chart into a big leather case.

'How would you rate that meeting, Father?'

The priest abandoned his efforts to salvage his pipe. 'I thought it went rather well except for the end, of course. Long Tom McCarthy is quite mad and should be packed off to an asylum before he does some real harm. I was surprised at Timothy Houlihan – though he may have a hidden agenda. At least you got the opportunity to explain your plans to the people and tell them the sort of money that's involved. Are you really using all your own capital?'

Divareli eyed the priest warily. 'Yes, of course. Like I said, I raise the money in New York in my own name and channel it through to the bank here as required. We will be setting up a holding company in Brulagh. That will give everyone a chance to participate fully in the project and have a say in what goes on. Right now Abe and I are inviting prominent local people to join the board. Would you like to be the first?'

'Indeed I would regard it as an honour but unfortunately canon law does not allow me to join a private company.' Father Jerry sighed to indicate his regret and hoped that Divareli was not familiar with the rules of priesthood – which had no such strictures as far as he was aware.

He need not have worried. Divareli had made the offer out of courtesy and without thinking, and had regretted it the moment it was out of his mouth. He was much relieved when the offer was graciously declined. The cleric seemed to be a curious type, likely to poke his nose into matters that did not concern him, like Gally's come-uppance, the blueprint for which was not yet completed. To be effective, it had to be secret – even Abe must not be in on it.

Aphra presented a further complication. Her father would have to be dealt with in a way that would attach no blame to Divareli. Anyone who called him a jumped-up Dago had it coming to him, and the Eleventh Earl of Gallerick was no exception. Divareli must take great care in exacting his revenge, however, so that Aphra would never know it was he who had planned the old reprobate's downfall. If she ever found out the truth, Divareli would inevitably lose her, and that was unthinkable, for he longed for her more than ever. Whether this was because their relationship remained unconsummated, or not, he did not care to consider. She filled his thoughts day and night. He was besotted.

'That's OK, Father,' he replied airily. 'I quite understand. It's just that we don't want anybody to feel left out of this thing. I was thinking of asking the Earl of Gallerick to head up the holding company. What do you think?'

Father Jerry tried to sound enthusiastic. Gallerick's previous business ventures all had one thing in common – abject failure. Yet the Orchid Project might well be his last chance to restore the fortunes of a fading dynasty. With Divareli and Linovitz overseeing his every move, his margin for error must surely be reduced to a point where success was at least a possibility, however remote. With Mick Flannery a virtual certainty to be on the board, Gallerick's title would be an added bonus.

'Yes, I think that's an excellent idea. Will you be starting work on the golf-course soon?'

'Oh yes, I think so. We have the preliminary permission from the planning authorities and I got the impression that the majority of those here tonight were solidly behind the project. Would you agree?'

'Difficult to say when we didn't have a show of hands. That McCarthy fellow is capable of anything when he has drink taken. I gather you have experience of that already?'

Divareli laughed as he made his way down the wooden steps that led from the stage to the floor of the hall. Already Abe Linovitz was striding purposefully towards the exit.

Father Jerry waited for the two Americans to leave before he sidled up so quietly to Charley Halpin that it gave the reporter quite a start.

'Oh 'tis yourself, Father. Now that you're here I suppose there's no chance of getting an exclusive interview about the Orchid Project?'

172

'You're right, as usual, Charley. How did the rest of the interviews go?'

'Yerrah most of the people I talked to seemed to think it was about time for the village to have the few quid spent on it. Naturally enough, they'll believe what the Yank says when they see it. After all of Mick Flannery's promises I suppose 'tis hard to blame them. Anyway, the most of them think your man the Yank is a decent skin and what he said about the jobs impressed most of them.'

The priest nodded absently, drew his coat about his shoulders and headed out into the dark night.

Divareli switched on the lights and closed the office door behind them. While Abe put away the projector and screen in the cupboard, he made for the filing cabinet and pulled out a bottle of Jack Daniels. Splashing the amber fluid into two stubby glasses, he handed one to Abe.

'Well, what do you think? Did we do all right?'

Abe took a deep draught, wiped a hand across his mouth and exhaled noisily. 'I guess so. Jeez, that Houlihan guy is some motherfucker. There was a moment there when I felt like ripping his head off his shoulders and stuffing it back down inside his neck. As for your old shooting buddy, they should lock that crazy bastard in a padded cell and throw away the key.'

Divareli sipped his drink and nodded. Abe had more on his mind than idle chit-chat about what, after all, had been a successful meeting.

'About the money,' Abe continued. 'You never did tell that limey how you were going to work it. I think it's about time you told me, old buddy.'

Divareli tried hard to keep the note of exasperation out of his voice. He failed to see why everyone was getting so excited about the money all of a sudden. Even the dogs in the street knew that he had got more than enough from selling the Italbank stock to cover the cost of the Orchid Project. How and when he used those funds was nobody's business but his own. The fact that he had decided to string up Gallerick in a financial noose of his own making just made things a little more complex. It also explained his unaccustomed testiness towards his business partner.

'Like I told you before, the money's OK. We just might have to change how it comes through, that's all.'

Abe pricked up his ears. His early-warning radar system homed in on the forced casualness in Divareli's voice. 'Oh yeah? Is there a problem of some sort?'

'Not really, why do you ask?'

Abe sighed as though the weight of the world lay on his broad shoulders. It was inevitable that it should crop up sooner or later. Might as well be now.

'The word is out that Italbank is in deep shit . . .' He held up a pudgy hand to forestall Divareli's protest. 'Now before you go jumpin' down my throat, why don't you hear me out first. Then when I'm through you can tell me I've got it all wrong. What I hear is that nowadays your depositors are mostly central banks and governments of Third World outfits. I hear that some oil sheikh bought those shares off you and that he's looking for his money back 'cos his bean counters didn't like what they found when they got a peek at the books.'

'That's rubbish!' Divareli exploded, his face white with rage. 'Abe, you should know better than to listen to that kind of loose talk. Our books are open to one and all. How could anyone in their right mind claim that there was anything hidden from them?'

Abe ignored the outburst, continuing as if there had not been the slightest interruption in what he was saying. 'The set-up threw them for starters. Those Arabs couldn't quite figure out why your bank is based on Wall Street but the head office is registered in Luxembourg. When they found out that most of its operations were channelled through the Caymans they almost shit themselves. Now they're telling everyone that Italbank is into money laundering, tax fraud and only Christ knows what else! They say they've proof that the big wheels on the Caymans bought stock in Italbank with loans that need never be repaid just so long as they're good little boys and don't rock the boat. The latest news item is that the Feds are going to pull the plug on Italbank. Is any of this a true bill of goods?'

Divareli sighed. Of course some of what Abe said was true. No one, least of all a bank, could pretend to be a guardian of morality. If some of their depositors were drug-runners, so what? All money looked the same on a deposit slip.

'Some of it probably is, but even so you can be damn sure that applies equally to every goddam bank on the Street. Why this sudden concern for Italbank? Are you worried that I won't come up with the money, is that it?'

174

'Yeah, that's exactly it. I don't want to be left holding the baby, especially if it's crapping all over me. You gotta remember I'm the guy that's gotta sell this project. Who's gonna want stock in the company or membership in the resort club with shit like that flying around? Why don't you come clean with old Abe here and maybe we can still work something out. I gotta tell you though, it makes me nervous as hell when I'm in the jungle with a guy who only tells me half the story.'

Divareli took a deep breath and tried to remain calm. 'OK, part of what you hear could be true, it's just that you've got the wrong angle on it. I'm not denying that from time to time Italbank may have laundered money, even drug money. What I do say is that we didn't *know* it was drug money at the time.'

Abe was writhing with impatience until he could contain himself no longer. 'So tell me somethin' I don't already know. All I'm worried about is that our own lines of credit are secure. That way I know I'll get paid and stay out of jail. It kinda worries me a bit when you start talking about changing the payment channels, that's all.'

Divareli put on his most soothing voice as he spoke. 'Don't worry about that – you'll get paid OK. You have my word on it. You don't think I'd be sitting on my ass in a dump like this if I didn't think there was going to be a big pay-off, do you?'

Abe sounded unconvinced as he replied, 'Naw, I expect not. Now fill me in on these new payment channels.'

Divareli tried to inject as much confidence as he could into what he said next. 'Because of the heat on Italbank, we'll have to work offshore, that's all. We might even use one of your shell companies.'

Abe brightened. In the past he had bought a few off-the-shelf companies from Italbank and they had proved useful at one time or another. He sounded more relieved at this news.

'Now you're singing my song. Off the top of my head, I seem to remember there's one I never even used. Can't remember its exact name but it had "Michigan" as part of its title. I'll call my lawyer and ask him to look it up. It could be just what we need – clean, empty and unused.'

Now it was Divareli's turn to be relieved. 'Now that's a great idea. Or better still, fly over tomorrow and set the thing up yourself. That way you can be sure it's exactly what we want. I think we should call it Orchid Investments. Make Gallerick the President,

Mick Flannery the Chief Executive and Aphra the Company Secretary. You and I will be just ordinary board members. Just make sure that we get over half the shares. That way there'll be no argument as to who is actually running this show!'

Abe took his feet down from the desk, squashed an evil-looking cigar out in the ashtray and drained the last of the Jack Daniels. Stretching the stiffness out of his back, he extended a hand to Divareli.

'Say no more. I'll book a flight and call New York and set up a few meetings. By the way, does the local guy, What's-his-name the banker, know anything?'

'Donnelly? No, I don't think so.'

Abe grinned evilly as he prepared to close the door behind him. 'Then let's keep it that way, eh?'

He was gone before Divareli could nod his agreement. Lost in thought, he stared at the closed door for a long time before locking up and crossing the street to the Brulagh Inn.

The next day, Divareli was driving fast along the narrow road, returning from the airport. Abe's plane had been late and now it was a mad rush to get back to the office to call New York before Italbank closed for the day. With the time difference, he would have to hurry. Rounding a corner too quickly he came upon a donkey and cart in the middle of the road. The driver was perched precariously behind the animal, his back resting against a large milk churn that was pitted with rust. He had a rope serving as reins in one hand and was holding a newspaper close to his eyes with the other. The milk churn was secured by another rope to prevent it falling off as the cart bumped its way along the road.

Divareli had but a split second to take in the scene. His options were limited to either crashing headlong into the donkey and its accoutrements or taking evasive active by throwing the car into a deliberate skid and sliding sideways into the clump of briars that had so obscured his view in the first instance. He prayed that they would act as a cushion, a buffer to slow down the hurtling Porsche before it slammed against the stone wall that skirted the road. The briars did their best, giving him the sensation of a giant hand arresting his inexorable progress. Just when it seemed that all might be well and that car and driver would emerge with nothing worse than a fright and a few scratches there came a sickening thud. This was

176

immediately followed by a scraping noise from underneath the chassis as the car rode over a large rock hidden in the undergrowth. Then the elegant nose of the Porsche smacked into the wall lurking behind the cushion of briars, causing the bonnet to fly open. For what seemed like an eternity he sat there, numb with the shock and listening to the ominous crackling of hot metal mingle with the steam hissing from a smashed radiator.

With a start he realised the damn thing might catch fire at any moment. Cursing quietly he scrambled out of the seat-belt and thrust his shoulder hard against the door. Mercifully it flew open and as it did so he was struck by the ridiculous thought that he need worry no more about the tardy delivery of the passenger door. As he pushed the briars aside, he looked back at the car. It had telescoped alarmingly, giving the front a Churchillian, bulldog look that suggested it was a total write-off.

Further thoughts on the matter were interrupted by a roar from beneath the upturned cart. The donkey had reared up, toppling over the cart and its cargo unceremoniously into the middle of the road. Then the animal had somehow broken free of its harness. Now it was grazing contentedly on the grass margin between the wall and what passed for a road, the rope that had once been its reins draped coyly about its grey neck. It looked none the worst for the adventure. The same could not be said for the face that glowered out at Divareli from under the cart.

'In name of sweet suffering Jaysus will you lift the fucking cart offa me before it has my back broke!'

Both the voice and its owner struck a familiar chord. With considerable effort Divareli raised the shafts just high enough to allow Long Tom McCarthy to crawl free.

'So 'tis yourself is after nearly killing me, is it?' The question could have been rhetorical, for he continued without drawing breath, 'First you try to drive me off my own land with that bloody mare of Houlihan's, next 'tis the shaggin' castle you're after and now you're after driving me off the same road meself and Parnell here have been travellin' since Adam was a boy. Well, thanks be to Jaysus and His Blessed Mother 'tis the last time you'll be drivin' that yoke of yours anywhere by the look of it. There's more steam coming out of it than from Mick Flannery the day before an election . . .'

Cackling throatily at this witticism, he launched a hawking spit that landed just short of Divareli's feet before resuming his tirade.

'If I said it once, I said it a thousand times and may I be struck dead this very minute if I'm telling one word of a lie but says I to myself "One of these fine days that Yank is goin' to kill himself in that motor-car of his if he doesn't watch out. There isn't a road in Ireland could hold him and the speed he's travellin'".'

A lengthy silence ensued. Divareli's reasons for preserving it were twofold. Firstly he wished to satisfy himself that the figure that was still removing gravel and other assorted debris from his threadbare dungarees was not accompanied, as heretofore, by a shotgun. The second was that he could not find anything meaningful to say. He sensed that this might not be the right time to upbraid McCarthy for driving his ass and cart in the middle of a narrow road. Then, of course, there was the matter of his own driving. He had been booting the Porsche at a ridiculous speed, preoccupied as he was with his plans to hoist the Eleventh Earl of Gallerick on his own petard. Even if he had been completely in the right he would not have chosen this particular moment to make the point. Long Tom had regained his feet if not his composure and was making sad, moaning sounds while watching the last of what smelt like stale beer spilling out of the churn on to the road where it left several dirty puddles with a brown scum on the surface. McCarthy was talking in a complaining whine.

'Johnny Slattery will have me life and no mishtake. Fifteen gallons all over the road and he waitin' for it this very minute below in the moat.'

Divareli's curiosity overcame his better judgement. He addressed his adversary for the first time. 'What was in the churn?'

Long Tom stared long and hard at Divareli as though weighing him up. Then, as if he had arrived at a momentous decision, he spat again, this time with more delicacy and further from Divareli's feet before replying.

'So well you might ask. That's the wash, so it was. The stuff Johnny makes the poteen from. The Sergeant is so busy trying to catch him that the poor divil makes up the wash in my place and I brings it to the milk-stand outside the fort. That's where the creamery lorry collects the milk in churns from the farmers round here. Except that I've the lorry driver tipped off to leave this churn

'. . .' he cocked a thumb at the now-empty vessel '. . . behind him. If the Sergeant spots a milk churn up on the stand, he'd think it nothin' out of the ordinary. Then after it gets dark, Johnny lifts it over the ditch and into the moat where he keeps the still.'

Divareli, though flattered to be taken into McCarthy's confidence and greatly relieved that he was not to be subjected to another outburst of invective – if not an assault – against his person, still didn't understand.

'How come someone passing by doesn't see the still and report it to the Sergeant?'

The answer came in a tone of condescension such as one might use to a backward child. ''Tis few are brave enough to go into that place, you know. They're afraid of the whitethorn tree and the power of the little people.'

He added helpfully, 'Leprechauns and that kind of thing. There's a sort of a cellar down in the middle of the fort, a big hole down where they used to hide from the enemy in the olden days. 'Tis down there Johnny has his still. He can boil away to his heart's content and no one will bother him, especially at night. If anyone has sharp enough ears to hear the hissing of the gas, they think 'tis fairy music coming from the fort and quicken their step along the road. Now what are you goin' to do about all this?'

The unexpected change in direction took Divareli completely by surprise. After a pause he said, 'Well, the car looks to be a write-off so the only way we can get back into town is on your cart. That means we'll have to turn it right-side up. Do you feel strong enough to try?'

McCarthy nodded and they soon had the cart ready to receive the donkey between its shafts. The beast, however, had other ideas. As Long Tom approached, it ambled off down the road – not actually running away but keeping just far enough ahead to avoid capture. After several fruitless efforts in which he launched himself at the recalcitrant animal only to end up clutching at fresh air, Long Tom shouted back down the road, 'I'm goin' to have to lep in over the ditch to get on the far side of the hairy bastard. You stay on the road and drive him down in my direction as soon as you see me on the far side of him. Apart from that hoor of a landlord, there's nothin' round here as stupid or stubborn as that shaggin' donkey.'

With that he crashed his way through what appeared to be im-penetrable undergrowth to reappear moments later, good as his

179

word, on the other side of their prey. 'Dhrive the hoor down to me now, like a good man. If he tries to double back on you, whatever you do don't let him past you or 'tis the long walk the two of us will have back into the town!'

With this warning ringing in his ears, Divareli stalked the animal much as he had seen matadors approach a particularly evil bull. Unfortunately the similarity did not end there. The donkey lowered its head, laid its ears back along its neck, bared its yellow teeth in a vicious rictus – not unlike Tom Donnelly's smile – and charged straight at Divareli. Before he could get out of the way, its head caught him squarely in the midriff, knocking the wind out of him for the second time in ten minutes. He regained consciousness seconds later to the sound of Long Tom's voice.

'Good man yourself. Faith then I promise you that put a sthop to the hoor's gallop. Look at him now, he doesn't know what hit him.'

Divareli looked up from the road to see Parnell, the donkey, quiet as a mouse and looking mildly apologetic as he stood between the shafts of the cart. He then transported his charges to the Brulagh Inn with commendable speed. In the course of their journey, Divareli made several discoveries. The first of these was that he had left his cigarettes in the wreck of his car. Long Tom proffered him a crumpled cylinder from a green cigarette packet. The brand was unfamiliar. Divareli took a deep drag which added to his mistakes that day. A curtain of red mist fell before his eyes, accompanied by a dizzy spell of such intensity that a cold sweat formed on his brow. Tadpoles with luminous tails swam through the mist, only to be put to flight by a bout of uncontrollable coughing. He threw away the offending cigarette in disgust.

'Jeez, where'd you get these?'

'Same place as I get them every day – Flannery's shop. Them's Woodbines. Take a bit of getting used to, so they do. Doctor Buckley has the heart put crossways in me from sayin' what'll happen if I don't give 'em up. Still and all, says I to him, 'tis one of the few pleasures left to the likes of me and myself with neither chick nor child. Like I say, sure a man must die of somethin' and it might as well be the oul' fag. What do you think yourself?'

Not trusting his vocal chords after the racking cough, Divareli just nodded and took a firmer grip on the shaft of the cart that provided the only handhold. The big spoked wheels had an iron band instead of a rubber tyre, and the prospect of falling beneath them did not appeal to him. He had already registered enough mishaps for one day. He wondered what he would do about the accident. He wasn't worried about the insurance element, for that was well provided for but rather the legal end.

'I'll have to report this to the Sergeant, won't I?'

'Begor an' you will. Otherwise your insurance won't pay up. I'd say that car cost you a fair few bob. Thanks be to God it's starting to rain. That way the wash will be well gone from the road by the time that shagger of a policeman gets there. Do you know somethin', he wanted to put me in jail last year? Just because I tried to fire a gun at that randy ram of a landlord, and his ancestors havin' all belongin' to me rotting in the grave.'

It appeared that one of Long Tom's ancestors had worked at Gallerick Hall. His job had been to feed the foxhounds, a more vicious pack than nowadays – so much so that they were housed in a small yard and fed by a huntsman who climbed a ladder and tipped the contents of the kitchen slops-bucket over the top of the wall to the ravenous dogs below. Long Tom's ancestor had apparently toppled over the wall and all they found of him afterwards were the brass buttons of his coat. His master explained to the widow that her man must have been drunk to climb over the wall, and refused to pay out any compensation. Instead, he offered to employ her daughter in the kitchens. A year later the girl was pregnant by a Gallerick son. Shipped off to America with a purse of gold sovereigns, she was never heard from again.

Divareli clucked sympathetically and hopped off the cart outside the Brulagh Inn. Though mindful of the fact that his fellow passenger had a tempestuous relationship with the demon drink, he thought it only courteous to invite him in for a jar to celebrate their survival of the crash. The original reason for Divareli's haste had long since passed into insignificance. While waiting for Abe's plane they had agreed to apply for a banking licence, deciding that setting up their own bank would be the most convenient way of funding the Orchid Project. Several exotic islands, one of them being Grenada, allowed favoured clients to set up shell companies that could trade as banks – but without the assets and banking licences necessary under stricter economic regimes. Of late it had been part of the service that Italbank offered its clients – an off-the-shelf bank of your very own for less than ten thousand dollars. To this end Divareli had bought a block of corporate registrations in Grenada and used the word 'bank' in their names. Offshore financial institutions were especially keen on these supermarket banking goodies. Certain multinationals were also buyers of these offshore 'banks', using them for legitimate purposes such as tax reduction and facilitating international deals. Divareli declined to sell any to known con-artists, though Abe had bought a few in his own name, a result of their working together on previous deals. It was one of these with the uninspiring name of Michigan Overseas Bank that was about to be reborn as the Orchid Investment Bank. The object of the phone-call had been to instruct Italbank's legal department to hire a lawyer in Grenada to effect the name-change. This lawyer would also write to Tom Donnelly in Brulagh to inform him that henceforth funds would be sourced from there.

There were no other customers in the bar. Sean's wife Jenny was in charge, and it was she who phoned Aphra some time later to tell her her employer was the worse for wear and inclined to sing *Did your mother come from Ireland'* to Long Tom McCarthy. The latter declined to accompany him on the wings of song, preferring to invite anyone entering the bar to fight. At one stage she had been called on to witness a barely legible agreement, scribbled on perforated sheets of toilet paper, the gist of which was, that in return for Divareli admitting liability for the accident, Long Tom would waive all rights to the ruined McCarthy castle on the foreshore. Lest Aphra should think that Jenny in any way condoned, much less encouraged, such behaviour, she repeated several times that were it not for Divareli, Long Tom would not have been allowed to darken the door of the Brulagh Inn. It transpired that he had been barred from there for the past five years. As for their condition, it was Jenny's opinion that this was due rather to the nips they took from a bottle Long Tom produced at regular intervals from inside his dungarees, than to the eleven pints of stout they each consumed before the party was declared to be at an end.

21

'I hear you ran into Long Tom – literally.'

They were standing on top of a sand-dune the size of an under-nourished Alp. It overlooked a long, narrow valley that ran between other dunes before coming to an abrupt end against the mound on which the old McCarthy stronghold lay in ruins. Divareli felt like Stout Cortez as he pointed out to the Doc the various hazards that awaited those playing the last hole of the new golf-course. The floor of the valley was pockmarked by tons of red earth, scattered in random heaps, awaiting the bulldozer's blade. It would mould them into a level highway that would lap at the base of the sand-dunes like a sea of red molten lava. At this stage it required considerable imagination to grasp what Divareli was talking about, though the wiry grass that trapped their ankles on the steep hillside was a considerable hazard in itself. The Doc decided that trying to hit a golf-ball from its grasp was something he would prefer not to try.

McAllister, the course architect, had wrought a miracle of sorts. The canny Scot had left the dunes untouched – and therefore the foreshore profile – much as they had been for the last thousand years or so. It was only in the valleys that his earthworks were visible. Bright yellow dump trucks darted to and fro, buzzing like angry hornets, to feed the giant blades of the bulldozers as they fashioned level fairways from the topsoil. In the midst of this bedlam gangs of men in yellow oilskins tidied and levelled the red earth neatly against the crevices in the dunes where the giant blades could not reach. Further away from the harbour two fairways had already been transformed into level roadways, seeded and fertilised so that they would become lush green ribbons of grass by the spring. The heavy grey clouds overhead had not yet emptied, indeed it had not rained for some time. Yet their menace gave added urgency to the work. Abe had dinned into every worker that if it rained too much, the work would have to be postponed and then the generous completion bonuses in their contracts would be cancelled. As it was, they worked in shifts late into the night under giant arc-lights that gave an eerie glow to the foreshore.

'Yeah, you might say that!'

Divareli had taken his time in replying to the Doc's question. There were several reasons for this. Among them would have been his uncertainty as to how well acquainted the Doc was with what had happened on the road and subsequently in the Brulagh Inn. The fact that a promise of secrecy – stronger than any *Omerta* – had been given by Divareli in exchange for Long Tom's revelations about the poteen business was another factor in his delay in replying. That Divareli had sought no such confidences but had merely been trying to extract from Long Tom an undertaking that he would not object to his turning his erstwhile ancestral abode into a resort complex was neither here nor there. The promise had been given and, to McCarthy's credit, no reward had been sought for his compliance.

As Divareli answered, he tried to grin at the Doc's feeble witticism but quickly abandoned the effort, deciding that to pull back his lips to the extent necessary for even the mildest of grins might easily cause his teeth to fall out. Already the inside of his mouth felt as though a small rodent had defecated, then died in it. The hangover he had experienced after the Race Dance was the merest trifle compared to what he was now enduring. Aphra had left a note on his desk. It stated that she was taking the day off. As a consolation she left a small box of Alka Seltzer and a large bottle of Perrier beside her note. Even the supposedly harmless mineral water blazed down his throat like a torchlight procession. Snatches of recollection bubbled to the surface of his memory, only to burst and disappear before he could quite get a grip on them. He seemed to recall writing down somewhere the brand of cigarette McCarthy favoured. Should he now find the slip of paper on which the name Woodbine was inscribed, he would treat it much as one might ask a badly dressed acquaintance the address of his tailor – as something to be avoided. Now the Doc was speaking again.

'Weren't you damn lucky he was on the ass and cart! He might have been driving Johnny Slattery's tractor and then you would have been killed stone dead for sure. Long Tom knows as much about driving a mechanically-propelled vehicle as his donkey, Parnell, does about the Theory of Relativity. And I wouldn't mind but he's not the worst of them. The trouble with most of the farmers round here is that they think they're still driving asses and carts – despite the fact that they now have powerful motor cars under their backsides. People criticise me for driving an old banger but Jaysus, I promise you if I had a dacent car under me I was dead long ago. It's only when the shaggers see you coming at them in something worth less than what they're driving themselves that they'll pull over to their own side of the road. Poor Father Jerry had the grandest car you ever laid eyes on after he came over here first. An Italian yoke, an Alfa something or other . . .'

'Alfa Romeo?'

'Yeah, that was it. A big black thing, sleek as a bullock raised on barley. Coming back from a sick call one night didn't he drive it straight into Johnny Slattery's tractor an' Johnny coming home from the pub without a screed of a light of any sort showing. There wasn't a mark on the tractor but the car was in bad shape afterwards. In the end it tried to drown itself . . .'

Divareli was mystified. 'How d'ya mean, *drown itself*?'

'Well, in the fine weather Father Jerry likes to go for a swim off the end of the pier and a fine swimmer he is, too. Anyway, while he was out in the bay, swimming away for himself, he must have forgotten to put the handbrake on properly. Didn't his grand car go down the slope of its own accord and topple off the end of the pier into the sea! The tide went out and in again over it four times before they could organise a JCB to lift it out. To be honest, I'd say the poor man wasn't sorry to see the end of it. Sure, what would a man want with a flying machine like that round here?'

Divareli wasn't quite sure if he was being got at in a subtle manner. The parallel being drawn between the fate of the priest's Alfa and his late lamented Porsche was a mite too close for comfort. He had yet to report the accident to the Sergeant. The agreement reached between McCarthy and himself last night would have to be taken into account when he reported the details of it. His version would have to shift the blame from McCarthy to himself, but subtly, without incriminating himself to the extent that the insurance company could wriggle out from its obligation to provide him with a new car. As for the firing of the shotgun in the hall, unless someone formally complained to the Sergeant the priest had said that probably nothing would result from it. He hinted that even though

185

everyone regarded Long Tom as being mad, nobody wanted to be the one responsible for putting him away.

The Doc was observing in an impressed voice, 'It looks like your McAllister's designed quite a tough course here. Do you think your visitors will be up to coping with it?'

By now Divareli was suffering from a hangover of such gargantuan proportions that he would have gladly donated substantial funds to any charity the Doc cared to name if only this long-standing appointment could have been broken, or even postponed until his body had had a chance to recover. As President of the Brulagh Golf Club, the Doc had been invited to 'walk the course' as a matter of courtesy. This meant picking one's steps with care along the steep sides of the dunes as Divareli pointed out where the tees, fairways and greens at each hole would be located.

The dunegrass was not only razor-sharp but downright slippery as well. More than once they had lost their balance and slid gracelessly halfway down the slope on their backsides. Walking along the fairways was out of the question. Some were already finished and to tread, however gently, on the soft seedbed would have been to undo much of the preparatory work. As for the unfinished holes, the many machines scurrying frantically forwards and backwards in their haste to finish before the predicted break in the weather would have constituted a very real danger to life and limb. With one accident already to his credit, Divareli did not intend risking another within the space of twenty-four hours.

The Doc's question was a good one. In fact it had been troubling Divareli for some time. McAllister was a taciturn Scot of the old school, and to any suggestion that his layout was too difficult for the middle-aged clientèle expected to play over it, he would just shrug his massive shoulders and grunt, 'They'll have to work for a par on my course. If they're nay good enough for that, then they can make do wi' a bogey. That's how this game was meant to be played.' Which, of course, was all very well for him. He would be long gone with his fee in his pocket before the first players showed up. The question also allowed Divareli to broach a delicate item that had not been included in the agenda of the public meeting.

'I guess so – I've been wondering about that myself, especially this par five we're looking at. There is provision made at some of the tougher holes to put in a few forward tees later on if we think it necessary. The question you have raised about the difficulty of this course is very much to the point. All along I have been meaning to ask you if your members would mind if some of our guests used your course now and again – as a nursery slope kind of thing. Somewhere that less accomplished golfers could get the hang of the game and build up confidence in themselves before they ventured out on this course. Obviously we'd be willing to pay for the privilege.'

The Doc was inwardly delighted as it was just what he had had in mind himself. However, now that Divareli had brought the matter up, his natural instinct for caution prevented him from sounding too enthusiastic.

'Well, I'd have to ask the members first but I've no doubt we could come to some arrangement. As you know, our course is empty most of the time so there should be no problem about overcrowding. It's also much shorter and the fairways look to be wider than yours so it should be easier for beginners to get started on. Just what you want, in fact. Naturally I would expect our members to have reciprocal rights to play here.' The thought had only just occurred to him but he tried to make it sound as if it was an obvious pre-condition.

This stopped Divareli dead in his tracks. The last thing he wanted was a crowd of unkempt locals clogging up the fairways – not at all the image that would be projected when the time came to market the resort. He paused for a while before answering in a voice that reeked of uncertainty, 'Yeah, I suppose that sounds reasonable enough. I'll talk to Abe about it when he gets back – I'm sure we can work something out. Now there's something else I want to ask you. I meant to approach you about it after the meeting but the damn thing broke up so suddenly I didn't get a chance. Would you be interested in coming on to the board of Orchid Investments? Like I said, we will be offering shares to everyone but there are certain people I would personally like to have with me at decision-making level on the board. I should tell you that Mick Flannery has already agreed to join us.'

The Doc gazed out over the dunes, wondering if this was how Christ had been tempted by Satan. While Divareli was not offering him half his kingdom, he made it sound not dissimilar. After what seemed like an age to Divareli, the reply came. For a while he thought that the Doc had either not heard, or else completely ignored the invitation to join Orchid Investments.

'You know, in the heel of the hunt that meeting didn't really decide very much. It generated more heat than light as far as I'm concerned. As President of the local golf-club, I would welcome the planeloads of tourists you promised us but as someone who has lived here all his life and likes Brulagh the way it is, I'd be less than honest with you if I said that I was looking forward to being crawled all over by gawping tourists. Naturally I realise that this is a very selfish point of view and that the jobs you have promised for the area are a damn sight more important than my personal preferences. And I'll tell you something else. When we planned something like this golf-course a few years back, there wasn't one word said about frogs or flowers. So we must ask ourselves, why all the fuss about them now? Especially when you have guaranteed off the platform to preserve the bloody things. Now as for your kind invitation, I must decline it . . .'

He saw the crestfallen look on Divareli's face but pressed on, hoping to soften the blow.

'. . . not because I don't think your project an excellent one, but because I think my place should go to a younger man. Of course I'll buy shares in the project and I'll give every support, both public and private, I can to it. But please don't ask me to sit on the board.'

Divareli waited for a while before he asked why.

'I'll tell you why and it's the gospel truth. The ordinary man in the street would say to himself that it's the same old crowd that runs everything in Brulagh who are now taking over the board of Orchid Investments. Far better to get a few new faces. That way everyone will know that it is a democratically-run show where everyone can have his or her say. Now why don't we leave that subject for the moment so that you can tell me what Long Tom said to you when you crashed into him on the road.'

The grin on the Doc's face was infectious. Divareli gave him a heavily edited version of the events that led up to the marathon drinking session in the Brulagh Inn. He did not mention that the milk churn had spilled its valuable cargo. Neither did he regard it as being any of the Doc's business that he had an appointment with Long Tom and the bootlegger for later on that night.

22

From the street, the police station was unimpressive. Only a blue ceramic tile above the door bearing the legend *Garda Siochana* identified it as such. The interior wasn't a whole lot better. A coal-fire spluttered in a metal fireplace. The walls were plastered with notices, many of them yellow with age. Some warned of what lay in store for those forgetting to licence their dog or television, while others reminded the reader that it was a serious offence, punishable by fines and/or jail to encourage the spread of noxious weeds, rabies or the warble fly. A more recent wall-poster, in glorious colour, appeared to give detailed instructions on growing your own marijuana. Closer inspection proved it to be an artist's impression, complete with helpful recognition pointers, to enable anyone stumbling across the weed to report its presence to their local garda station. Divareli had plenty of time to take all this in because there was no one about. This was odd in that Gus had just phoned minutes before to ask him to drop in. Then from offstage came the unmistakeable sound of a toilet being flushed vigorously. Moments later Gus entered stage left through a side door.

'Thanks for coming over so quick. Not that there was any great rush. It's just that I wanted to make inquiries about the crash. I have to send a report to my Superintendent, you see. Then he'll have to make up his mind if he's going to prosecute either of you for driving in a manner dangerous to the public . . .' He stopped suddenly in mid-sentence as a thought struck him. When he resumed it was more as though he were thinking aloud in a mournful voice than addressing Divareli. 'Of course I was forgetting for a moment there that a donkey and cart is not a mechanically propelled vehicle.'

He fiddled thoughtfully with a sheaf of offical-looking papers on the large table that served as a desk. An elderly 'sit-up-and-beg' typewriter formed a barrier so effective that it forced them to peer round it to get a clear view of each other. Divareli sensed that before long there would be an even greater barrier between them. His

189

pledge to Long Tom that he would not mention the shot fired at the meeting and that he would report the accident so as to attach no blame whatsoever to him might prove to be somewhat more difficult now than it had seemed at a late hour last night. In doing so, he would also have to avoid incriminating himself.

'And that being so Long Tom, unlike yourself, could not be charged with dangerous driving even if we had a strong case against him – which at the moment we do not. Unless, of course, you can come up with sufficient evidence to convict him in a court of law. Maybe even something to do with a shotgun?'

As he spoke the Sergeant shot a covert glance around the typewriter to gauge the effect of his last remark. Divareli remained poker-faced though inwardly he was wondering whether Gus was trying to lure him into believing that no matter what accusations he laid at Long Tom's door, no charges could be preferred against him because of the indisputable fact that Parnell was not an internal combustion engine. Compared to Gus the Oracle at Delphi had been a mine of information.

Because he couldn't think of anything better to do, Divareli shook his head slowly – a mistake, since immediately set in process once more the drilling rig that Divareli hoped had shut down, at least temporarily. Across from him and still partially concealed by the enormous typewriter, Gus was now seeking details of the crash.

'What speed would you say you were doing at the time?'

'Hard to say, Sergeant. About fifty-five, I guess.'

'Ah, go on with you. Sure you couldn't be doing half that speed – not with the road the way it is. The last time it had a hand laid next or near it was just before the election. Even then, the County Council workmen only threw a few shovels of gravel into the po-tholes – the bigger ones, that is – and promised they'd be back shortly to finish the job properly. That was six years ago, for God's sake. Sure if you were to tell me – seriously, that is – that you were doing fifty-five miles an hour on that stretch of a road, it isn't dangerous driving I'd have to be charging you with but attempted murder. Apart from that altogether, there's a countrywide speed limit of fifty miles per hour – not that anyone takes a blind bit of notice of it. 'Twas only brought in when them hoors of Arabs cut off the oil on us. After the petrol rationing was over, them shaggers up in the Dail never bothered to change the law. Now tell me again because I'm a bit hard of hearing. What speed did you say you were going just before the crash?'

'About twenty, I think. Like you say, it's a bad road.'

'And how did it happen?'

'Well, there was a big thornbush blocking my view. When I came round the corner, there was an ass and cart in my way. I skidded the car deliberately to avoid hitting them and . . .'

The Sergeant interrupted. 'You couldn't skid if you were only doing twenty miles an hour, for God's sake. My Superintendent would never swallow that – neither would your insurance company, for that matter. Are you sure you didn't just pull into the side of the road to avoid hitting the ass and cart, which was bang in the middle of the road without room for even a bicycle to pass, much less a motor car? What's more, I'd bet money that Long Tom was reading *Clarion* and leaving the donkey to find its own way home. He claims he's as blind as a bat, did you know that?'

'The donkey?'

'Ah no, for God's sake – Long Tom. He's been drawing the blind pension for years though the same man could knock a flea off a greyhound's back from fifty yards with that gun of his! An inspector from the Social Welfare called to his home one day to try and find out if he was really blind. As your man was leaving, he asked Long Tom which direction he should take for Brulagh, hoping to catch him out, you see. But Long Tom is nobody's fool, I'll grant him that much. What did he do but answer the inspector nice as you please, "Sure that would depend, sir, on which way your car is facing". Oh, they don't make them much cuter than that.'

Divareli laughed politely. He appreciated the Sergeant's efforts to prevent his incriminating himself but in doing so, he must not forget to keep faith with Long Tom. Something he had said in the Brulagh Inn about having the Sergeant in his sights more than once but being afraid to pull the trigger would clearly indicate that there was no love lost between them. So, Gus might be understandably keen to put the lunatic away before he shed his scruples about shooting policemen but that, however, was not Divareli's problem. Meanwhile Gus was scribbling furiously on the Accident Report form. Now and then he would pause for a moment and gaze at the fly-specked ceiling in search of further inspiration before licking the tip of the pencil and pressing on with his task. After some thought

Divareli answered the Sergeant's question about how he could skid if he was travelling at such a low speed.

'Look Sergeant, thanks for trying to get me off the hook but the whole thing was really my fault. I was going too fast and thinking of something else at the time. When I saw the ass and cart, it was too late to do anything else but slam on the brakes and hope for the best. What happened after that was out of my control. As it was, I nearly got away with it. If the damn car had stopped ten seconds earlier, there would not have been a scratch on it. As it is, the thing is a complete write-off.'

The Sergeant appeared to hear none of this. Instead he appeared to want to talk golf. 'That's a great course you're making down by the shore. I took a walk around there last night when the lads were working under the lights. That last hole is something else.'

Divareli was growing increasingly exasperated by these sudden changes in direction but thought it best to humour the Sergeant.

'Yeah, it's one of the longest in the country, I'm told. McAllister claims it will be one of the best par fives in the world.'

'I noticed that it finishes up under the old castle, too. Do you know what's been puzzling me this past while . . .', the question had to be rhetorical because there was no time for an answer before he was off and running again, '. . . isn't it amazing that Long Tom didn't lodge an objection against you with the planning authorities, especially after his carry-on at the meeting? There was a moment there when I thought I'd have to arrest him for threatening you with the gun. You'll be pressing charges against him, of course?'

Another pregnant silence ensued. While by nature Gus was a man not to be rushed, Divareli felt that there was nothing to be gained by answering. While waiting for a reply, Gus had found something of interest at the tip of his fingernails and was engrossed in examining it minutely. When it became clear that no answer was forthcoming, he cast his net in different waters. 'Before you decide one way or another, do you know what I'm going to tell you?'

Another rhetorical question. Divareli did not risk shaking his head to confirm that indeed he did not. It scarcely mattered because the Sergeant was clearly intent on adding to the sum of human knowledge.

'For the last twenty years I've been trying to arrest Johnny Slattery in the act of making poteen. There were a couple of times I thought I had him caught, but he's slippier than an eel. With the Government increasing the tax on spirits every budget, business has got so good for the hoor that he's after taking on a partner if you don't mind – and do you know who it is?'

This time Divareli risked an almost imperceptible shake of his head.

'Your friend Long Tom, no less.' There was no mistaking the contempt in the Sergeant's voice. 'And a perfect match they are, if ever there was one. The both of them are as crooked as a ram's horn. The trouble with Long Tom, though, is that he's mad as well. That poteen Johnny distils would drive a rabbit to attack a pack of greyhounds. Put a few belts of it inside someone like your friend McCarthy and he would shoot you just as soon as bid you the time of day.'

Divareli noticed with some nervousness that this was the second time Long Tom had been described as his friend. Before this impression could be corrected, the Sergeant had resumed his remarks, this time in a quieter, more confidential note.

'To tell you nothing but the truth, you'd be doing everyone round here a big favour if you helped me bring him to justice. That way I'd be able to have him put out of the way for a while. Doctor Buckley is blue in the face from telling me that if they could only get him into one of those institutions, they'd give him some class of a pill that would nearly turn him into a normal human being.'

This observation was allowed to hang in the air for some time. Divareli was learning to appreciate the virtues of long silences. It was developing into a battle of wills as each waited for the other to crack first – the exact opposite of everything he had been accustomed to up till now. In tense boardroom battles, his strategy had always been to charge in with all guns blazing. The thinking behind this had been that those who were 'firstest with the mostest' usually came out on top. Not so in this instance, he reflected. He had to pinch himself to get this very minor irritant into proper perspective.

Such reflections were interrupted by the Sergeant, who had taken to reminiscing on the life and times of Slattery the bootlegger – though to what purpose Divareli could not even begin to fathom.

'The maddening thing about Johnny is that I can't for the life of me find where he hides the wash or the hard stuff. It's easy enough to hide a still, for it comes apart and could fit under a bed, up in the attic or inside a plastic bag hidden in a ditch. But the wash is a different kettle of fish altogether. It has to be made up in big quantities so that it can ferment a bit first before 'tis run through the worm. As for the poteen, that has to be kept in bottles and they takes up a fair bit of space, you know. If I've searched Johnny's farm once, I've searched it a hundred times but never seen sign nor light of a barrel or a bottle anywhere. Isn't that a mystery for you now?'

This time Divareli had an inkling of where the apparent *non sequitur* was leading but again he held his peace. He gave no indication that the Sergeant's failure to catch the bootlegger with the goods was of the slightest interest. Instead he glanced in the most obvious way possible at the chunky Rolex on his wrist. This, he hoped, might bring matters to a speedy conclusion. He was to be disappointed.

'The reason I brought the matter up at all . . .' Gus spoke so slowly and ponderously that each word seemed to be drawn out of him much as one might have extracted his eye-teeth – without an anaesthetic '. . . is that when I went out to measure the road and draw up a map of the accident I got a strange class of a smell around the place. 'Twas for all the world as if beer had been spilt all over the road. I couldn't actually lay hands on a sample because the rain had washed it away – but not the smell. You weren't drinking by any chance, before you had the accident I mean?'

The very mention of the word *drink* sent shivers up and down Divareli's spine. Though the agony had eased somewhat since giving the Doc the five cent tour of the golf-course that morning, it had not yet taken its departure. A dull throb of pain still persisted behind his right eye. It quickened its tempo at the Sergeant's suggestion that drink might have caused the accident. Remembering what Aphra had said about his views on drunken driving, Divareli tried to work as much indignation as possible into his reply.

'Certainly not! I wouldn't dream of driving if I had been drinking. I was on my way back from the airport having put Abe Linovitz on a plane. Like I said, I was doing about twenty and even though McCarthy did his best to avoid me, the road was just too narrow. I tried to avoid injuring the donkey by driving my car on to the verge of the road, and in doing so, I struck a stone wall hidden behind the undergrowth. That's about it, Sergeant. What'll I do about the car?'

'Oh I've made arrangements to have it towed . . .'

A telephone shrilled at the back of the room. Gus raised his eyes to heaven at the interruption, then got out of his chair and lifted the receiver. 'Hello, hello, Sergeant Moriarty here. Who's speaking, please? Ah, 'tis yourself, Superintendent. I see . . . So what you're telling me in plain language is that I can't have anyone after dark, is that it? No over-time due to cutbacks, you say? Well, I suppose what cannot be cured must be endured, isn't that the truth of it? Right so, send them on soon as you can and tell them to check with me here in the station first and not be running around the place like headless chickens . . . and good day to you, too, Super.'

Gus replaced the receiver thoughtfully and returned to his seat across the table from Divareli. Before he picked up the conversation where he had left off, he moved the typewriter to the side so that he could get a clear view of his quarry.

'Like I was telling you, I've arrangements made to have your car towed back here. 'Twill be kept in the garage under lock and key until an insurance inspector has a proper look at it. The insurance crowd are fierce strict about that sort of thing nowadays. Some smart aleck pulled a fast one on them a while back and they've been on their guard ever since.'

Divareli thought it time, anxious though he was to bring the proceedings to a close, to demonstrate that the power of speech had not completely deserted him. 'What happened to make them so suspicious?'

Gus sighed and steepled his hands beneath his chin. 'Yerrah it's a long story but I'll make it short as I can. A while back this friend of Mick's smacked his new Mercedes into a wall. Unlike yourself, he had a drop too much taken. Not too much though to cloud his brain for didn't he drive all the way up to Johnny Slattery's farm and tell him what was after happening. Johnny told him not to worry and to leave everything to him. He went into the city and hired a car but not before he had hit the Mercedes a few belts with a sledgehammer. When he brought the hired car back, didn't he do the same thing to it. Then off with him back to the crowd he had hired it from. "I'm after running into a Mercedes," says he to them, "and as God is my judge wasn't it all my own fault. I even signed a statement saying as much and I know that whatever damage I did is covered by the insurance of the car I got from yourselves." Of

195

course it was and Mick's friend got a new front to his grand Mercedes car for nothing. The hire company cursed Johnny to the pit of hell but that was all they could do about it and he after admitting full liability. I suppose Johnny got a fair few quid out of it as a backhander for dreaming up the whole thing. It only goes to show that the hoor is cute as a fox.'

There didn't seem to be much to add so another silence ensued as Divareli marvelled at the bootlegger's ingenuity. It was much the same as he was seeking for Orchid Investments – the perfect scam.

Gus was speaking again. 'Did you know I'm due to retire at the end of the year?'

Accustomed as he was to *non sequiturs* cropping up where they were least expected, this one seemed to have attained new heights of irrelevance. Nevertheless, this was the time to humour the Sergeant, now that the accident thing appeared to have been sorted out. Divareli was still wrestling with what Gus had just said when the veil of mystery was miraculously lifted. With a deep sigh, the Sergeant suddenly made the reasoning behind his devious approach to the accident and the clumsy but well-meaning efforts to absolve Divareli from blame absolutely clear.

'Why I mentioned my retirement at all was that I was wondering if you had made any arrangements about security for your resort. I've spent a lifetime in the force and what I don't know about what goes on round here isn't worth knowing. While a sergeant's pension is generous enough, it wouldn't be any harm to have a bit extra coming in – something to put aside for the rainy day. Apart altogether from the money, to tell you nothing but the truth I'm an active class of a character and I'd be very anxious for something to keep me occupied as much as anything else.'

Divareli felt the pain behind his eye lance backwards through the matrix of his brain tissue and then rush out through both ears simultaneously. It was nothing, however, to the blinding flash of inspiration that assailed him. 'I think we can do better than that, Sergeant. How would you like to join our board of directors?'

The arrangements for meeting had been vague. All that Divareli could clearly recall was that he should walk along the road leading to the fort at around eight o'clock. From there on, it would be up to Long Tom to make contact. The invitation to watch the still working had been extended towards the end of their marathon in the Brulagh Inn at a time when Jenny, Sean's wife, had been trying to persuade Long Tom to leave.

After an amazing sunset in which Mount Brulagh stood black against a fiery sky, the grey mist rolled in from the sea and lay on the ground like a fluffy eiderdown. The flocks of starlings that had skittered overhead, darting to and fro like a swarm of demented mosquitoes, had long since found shelter for the night. As dusk turned to darkness, even the crows ceased their squabbling and now only the occasional angry caw rent the night air, a stark counterpoint to the piercing shriek of a seagull seeking its mate in the darkness that had banished the flaming orb of the sun beneath the horizon. The road was darkened by huge trees that towered above him, their network of bare branches already glistening in the moonlight with the night frost. The pale moon had turned the gossamer draped over the hedgerows into delicate threads of spun silver. More and more stars leaped from the dark ceiling with an almost audible pop. The only other sound was that of waves gently lapping against the distant harbour wall. Divareli shivered and quickened his step. It was not just the cold that had brought on this involuntary *frisson*. He switched on the torch once more, this time as much to comfort himself as to see where he was going. Indeed the light of the moon allowed him to pick out the salient features of his immediate surroundings.

A voice hissed urgently from the inky blackness, 'Quench the lamp for Jaysus sake!'

It was so close that it made him jump with fright. The figure of Long Tom was at his shoulder. Divareli could not shake off the impression that it had materialised from nowhere, from out of the mist like one of the little people about whom Long Tom had waxed so eloquent the previous night. Indeed, he had explained to a wide-eyed Divareli, it was the little people or *Pookas* as he called them who ensured that Johnny and he were safe from prying eyes when they were making 'the pure drop'. The Pooka, he said, was a thoroughly bad sort reputed to infest the branches of the thorn trees that grew in the fort. This was enough to ensure that unwelcome vistors did not arrive there unexpectedly, especially at night, for then the Pooka was believed to take on the form of a black pony with a shaggy coat and eyes that blazed in the dark like hot coals. It delighted in waylaying late-night revellers and offering them a lift home on its back. It would then set off at a mad gallop over mountain and stream only to buck off its unfortunate rider into a ditch far from home. In this, it seemed to bear a marked resemblance to the animals Houlihan hired out to unsuspecting visitors. The Pooka's other main task, apparently was to breathe on the berries that grew on the hedgerows at Hallowe'en, thereby making them unfit for human consumption.

Before he switched off the torch, Divareli noticed with trepidation that his guide cradled his trusty shotgun in the crook of his arm as nonchalantly as another might carry a walking stick. Walking wordlessly down the road, they paused beside a wooden platform that might have been for the milk collection, though no churns were visible. Looking around carefully to make sure they were unseen, Long Tom steered him by the elbow through a narrow gap in the ditch, much as one might help a blind person cross the street.

They walked through a muddy field, the frozen grass crunching against their feet. Here it was much brighter, for there were no trees to blot out the moon. Out of nowhere, in the middle of the empty field, a circle of trees sprouted from a wall of dense undergrowth and loomed before them. Luke was led around to the side furthest from the road to a narrow gap in the brambles that snatched greedily at his jacket as he forced his way through. Now they were in a circular clearing with ferns and bracken growing knee-high. A smallish tree, presumably the Pooka's residence, grew in the centre. This, too, was guarded by seemingly impenetrable brambles. To Divareli's surprise his guide lifted an entire bramble outwards – much as one might remove a section from an orange – to expose a bare patch of ground on which lay a rusted sheet of corrugated iron. This he placed carefully against the trunk of the fairy tree, revealing the mouth of a quite large tunnel. Making a gesture at Divareli to mind his head, he disappeared down a short wooden staircase. At the bottom stood a crude door made out of another sheet of rusted tin.

With a greeting of: *'It's me and I have someone with me!'* Long Tom rapped on the metal with the butt of his gun. The door was opened gently from the inside to reveal a large chamber. The earthen floor was covered with strips of cracked linoleum, and the slatted ceiling was supported by wooden posts driven into the ground. A blast of heat, mingled with the cloying stench of fermenting beer, greeted them. Two spluttering storm-lamps hung from the posts while a small transistor radio crackled with static. Johnny Slattery extended his free hand. He held a blow-torch attached by a thin rubber tube to a bright yellow gas cylinder in the other. This had been turned back to the minimum setting and so gave off a wavering tongue of orange flame rather than its more usual hissing blue streak. Johnny was waving it, as though he were trying to paint with fire, along the side of a milk churn similar to the one that had emptied its contents all over the road after the collision.

From a hole drilled in the lid of the churn protruded a length of curled copper piping less than an inch in diameter. After several loops the size of a car-wheel it disappeared into a barrel filled with water which acted as a crude condenser. From the other end of the copper 'worm' came a spasmodic trickle of clear liquid. Withdrawing his hand, Johnny barely nodded to Divareli before returning to his task. It soon became obvious that the flow at one end was controlled by the amount of heat 'painted' on to the side of the churn by Johnny's blow-torch.

'Will you be long more?' Long Tom's voice broke the spell.

Johnny wiped his nose with his free hand, winked at Divareli for some reason and muttered, 'Another few minutes is all that's left in this lot, I'd be thinkin' . . .'

He lovingly caressed the flame against the steel until the flow satisfied him then, turning back to the two newcomers, he addressed Divareli. 'I found it hard to believe 'twas yourself Tom told me was comin'. I couldn't for the life of me make out what a gentleman of your means would want with a pair of poor moonshiners like ourselves in a lonesome, out of the way spot like this.' There was a definite note of suspicion in the voice which Divareli did his best to allay.

'When I crashed into Tom . . .', he was careful to choose his words carefully so that the lunatic and his shotgun would realise that, as promised, he was shouldering complete responsibility for the accident, '. . . I asked him what was pouring out of the churn and after a while he told me of your operation here.'

When Divareli saw Johnny glaring balefully at his partner, he thought further amplification might be in order. 'It was just as well that he did, because when I was with Sergeant Moriarty this afternoon, he was asking me what was in the churn. I told him that all

I saw coming out of it was milk, but I'm not sure if he believed me. Had Tom not told me the truth of the matter, I mightn't have known any better and said that it was brown stuff smelling like beer.'

Johnny seemed mollified by this. 'Well then, maybe 'tis all for the best in the end. You'll understand we don't encourage sightseers – to tell the truth you're the first that has laid eyes on this place apart from the two of ourselves.' Divareli signalled his appreciation of the great honour with a curt nod. 'Is there anything special you'd like to know?'

Divareli racked his brain for something that might sound like an intelligent question. Eventually he could come up with no better than, 'What's your market? I mean, do you supply individuals or bars?'

Johnny thought for a moment before answering. 'A bit of both. We have someone who sells it to the pubs – but that's different stuff to what we give our own customers.'

'In what way?' Divareli was genuinely interested now. His ancestors had been rum-runners during Prohibition, though it was not a part of the family history often referred to, especially in the Annual Reports of Italbank.

'Yerrah some of the pubs put it straight into the whiskey so we have to make up the mash with barley and colour the drop with a shake of Bisto. That way it tastes and looks like the real thing. To my mind, 'tis better than a lot of the whiskey that comes out of the bottle but that's a matter of opinion, I suppose.'

It transpired that Johnny's credentials as a bootlegger were impeccable. 'My poor father was the best respected poteen-maker in the land and that's not one word of a lie. They used to say that the stuff Mikey Joe Slattery made wasn't poteen at all, but pure nectar. He was so famous that they offered him the price of several farms of land to go to America during the Prohibition to show how 'twas made but he refused. Said a fortune-teller had warned him that he'd be drowned if he crossed water. Anyway, he couldn't leave his stock after him for, you see, he used to keep the poteen in sherry casks for a year or so. Every so often he'd go down to where he had them hidden and give them a bit of a turn. He'd tell no one but meself where they were and sure I was only a slip of a child at the time. God rest his soul but he always said that that was the most important part of the whole business – the moving of the casks. When there

200

was rationing of every sort during the war, sure the so-called respectable citizens had a path beaten to his door for "a cure" – judges, politicians and, of course, the clergy. That's not to say that the present man touches the stuff. In fact he's dead down on it. The poor, dacent man makes out 'twas the poteen killed his own father.'

'And did it?' Divareli could not contain his curiosity any further.

Johnny seemed deeply offended by the question. 'Indeed and it did no such of a thing. Poteen never killed anyone and that's the gospel truth.'

Divareli was unconvinced. He had heard many stories to the contrary. 'I was always told back home in New York that if you drank moonshine you'd go blind or die – or both!'

'Yerrah that's only nonsense, man. The only poor divils I ever heard of who were killed from it came from the north. All of a sudden they decided to go into the business for themselves without knowing the first thing about it. Sure didn't they go and buy an iron barrel off a tinker without even bothering to wash it out properly. What the poor shaggers didn't know was that the barrel had held weedkiller, stuff called paraquat that's pure poison. It was that and downright ignorance that killed them – not poteen. Mind you, I'm not advising you to take stuff off a complete stranger. Some of the blackguards in the business don't care tuppence about making "the pure drop". 'Tis just the quick shilling they're after! They use washing soda to clear the poteen, for Jaysus sake! It looks fine and of course, it's much quicker to make, but the stuff is pure poison. 'Twould put the eyes crossways in your head. You can always tell it's bad stuff by the way a drop of it will curdle milk. 'Tis greedy bastards like them that are killing the trade – and the Guards, of course. That Sergeant Moriarty above in the town will never give me a minute's peace. I never use anything artificial when I'm making the drop, only barley, yeast and water. I can promise there's some that would travel ten miles on their bare feet for the first sip of the pure drop.' He lapsed into silence as he held a glass up to the light.

Long Tom spoke for the first time. 'What about the fairies?'

His partner nodded and poured what was in the glass on to a patch of bare earth. Feeling that some explanation was in order, Long Tom said, 'I make him do that every time. If the little people don't get a drop to keep them happy, there'll be nothing but trouble! And God knows we've enough of that as things stand with that shagger of a Sergeant.'

Johnny winked again at Divareli before elaborating on their problems with the Law. ''Tis true, for that Sergeant Moriarty has the heart put crossways in us. Things have got so bad that Tom has to make up the mash in his own place.'

'Aye, on the blanket!'

The two bootleggers were shaking with laughter. Divareli, though he could not see the joke, thought to join in as Johnny explained.

'The mash needs a steady heat and because the Sergeant knows we work together, he'd be watching Tom's place too. The only way we could think of to keep the milk churn warm while the mash was fermenting was to wrap an electric blanket round it.'

'And does it work?'

'Oh, the finest! The trouble is in getting from his place to here. That's where you came in. Would you say the Sergeant caught the smell of it off the road? I know Tom told me it rained after you running into him but still and all 'tis a fierce strong smell it has and no mistake.'

Divareli considered his reply carefully. 'I guess he did at that. At least, he asked me if I'd been drinking beer before the crash because he got the smell of it from the car.'

'And what way did you answer the hoor?' There was no mistaking the sharp edge in Johnny's voice.

'I told him that I hadn't been drinking and then the telephone rang. After that, he didn't mention the matter any more.'

The bootleggers eyed one another silently. Johnny stroked the stubble on his chin a few times and then gave his nose a ritual wipe with the same hand before lifting the far-from-clean glass and offering it to Divareli. 'You might as well have the first sup.'

There was no escape. Should he savour it with all the deliberation of a *connoisseur* sipping a rare single malt, or would it be wiser to knock it back straight off, like a schnapps, in the hope that it would not remain in the mouth long enough to remove the enamel off his teeth *en passant*? Opting for the latter, he put the grubby glass to his lips and swallowed its contents in one gulp. Nothing of any consequence happened for a moment or two. This lull proved to be the calm before the storm: without warning, a hand-grenade ex-

ploded in the pit of his stomach, belching flames and metal frag-
ments upward and outward through his nose and mouth. The fireball
eventually settled down to a mere seething inferno, but even then
he still couldn't catch his breath. As his eyes watered uncon-
trollably, he tried to rid himself of the notion that he had, in some
way as yet unclear, swallowed the blow-torch as a chaser to the
'pure drop'. When he regained control of his vocal chords, the best
he could manage was a hoarse, 'Keerist Almighty!'

The pair were watching him with ill-concealed mirth. After a
while Johnny sought to console him.

''Tis best to take a small sip first, I find.'

Long Tom nodded solemnly in agreement.

23

As he walked back towards the Brulagh Inn, Divareli was unaware that another pair of eyes were watching him. The Sergeant's curiosity had first been aroused by Divareli's eagerness to take the blame when it was clear as daylight that Long Tom had been in the wrong. Then the unmistakeable smell of 'wash' at the scene of the accident heightened his suspicions. Add to that the Superintendent's unprecedented second telephone call of the day that came through shortly after Divareli had left the station, and Gus knew he would have to keep an eye on the Yank. Apparently the American Embassy in Dublin were interested in him and the other fellow, Abe something or other.

Tailing Divareli was a long-shot but it just might pay off. From bitter experience, he knew he was just wasting time in trying to track Johnny or Long Tom to where they had hidden the still. They could sniff the Law at fifty paces in a high wind before vanishing like a pair of will o' the wisps. Instead the Sergeant had to settle for following Divareli, whose progress was punctuated at irregular intervals by the flash of a torch. From a distance it was impossible to say whether the Yank did this to see where he was going or to signal to someone trying to make contact.

Suddenly, the Yank disappeared into the mist. When Gus realised that he had lost him, he cursed silently for a solid minute before mulling over where his quarry might have gone. He reminded himself that it was quite possible that the man was just going for an innocent walk on a frosty, moonlit night. The road passed the Golf Club. If this were his destination, he would have no option but to come back the same way. Perhaps the Yank wanted a quiet drink there, though to judge by the look of him in the station, drink was the very last thing the man would want. Still and all after Jenny's description of his performance last night, especially his rendering of *Galway Bay* and *My Wild Irish Rose*, it would be quite understandable if he were to give Sean's place a miss for a day or two until the memory had passed into a welcome oblivion.

Another possibility was that, unseen by Gus, he had met his contact and they had taken to the fields. It could be a tryst with the Lady Aphra but that seemed hardly likely. They did not strike Gus as a couple who would make love in a ditch, especially a frozen one. Still, as Jenny had sniffed when she described how Aphra had helped her put Divareli to bed last night, there was no accounting for tastes. Afterwards the two women had chatted over a cup of coffee, in the course of which Aphra had hinted that her relationship with the Yank was not progressing as speedily as she would have wished, due to a series of mishaps that always seemed to occur at the critical moment. The pleasure Jenny took in imparting this nugget of information to the Sergeant was unmistakeable.

If Gus were in luck the suspect, as he now reluctantly regarded Divareli, was meeting Long Tom for some reason connected with their drinking session of the previous night. If that were so then it was more than likely something to do with poteen. Jenny had unwittingly supported this theory when she angrily disclaimed responsibility for their sorry state by hinting that it was due to the bottle in Long Tom's pocket rather than what had been legitimately bought over the counter.

Gus waited behind a low stone wall across the road from the milk platform and reviewed his options. These were either to wait a while longer, or cut his losses and go home to bed. His dark blue uniform and peaked cap gave him all the cover he required to melt into the darkness. He had just decided that he was on a fool's errand when a flash of light came from the direction of the fort. Others more gullible than himself might have attributed it to the fairy lights. If Johnny Slattery's aunt were to be believed, they shone from the magical bodies of the *sidhe* or little people who liked nothing better than to dance the night away in fairy forts.

Even his own mother had warned him that should he ever come across the little people and be invited to dance that it would be wise to do so with good grace. They were a tetchy lot by all accounts and refusal to join in their merrymaking would cause them to cast a spell that would make him dance till he dropped from exhaustion. Then he would be whisked away to Tir na n-Og, the home of the fairies. This did not seem as unattractive a prospect now as it did at his mother's knee. With retirement just around the corner followed by the inevitable slide into a lonely decrepitude, Tir na n-Og

– which meant the Land of Eternal Youth – seemed a better alternative.

Retirement though, despite its drawbacks, would provide a welcome relief from the mounting pressures of his job. Until quite recently the most he was expected to do was to keep an eye on Brulagh and its immediate surroundings. This involved reminding the villagers to tax their cars, pay their TV licences and desist from riding bicycles at night without a light. And, of course, keeping a beady eye on the pair of moonshiners. Of late all this had changed – and not for the better. A directive from the Department of Justice ordained that the evil of illicit distillation be weeded out root and branch once and for all. This, it had to be admitted, was not in response to any outcry from a gullible electorate. In fact it was at the behest of the Minister for Finance who strongly objected to missing out on Excise Duties that otherwise would have swollen his coffers. At a more local level, the Brulagh Pioneer Total Abstinence Association in the persons of Julia May – the priest's housekeeper – and Maggie, long-suffering spouse of Mick Flannery, indicated a view similar to that of the Minister for Justice.

That brief flash of light from the fort continued to bother him. He could not know that it had been caused by the door of the underground chamber opening to let out Divareli. A minute or two later he suddenly appeared from nowhere, walking briskly in the direction of the village. Gus did not make the connection between the two events until much later that night. When it finally dawned on him that the fort might be the latest hiding place for the still, he had seriously considered getting out of his warm bed and raiding the place there and then. However, wiser counsels soon prevailed. There was an intricate fretwork of ice on the bedroom window, refracting the moonlight into delicately wrought abstractions. Lying in bed he reflected sadly that if his previous forays were anything to go by, the most he could hope to capture was the still and its attachments. The two blackguards would be long gone before he got within a stone's throw of the fort.

Of course, seizing the equipment would be better than nothing and in ordinary circumstances he would have probably gone ahead and done so. At the very least it would have guaranteed a front-page picture in the *Clarion*, which he would send post-haste to the Superintendent. It would portray himself in full uniform with an axe raised over the timber barrel of wash and its tell-tale copper worm. The caption would read '*A good night's work. Sergeant Moriarty about to destroy an illicit poteen still.*' Below that would be the headline: *HUGE QUANTITY OF POTEEN FOUND IN RAID*!

Charley Halpin's purple prose would in no way be coloured by the fact that he was the sole distributor for 'the mountain dew' – a profitable sideline to his journalistic career at a princely commission of two pounds per bottle. The fact that he sold advertising space for the *Clarion* in the same area as his poteen concession gave him access to all commercial premises, including public-houses – thus providing him with a perfect cover. Though Gus knew this as well as the twin Cassandras, Julia May and Maggie Flannery, it was a very different matter altogether to actually prove it.

From between the warm sheets he savoured the prospect of such public praise but a tiny, nagging voice reminded him that neither his Superintendent nor the Pioneers would be satisfied with the mere seizure of poteen and a still. Both could be replaced at short notice and set up again in any one of a thousand places. It was the heads of Johnny and Long Tom on a plate that the hoors were after, and they would continue to snap at his heels until they got what they wanted. Which was the reason the Superintendent had promised him reinforcements, albeit day-time ones. He hoped they wouldn't be raw recruits, red of face and neck, fresh out of training school with their notebooks and pencils at the ready. More the pity that the stupid Government cutbacks did not allow a night raid, now he knew for certain where the two blackguards kept their still.

Before he fell asleep, he chuckled happily to himself at the start he had given Divareli when he had sidled up beside him on the dark road and bade him goodnight. His future employer had jumped like a gaffed salmon with the sheer fright but not before Gus had got a familiar whiff of liquorice off his breath. As even the most ardent teetotallers knew full well, the best poteen smelled of those sweets that every schoolchild would have given their eye-teeth for after mass on Sundays. They were called liquorice allsorts.

As for Divareli, he had far greater difficulty in getting to sleep. The events of the day cascaded through his mind in a kaleidoscope of jumbled thoughts. How in the name of all that was holy could he possibly have got involved with a pair of bootleggers, much less become hopelessly drunk with one of them? Then there was the business of bumping into the Sergeant on the road. Had he been 'tailed' to the fort? Would he be prosecuted for aiding and abetting known criminals or would the Sergeant's guns be spiked by the prospect of joining the board of Orchid Investments? Which reminded him, the matter of inviting Gally on the board could not be put off much longer. Divareli was damned if he was going to ask the blue-blooded bastard himself after his 'Dago' remark. Abe was due back the day after next and he could do the dirty work. That way, Divareli would stay in the clear with Aphra when the time came to hang her father out to dry.

A further complication arose as he passed through the deserted bar of the Brulagh Inn and climbed wearily up the stairs to his room. Sean called after him, 'How's the head? I hear you went on a bit of a tear with Long Tom last night. Jenny was telling me that every so often, in between singing, the two of ye were taking a nip from the bottle as a chaser for the pints of stout. I'm sorry I missed that, though I couldn't admit it to herself or she'd have my life. Oh, I nearly forgot! Father Jerry phoned looking for you earlier. Said to tell you that himself and the Doc are going shooting pheasants after lunch tomorrow if you'd like to join them. He told me to be sure and tell you that he even has a spare gun organised for you. Sleep well!'

24

Everything looked very different in daylight. The overnight frost had gone and the ground was soft and muddy. Their wellington boots squelched noisily as they walked towards the fort. Far above them a wedge of wild geese were silhouetted stark against the evening sky. Crows and wood-pigeons cawed and clucked from the topmost branches of the tall, skeletal trees that encircled the fort. But it was pheasant they were after. It would seem that these, survivors of the great escape from Gally's orchard, had grown wary. Divareli wondered if the two bootleggers were even now at their still. Would Long Tom again find the courage to pull the trigger of his elderly weapon that was held together with wire? This time his aim might be truer. Whatever happened, Divareli hoped that the bootleggers would realise that the fort had not been his choice to shoot over. This had been the decision of the Doc and Father Jerry, who were crashing around noisily in the open clearing that he had visited last night.

Suddenly a blue car roared up the road and skidded to a halt in front of the milk-stand. From where he stood outside the fort, Divareli could just make out the word GARDA etched in black on a plastic roof sign. This was flanked on either side by a chrome spotlight. A number of uniformed men, including the familiar figure of Sergeant Moriarty, piled out of the car. They filed through the narrow gap in the ditch and immediately started to fan out wordlessly, striding towards Divareli in a determined manner. It began to dawn on him that this was a raid. He recalled the Superintendent's telephone call to the Station yesterday. Gus had said something like, 'Send them on soon as you can . . .' Well, it looked as though the Sergeant's reinforcements had arrived.

Just then a pigeon rocketed out of a tree at the far side of the fort, disturbed by the noise being made by the Doc and Father Jerry. Without a moment's hesitation Divareli raised the gun to his shoulder, flicking off the safety catch with his thumb as he did so, and let fly with both barrels. The noise was tremendous. The bird was never in any danger. From the first moment it appeared it had been well out of range. By now it was halfway to Brulagh. The ricochet from the double burst of gunfire caused the stock of the barrel to jump from his shoulder and strike him sharply on the nose. His eyes began to water and it was a moment or two before he could congratulate himself that his efforts had not been in vain. Like a pair of foxes breaking cover, two figures emerged from the far side of the fort, one with a gun in his hand and the other with a gunny sack slung over his shoulder from which protruded the familiar shape of the copper 'worm'. Though almost bent double to avoid being seen, they scurried across the stretch of open ground between the fort and the ditch at the far end of the field with commendable speed. They had disappeared from view by the time the posse reached Divareli.

When the Sergeant spoke, his voice was heavy with sarcasm. 'That was the lucky pigeon and no mistake. He must have been a good quarter of a mile away by the time you let fly at him. 'Twas a miracle that he didn't drop down dead of the fright. That's the only thing that would have killed him from this distance, so it was!' The Sergeant's uniformed colleagues, their heavy black shoes now caked in mud, nodded their wholehearted agreement.

'Come on, lads, and we'll see if there's any more game left inside this place. At a guess, though, I'd have to say that Mr Divareli here is after frightening off whatever might have been in there!'

As they headed for the entrance at the far side of the fort they were met by the priest and the doctor. The latter was first to speak.

'If it isn't yourself, Sergeant – and a search-party along with you, if I'm not mistaken. It wouldn't be the little people you're after, by any chance?'

Before any of the *gendarmerie* could reply, the Doc was off again. 'Well, all I can say to the lot of you is that if it's pheasant you're after, you're in the wrong place. There's neither trace nor tidings of them to be found anywhere inside that Godforsaken place. Isn't it true, Father?' The Priest nodded in a noncommittal manner.

The Sergeant looked the Doc directly in the eye and answered with a straight face, 'It's a different class of a bird altogether that we're after.'

210

The Guards tipped their caps respectfully at the man of God and nodded to the Doc before making their way past him into the fort, hard on the heels of the Sergeant.

As they walked back towards the village, the three stopped beside a low wall crowned with a strand of rusted barbed wire while Father Jerry tried to light his pipe. A north wind of Siberian bleakness made his task impossible. He sighed and expressed the view that their excursion seemed dogged with ill-luck. They had flushed out nothing better in the fort than two bootleggers, and now he couldn't light his cursed pipe. It was the first reference anyone had made to those who had fled across the fields. Until that moment Divareli had thought that he alone had seen them. On reflection he realised that they could hardly have climbed out of the tunnel, replaced the sheet of corrugated iron and the section of briars and made a run for it without being observed by either the Doc or Father Jerry. Inwardly he wondered whether their silence to the Guards on the matter could be construed as aiding and abetting a felony. One thing was certain, the Sergeant was displeased at his firing the loose shots after the distant pigeon. Further consideration of the implications of this were interrupted by the Doc.

'I wonder would it be worth our while to give a bit of a walk through the bog over there? We've time yet before it gets dark and we might bag a snipe or two for our trouble. God knows there's not much eating in them but 'twould be better than nothing. As it is we can hardly send Father Jerry home to Julia May empty-handed. He'd never hear the end of it.'

Father Jerry confirmed this without rancour. 'You're right there.' He turned to Divareli and said by way of explanation, 'My house-keeper has a reputation for being something of a tartar. I think I may have referred to her views on punctuality that time we played golf together.'

Divareli remembered it well. That was the conversation in which Marcinkus and Italbank had cropped up. He hoped those twin topics would not be resurrected now. A hurried call from Abe earlier in the day hinted that all was not well with the New York end of things. He had cut short Divareli's questions with a curt, 'Can't talk now, gotta go and sort out a coupla things. I'll be on the two-fifteen flight tomorrow. See you then.' This worried Divareli. Until now, Abe had looked after the projects *in situ* and financing had been Divareli's province. This seemed to be changing for no good reason and he did not like it. After all, Abe *did* have a certain reputation though, to be fair, the guy had never got out of line on anything they had been involved in. Up to now. Brulagh was a fine place but it was a long way away from The Street. That had been a definite plus in the beginning when all he wanted was to relax and get away from it all.

Then he had dreamed up the Orchid Project. Ever since then the damn thing felt like it had taken on a life of its own. He wished he wasn't so much in love with Aphra. Love complicated everything. This was especially true when it came to settling scores with her father. Well, whatever it was that was bothering Abe, it had better not prevent the old conman from putting on his snake-oil salesman act for the Eleventh Earl of Gallerick.

Before long, they were wading through soggy marshland, their guns at the ready. Suddenly ten yards ahead a flock of small birds popped out of the waterlogged reeds like corks from a well-shaken champagne bottle. Three guns blazed and four snipe dropped to the ground. Their companions zigzagged out of range as the three collected the corpses and reloaded. This was repeated several times in the next hour, during which Divareli inquired, 'Won't people object to our shooting over their property?'

This thought had been occasioned as much by Donnelly's mind-numbing dissertation on the love the Irish bore for every blade of grass on their land as by the fact that, at this rate, they would soon make the snipe – along with certain orchids and frogs – an endangered species. The body count currently stood at fourteen.

'Yerrah not at all. Where we are is only a bog – good for snipe and damn all else. The widow who owns it is a patient of mine. We'll offer her a few snipe though they wouldn't go far with the number of mouths she has to feed. A brace of mallard or a greylag goose would be of more use to her. Since her husband left her, Johnny Slattery is helping out around the farm. He's probably hiding in her cottage this very minute until the coast is clear of the Guards.'

'When you say her husband left her, what exactly do you mean? I thought there was no divorce in Ireland?' Divareli was perplexed and he showed it.

Priest and doctor exchanged meaningful glances. After a moment's hesitation they shrugged their shoulders as if to say, 'What

212

the hell does it matter now, anyway?' and then the Doc growled, 'You're right, there isn't. The poor divil hanged himself a while back. He was in trouble with the bank. Left a rake of children after him, so he did. I'd say the widow's going to marry that blackguard Johnny one of these days. Could be the making of him for all anyone knows. What do you think, Father – will the widow catch him this time?'

'If he shows the same turn of speed to her as he did haring across that field with the still on his back, I wouldn't bet money on it. Anyway, what would a celibate like myself know about things like that? More to the point, would you tell me if that's a grey goose over there by the lake, or do my eyes deceive me?'

The Doc shaded his face with a hand as he stared into the dazzling sunset. He looked long and hard before replying. 'Hard to say from this distance. We'd want to be damn sure that it isn't one of Joe Gallagher's swans before we open fire.'

Some sixth sense must have warned the bird of their intentions, for it veered sharply for no good reason and flapped off gracefully until it was lost forever behind the mountain.

Nine tiny bodies stared back up at them from the silver dish. Spindly legs pointed skywards in a perfect 'dead budgerigar' pose. What set them apart was their beaks, which were every bit as long as their dainty carcases. Julia May had skewered the beaks through the breast – giving the impression that the snipe had engaged in a ritual *hari kiri*, rather than fallen victim to a hail of buckshot in a bog.

Two bottles of a Chianti *riserve* stood guard over them, while a bottle of The Macallan, Divareli's contribution to the proceedings, waited patiently on the sideboard. One silver dish held creamed potatoes, and another was filled to the brim with chopped celery in a delicate butter sauce. Julia May cleared away the empty soup plates as Father Jerry splashed wine into enormous goblets with the Vatican crest emblazoned on their bowls. Divareli asked his host about the wine. It bore an unfamiliar *classico riserva* label from the district of Panzano.

'Where's that exactly?'

The Doc had been to Rome with the previous parish priest of Brulagh and thus regarded himself as an authority on all things Italian. As proof of this, he used the bronze head of a Florentine

213

lion as a door-knocker. 'Up in the mountains outside Siena. Bang in the middle of the Chianti region, isn't it, Father?'

The priest confirmed this. 'Yes, indeed. I have an old friend who sends me a few cases of it every Christmas.' He broke off to turn to Divareli.

'I hope you'll like it. One of the reasons I chose it for tonight is that I believe your ancestors come from quite near there. Another reason is that it's a *vino nobile*, my favourite of all the Chiantis though connoisseurs seem to think it a bit rough. At least, the only book I ever looked it up in said as much. I thought it would go well with the snipe.'

It did. The birds had a delicate quail-like taste without being too gamey. Julia May had dismissed them peevishly when the priest laid them out on the kitchen table. 'God love us but you'd get more meat off a fieldmouse.'

In fact there was more flesh than one would have expected. As he concentrated on removing delicate strips of meat from the tiny bones, Divareli pondered long and hard on where the priest had got his information about his ancestral seat. Old Cesare had put out that the Divarelis were a once-proud Sienese family, when the truth was that they were debt-ridden *pezzanovante* who had had to flee the wrath of their creditors and seek a fesh start in the New World.

Just as Julia May had once again cleared the plates from the table and was bringing in a steaming casserole of bread pudding from the kitchen, the telephone in the hall jangled.

'Heads it's for you, tails it's for me.' The Doc recited this in a sing-song voice as though it were a favourite nursery rhyme. In fact it was for him. He took the call, then reappeared in the doorway. 'Thanks for the dinner, Father. Be sure to say the same to Julia May for me. I must be off so I'll let myself out. It's the old blacksmith on the far side of the mountain. I'm afraid there's not much I can do for him, but he's been a patient of mine since I first came here so I'd better give him a proper send-off. If I think you're needed before tomorrow, I'll phone you from there.'

The last sentence was delivered with an impish grin as he let himself out through the dining-room door. The priest divided the bread pudding evenly between them, helped himself to whipped cream and started in on the *mélange* with apparent gusto. Divareli, preferring his bread in slices or bâtons, moved great gobs of the dessert around his plate to give the illusion that it had been sampled if not actually consumed. When Julia May came in later after they had adjourned to what Father Jerry called his 'den', she harrumphed at this slight to her culinary skills. Turning to a framed woodcut hanging on the wall of the dining room depicting Mary the Mother of God emerging from a fiery cloud, she confided to the Blessed Virgin: ''Tis easy known that Yank doesn't know what's good for him. I never met one of them yet that wasn't contrary about what they ate. Well, if Julia May's Queen of Pudding isn't good enough for him, I know of one that won't say no to it!'

With that she scraped the dessert on to a tin plate and fed it to the cat.

25

The contrast between the den and the almost clinical tidiness of the rest of the house suggested that Julia May's writ did not run this far. Shelves of well-thumbed paperbacks, many supporting one another at crazy angles like amiable drunks, lined the walls. A fireplace with a pot-bellied grate glowed warm with spark-spitting logs and slabs of turf that flamed blue against the soot-blackened chimney breast. A large oil portrait stared down from above the mantelpiece. It was of a young cleric, stern and gaunt, in the sort of pose that the more powerful Renaissance Bishops liked to strike. Arrogant and proud, they clasped a globe in one hand and a crucifix in the other – a statement that Divareli had always felt left little doubt as to their plans for the immediate future.

He stared long and hard at the features before it dawned on him that he was gazing at a younger version of his host. Though the cleric above the fireplace bore neither orb nor sceptre, he had a power-hungry look that was absent from the face of the cheerful fellow seated on the far side of the untidy desk.

A Smith-Corona with a sheet of paper protruding from it had been pushed to one side. Some typing on the exposed page indicated that work on it had been interrupted – or abandoned. Until now, Father Jerry had been preoccupied with lighting his pipe, something that seemed to take up a sizeable portion of his waking hours and greatly exceeded the time he spent actually smoking it. Through the haze of swirling smoke he saw Divareli looking at the portrait and noted with amusement the slow realisation as to who the subject was. It was only when his guest's gaze drifted towards the typewriter that he felt some explanation might be in order. In it there was a letter, as yet unfinished, to Gianni Manolo Agostini, shepherd of the tiny Boggola flock, of which he did not wish his guest to see any part. That which was visible above the rollbar expressed thanks for the information on Luca Divareli and Italbank, especially the rumours of its impending collapse, and requested further details on its off-

216

shore funding methods as soon as possible. It also asked for any information Agostini might have on one Abraham Solomon Linovitz of New York, expressing regret that no further details of him were currently available other than the fact that in the recent past he had worked closely with Divareli.

With a sweep of his hand, Father Jerry removed the letter and crumpled it into a ball. Dropping it into the wastepaper basket, he lied with as much conviction as he could muster, 'My sermon for next Sunday. It's supposed to deal with the seventh commandment. *"Thou shalt not steal"*,' he added helpfully, lest Divareli had forgotten them – a racing certainty if but a fraction of what Agostini had said of Italbank and its former owner were true.

'I have always found it the most difficult of the commandments to explain to my flock,' he went on smoothly. 'They have no trouble in accepting that things like adultery are morally wrong, even killing – though one might have difficulty in believing this to judge by what's happening every day in the north. Nevertheless, your average mass-goer will take my word for it that murder and fornication are wrong. What they refuse point-blank to accept is that the seventh commandment is not automatically suspended whenever a business transaction takes place. Now tell me this: do you find the same thing applies in New York?'

'If you mean about stealing, sure. Only they dress it up in fancy names like insider trading or arbitraging. But, yeah, I guess it's plain stealing just the same.'

The priest busied himself pouring The Macallan into chunky cut-glass tumblers. There was a jug of water, its crystal cut to the same pattern, but neither of them used it. The priest took a sip of the dark malt whisky and murmured appreciatively, 'I haven't tried this one before. It's smokier, heavier I suppose than the Glenmorangie I bring out on State occasions. Not unlike the best poteen in some ways, I suppose. Did you know that there are still people who will tell you that the poteen lost its smokey taste when it was no longer made over a turf fire? That, of course, is absolute nonsense since the heat source, be it gas, turf – or nuclear fission for that matter – has absolutely nothing to do with the taste.'

'Why so?' Divareli was genuinely interested, though he wondered whence this line of talk was leading.

'For the simple reason that the heat source cannot possibly affect the taste of what is in a container. The water used in the "wash" could have an effect, of course. Obviously that from a brackish stream tastes different from water straight out of a tap. Speaking of poteen, that was a timely burst of fire you let loose just as the Sergeant and his troupe appeared on the scene. Johnny and Long Tom have a lot to be grateful to you for. Did you do it on purpose?'

Divareli eyed his host for a while before replying. 'I guess so. I had been watching them make the stuff last night down in the tunnel.'

'Souterrain, that's what it's called. An underground chamber where the tribes of old took refuge from their enemies. The Brulagh one is bigger than most of them. It was clever of them to choose it. Most of the people round here think it's an ancient burial site and keep well clear of it, especially at night. Obviously the two buckos have no such qualms. There was great excitement around here a few years back when a new spade was found abandoned inside the fort next to a freshly-dug hole in the ground. Some said it was a treasure-hunter digging for treasure who was frightened off by something – or someone. Anyway, it was enough to keep most people away from the place. At a guess I'd say it was Johnny who left the spade there with that very intention, though it's not like him to waste money on a new spade.'

'Mebbe he wrote it off to protection, like a burglar alarm on your house or a timelock on a safe?'

'That may well be the case. I wonder if the Sergeant and his colleagues have discovered the souterrain by now? Not that it matters so much once the worm is safe. That's the only really valuable bit of equipment in a still, you know. Everything else can be replaced quite easily but a good worm is like a favourite violin – you can play beautiful music on it if you have the right skill.'

'You seem to know a hell of a lot about bootlegging, Father, if you don't mind my saying so.'

'Why wouldn't I? I might as well admit it. All my family were in "the business" up to their necks. The money they made from it sent me to the college in Maynooth so you could say that it actually made a priest out of me. Whether that is an example of good coming from evil I'll leave yourself to decide. My father died because of it . . .'

Divareli could not believe the coincidence and just had to inter-rupt. 'So did my mine! Not my father but my grandfather, to be precise. The Mob killed him when he tried to muscle in on their rum-running operation!'

'How very interesting. Do you mind if I ask his name?'

'Farrell. Kevin Farrell. When he got killed my mother remarried, this time to an Italian – Luca Divareli, my grandfather.'

Bells jangled in the dim dark recesses of his memory. The name Farrell had cropped up in another context quite recently. Could it have been when the Lady Aphra persuaded him to write to the Office of Diocesan Studies in New York? He would check it out the first chance he got. Not now, however. The conversation was far too interesting to risk an interruption that might break the flow. Agostini had been on the phone just before his guests arrived. He had further alarming news of Italbank and its connections, which had made the crumpled letter completely redundant.

'And the founder of Italbank, isn't that so?'

'Yeah, he started out as a mobster, then cleaned up his act and founded a bank. He often joked that it was much easier to rob someone with a suit and a briefcase than with a bulletproof vest and a machine gun.'

'You are quite certain it was meant as a joke?' Father Jerry smiled with his mouth but not with his eyes as he posed the question, then without waiting for an answer he pressed on: 'I seem to recall you saying that his son – your father, that is – was a friend of Archbishop Marcinkus, did you not?'

'I did, though I don't think either of them ever boasted of the fact. Like I told you, my father was Kevin Farrell's boy. When the Irish gangs shot Luca, he couldn't have any kids of his own so young Charley Farrell became Cesare Divareli – my old man.'

'How very interesting . . .'

As indeed it was. If the perfectly outlandish theory that was beginning to form in Father Jerry's mind had any basis whatsoever in reality, it could really put the cat among the pigeons. For the time being he would just have to be patient and wait until his guest departed, then he would have to find that damn letter. In the mean-time he would put out a feeler or two to check if Agostini's infor-mation was correct. There was always the possibility, of course, that the news had not yet reached Divareli.

219

'I believe that Italbank is encountering some rough weather just at the moment. Did you know that?' The priest's eyebrows arched inquiringly as he put the question.

Divareli wondered where the hell this cleric in the asshole of nowhere was getting sensitive information like this. He took a deep draught of The Macallan and shook his head. 'Not really. Abe was on a few hours ago and said that there seemed to be one or two problems in New York but he didn't spell them out, not over the telephone.'

'I'm afraid that my informant had no such reservations.' Father Jerry was too polite to add that perhaps he didn't have as much to hide from prying ears as the tough little Jewish streetfighter from Queens.

Divareli accepted another tumblerful of his own whisky and could barely hide his impatience. 'So what had this guy, whoever he is, to say about Italbank? I gotta tell you the last time I checked it was doing fine, just fine.'

'That may well be the case. I do not dispute that, not for a moment. All I want to say is that my informant tells me that Italbank bonds were being traded in Zurich this evening at a discount of thirty per cent. That means little or nothing to me but he seemed to think it was a straw in the wind.' Until this, the priest had barely touched his drink. Now that he had said what he wanted to say, he felt he had earned it. He reduced the level in his glass by a third as he waited for a reaction.

'Jeezuss – sorry, Father – but that can't be right! If it is, you sure could describe it as rough weather. Hurricane stuff would be nearer the mark!'

As the thunderbolt sank in, he blew out through his lips, making a noise like air escaping from a balloon. Then he straightened in his chair and his voice took on a sterner tone. 'You wouldn't care to give me the source of this information?'

The priest shook his head firmly. 'Afraid not. The best I can do is to describe it as "a usually reliable source". Is it really that bad?'

'I'll tell you how bad it is – if it's true, that is. I sold most of my stake in Italbank last year to a Swiss banker. Because Italbank is a privately owned Corporation with restrictions on whom I – or anyone else on the board – is allowed to sell its paper to, the only buyer I could find was this Swiss outfit. My board approved the deal and it went through in bearer bonds. The value of those bonds is an indication of the health of a company – in this case Italbank – when it is not publicly quoted on any Stock Exchange. Even though it's supposed to be a private matter, word gets out sooner or later, especially in Switzerland. Those bastards can smell trouble a mile off.'

It was Father Jerry's turn to be surprised. 'I was always led to believe that the Swiss were the very soul of discretion, with their banking-secrecy laws and all that sort of thing.'

'Naw, not any more. It may have been true once though I have my doubts about that, even in the good old days. They're a funny race, the Swiss. Everyone pictures them as solid burghers with cuckoo clocks and funny hats who run banks and ski-resorts. People tend to forget that they were mercenary fighters for most of their history . . .'

Father Jerry interjected. 'Of course, the Swiss Guard at the Vatican . . .'

'Yeah, that's right . . .', Divareli was in full flight now and nothing was going to stop him, '. . . and dozens of brigades just like them. The Swiss – and the Irish, too – sold their swords to the highest bidder. Then the Swiss woke up one morning and realised that they were really only fighting each other. So they gave it up – the fighting, I mean – and settled into running banks and ski-resorts. They made more money that way and didn't get killed doing it, either. Not often, anyway!'

'Calvi did.'

'Aw come off it, Father! That's a cheap shot if ever I heard one. Surely you're not comparing Italbank to Banco Ambrosiano? By the time they found Roberto hanging from a girder under Blackfriars bridge, the poor guy was more of a politician than a banker, no matter what the Press – or the Vatican said. What am I saying? You must have been in the thick of it in those days, am I right?'

'Not quite. I was in South America till early 1983. "God's banker" was dead almost a year by the time I got back to the Vatican.'

Father Jerry felt it unnecessary to reveal his work for Pro Fratribus, a rather shady religious organisation. It was ostensibly there for the distribution of aid to Eastern Europe and South America. As a political-religious operation it was widely suspected of supplying money, if not arms, to left-wing rebels in some South American countries. Father Jerry, even then, believed that this was carrying the Liberation Theology so popular at the time a trifle too far. When his involvement with social causes became too much for the Brazilian government, they shipped him back to the Vatican. Divareli was speaking again

'I'd forgotten the handle they stuck on him. "God's banker" was a good one. Didn't the London Coroner bring in a verdict of suicide?' Father Jerry stroked his chin as though trying to remember before making an answer.

'The first one did, as far as I can remember . . .'

In fact he remembered only too well. His boss, Cardinal Castelli, had him filing clippings for months afterwards from every major newspaper in the world.

'. . . then a Milan Insurance Company – I forget which one – proved that Calvi could not have hanged himself under the bridge so London held a second inquest. This time they brought in an "open verdict".'

'Which means you can believe anything you want, right Father?'

'Precisely.'

Father Jerry decided that this would be as good a time as any to call a halt to the proceedings. They both had a lot of information to digest and the bottle of The Macallan had suffered terminal damage. Without further ado he rose to his feet, murmuring as he did so, 'I trust the work on the golf-course is progressing favourably?'

Divareli's mind was obviously still miles away. It took a moment for him to realise that the priest was politely but firmly indicating that the night was at an end. His asking about the work in progress was merely a courtesy.

'Oh, fine. Well ahead of schedule, in fact. We're rushing things along as much as we can. There's a big storm out in the Atlantic, apparently. The weather people say it's static for the moment but they expect it to move in over here shortly.'

Father Jerry nodded as he showed him out through the front door. Julia May had long since retired to her bed. If either of them made the connection between the threatening weather pattern poised in mid-Atlantic and the stormclouds gathering over Italbank he declined to say so.

222

No sooner had he closed the door behind his departing guest than the priest hurried back to the filing cabinet in his den. After some frantic rummaging he at last found what he was looking for. As he read the letter from the New York presbytery, his frown deepened. It took even longer than usual for sleep to come that night.

26

'But Aphra darling, can't you see that's the whole point of the plan! If we can only persuade your friend that he's the rightful heir to this place, he won't hesitate to splash out absolutely zillions of dollars on refurbishing the Hall. That way we won't have to go cap in hand to slimy creatures like Donnelly or Mick Flannery to beg money off them to fix the blasted roof. Nor spend every waking hour trying to be nice to Daft Daphne, I might add. Just think what a difference a million dollars would make to this place. Tennis courts back in action, the gardens bursting forth in all their splendour, croquet on manicured lawns, no more potholes in the avenue, dredge the lake and acres of raked gravel. In fact, everything this blasted place should have but doesn't. And why?'

She knew it was a waste of time to ask, especially when she had heard the answer a thousand times before.

'I'll tell you why, my girl! Because we haven't two bloody brass farthings to rub together, that's why! I had Harmon in here again a few minutes ago, would you believe? Looking for another blasted raise if you don't mind.'

'You mean the same one he has been asking for all along. What excuse did you give him this time?'

'Told him these incessant demands on my slender purse must cease forthwith, that's what I told the old blighter.'

'How did he react to that?'

'Asked me for next weekend off, that's how! Had to give in to him of course, when he claimed that he still had a week's holiday coming to him from last year. Anyway it's better than having to pay him hard cash, especially when we haven't any. You know that as well as I do. And another thing, to get back to your Yank. This male heir thing won't affect your marrying him, y'know, if that's what you had in mind.'

He raised his hand sternly to forestall her yelp of protest before continuing. 'He would be miles outside the forbidden degrees of

224

kindred as dear Father Jerry would call it. So that's no problem either. Now all you've got to do, Aphra my dearest, is to toddle along and tell him that your researches have revealed that he's the nearest living male relative and that if he plays his cards right, he stands to inherit Gallerick Hall the moment the Grim Reaper gives me the nod. That ought to loosen his purse-strings, eh what?'

'Oh God . . .' Aphra stamped her foot in temper. It infuriated her that Gally could be so bloody stupid, especially at times like this.

'That's about the most focking ridiculous idea you've ever come up with – and that includes the deer and the pheasant breeding, let me add. *My* Yank, as you call the poor darling, is nobody's fool, least of all yours. Before I got even halfway through your crazy focking story he'd spot the missing link a bloody mile off! Surely to God even you can see that?'

He couldn't. In fact the Eleventh Earl of Gallerick was completely mystified by the introduction of missing links. What the blazes had monkeys and apes got to do with it? All he was asking the bloody woman to do was to tell a tiny white lie to her man about their shared ancestry. Surely that wasn't too much to ask of one's own flesh and blood? As for her language, it was getting worse by the day. No one, not even a jumped-up Dago like Divareli, would want to marry someone with a tongue like Aphra's. Still, this might not be the perfect time to rebuke her on that score. As for her totally unnecessary reminders of his unhappy forays into deer and pheasant breeding, what had they to do with it? In his latter years his own father used to cry out in anguish on occasions like this, 'How do you account for women?' to which he would instantly reply, 'There *is* no accounting for women!' At the time, Gally had thought it a sign of creeping senility. Now he saw it for what it truly was – an incisive and telling insight into the female psyche.

'What damn missing link, for heaven's sake? Try not to talk absolute drivel, Aphra my love!'

Another furious stamp of her foot as she blinked back tears of rage. 'Oh you can be so focking maddening at times . . .'

'Here steady on, no need for that sort of language, y'know. Kindly observe the decencies of civilised debate or we'll just have to chuck the whole thing here and now.'

He tried hard to sound stern. It was, after all, a risky line to take. Nothing would have suited him less than to have her stalk off in high dudgeon at this critical juncture. For days he had been trying to work around to this very subject but with no success – until now. He waited anxiously, watching her swallowing hard, then taking a deep breath to compose herself before answering him quietly rather than shrieking at the top of her voice as she quite obviously longed to do. With exaggerated slowness she spelt it out patiently like a mother explaining something to a backward child.

'The missing link to which I refer is that between Jessie Kelly going to New York, pregnant by our ancestor, dear Rodney, and us having even the slightest shred of evidence that she ever laid eyes, much less anything else for Christ's sake, on someone called Divareli. To prove that Luke is a direct descendant she would have had to marry a Divareli or at least leave some tangible record that she had a descendant who did – eventually. The only suggestion we have so far that Jessie Kelly ever married a Divareli is Johnny's aunt. Even then all she remembers – and I've questioned her on this point often enough, believe me – is *her* own mother telling her that Jessie finished up marrying someone called Davey Leary. Recollection and hearsay, that's all it is. That's a long focking way from proving that she married an Italian called Divareli. I had hoped that even *you* could grasp that blindingly obvious fact!'

If Gally were peeved by this further example of filial rudeness he kept it to himself. It was much more important to drill into this young girl's head the absolute necessity of convincing her *beau* that blue blood was sloshing through his veins. Oh well, he admitted to himself, maybe that was pitching it a bit strong. Trickling would seem to meet the case nicely.

'Oh I don't know so much about that, Aphra my dear. The Yank hardly fetched up in Brulagh entirely by chance, y'know. Maybe he was into this dreadful American thing of tracing one's roots. Always thought myself it should be a relatively easy thing for most Americans. All they need do is to look up the deportation orders served on criminals by Her Majesty's Government.'

Aphra's patience had come to an end. Once mounted on his favourite hobbyhorse, it required plain talking to persuade her father to stable the animal before it had cantered at a leisurely pace over hill and dale. Unfortunately she still had a day's work to do and so was anxious to bring the discussion about Divareli to some sort of sensible conclusion.

'That's absolute focking nonsense, Father, and well you know it! Anyway, it's Australia you're thinking of. The immigrants to America were a respectable lot by comparison. Give me your poor and your hungry sort of thing – and your pregnant, as in the case of poor Jessie Kelly.'

'Not so sure about the poor bit, darling,' Gally interjected with some spirit. 'She did, after all, collar fifty gold sovereigns off Rodney's poor father. That is, of course, always supposing the parish priest handed it over to the deserving poor rather than trousering it for himself. Never did trust those chaps who wear their collar turned back to front!'

Further discussion along these lines was interrupted by a discreet knock. Harmon put his head around the door, coughed discreetly, and announced: 'Mr John Slattery is at the Hall door. He wishes to have a word with your Lordship . . .', seeing Aphra, he added, '. . . in private.'

Aphra raised her eyes to heaven and said a silent prayer in gratitude. But for this, she could still be closeted with her father an hour from now. As she left she couldn't resist teasing Harmon and his master.

'Hope you two are not buying poteen from Johnny to replenish the cellar after the hunt and the dinner party. Not that Johnny's poison could be any worse than the last brandy you bought. Tom Donnelly's wife told me her husband was sick for a week after the dinner party and he blamed it on the brandy you served him. Where on earth did you get it from, Harmon? I took one sip and it almost focking choked me. Absolute gutrot.'

Harmon remained unruffled by the onslaught. 'I bought several cases off the captain of a Spanish trawler that was sheltering in the harbour, your Ladyship. With his Lordship's approval, I might add. The price was quite reasonable, as I recall.'

'I'll bet it was. Probably paid you to take the focking rubbish out of his sight if the truth were known. Well, it's nice to know you've taken to consorting with sailors, Harmon. What next, I wonder? Sheep, perhaps? Oops, here comes the sheep-man himself. Hallo Johnny – and goodbye. *Ave atque vale* everybody, I must rush. Some of us still have jobs to go to.'

After she had left, Harmon ushered in an almost unrecognisable Johnny Slattery. Apart from the cap, which he was reputed to sleep

227

in, everything had changed, changed utterly. He wore a suit with leather patches at the elbows, a shirt that might once have been white and a tie with a knot as big as his fist. Instead of the usual dung-caked wellingtons, he wore a pair of black hobnailed boots that clattered on the floor as he approached Gally's desk.

With reluctance Gally allowed the dream of Divareli becoming the reincarnation of old Nabob to be shelved for the nonce. There was little doubt that the family fortune needed to be restored, and Gally was not especially worried whether the required funding came from the Nabob's India or Divareli's New World. It was to be hoped, of course, that in his dotage Divareli would not take to wandering around the grounds stark naked with a cowbell round his neck to warn the servants of his approach. Perhaps he might emulate the Nabob in riding his horse into the lake in the mistaken belief that it could walk on water. Such was the stuff of legends, Gally decided ruefully as he turned his attention to the latest arrival.

'Well, Johnny, what can I do for you?' A keen observer would have noticed an almost imperceptible change in accent. It was the one his Lordship assumed when addressing the lower orders.

'Well, your Lordship, I was thinking . . .'

Gally resisted the temptation to express surprise that Johnny should attempt such a feat. Instead he steepled his fingers beneath his chin and looked the bootlegger straight in the eye.

'. . . There's an awful lot of your deer running wild around the mountain. Hardly a day goes by but I don't see one or two of them peeping out from behind a furze bush or galloping like the Divil himself was after them over the top of the mountain. So sez I to meself "One of these fine days, some cute hoor will destroy the lot of them with a rifle and then where will his Lordship be?" '

A silence ensued while both parties eyed each other warily. Gally soon gave up trying to tease out whatever it was that could have been rattling around in that great, grey wilderness that was Johnny's mind. What the Eleventh Earl of Gallerick wanted to discover at the earliest possible opportunity was what Johnny's plan was and how much it was going to cost. When no encouragement was forthcoming from across the desk, Johnny pressed on regardless.

'What I was thinking was that if your Lordship was to give me the loan of the Land Rover and the horsebox, I could catch the deer and carry 'em back to the orchard where the divils escaped out of.'

228

Johnny now had the full attention of the meeting. Anything that would get those blasted deer back in captivity before Donnelly came looking for his money automatically guaranteed his Lordship's undivided attention. However, certain elements of the plan were, to put it mildly, as yet far from clear.

'How the blazes would you get the mad buggers to go near the bloody horsebox, much less expect them to walk meekly into the damn thing?'

Johnny remained silent for some time. To tell his Lordship how he proposed to accomplish this was to run the risk of the crafty old bastard doing the job himself – and then where would poor Johnny be? Eventually candour won the day. 'First of all I'd park the jeep and the box way up the mountain, leaving the back door held open with a bit of a stick attached to a long cord. Then I'd shake a few buckets of those calf nuts you used to feed 'em, inside in the box. As soon as one of the deer smells the nuts, it'll walk into the box if it sees no one around, and start in at the nuts. That's where he'll be after making his big mistake, don't you see?'

Gally shook his head to confirm that he did not.

'Well, your Lordship, you see I'll be well hid behind a furzebush and the very minute I see your man safe inside in the box, I'll give a pull to the rope. That'll make the door fall shut with the animal caught inside. Then all I have to do is bring him back to the orchard.'

The idea seemed sound enough. If it worked, Gally got some of his deer back for nothing. If it failed, all he was at the loss of was a few days without the Land Rover. As the next hunt wasn't for some time, that wasn't a problem. He decided to go along with the idea.

'All right, Johnny, you might as well give it a try, I suppose. You can take away the jeep and horsebox with you. Ask Harmon for the keys on your way out. Oh yes, now that I come to think of it, you'd better tell him to fix the wall of the orchard where they broke out the last time. In fact, you had better get him to do it right away as the damn fellow is taking the weekend off, if you please! What next, I ask myself? Anyway, we don't want the deer escaping again the minute you bring them back, now do we?'

'Faith then we don't, your Lordship. I'll even give him a hand to mend the wall first before I leave, then I'll take away your jeep and horsebox. When do you want it back?'

'Oh, a week's time I suppose. Be careful of it now, do you hear? Do any damage to it and you'll jolly well have to pay for it out of your own pocket, deer or no deer. Understand?'

'Indeed I do, your Lordship. You won't regret it, I promise you. You'll have all them grand deer back safe and snug in the orchard before you know where you are.' With that he tipped his cap respectfully and was gone out of the study before Gally could change his mind.

Seconds later the phone on the desk rang. It was Abe Linovitz. 'Hi, is that the Earl?'

The way the American pronounced it was beyond belief. It sounded like *oil*, as in castor. Gally was racking his last remaining wits to try to recall the owner of this familiar but quite dreadful accent. Linoleum? No, not that. Linotype? Hardly. Linovitz – yes, that was it! Smallish chap with no neck, just a succession of chins that began somewhere due south of his lower lip and disappeared into his barrel chest. With a name like that he should have been a pawnbroker – or a moneylender like that damned Donnelly. Then in a welcome flood of recognition he remembered the meeting the parish priest had chaired in the Community Centre. Abe was the low-sized chap who operated the slide projector and fielded the technical questions Divareli couldn't handle. Not a very pleasant individual, if appearances were anything to go by. Nevertheless it would be only civil to find out what the little bounder wanted.

'Yes, this is the Earl of Gallerick. What can I do for you?' With difficulty he suppressed the urge to add a *pray tell me*? – with loads of backspin. Such subtleties would have been wasted on the little sod.

'I wanna see you. Have you gotta minute or two to spare?'

Curiosity struggled furiously with his umbrage at such a sudden change from servility to instant *camaraderie*. This was all the more objectionable since the sudden chumminess was based on only the slightest of acquaintances. Gally paused before replying, as though to give himself ample time to leaf through an overloaded but nonetheless imaginary appointments book. 'Well, it just so happens that I can see you briefly in about half an hour's time. Drive to the Hall and I will instruct Harmon, the butler, to let you in. Don't mind the dogs, by the way. They bark a lot but they are quite harmless.'

Soon afterwards, the whine of an overstressed engine, followed immediately by the screech of wheels skidding to a halt in a shower

230

of gravel announced Abe's arrival. Moments later, Harmon deposited him in the study, where Gally greeted him with as much enthusiasm as he would have shown a dead rat that the dogs had left in the pillared portico.

Abe extended a hairy paw in greeting across the desk and rasped, 'Good of you to see me. What do ya want me to call ya? Dracula back there suggested your Lordship but that kinda sticks in my gullet. Back where I come from, the only titles we use are the ones black guys get for beating the shit outa one another in the ring. Even then at that, the fights are usually fixed, I guess!'

This amazing outburst was followed by what sounded like a clap of thunder as depicted offstage by the Brulagh Amateur Dramatic Society. This proved to be Abe laughing heartily at his own joke. Gally salvaged what dignity he could from this frontal assault.

'Everyone round here calls me Gally. You may do the same.' He tried, without success, to inject a note of enthusiasm into the suggestion.

'Great – Gally it is, then! Well, Gally, without beating around the bush I'll come to the point right away. Luke, that's Luke Divareli I'm talkin' about, and me want you to head up the board of Orchid Investments. He and I started the company and we'll be transferring fifteen million dollars to the bank here real soon. You get one golden share in the firm which entitles you to fifty thou American a year, a damn good expense account and several trips a year to New York – starting this weekend, by the way, if you accept our offer. We'd need you to sign papers and all that kinda legal shit right away with our lawyers over there if you want the job. Only thing is, I need an answer right away 'cos if you turn me down I have to move right on to the next name on my list. So what's it to be, Gally, ole buddy? Do we have a new Chairman of the Board or am I still chasing around for one like a blue-arsed fly?'

27

In a rather more expensively furnished office, Pat Mullarkey sat in a deep leather armchair. He was facing a grizzled hulk with close-cropped grey hair and an impressive array of jowls that gave him the appearance of an elderly St Bernard who was getting too old for the job. The Ambassador had devoted a lifetime of service to the American fast food industry and the Grand Old Party. As a youngster he had developed a bun in his father's tiny bakery in Milwaukee that stayed fresh for weeks rather than hours. As he explained to the hamburger and hot-dog sellers who were then graduating from the corner drugstore to the vast chain of fast food joints that blight the American landscape, the average punter equates softness with freshness where their bread is concerned, and his buns stayed *softer longer*.

As his business grew, so did his contributions to the Republican Party. These were rewarded last year with an Ambassadorship. His wife had hoped for the Court of St James but as he reminded her several times a day, Dublin was less than an hour's flying time from London. He had a large staff, comfortable surroundings, and his duties were not onerous. They lay mainly in preventing undesirables from entering the USA via Ireland and blocking funds from misguided Irish Americans in Boston and Chicago who wished to aid the armed struggle, as they termed it, in Northern Ireland. Today's problem presented a welcome change. As Washington said, all it would require was bit of gentle arm-twisting. It might even be necessary to remind the host country on which side its bread was *really* buttered. Well, he chuckled, as he took stock of the representative of the Irish Government sitting opposite him, there was no better man in the world to talk about bread.

The problem was quite straightforward. Two of his countrymen were investing in a resort in some dump called Brulagh – so small that his staff had trouble finding it on any map. The office of the US Attorney wished to interview one of the men, a con-artist called

Abraham Solomon Linovitz. The other, Luca Divareli, was the previous owner of Italbank, currently being quietly investigated for laundering drug money for the Mafia and the Colombians. That investigation was getting nowhere fast so someone in Washington thought that it might be a good idea to put pressure on Divareli to testify. It was then they found out that he had set up shop, quite legally, in Ireland and was partnered by the lowlife called Linovitz.

The Ambassador's brief was to persuade the local yokels to impound Divareli's passport and freeze his assets in Ireland. As for Linovitz, he was to be extradited back to the States where he would face charges of fraud and non-disclosure of assets. His staff had briefed him that the highest-ranking politician available was the Tanaiste. He was the equivalent of the Vice-President. It seemed that Patrick Mullarkey – by one of those strange coincidences that happened all the time in this land of leering, lying, lazy leprechauns – hailed from Brulagh. Suddenly Brulagh had become the buzzword in the circular fortress that served as the Irish Embassy of the greatest country in the world.

'So what I want you to arrange, Mr Mullarkey, is for this guy Linovitz to be extradited immediately and for Divareli's passport to be confiscated and his assets frozen. No more and no less.'

Mullarkey was unimpressed. His leader, the Taoiseach, was at a meeting of the EC Heads of State which might go on for three more days. With an already taxing workload, this made life almost unbearable. Now as an added aggravation this doddering Republican hack wanted him to bend, if not actually break, every law in the Statute Book. The anti-terrorist laws in Ireland were among the toughest in the free world. They had to be. By contrast, those relating to personal freedoms – where offences against the State were clearly not involved – bent over backwards to protect the rights of the individual. Evidently this was something the Ambassador had either overlooked or preferred to ignore. In either case, it made Mullarkey's position difficult. More so because of the unhappy coincidence that the two men were operating on his very doorstep.

If he were to do anything that might be construed, however remotely, as stunting the development of his native village by putting the stoppers on the Orchid Project, he would be a dead duck politically. Not only would he *not* make Taoiseach and leader of the largest political party in the land – a post for which he was already being hotly tipped by knowing insiders – but he might not even be re-elected next time. The annals of Irish politics were full of such cases. Indeed he need search no further than Mick Flannery for a perfect example of the fickleness of the electorate. Once a legend in his own lifetime, Mick Flannery would have been booted out of political life by those who had once worshipped him if he had not secured for himself the position of Euro MP under what could only be described as rather unusual circumstances. Mullarkey had no intention of suffering a like fate, no matter what the geriatric representative of the most powerful nation on earth might wish him to do.

'I see. Well, Mr Ambassador, as you know the Taoiseach is out of the country just now but I will see what I can do. Extradition, as you must be well aware, is something of a hot potato at the moment. The big protest march last weekend for that IRA man we sent back for trial in the north proved that beyond any doubt. We're still trying to clean up the mess after the riots. The fact that our northern brethren appear to be making a complete cock-up of his trial doesn't help either . . .'

He didn't quote his Taoiseach to the effect that 'those thick shower of public-school yobboes couldn't find their arses in the dark, much less get the paperwork right in the simple matter of jailing a murdering Provo and then throwing away the key'. He sensed that the Ambassador might fail to appreciate the *nuances* of that particular situation.

'. . . As for Divareli, I have met the man once or twice, socially. He appears to be nothing more than a wealthy philanthropist who wishes to invest heavily in my home town. I suspect that getting a court order to confiscate his passport and freeze his assets might be difficult, if not actually impossible.'

The old man in the chair exploded, spraying the elegant Scandinavian glass table that separated them with a shower of spittle. Mullarkey thanked his stars that he was out of range.

'Are you trying to tell me that your Government is going to do sweet damn all about two cheap crooks who have ripped off Uncle Sam for millions of dollars? Like hell you are! Let me tell you somethin', young feller. My country has kept you lot going since before the goddam famine. When no one else would take your ditchdiggers and sod-busters, Uncle Sam welcomed 'em with open arms. Now since you guys joined Europe you think you can tell Uncle Sam to go play with his marbles. Well, let me tell you somethin' else, young feller . . .'

His jowls quivering with rage, he waved a pudgy finger at Mullarkey as though it were a loaded gun.

'. . . When the goddamn EC has broken up, as it undoubtedly will, into a gang of squabbling bums and panhandlers that'll make the Tower of Babel sound like a retreat in a Trappist monastery, you guys are going to come right back here with your begging bowl. I wouldn't count on us putting anythin' much in that bowl, son, if your Government doesn't act a bit more cooperative. Do you read me loud and clear?'

Mullarkey rose to his feet. Until now he had only met this old fool on the diplomatic Martini circuit or at the races. The Ambassador had invested heavily in horseflesh under the guidance of one of the more notorious Irish trainers. It was whispered that when one of his horses won a race, an exceedingly rare event, the whole of the country had backed it with the exception of its owner. Perhaps this accounted for his ill-humour. Whatever the reason, Mullarkey had taken enough of it for one day.

As he picked up his document case from the table, pointedly wiping the Ambassadorial spittle off it with his sleeve, he replied, 'Indeed I do, Mr Ambassador. I have tried to outline the difficulties in doing what you ask. I will consult with the appropriate departments and they will let you know our decision in due course.'

Before the old man could erupt again, Mullarkey let himself out of the study. The moment his official Mercedes pulled away from the kerb, Pat lifted the carphone and punched in Mick Flannery's number.

They sat in the Saab looking out on the machines and men buzzing like bees around the dunes. Divareli reached over and switched on the radio while Abe checked some detail on the blueprint spread across his lap. After a few advertising jingles, a woman's voice announced solemnly, 'And now here is the weather forecast for all regions . . .'

She followed this with a litany of wind strengths and atmospheric pressures that rose and fell around obscure lighthouses and unheard-of headlands. Just before she ended she offered a long-range forecast up to and including the coming weekend.

'The storm pattern that has remained static in mid-Atlantic for some time now is expected to reach the west coast by Friday night. This will bring with it high winds rising to severe storm force eleven in all coastal areas. These winds will be accompanied by heavy rain and lightning. Some structural damage may be expected. That is the end of the forecast. *Beannacht Dé libh.*'

'What's she sayin' for Chrissakes?'

Divareli thought it was fairly clear but allowed that Abe might have been absorbed in the blueprint and missed something. 'She said it was going to blow like hell over the weekend. Better get them to cover the topsoil dumps with tarpaulin in case it gets blown away . . .'

Abe cut him short. 'Christ Luke, I can hear, ya know! I meant what did the broad say at the end?'

'Oh that – that's Irish for goodbye. Means "God be with you". Nice, isn't it?'

'I dunno, is it? Tell ya the truth, this place is beginnin' to give me the creeps. Sooner I'm outa here, the happier I'll be. Not you though, from the look of you. You're really hooked on Aphra, aren't you?'

Divareli was appalled. He thought he had managed to conceal this indisputable fact remarkably well, considering the amount of hours in the day they were thrown together. He thought long and hard before confirming it in a distant voice.

'Yeah, I guess I am at that. Thought it might just be a fun thing at the start. Not now. I want to marry that girl, Abe.'

'Jeez. That bad? Well, you know my views on marriage.' Everyone did. Abe never tired of telling anyone who would listen that he had been married four times until he discovered that he didn't need to buy the orchard to steal the apples.

'I sure do. How did you get on with her father? Did he take the job?'

Abe chuckled huskily. 'Did he what? He practically jumped out of his chair with excitement. I could see dollar signs flying round where his eyes used to be – like a Reno fruit machine with the trots! Of course he played it real cool at the start and said he'd have to consider it, what with his other commitments an' all. That was all just a load of crap. That guy does sweet fuck all – all day every day. Unless you call sitting on your butt and watching the building fall down around your goddamn ears doin' somethin'. Anyway, he jumped at it in the end. Can't wait to get to New York, he says.'

'When's he going there?'

'At the weekend. I'll probably go over with him – to make sure he signs the right papers and doesn't get lost. I gotta couple of things of my own to attend to while I'm there. Didn't get a chance to look after 'em the last time.'

There was something in Abe's voice that made Divareli shoot him an inquiring glance. It could have been a trace of anxiety but the moment passed.

'Just so you remember, Abe. When he signs up, he *must* accept full liability for the debts and assets of Orchid Investments Ltd. That's how I'm going to screw the bastard when the time is right.'

'Yeah, I know. We've been over it often enough by now, haven't we? Beats me why you want to waste time nailing a creep like him, especially when you're sweet on his daughter . . .' seeing Divareli suddenly stiffen in his seat, he hurriedly corrected himself '. . . but then that's your business, ain't it?'

'Like you just said, that's *my* business. Now let's get back to *our* business. The planning permissions have all been okayed while you were away. Oh yeah, I almost forgot. The EC grants are approved – or so Mick Flannery says.'

'Hey, that's great! Didn't expect approval that quick, did you?'

'No. I expect it helps to have City Hall pulling for you, though.'

'You can set that to music, Luke, ole buddy. Now I gotta go down there and crack the whip a bit.'

'Don't forget to tell them to tie everything down that might be blown away. It sounds like a real big one coming in from the Atlantic.'

Abe nodded and made his way down the side of a sand-dune to where the nearest bulldozer was carving brown swathes in the valley that was to be the eighteenth fairway.

Divareli turned the key in the ignition and accelerated smoothly away. The Saab was a replacement for the late-lamented Porsche. Now that he had got the hang of the turbocharger, he actually preferred it to the German thoroughbred. It certainly handled the Irish roads a damn sight better, though this might be due, in part, to the caution with which he now approached blind corners since the accident.

The news that the Eleventh Earl of Gallerick was about to visit the Colonies suggested that his country seat might be empty at the weekend – save for Aphra. She had mentioned that Harmon was to have the weekend off, too. As he parked the Saab outside the office, Divareli wondered if the fickle finger of Fate was pointing in his direction for once – thus shortening the odds in his favour of spending an uninterrupted night with Aphra.

28

Abe was furious. That bastard in charge of First Island was refusing to take his calls. An underling with a Yale accent told him politely but firmly, 'As you are already aware, Mr Linovitz, our current policy is to accept written instructions only from clients. If you wish to transfer your account, we must receive your instructions on the matter by . . .'

Abe could take no more. 'Lissen t'me, you little asshole, you tell your boss that I want my fuckin' money outa your fuckin' bank today! Not tomorrow, nor the fuckin' day after that. I've written you a letter saying just that over a week ago for Chrissakes! What do ya use for postal deliveries on that fuckin' island, carrier pigeons? In the letter I wrote I even used big fuckin' letters and short words so that stupid bastards like you could understand it . . .'

Just as he realised the party at the other end had hung up on him, the door of the office opened. Aphra was coming to work. On her way from Gallerick Hall, she had stopped off at Sean's place to have lunch with Divareli. As she hung up her coat and put her handbag beside the typewriter, Abe was still barking into the phone. The moment he saw her, he clamped his hand over the mouthpiece and whispered hoarsely out of the side of his mouth, 'Honey, write this down as I call it out to you, will ya? And make sure you get it word-perfect! It's fucking important!'

He unclamped the mouthpiece and spoke into it. 'Would ya sing that out for me again. I've just got someone here now to take it down this time.'

There was a pause. Abe resumed eye-contact with Aphra and repeated in a parrot-like voice. Aphra started scribbling furiously, hoping that her shorthand could match Abe's staccato delivery.

'What started out as a routine investigation by the US Treasury and the Federal Reserve Board into accusations that Italbank was laundering drug money has suddenly taken on a new and sinister twist. Investigators have turned up evidence that directly implicates

Italbank in a massive share scam. The "sting" would have worked like this. Feed the investigation false evidence linking Italbank to a global money-laundering operation. This would depress Italbank paper to rock bottom as investor confidence ebbed. The Italbank paper is already heavily discounted and shows no immediate signs of recovering lost ground. As soon as Divareli decides that the price has touched bottom, he mounts a "dawn raid" and buys all the paper he can lay hands on. Later, when the evidence against Italbank does not stand up, all charges will be dropped and the value of the bank's paper will rise again. This would leave Divareli owning the bank once more and sitting on a hefty profit as well!

However, because it is illegal for Divareli to trade in Italbank paper except on one day a year – this to avoid just such price manipulation as is going on right now – he has arranged for a shell company to buy Italbank paper on his behalf. This paper has learned that a company – Orchid Investments – is to be the vehicle whereby Italbank paper is snapped up at firesale prices and put on hold under Irish Nominee Directors until Divareli can legally buy that paper from them, seven months hence. It will be remembered that Luke Divareli sold his stake in Italbank for twenty-five million dollars some time back. It now looks like he is going to get the whole bank back for a fraction of that amount.

As of this morning, Mr Divareli could not be contacted in New York. A spokesperson for Italbank thought that he was "holidaying somewhere in Europe". This paper has discovered that Divareli is in Ireland where he is setting up a holiday resort, and the name of the holding company for the resort is – guess what? You got it first time – Orchid Investments! It remains to be seen whether the notoriously lax Irish Central Bank will interest itself in what is essentially an American problem. It is even possible that Divareli may not have broken any leprechaun law and is therefore untouchable. In view of the Emerald Isle's hatred of extradition, it may well be that Luke Divareli will take an extended holiday – at the expense of the US Treasury – on Erin's green shores.'

'That's it, you say. Well, thanks for calling me, I sure appreciate it.' With that he hung up and looked quizzically at Aphra. 'Did ya get all that, honey?'

When she nodded, he asked her to type two copies and to give one to Divareli as soon as she saw him. 'It's real urgent, honey, that he sees that right away. That piece is goin' to appear in the *Wall Street Journal* next week. When it does the shit will really hit the fan. By the way, I was with your father a while back . . .'

He put on his coat and was heading for the door when he dropped the bombshell. 'He's agreed to head up the board of Orchid Investments.'

Before she could register her disbelief, he had gone. As she was typing up her shorthand notes the sound of something being pushed through the letterbox of the outside door distracted her. She resolved to finish typing before she went to see what it could be. There was only one postal delivery in Brulagh and that was always on the floor to greet her first thing in the morning. This time there was just one white envelope with her name on it. It was marked PERSONAL and BY HAND. The heading on the notepaper showed it to be from Father Jerry. It read:

Dear Aphra,

Attached is a letter I have just received from St Malachy's Presbytery, Essex Street, Lower East Side, New York. As you can see, the letter confirms that a Jessie Kelly was in their care for five months during 1867. She died giving birth to a little girl called Mary who later married one Joseph Farrell, a bricklayer by trade, in 1890. They had one son, Kevin, in 1892. From my discussions with Luke Divareli and others, it would appear that this Kevin was killed in a shooting in 1925. Before this he had married an Eileen O'Connor and they had one son in 1922 whom they called Charles. In 1929, Eileen married again. This time her husband was called Luca Divareli and they had no issue. Charley's name was changed to Cesare – who appears to be our Luke Divareli's father!

Hoping this will be of some assistance to you in your researches, I remain,

> *Yours in Christ,*
> *Jeremiah O'Sullivan, P. P. Brulagh.*

Her shock was so great that it wasn't until some time later, when she was tidying up before going home that she noticed a sheet of paper beside the telephone. In Abe's handwriting it reproduced almost word-perfect what she had just been typing out. She read it through once more to make sure, then put it back where she had found it.

The two men sat comfortably in the plush leather at the back of the car that sped through the countryside at high speed. Alone in the front, the driver squinted as the morning sun glinted off the almost deserted motorway. The drive from Dublin to Brulagh was a long one and this was the only decent stretch of road on the journey. If time were to be made up, he knew that the next twenty miles would provide the only opportunity to do so. He watched the needle slide past one hundred miles per hour with only the slightest increase in wind noise. Ahead of him, scruffy black crows delayed their takeoff from the tarmacadam road until the very last milli-second before being crushed beneath the humming tyres of the State car. The black limousine was the ultimate goal of every politician. As Mullarkey's passenger was wont to complain when drink got the better of him, 'With one of these under your arse, you can call the Pope your uncle'. The 'State Merc', as it was known by one and all, was every bit as important as the seal of office each Government Minister received on his appointment to the Cabinet. Mullarkey had received his Merc after a brief but meteoric political career in which he had replaced his passenger, Mick Flannery, as TD for a constituency that included their home town of Brulagh.

Both men were engrossed in the contents of their briefcases. Mick was reading with mounting disbelief the report Mullarkey had received from the American Embassy's Commercial Attaché. It stated baldly that Divareli had fifteen million dollars in a deposit account labelled Orchid Investments Ltd. In the same bank, the First Island Bank of Grenada, Abraham Solomon Linovitz had a personal account in excess of five million dollars. While the Divareli funds appeared to have been legally transferred from Italbank in New York, there was still a question mark over them in that Italbank itself was under investigation for money-laundering activities. An official inquiry by the office of the US Attorney had so far failed to turn up solid links between Italbank and either the Mafia or the Colombian drug barons. This was due to subpoenaed witnesses 'taking the Fifth' and declining to answer questions on the grounds that by doing so they might incriminate themselves. The Inquiry felt it could be helpful if Luca Divareli were to testify, and recommended the Irish Embassy to employ its best offices to this end.

Another confidential report marked *'For Your Eyes Only'* and addressed to the *Minister for Finance, Dáil Éireann, Dublin Ire-*

land explained the connection between the Grenada bank and Italbank. When Luca Divareli sold his stake in Italbank it was to a
discreet Swiss bank in the Canton of Vaude. Crédit Vaude had
recently expanded its business into international operations. Its first
step was to purchase Divareli's stake and soon after, take a control-
ling interest in the First Island Bank of Grenada. As a result they
were very much on the lookout for wealthy clients and Abe Linovitz
must have seemed to fit their bill perfectly. His close connections
with Divareli would indicate to them that he was 'a big hitter'. As
a result, First Island bent over backwards to accommodate Abe in
every way. His trading instructions were executed swiftly and effi-
ciently by telephone, where other clients were expected to send
written instructions. The fact that some of his deals appeared to be
borderline was overlooked, especially when his net worth jumped
from nothing to over five million US dollars in a matter of weeks.

A third document addressed to *The Commercial Attaché, American Embassy, Ballsbridge, Dublin* and also stamped '*For Your Eyes
Only*' was a report from someone called Stephen Makowski, Jnr. He
was an investigator attached to the office of the US Attorney in
Miami. His researches into Abe's transactions made interesting
reading. It appeared that Abe had brought several other resorts
onstream and so had live contacts in the industry. These he had
contacted within the past few weeks, offering wealthy individuals
and corporations membership in an exclusive resort operation shortly to open in the south of Ireland. In return for sums varying from
one thousand to ten thousand dollars, memberships of various
grades were offered to Americans. Cheap flights, cut-price accommodation of the highest standard and free golf and sailing were
among the baits used to hook the unwary.

It was from this operation that Abe derived his healthy bank
balance. The problem was that in the US it was illegal to sell
membership in something that was not already up and running. To
do so was a federal offence attracting heavy fines and/or imprison-
ment. Offshore trading in such illegal memberships was an even
more serious offence since moving funds out of mainland USA to
places like Grenada without the permission of the US Treasury
contravened several fiscal regulations. The investigator concluded
his report by stating that he had now completed his investigations
in Grenada. He had instructed the officers of First Island that when

243

Abe next telephoned his instructions, he was to be told that he would have to confirm them in writing before they would be executed. This would provide sufficient evidence to go before a Federal Judge and obtain a signed warrant for Abe's arrest. He would then fly to Ireland and execute the warrant with the cooperation of the Irish authorities. He hoped the Attaché would see to it that no obstacles were put in the way of extraditing Abraham Solomon Linovitz back to the State of New York to stand trial.

The last sheet of paper Mullarkey had handed to Mick without comment. It bore the imprint of the Central Bank and was a note to Mullarkey from its Governor.

Dear Pat,

Many thanks for lunch the other day. I checked out that matter and from what I can gather Italbank is in terminal decline. The Judicial Inquiry into its activities will see to that. Even if no charges result from it, the reputation of Italbank will have been damaged beyond repair. Indeed its paper is trading very much below par at the moment and is unlikely to recover. I checked out Luke Divareli, as you requested. As far as we can see from here, the man appears to be clean. The suggestions of links with either the Mafia or Colombian drug dealers just do not stand up. As for money-laundering, those of us without sin must cast the first stone. You will recall the recent Tribunal set up to investigate campaign contributions to your own – and other – political parties. When a lawyer suggested that such contributions were merely another form of money-laundering he was severely censured by his own Bar Association and warned as to his future conduct! On that basis, your Mr Divareli would have, in the opinion of the Central Bank and its legal advisers, no charge to answer under Irish law. Furthermore, we think it unlikely that any charge could be sustained against him under the laws of his own country. It would be unwise, therefore, in our opinion to take any action against him whatsoever. Whatever assets he has in Ireland, therefore, should not be frozen. What you might care to do with his passport is not a matter for us at Central Bank, but since you asked, we would counsel extreme caution in this matter also!

Yours sincerely,
Brian.

When he had finished reading he turned to Mullarkey who was staring out the window at the passing scenery.

'Jesus Christ Almighty, that's a fine kettle of fish. This Linovitz character seems a crook of the first order. I wonder if Divareli knows what's going on, about the memberships, I mean?'

Mullarkey pursed his lips before replying, choosing his words with care. 'I wouldn't think so, not yet anyhow. There's always the off-chance that it might be something they agreed on ages ago, but I don't think so. Why would Divareli risk losing his millions of bucks because of a cheap scam like flogging dodgy memberships in something that isn't even built yet? No, my guess is that our friend Abe is in business for himself – and as it says in there somewhere . . .' he gestured towards the papers on Mick's lap '. . . the guy would have plenty of contacts in that line of business if he had started up other resorts before this one. Which is probably why Divareli brought him in at all, I expect. Anyway, you and I are going to have to work together on this one. Whatever our past differences, I think it will take our combined efforts to sort out this mess for the good of Brulagh.'

Mick nodded slowly and extended a hand. 'Yeah, you're right. When a ship is nearly on the rocks it's better to have two men at the helm. We'd better shake on it.'

The driver, who had been keeping a weather eye out for a signpost indicating the last few miles to Brulagh, happened to glance in the rear-view mirror and was just in time to see the two old rivals shaking hands. He spared a moment to mentally sympathise with whoever it was would be the victim of this unholy alliance.

29

'Jesus, Luke, can't ya see? The fucking *Wall Street Journal* or the Federal Reserve or the Attorney's Office – or maybe all three – are goin' to send guys over here right away to try to get a fix on you and Orchid Investments. I'd advise getting the money out of Grenada and over here real fast before the Feds try to freeze it. When that piece is printed, the balloon will go up for sure.'

'Who did you say again was your source in the *Journal*?'

'I didn't. What's more I ain't gonna tell you. In dirty things like this, the less you know the better. That way you can put your hand on your heart in front of a Grand Jury and say "I don't know".'

'Still and all, Abe, I'm telling you that the guy who wrote the piece, whoever he is, is just making it all up. What he says about the value of the bank paper dropping may be correct – I heard about that already from the priest of all people, and where *he* got it from God only knows – but I promise you there isn't one shred of truth in all that crap about the scam to buy the bank back. With the investigation going on, I wouldn't take a present of it right now. You do believe that, don't you?'

Abe nodded vigorously but his words were less reassuring. 'Sure I do, ole buddy. But who else will?'

Divareli was perplexed by Abe's attitude to the tissue of lies that made up the threatening piece in the *Journal*. 'I'm innocent, for Chrissakes, so why are you advising me not to call the *Journal* and tell 'em it's all a pack of lies?'

Abe raised his eyes heavenwards as if to request a benevolent God to give him patience. 'Jeez, Luke, have I ever given you a bum steer yet in all the years we've known each other?'

Divareli was sure he had but couldn't remember any just at that moment. 'Not as I recall, but . . .'

'No buts. If you contact the *Journal* they'll just figure you're panicking because the story is true. As for threatening 'em with libel, forget it! That lot of arrogant bastards would just laugh right in your face. You'll also get the guy who phoned me into deep shit, but mostly you'll be harming yourself. The only thing to do is to let it go. If they do run the story then you can sue 'em blind if you want. If they don't print it, well where's the problem?'

Divareli just shrugged his shoulders. None of this made any sense to him and he was beginning to get a headache. What he really wanted to do was to get back to his room, have a long shower and then take Aphra out to dinner at a little restaurant they had discovered about an hour's drive away. Abe was in full flow again.

'Another thing – we'd better hold an Extraordinary Meeting of Orchid Investments right here and now and vote in the Dook or the Earl of What's-his-name as Chief Executive Officer. Better make him Chairman of the Board while we're at it – it'll look good on the notepaper. He'll need that handle and a letter confirming his appointment signed by both of us. He may have to go Stateside on his own now that this *Journal* thing is flying around. Suppose someone alerts Customs to hold us at Kennedy? Those guys are all computerised nowadays. All it takes is a phone-call from the right person and anyone can be held without a fucking lawyer for twenty-four hours at the airport. Who the fuck needs that, even if they are as innocent as a newborn babe?'

'I still think you may be going overboard on this one, Abe, but if that's what you really want, then we might as well hold that meeting and agree to send the Earl of Gallerick as our legal representative to sign the papers in New York. Remember he'll need power of attorney to sign some of that stuff. You don't think he'll high-tail it down to Mexico with our money, do you?'

Abe gave this some thought before answering. 'Naw, I don't think he would. Still, to be safe why don't we restrict his control of the money to here. I mean, only give the guy authority to handle it out of the bank here in Brulagh. That'd spike him if he wanted to do a runner like you said. If your pal Johnny Slattery is anything to go by, the Earl has so much interbreeding in him that it's amazing his ears ain't growing out of his shoulders.'

'How do you know Johnny?'

'Met him and his buddy, the guy that tried to plug you with the shotgun last night over a drink. Several, in fact. Seems they don't love you no more, by the way. I tried to tell 'em you were an all-right guy but nuttin' would persuade them that you didn't blow

247

the gaff on 'em to the Sergeant. They said you were there just when the cops raided their still. Is that true?'

'It is and it isn't. I was in the fort, shooting pheasant with the priest and the Doc when the police raided. Godammit, I even fired my gun to warn those two guys!'

'Well, whatever you did, they blame you for the raid. Did you know they've gone mobile?'

'How do you mean, *mobile*?'

'Well, I promised to keep my mouth shut about this but I guess there's no harm in telling you. They got hold of a jeep and a horsebox somehow and they have the whole works inside it. They move from place to place so that the cops can't get a fix on 'em. Neat, huh?'

Divareli nodded. It certainly was neat. Then he shook himself out of the gloom of Abe's story and put the two bootleggers out of his mind as he became more businesslike.

'Ok Abe, let's get the paperwork done on this Gallerick business.'

Gus was eyeing the clean-cut young man with interest. Minutes earlier he had introduced himself as Steve Makowski of the US Attorney's Office and he had a warrant for the arrest of Abe Linovitz. It was this piece of paper that Gus was pretending to examine carefully as his mind raced ahead, vainly trying to grapple with the implications of his complying with this quietly spoken American.

'Would that be valid for this part of the world, I wonder now?' Gus stroked his chin thoughtfully as he waited for a reply.

'I guess so. That's what they told me back in the Embassy. What's more, they said I'd get your wholehearted cooperation.'

'Oh begod you'll have that and no bother. No, what's worrying me now to tell you nothing but the Gospel truth, is that this scrap of paper . . .', he waved it aloft lest Makowski should think he was referring to the *Clarion*, which was spreadeagled across his desk, open at the large picture of himself and the raiding party smiling contentedly over two barrels alleged to contain 'wash'. It had not escaped the *Clarion*'s more sharp-eyed readers that there was no sign of a 'worm' in the photograph. Beneath this was the caption *'Sergeant Moriarty and his colleagues make important seizure of illicit spirits in pre-Christmas raid.'* This was followed by Charley Halpin's piece which was notable more for what it left out rather than that which was included in his brief report.

248

'. . . That I have in my hand might prove to be no good at all. Then where would we be, I ask you?'

Not realising that the question was purely rhetorical, Makowski attempted to answer it. 'Well, I dunno Sarge. Like I said, the guys in the Embassy said it was OK and that I could count on you. Did they phone you?'

'No, they did not. But then again I'm out a lot these days. This is our busy time of the year, you know.'

He did not feel like telling him that both his Superintendent and Mick Flannery had been speaking to him already by telephone. The thrust of their remarks was similar. Gus was to give every appearance of cooperating with Makowski without actually doing anything. If absolutely necessary he could hold Linovitz in the station for questioning, but under no circumstances was he to arrest him. When he made to inquire why, he was told – more or less – to mind his own business. Mick was slightly more forthcoming than the Superintendent, as might have been expected from one old friend to another.

'Yerrah the Yanks are bullin' like mad to get this Abe fella back to America and throw him in jail. The thing is, we can't do it – even if we wanted to – under Irish law. However, we have to keep the Ambassador happy though between you, me and the wall the man is nothing but a roaring bollix. Pat Mullarkey is running the show while the Taoiseach is away. Pat says we're to keep the Yanks happy if we can at all. At the same time we don't want to banjax Brulagh's best chance yet of a better life for its people, now do we, Gus? One thing is for sure, if your man Abe is arrested and jailed in America, the money for the Orchid Project will dry up before you can blink. Now neither yourself nor myself want to see that happen, do we? So it comes down to this. Pat and myself are relying on you to keep Makowski happy. If you find the going too rough, give me a ring at home and I'll be up to the station to give you a hand.' Some help, Gus thought bitterly, as he turned again to Makowski.

'Anyway, be that as it may, whatever the men at the Embassy said to you, I'm not so sure about this piece of paper, my friend. You see, there's a thing here in Ireland called "wrongful arrest". For example, if I go and arrest you for something and afterwards some smart lawyer goes off and proves to some auld judge that I had no business in arresting you at all in the first place, then you, do you follow me, you can come back at meself and hit me a slap of a summons. And that summons will be for . . .'

'Wrongful arrest. I think I read you, Sarge. So are you telling me that I'm going to have to arrest Linovitz myself, then?'

Gus gathered up as much dignity as he could. 'Oh, indeed I'm not. Nothing of the sort. Anyways you couldn't even if you wanted to.'

'How come?'

'Because as I'm nearly blue in the face from telling you, you haven't the authority to arrest anyone in this country and that's the long and the short of it. Until such time as you come back to me here with a piece of paper signed by my Superintendent or, better still, the Garda Commissioner, there isn't a damn thing I can do about your man Abe. Can't you see, he hasn't done anything wrong around here or at least anything that we're aware of. And neither has Mr Divareli either so you can forget about me asking that fine gentleman to hand in his passport. 'Tis more likely that he'd give me a belt in the eye for my trouble and he'd be fully entitled to do so, the dacent man and he after comin' all the way from America to spend his money in a place like Brulagh!'

'Look Sarge, I've got to report back to my people right away. I just want to get this straight once and for all. Are you telling me plain and square that you're not going to arrest Linovitz or confiscate Divareli's passport?'

'Yerrah don't be talking nonsense like a good man. I'm saying no such thing. All I'm trying to get into your head is that I haven't the authority to arrest anyone unless they've done something wrong in this country. As far as I'm concerned, those two American gentlemen are free to go and come as they please. Now if yourself was to walk in here one of these days with a proper warrant sworn out by an Irish Judge and some proof against either of the two gentlemen we're talking about that they had broken an Irish law, why then that would be a different thing altogether, do you understand what I'm gettin' at?'

'OK, Sarge . . .' The exasperation in the younger man's voice was unmistakeable. 'I must ask you to let me use your phone and we'll sort this thing out right here once and for all.'

He consulted a notebook he produced from an inside pocket as Gus answered him, 'Go ahead, use it all you want. That's what it's there for. If you can get your crowd to arrange that I get the proper authority to do what you want from *my* superiors then we can save each other a lot of time and trouble.'

Makowski dialled a number and stared at the ceiling as it rang out. He drummed his fingers impatiently on the desk as he waited for someone to pick up the receiver. Makowski kept the phone glued to his ear so that Gus could not hear the voice at the other end. The message was brief.

'I'm getting nowhere down here. One policeman and that's it. He can't do anything for me till he gets the OK from higher up. Right, I'll wait here at the station. The number is . . .?' He raised his eyes quizzically at Gus who called it out to him. 'So, try to get back to me soonest. OK, 'bye.'

Makowksi fished out a pack of Marlboros, offered one to Gus and then lit one himself. He forced the smoke out through clenched teeth and tried to keep a patronising tone out of his voice as he asked, 'So this is your busy time, huh?' He refrained from adding that he would hate to see how quiet things got around here in the slack times.

'Yes, before Christmas the poteen boys work all day and all night. It's my job to catch them.'

'Moonshiners, huh? And *do* you catch 'em?'

Gus handed him the *Clarion* without comment, pointing to the relevant section. Makowski read it through and registered commendable appreciation. 'Hey, that's pretty good. Any time the papers write about us back home, they usually tear strips off us for not getting convictions. Reckon they'll do the same if I don't bring back Linovitz in handcuffs.'

Gus was saved from commenting on this by the ringing of the telephone. Makowski with a polite 'May I?' picked it up and almost immediately handed it over to Gus with a smiling, 'I think it's for you.'

'Hallo Gus, the Superintendent here. You'd better bring your man in for questioning. Let your friend there with you ask him anything he likes but make sure you have plenty of witnesses to what's going on between the two of them. The more the merrier, if you get me. Now put me on to him again.'

'Hi, Superintendent. Makowski here . . .' A long pause as chattering poured from the line, far louder than the whisper he had employed with Gus. 'That's fine – I appreciate your interest. Sure, I understand. I hope to have something official pretty soon but until it comes I won't arrest him, OK? I presume Sergeant Moriarty here can hold him in custody? Oh I see . . .'

Another long pause as the babbling from the far end became even more animated.

'Well, the two us will just have to play it by ear then, won't we? I just gotta hope and pray that my authorisation comes through in time, I guess. G'bye.'

There followed a pregnant silence which neither man was in any hurry to break. Eventually after what seemed like an eternity Gus suggested, 'What I think we should do is this. You hold the fort here until your authorisation comes through. In the meantime I'll hop on my bike and start making inquiries as to where I might find Mr Linovitz. When I find him, I'll invite him back here to answer a few questions. If I can get Mr Divareli to come along too, will I ask him?'

'No, that wouldn't be a good idea at all, Sergeant. In fact, if you know where I could find Mr Divareli I'd like to have a quick word with him first thing, even before you go looking for Linovitz. Do you think that would be possible?'

Gus nodded and said, 'Let's see first where he is.' He phoned Sean at the Brulagh Inn and was told that Divareli was in his room upstairs. Gus gave Makowski instructions on how to find the place and he left.

Divareli was in the shower when the knock came on the door.

'Come in!' he bawled. 'I'll be with you in a minute.'

The noise from the shower prevented any further meaningful conversation. As he emerged wrapped only in a towel, he was surprised to see a stranger sitting by the writing desk, reading his copy of the *Clarion*. The young man in a Brooks Brothers suit extended his hand. 'Steve Makowski, I'm from the Attorney's Office.'

'Jeez, that was quick. I'm Luke Divareli, as you probably know. If you've come about the piece in the *Wall Street Journal* – the Italbank scandal – I've nothing to say.'

'That's OK, Mr Divareli. I've got nothing to ask you about Italbank, though I did notice you had several million dollars lodged in First Island of Grenada last week. Would that be money you got from the sale of your stake in the bank?'

'Yeah, as a matter of fact it would. But what has that got to do with you?'

Makowski was all smiles, trying hard to please rather than offend this prickly customer. He raised his hands defensively as though to ward off a blow. As a gesture, Divareli thought it rather too dramatic.

'Nothing, absolutely nothing to do with me. Or with anyone else as far as I know. As for the piece you mentioned in the *Journal*, I know nothing of that either. I just happened to come across your account when I was investigating Abe Linovitz's affairs in Grenada.'

'In Grenada?' This was news to Divareli. Abe had never mentioned that he had an offshore account there.

'Yeah, First Island, same bank as yourself, Mr Divareli.'

'I gotta say I didn't know Abe banked there. Look, it's been a long day, Mr Makowski, would you just tell me what you want. I got a dinner date in a few minutes.'

'I'm here, as I say, representing the Attorney's Office. I have an arrest warrant for Abe Linovitz.'

'What!' Divareli was flabbergasted. He guessed that Abe had sailed pretty close to the wind from time to time, but a warrant for his arrest . . .

'That's right, sir. He's been selling memberships which we suspect might be fraudulent. That's why we came to you. We hoped you might be able to help us with our investigation.'

'Keep talking, Makowski. I'm listening.'

Indeed he was. But he was also trying to fight down the panic mixed with nausea that was rising in his gorge. What Makowski was saying had to be true. It all added up. Abe's story about the *Wall Street Journal* was just a load of crap to get him to move his money to Ireland. Over dinner he'd check out with Aphra just precisely how that story came through on the phone. In the meantime, as Makowski unfolded his tale, Divareli found that he had suddenly lost his appetite.

30

In the restaurant, Aphra told him of discovering the duplicate of the *Wall Street Journal* piece – in Abe's scrawled handwriting – beside the office telephone. Divareli gritted his teeth and said in a low voice, 'You might just see if it's still there when we pass the office. If it is, get it for me, would you?'

She agreed and then he became very quiet. It was as if there was something else he had wanted to ask her and then either he had changed his mind or his nerve had failed him. After dinner, they drove back to Gallerick Hall, collecting Abe's scrap of paper on the way. The changing of the guard ceremony was performed with Harmon greeting them at the top of the steps leading to the front door, and informing her Ladyship that the fire in the drawing room was lit, as she had requested. Aphra did not wish to delay him further.

'Have a splendid weekend, Harmon, and try not to overdo it!' she trilled.

With an 'I wish you the same, your Ladyship,' he threw his leg across the bar of an ancient bicycle, fiddled with the lamp mounted on the handlebars until it glimmered feebly and wobbled off slowly into the night. Standing beneath the draughty portico, they watched Harmon's flickering light slice through the dark until it vanished round a corner of the avenue. Then they kissed – gently at first – then with increasing passion. Before it could reach a crescendo Aphra broke free for a moment, held him away from her at arms' length and struck what to Divareli seemed an exceptionally wanton pose. He was consumed with desire, all thoughts of Makowski's tales of chicanery and Abe's double-dealing now wiped clean from his mind.

She murmured in a voice hoarse with passion, 'Welcome to your inheritance, Milord!'

For once her voice held not a trace of mockery. She had shown Divareli Father Jerry's letter and the note from St Malachy's Presbytery in New York. Amid a heady mixture of excitement and amazement, he had confirmed that the Farrell part of the story did indeed agree with his own recollection of his family history. He had become so caught up with the whole thing that he left her for ten minutes during their meal to call New York collect. The family lawyer confirmed that the story was quite likely to be true and promised to check out the details immediately. He could also confirm that nothing untoward had emerged from the Italbank investigation so far. He added that should the *Wall Street Journal* be foolish enough to even contemplate publishing anything of that nature, they would almost certainly have contacted him first. In which event, he concluded frostily, '*We would sue them to hell and back*'. It was a much relieved Divareli who had resumed his seat at the table and called for two more Irish Coffees.

They kissed again, this time with the wind snapping at their clothing. It had sprung up, as forecast, quite suddenly. Huge stormclouds threatened to engulf the silver crescent of a moon that reclined comfortably on its back, seemingly supported by the murky silhouettes of the giant oaks, looming dark against the night sky. From somewhere high above their heads, a lone skylark warbled a mournful aria. Divareli put his arm around Aphra and held her close to him. Just as they turned to go inside he pulled her towards him yet again but this time he had something to say.

'My love, this has been quite a day for both of us. Looks like Abe's hash is cooked and the Orchid Project is going ahead after all, so there's just one outstanding matter that needs attending to. It's a fairly straightforward one and it largely depends on you.'

'Oh yes? And what might that be, my darling?'

'I want you to marry me. What's more, I want your answer before we step inside this door.'

For a fleeting moment he had thought to joke about it not being right for the heir to the Hall to be seen messing on the doorstep with the hired help unless they had 'an understanding' – as engagements were called around Brulagh. Then he decided it might be too close to the bone. After all, Jessie Kelly *had* been a maid here all those years ago. This was no time to risk Aphra climbing up on her high horse and flinging the ring which he was about to take from his pocket over the parapet.

She put her arms loosely around his neck and stared into his eyes. 'I thought you would never ask. Of course I'll marry you, you silly person. Tomorrow if you like! Now let's go inside before we catch our death of cold. That's a favourite phrase of Harmon's and nobody quite knows what it means. I hope he left us a decent fire before he scuttled off. The poor chap looked like a schoolboy raiding the orchard, didn't he? Hard to blame him – it's his first weekend off in ages.'

'Just before we go in, I want to give you this. Hope you like it. I asked Abe to get it for me in New York.'

With that he handed her a small square casket. She pressed the clasp and the lid sprung open. Inside, a single diamond sparkled more brightly than any star in the sky. Excitedly she tried it on and then held her left hand outwards so that it would catch what light there was coming from inside the door.

'Oh my darling, it's absolutely divine. And it fits perfectly!'

'Good. That's not surprising, really. You see, that ring has been in the family for as long as anyone remembers. It's the same one old Luca gave to Eileen Farrell back in twenty-nine. In a way, it's just coming home. Like me, I guess . . .'

Before he could finish, he was smothered in another kiss, this one deeper and more searching than the one before. Then she broke free and giggled, 'Shouldn't you carry me across the doorstep or something? Or is that only when people are already married?'

'It's a damn good idea anyway. We can always pretend we're married . . .'

'What a superb idea, Luke. I was just thinking along the same lines myself.'

He carried her through the door, across the hall and into the drawing room. Harmon had done well. A welcoming fire blazed in the grate. He laid her down gently on the lambswool rug and together they examined the ring. After a while they kissed again – and again. As they did so the first peal of thunder rumbled overhead, a suitable accompaniment to their hurriedly discarding the last of their clothing. As they embraced again and started to make slow, passionate love on the rug in front of the blazing fire, the first flashes of lightning lit the room with an eerie blue light. For a moment Aphra imagined herself to be Jessie Kelly succumbing to the wiles of an earlier Gallerick. Arching her back to meet his ever-faster thrusting, she cried aloud as she climaxed. Seconds later Divareli, too, had climaxed to a crescendo of thunder and lightning that was Wagnerian in its intensity. Neither of them had ever experienced anything remotely like it before.

Aphra was first to regain her composure. Wearing nothing but her newly-acquired ring, she whispered tenderly, 'Well, my darling, that was worth waiting for, wasn't it?'

Before he could agree, a window caved in with a splintering crash, followed instantly by a screaming gust that caused the heavy velvet drapes to flap like the flimsiest of handkerchiefs in the wind. Divareli could just manage a 'Jeez, what was that?' as he grabbed for his clothes. In the broken window that framed the night sky, a head was silhouetted in a faintly familiar profile before it ducked low and was gone. Not, however, before a hoarse shout of triumph floated through the broken glass.

'This'll fix the both of yez. No land-grabbers will ever . . .'

The rest was lost forever on the wind. A bottle with a flaming rag stuck in its neck sailed in through the window and shattered in an explosion of flame against the drapes that concealed the French windows in the gable wall. Within seconds the far side of the room was a blazing inferno, fanned by the wind from the broken window and fuelled by whatever was in the bottle.

Aphra, too, was struggling frantically back into her clothes. Then they made a hasty retreat out to the relative safety of the hall. Divareli wrenched what looked like a nineteenth-century fire extinguisher from its bracket beside a stag's head.

'You phone the Fire Brigade while I try to get this damn thing working!' He banged it off the wooden floor and a thin stream of brownish liquid emerged from its nozzle. As he dashed back into the drawing room, he could hear Aphra screaming into the telephone.

'And please, PLEASE, do tell them to hurry, won't you? Yes, Gallerick Hall. Please hurry, I think the fire's already out of control.'

In that she was almost correct. The drapes against the gable wall were blazing merrily, the fire was taking a firm hold of the wooden panelling on the walls and also on the varnished pelmets from which the blazing drapes were suspended. To make matters worse, the delicate plaster moulding on the ceiling was also feeding the hungry flames which were steadily working their way towards the bedroom overhead.

As for the fire extinguisher, it was worse than useless in that valuable time had been lost in trying to get the damn thing working. When it eventually did, it had no apparent effect on the ever-growing inferno. Divareli decided that the best they could do in the circumstances was to try to limit the damage to one end of the house until the Fire Brigade arrived. They frantically collected every bucket, chamber pot and basin they could find and filled them from the tap in the kitchen sink at the far side of the house. Scampering to and fro, they poured water on the outer fringes of the fire in a desperate effort to prevent it spreading.

They had reached the stage where they had closed the heavy wooden doors of the drawing room and the bedroom directly overhead and were splashing water against them in a last desperate effort to contain the fire when the welcome sound of a siren was heard above the angry crackle of the flames. The fire engine screamed to a halt on the gravel, beside the Saab. Exhausted and wrapped in blankets they had salvaged from the other bedrooms, they sat in Luke's car and watched the titanic struggle that ensued between man and the elements.

Divareli was impressed by the modern equipment and obvious professionalism of the firefighters. Once they had secured a water source from the lake, they played six hoses, two of them from telescopic ladders high above the roof, at full blast on the fire and the roof of the west wing from which smoke was now beginning to ooze in an alarming fashion. Holding Aphra close, Divareli watched helplessly from inside the car. He wished that there was something more he could do to save what had so recently become his home. Suddenly it struck him that his whole life would centre round this ungainly pile from now on. It became vitally important to him that the house be saved – otherwise his own future happiness would go up in flames with it.

'Excuse me a moment, my love. I want to have a word with the Fire Chief.' He had some trouble in locating him as all the firefighters looked the same. After a brief and hurried conversation, Divareli was back at Aphra's side, clutching her to him more tightly than ever.

'Does he think he can save the house?' Tears were streaming down her face, glistening like pearls in the light of the flames.

'He says he's gonna give it his very best shot.'

Which he did. The fact that Divareli had just promised him and his men a bonus of a thousand pounds each if the fire were confined to the west wing made them work like dervishes and take risks that they otherwise might not have considered worthwhile. Two hours later the fire was under control. It had never got beyond the two doors Aphra and he had closed those few precious hours ago. The Fire Chief approached them, a triumphant grin on his begrimed face.

'We have her under control now, sir. She'll be out in an hour or so. I'll stay on here with the lads to keep it damped down and make sure that no one helps themselves to anything from the house. The two of ye should go off and get a wink of sleep now that everything is secure.'

Aphra could just about get the words out. 'Is there much damage?'

'I'm afraid so, your Ladyship. The drawing room and the bedroom above it are gutted and the roof of that section will have to be replaced. But we managed to save the rest of the building, thanks be to God . . .' Here he paused to wink knowingly at Divareli before ending with, 'There's no damage anywhere else apart from a bit of smoke and soot and maybe a drop of water from the hoses.'

As Aphra was shaking with some sort of convulsion, Divareli answered for her. 'Well, thanks again, Chief. I'll contact you later to settle that matter we agreed on. I think we'll take your advice and go back to the village to get some sleep. Good night – or should it be good morning!'

He ushered Aphra, still shaking, into the Saab and gunned it down the winding avenue. It took him a while to realise that she was shuddering not with grief or shock but with uncontrollable laughter. As soon as she could compose herself sufficiently to speak, she explained.

'When the insurance premiums fell due the last time, Gally nearly had a stroke. To insure the contents of the Hall against theft would have cost a fortune. Instead, he said "Bugger the theft bit, we'll increase the cover on the place for fire and storm damage instead".'

Divareli tried hard not to ask the obvious question. After all, he had a stake in the place now. Instead, in as calm a voice as he could manage he inquired, 'Is that why you're laughing. Jeez I thought there for a moment you were crying your heart out.'

'Yes, my darling, that's why I'm so happy . . .' She had to break off as another wave of hysterical laughter engulfed her. Finding her breath again and drying her eyes, she continued, 'He doubled the cover, the old darling. Now we get a new roof over our heads after all these years. And for sweet fock all! Isn't that absolutely wonderful?'

It was so wonderful that he steered the car carefully into a gateway at the side of the road. This time there were no interruptions to their lovemaking, save for two sheep which registered their approval by baahing happily.

31

'Now, gentlemen, I really must call this meeting to order, if you please. There is a lot to be gone through and the sooner we begin, the sooner we can finish.'

As the chatter subsided the Eleventh Earl of Gallerick sounded pleased with this glimpse of the blindingly obvious that he had so kindly afforded the rest of those gathered round the desk in the office. Mick Flannery who was seated between Divareli and the Doc gazed out through the window at Joe Gallagher's boat heading out to sea for another day's fishing. The cane lobster pots were piled high on the deck and the luminous orange buoys were heaped beside the pots, tied to carefully coiled lengths of nylon rope. A raucous horde of seagulls followed in his wake, the chug of the diesel engine acting as metronome to their squalling chorus.

'I would ask Aphra to take note of the proceedings in the Minutes. I take it there is no need to read out the Minutes of the Extraordinary Meeting that was held between Mr Divareli . . .', he paused here to nod in Luke's direction for some reason known only to himself, '. . . my future son-in-law, I might add . . .'

This wholly superfluous news item was greeted by an uncertain murmuring around the table that might possibly have been congratulatory. More likely, Divareli decided, it was intended to convey to his Lordship that he should cut the cackle and get on with it. Lunch beckoned and he hadn't even got to the first item on the agenda.

'. . . And the recently departed Mr Linovitz. It was held to agree the transfer of certain funds to the Orchid Investments account here in Brulagh. The sum in question was fifteen million dollars . . .'

Which I was going to hang you with, Divareli chuckled to himself. What Gally could not know was that the original plan was to allow Gally to write cheques drawn on an invalid Credit Transfer from a bankrupt Italbank. Under his terms of contract, Gally would have been liable for the amounts outstanding in Donnelly's Bank –

which would have been more than enough to ruin him. When, at Abe's insistence, the funds were suddenly moved to Grenada and sourced from there, the effect had been the opposite to that which was intended. Gally now had control over all those millions of dollars and this had given him the clout to have the resort centre relocated at Gallerick Hall. Reason enough to forgive and forget the Dago slight, Divareli decided, as he turned his attention back to the speaker.

'. . . That brief meeting also appointed myself as Chief Executive Officer and Chairman of the Board of Orchid Investments Ltd. I am glad to be able to report to you all that our company is now legally registered under Irish Law and that the authorities are quite satisfied that, despite Mr Linovitz's best efforts, we are a thoroughly respectable – and solvent – company . . .'

The reference to Abe brought differing reactions from those gathered around the table. Mick shot a covert glance at Divareli before nodding towards Joe Gallagher's boat that was now the merest speck on the horizon. Abe was on board after 'escaping' from custody. Yielding to pressure from above, the Sergeant had brought Abe to the station for questioning by Makowski. He had also invited along Mick Flannery and Divareli to witness the proceedings. This did not please Makowski but in his position, beggars could not be choosers. When faced with Makowski's arrest warrant and the incontrovertible proof that he had been selling bogus memberships behind Divareli's back, Abe caved in and confessed all. Armed with the draft of his statement, Makowski and Aphra retired to her office next door to type it up, ready for Abe to sign.

While they were thus engaged, Abe was persuaded to sign a handwritten document that waived all past and future claims he might have against Orchid Investments Ltd, and one Luke Divareli. This specifically cancelled their original agreement in which Abe was to receive his seven points of the total cost of the project, and was witnessed by Augustine Moriarty, Sergeant of the Garda Siochäna and Michael Flannery, Member of the European Parliament. In return, he was told that he would be allowed to 'escape' later but first, after he had signed the confession for Makowski, he would have to pretend to become unwell. When the Doc examined him, Abe would be declared unfit to undergo further cross-examination.

To allay Makowski's suspicions, the Doc would offer to keep Abe in his own house until he was well enough to resume his discussions with the investigator. Then, under cover of darkness, he would be 'rescued' by Long Tom McCarthy who would use his Lordship's horsebox to bring Abe to the pier where he would board Joe Gallagher's fishing boat. This would bring him to the port of Cork where he could board a ferry to France. From there it was suggested that he pay an extended visit to relatives in Israel, at least until the heat died down. Long Tom's fullest cooperation in the matter was secured by Divareli agreeing to 'forget' that the face he saw throwing the Molotov Cocktail through the drawing-room window was none other than that of the gun-toting bootlegger. He felt it unnecessary to explain to Long Tom – or anyone else save Aphra – that the terms of the fire insurance stated that payment would only be made if the fire were accidental. To accuse Long Tom of arson – even if the charge could be proved – would only confuse matters.

'Now the first item on the agenda is for the Board to accept Mr Abraham Linovitz's letter of resignation as director of Orchid Investments Ltd on the grounds of ill-health and some rather pressing personal business elsewhere. All those in favour kindly raise their hands and say "Aye".'

The room was filled with 'Ayes'.

'The next item is the rescheduling of the original plan for the Leisure Resort and Conference Centre. I call on Mr Divareli to enlighten us on the most recent changes.'

Luke rose from his chair, coughed to clear his throat and began, 'Right Honourable Chairman, ladies and gentlemen. As you know, we had originally intended to incorporate a rather lavish clubhouse and marina in the overall plan for the Orchid Project. At one time we had even thought of lining the fairways and sand-dunes with holiday chalets, some of which we would have sold to corporate clients and leased others out on a timeshare basis. I am now glad to tell you that this aspect of our original plan has been shelved. There are a variety of reasons for our doing this. One is that your Chairman and I sensed that there might be quite understandable local objections to what would, in essence, be a satellite town on Brulagh's doorstep. The benefits of such an operation for the people of Brulagh would be doubtful, to say the least. As the public meeting we held earlier suggested, it could also result in little or no mingling of the visitors with the people of the village. This, I believe, would be a serious loss for both sides because the greatest asset we have here in Brulagh is not the scenery, not the unpolluted air and sea, but the people. I can pay them no higher compliment than to remind you that I am about to marry one of them . . .'

When the cheering died down, he pressed on. 'So now in our restructured plan we have scaled things down to a size which I feel is more in keeping with the aims and objectives of Orchid Investments Ltd and should please the good people of Brulagh better as well. We have, therefore, decided to build a very modest clubhouse on the site of the old McCarthy castle. Here I would like to pay tribute to Mr Thomas McCarthy who was most cooperative in signing away whatever claims he might have had to the site and providing your company with a written undertaking that he will not pursue the matter at any future time. I think . . .'

It took him all his time to keep a straight face as he said this. In fact, to avoid breaking up he continued to stare out of the window at the now-empty horizon as he said, 'Therefore that our new idea should fit the bill perfectly. The new Conference Centre will be based in Gallerick Hall . . .', he paused while a ripple of surprise coursed around the table, '. . . which, as you all know, is already being extensively refurbished. The basic cost of this will be met by the insurance company, isn't that so?'

He looked for confirmation of this to Gally who nodded his head. It had taken a lot to persuade his future son-in-law that this was the way to go but it had been worth it in the end. Now he wished the blighter would get a move on. His very soul cried out in anguish for a gin and tonic.

'Orchid Investments will meet the extra cost of bringing the rooms up to the highest standards. It is the view of the board that superb accommodation and excellent food served to a wealthy and discerning clientele in the splendid surroundings of Gallerick Hall is a surefire formula for success in the international tourist market. I need hardly remind you that we are proceeding with the golf-course project and expect to have all eighteen holes in play by next summer. In addition, we propose to build an extensive indoor riding centre at the Hall and have secured the services of Miss Gillian Flannery to run it for us. Another facility we will be offering our guests is a pheasant and deer shoot over the estate at certain times

264

of the year and with the full cooperation of the local game clubs. Last but by no means least, our Right Honourable Chairman has kindly extended membership of the Gallerick Hunt to all guests staying at the Hall on payment of a nominal fee . . .'

Gally thought to himself that if two hundred dollars a day was a 'nominal' fee to hunt with his pack of hounds, then the lad was entitled to his opinion.

'And I know that this will be of great benefit when we come to market the project abroad. Sorry for taking so long and thank you for your attention.'

There were several other mundane items regarding staffing levels, playing rights for members and visitors on the old and new golf-courses, the preservation of the Bee Orchid, Natterjack Toad and Joe Gallagher's swans before Mick Flannery brought the matter up under the heading of 'any other business'.

'Could the Chairman enlighten us as to the situation relating to the bogus memberships Mr Linovitz was dealing in before he had to leave us so hurriedly?'

Gally shrugged his shoulders and referred the question to Divareli.

'Yes, Mr Flannery, I think I can help you there. The bank which Mr Linovitz was using for his illegal transactions was so embarrassed by all of this that they have frozen Mr Linovitz's account there and have undertaken, of their own free will, to reimburse all his clients. The sums involved ranged from one thousand to ten thousand dollars, depending on the grade of membership Abe conned his unfortunate clients into taking. Because I have had dealings with that same bank, all of them perfectly legal and above board, I assure you . . .', this was greeted with an embarrassed titter, '. . . they offered to write to each client, some four thousand six hundred of them in all, offering them an Overseas Membership for one year in our resort here in Brulagh for the modest sum of fifty dollars. It was felt that the clients would be so grateful to get the bulk of their money back that they would not balk at the First Island Bank of Grenada retaining a mere fifty dollars on their behalf. This will enitle the Overseas Members to special rates should they choose to visit us here in Brulagh. Realistically, we would have to admit that while we expect the bulk of the clients to pay the fifty dollars, we do not expect many of them to fly over here for the sole purpose of saving a few dollars on green fees and accommodation. Of course if anyone wants their fifty dollars back, First Island will reimburse them. When we explained to First Island that all the proceeds from this would be invested in the Flannery Leisure Centre, they kindly agreed to waive their usual charges . . .'

They sure did, he chuckled to himself as he shot a quick glance at Mick Flannery who was grinning from ear to ear, but only after it was agreed not to hit them with a malfeasance suit that could have cost them their banking licence.

'It was suggested that the pitch needed re-seeding and that the provision of floodlights would help popularise sport among the youth of the village. Also the amenities both in the stand – and underneath it – will be improved. We had thought of providing a theatre-cum-meeting hall in one section, and modern showering and changing facilities in another. If funds are sufficient, we would also envisage erecting two squash courts. In conclusion, I would remind the meeting that the First Island Bank are providing their services free to the Flannery Leisure Centre – an example I would hope and expect Mr Donnelly to follow in view of the large volume of business we are transacting through his bank. Perhaps our lady secretary, my wife-to-be, might convey this to the gentleman in question?'

'With pleasure!'

Aphra smiled – and she meant it.